Gabriel Beyers

Beauty & Power
Perpetual Creatures 2

Chapter One

Jerusa Phoenix perched in a high limb of a walnut tree, relishing the chilly October wind as it tugged at her hair. The breeze brought the scent of decaying leaves and pine cones from the surrounding forest. Had she been human, that might have been all she could smell. But her vampiric senses were a thousand times more powerful than her human ones had ever been. She could smell the fermenting of rotten apples coming from a tiny orchard several miles to the west. To the east came the pleasant aroma of hickory burning in a fireplace. A skunk, startled by a coyote, had sprayed somewhere to the south. And to the north, not too far away, she detected her prey.

She steadied herself on the tree branch, preparing to swoop down like an owl on a mouse.

Soft and wary footfalls sounded in the overgrowth up ahead. Jerusa's prey stopped to check his surroundings, making sure he was not pursued. He gave a soft grunt then continued on. He was following the dry creek bed at the bottom of the hollow, just as Jerusa hoped he would. If he kept on, he would pass right below her.

Loose slate rock clattered in the creek bed below and Jerusa held her breath. Her prey stopped to drink from a puddle remaining from the last rain and she bit back a scream of frustration. She had been a bit short on patience of late, though no one could blame her. She hadn't fed since becoming a vampire, nearly six months ago. That was enough to put anyone on edge.

The underbrush stirred and then the whitetail buck emerged into sight.

He was a magnificent specimen. The envy of every hunter. His chest was broad, with a thick shiny coat. He stood with the confidence of a king, shaking his crown of antlers back and forth. Jerusa counted fourteen points and wondered how many years the deer had been evading arrows, bullets and the occasional automobile. He scanned the shadows for danger, then lifted his snout and gave a loud grunt.

Jerusa took in his musk. She listened as his powerful heart beat and the blood-thirst rose in her like a terrific storm. She ran her tongue across her small but deadly fangs, tasting a few drops of her own blood from the tip. The buck stepped beneath the walnut tree and Jerusa prepared to pounce.

Just as Jerusa leaned forward, committing herself to the jump, the cell phone in the pocket of her pants began to ring.

The buck flinched. Though he seemed unsure of the sound, he darted down the creek bed. Jerusa landed on her hands and knees in a pile of jagged slate, missing the buck by mere inches. The buck, now sure of the danger behind him, turned and ran up the hill. His speed and agility were impressive for such a large animal, especially one with a hat-rack on top of his head, but he was no match for Jerusa.

The buck moved side to side, zigzagging around the trees, trying with all his might to put some distance between him and his attacker. Jerusa evaded the larger trees and smashed through the smaller ones. She caught up to him at the top of the hill, leapt ten feet into the air and landed on his back.

The buck stumbled, but didn't fall. Jerusa gripped his antlers with her left hand while wrapping her right hand around his thick, muscled neck. The buck stopped and reared in an attempt to shake her, but when it didn't work he took off again, at a run, slamming his body against the trees and darting under low lying branches. Jerusa took each blow with clenched teeth. She would not let the deer throw her. His blood would not strengthen her as human blood would, but it just might quench the fiery thirst tearing through her core.

Jerusa yanked back on the buck's antlers, twisting his head to the side. The beast lost his balance and fell on his side, rolling over

Jerusa as he attempted to regain his feet. The deer weighed at least three-hundred pounds, but it didn't even knock the wind out of her. She held tight to him, wrenching his head back and giving her a clear shot at his throat. The buck kicked at the air, bleating in horror. Jerusa rushed in for the kill.

A blinding pain exploded within her chest, as though her heart were being cooked by lightning. Jerusa struggled to hold on to the buck, but the unbearable agony burned all conscious thought from her mind. She arched her back and would have screamed had she had the power to pull air into her lungs. Her hands, pried open from the electrical pulses firing with every throb of her heart, fell at her sides, and the buck jumped up and fled into the forest, without even a grunt of thanks.

When the buck was out of sight, the pain cut off as though someone had thrown a switch. Jerusa turned her head. Alicia lay beside her, wearing her beautiful blue prom dress as she always did. The ghost's eyes were weary and her pain-filled panting matched Jerusa's.

She didn't know how much more she could take. The blood-thirst was growing worse every day and every time she tried to feed, Alicia would send that inexplicable pain rushing through her. Her only consolation was that Alicia felt every bit as much agony during this as Jerusa did.

"You know, when you're hunting, it's best to turn off your phone."

"You don't say," Jerusa said, without looking up. She recognized Taos's voice and sarcasm anywhere.

"Who's calling you at this hour?"

"My mother," she said with a sigh.

"How do you know? You didn't even look at your phone."

"Because she calls me every day. Sometimes nine or ten times."

"Maybe you should call her back."

"I will later. She wants to see me, but I can't go to her

looking like this."

The vampire spirit—as Shufah liked to call it—had worked a wondrous magic in Jerusa. Besides giving her eternal life, immeasurable strength and speed, it had also enhanced all of her natural beauty, leaving only the scar from her heart surgery as a reminder of her mortal years. Be that as it may, she had not yet fed since becoming a vampire and signs of her hunger were starting to show. Her skin had paled to a snow-white pallor. Her lips, however, were a dark shade of crimson, as though she were wearing a thick coat of lipstick. Most unnerving of all, though, were her eyes. The vampire spirit had turned Jerusa's dull green eyes into burning emeralds, but the lack of blood had left a thick ring of red visible around the irises.

This was all just an excuse, though. She could hide all of the physical signs from her mother. It was the mental signs she feared. On occasion, the thirst for blood overwhelmed her senses, driving her mad with rage. In those moments, all she could think of was feeding on blood and she didn't care from whom or what. Had it not been for Alicia, Jerusa would have taken Thad's life a few months back. For this reason, Shufah demanded that Jerusa not be alone with any humans until they could figure out why and how Alicia was preventing her from feeding.

Jerusa reached out and touched Alicia's hand. It still amazed her, even after six months. Ghosts don't have bodies. And you can't touch what doesn't have a body. Yet, somehow, since her transformation, Jerusa could touch Alicia. She wove her fingers into Alicia's and it felt no different to her than if she had taken Taos's hand.

No one else could feel Alicia, of course, but they could sometimes see her, or Foster, if they were touching Jerusa. Foster appeared above Jerusa's head as if bidden. He looked down on her with a wry little smile. She reached up for him and he extended his hand, as if to help her up, but her fingers passed through his palm with no resistance, leaving only a slight numbing chill to her skin.

Why Alicia and not Foster?

Jerusa sat up. Taos squatted on a boulder of limestone jutting out of the ground. The handsome hulk, with his ice-blue eyes and long blond hair, seemed a Nordic god come to life.

Jerusa stood to her feet and dusted away the bits of crumbled leaves clinging to her clothes. "It was worth a try. The buck, I mean. I'm getting desperate."

"You think you're desperate now," Taos said with a small laugh. "Just keep letting that ghost push you around, not letting you feed, and eventually the Gray Death will set in. Then you'll know desperate."

Jerusa shuddered, though from the cold breeze or the thought of what awaited her if she didn't start drinking blood, she couldn't say.

"Yeah, I hear it's pretty bad."

"The Stewards sometimes use it to punish the worst of offenders." Taos brushed his wind-tossed hair from his face. "Most times they just have the Hunters burn you up, but if they are in an especially cantankerous mood, they'll drop you down a deep pit or lock you in a box and let time turn you into a rock."

Jerusa waved him off. "Yeah, yeah, I got it. It's not exactly what I want to hear right now."

Taos shrugged. "Sorry. I tell it like it is."

Her relationship with Taos hadn't started off on the best of terms, seeing as he had once tried to kill her and Thad. Things were different now, though. Taos liked to play the uncaring scoundrel, but Jerusa had learned to see through his façade. Behind those cold blue eyes, he was concerned for her.

"Let's change the subject."

Taos shrugged. "Okay. What are you going to do about your mother? You've put her off for as long as you can. Eventually she will force a meeting with you. You don't want her dropping by the house unexpected. You remember where that got you."

Jerusa smiled. "Hey, if I hadn't dropped by that night, I

would have never known the blessing of your company."

"Or the beauty of my face."

"Too true." Jerusa sighed. "What do you think I should do about my mother? Maybe I should just tell her the truth. She's a smart woman. She'll understand."

"I'm not so sure about that," Taos said. "I tried to tell my father the truth."

"How did he take it?"

"He ran me through with a broadsword and tried to set me on fire."

"No offense," Jerusa said, "but most people that meet you want to do that." Taos smiled at her. "So, what happened to your father?"

"The truth drove him insane. He spent the rest of his life as a raving madman, proclaiming to whoever would listen that his son was the devil. Eventually, they locked him up in a sort of sanitarium."

"I'm so sorry," she said. Taos shrugged it off as if it made no difference to him. "Did he die?"

Taos raised an eyebrow. "Well, yes, a little over three hundred years ago, but not in the sanitarium, if that's what you mean."

"So, he got out?"

"Yes. He finally found someone willing to listen to his stories."

"Who?"

Taos hopped down from the limestone boulder. "It was a group known as The Light Bearers. A sect of humans obsessed with discovering the 'truth' hidden in the darkness of the world. My father joined the Light Bearers and eventually rose to some lofty position in their ranks."

"The Light Bearers? They sound like some kind of crazy cult."

Taos walked up to her and brushed the hair from her

forehead, sending a shiver down her spine. "Oh, they are that, for sure. But they are also well financed and insanely dedicated to their purpose."

"And what is that purpose?"

Taos shrugged. "Beats me. There have been a couple of them milling around town for the past few days. We can go ask them if you like, though, I suspect they'd die before telling us anything."

"The Light Bearers still exist? And they're in town?"

"Oh, they still exist. They've been around for the better part of a millennium. These days they've broken into splinter-cells that latch onto various governments, acting as some sort of secret research firm, but all along, they are funneling money to their true purpose."

"Which is?"

Taos sighed. "I told you, I don't know. Nor do I care, any more than I care about the mission of fruit flies."

"But why are they in town?"

"I'd say they caught wind of our little escapades a few months back. Don't worry. Soon their trail will go cold and they will leave."

"And what if they find us?"

Taos shot her his patented mischievous smile, showcasing his fangs. "We turn them into dinner."

Jerusa glanced back at Alicia.

Taos turned and followed Jerusa's gaze. "Come on, ghost-girl, cut Jerusa a break. If you want to pick on someone, pick on me."

Taos pulled his hands toward his chest, pressing them close together, as if squeezing a basketball. An orb of fire appeared between his palms. The flames licked the air, writhing and twisting around each other like a mound of fiery salamanders. Waves of heat distorted the air, turning Taos's handsome face into a grinning fiend's.

Taos thrust his hands forward and the ball of fire shot forth, soaring through the air like a comet. Though Taos couldn't see Alicia, his aim was strangely accurate, hitting the ghost in the chest. Alicia lacked a corporeal body, of course, so the fire passed through her, doing no more damage than it did to the air. The fireball hit a tree behind Alicia, exploding the trunk and raining bits of smoldering bark down on them.

Jerusa slapped Taos in the shoulder. "Shufah would be mad if she knew you did that. Besides, all that's going to do is make Alicia angry." Indeed, the ghost girl shot Taos a rude hand gesture. "That was a good one, though."

"Thanks," Taos said. "I've been practicing."

"Still hoping to join the Hunters?"

The corners of Taos's mouth turned down as he considered the idea. "Maybe. Or perhaps I just want to be ready if we have to defend ourselves from them."

That meant more to Jerusa than she could express to him.

The Stewards were tyrannical when it came to who they allowed to be a vampire. They respected only two things: beauty and power. Jerusa's gift with the spirits was truly unique. Vampires couldn't see ghosts, even if they could when they were human. And though she had great strength and speed to go along with her other talents, there was one major factor working against her.

The vampire spirit perfects the vessels it inhabits, yet it will not remake you. Jerusa still bore the large scar on her chest, given to her on the day she received Alicia's heart. There was a very good chance that the scar, which symbolized her fight for life, would be the cause of her death.

Oh, life and its hilarious ironies.

Jerusa slipped her arm into the crook of Taos's elbow and the pair strolled through the forest, leaving the obliterated tree to smolder in the darkness.

"I know I've asked this before," Taos said after several moments of blissful silence, "but I'm going to ask again, because you've never given me an answer that I can swallow. Why, do you think, is your ghost friend preventing you from feeding?"

"Her name is Alicia. She doesn't like it when you call her a ghost."

"Oh, I know," he said, wielding his arrogance like a sword. "I can see her over there, looking all morose." Alicia stood just ahead of them, leaning against a tree with her arms crossed over her chest—her favorite pose. "I know Shufah is fascinated by this little *touch-and-see* gift you have, mainly because she can visit with her lost love." Jerusa's chest knotted at the thought of Foster's death. Taos continued, "I, however, find it rather creepy. No offense to the lingering dead. But let us not be distracted from my original question."

Jerusa shrugged, as she always did when asked this question. "She knows something. She can't tell me what it is, but it's important. I think Foster knows it as well, though he doesn't seem to share Alicia's conviction on the matter."

"Ah, so there is trouble in ghost paradise."

"No, not exactly. They just have a difference of opinion."

Taos nodded. "Are you sure she isn't doing this out of spite or jealousy? Perhaps she even wants you to die, so that she can reclaim the heart you took from her."

Jerusa shook her head as if she could rattle this idea right out of her brain. "No. She's not like that at all. When she hurts me, it hurts her just the same. She's trying to protect me from something."

"She's going to kill you."

Jerusa hugged his arm tighter. "Well, then you'll be rid of me and free to continue your immortal trek around the world."

"I've seen the world," he said gruffly. "Nothing in it near as entertaining as you."

"Careful now. You keep showing your soft side like this and people are going to start saying you have a crush on me."

Taos pulled his arm free from her and tried to give her a playful shove. Jerusa rooted her feet to the ground, and though Taos was older and much larger than her, he managed to move her no more than an inch. Jerusa reached under Taos's arm, placing her palm flat on his ribs and shoved, sending him several feet to the side, into a tangled knot of vines.

"Man, I need to get me a taste of that Divine blood." Taos ripped free of the snaring vines. "Do you suppose Silvanus would let me have a drink, if he ever gets back around this way?"

Jerusa made a sarcastic look, as if she were pondering the question. "Um . . . I kinda doubt it."

Taos strolled back over to her, not one ounce of his bravado wounded from the push. "How about you give me a drink? I bet your blood would do wonders for an average vampire such as me."

"I'm gonna hafta go with a no on that one. If you want some strong blood to give you a boost then you'll have to ask Shufah to make the donation."

Taos rolled his eyes and offered his arm back to Jerusa. They walked in silence the rest of the way back to the house. They passed through the hidden laser perimeter set just on the edge of the open property, knowing it would ring their return to Shufah in the house. The warm glow from the windows invited them like a gentle smile, and the sassafras and hickory smoke billowing from the chimney embraced them as they approached.

Jerusa typed the passcode into the digital display panel near the front door then walked inside. Taos followed her, shutting the door behind them. The stillness of the house was nothing new, yet something seemed off. A subtle scent wafted in the air, not of cologne or body odor, but something alien to the house.

They found Shufah in the living room sitting on the plush leather loveseat. She sat, back straight, legs crossed, her dark skin magnificent in the firelight. She turned to look at them as they entered, as did the pair of vampires sitting on the matching couch across from her.

"Welcome home, my lovelies," she said with a forced smile. She gestured to the pair of vampires. "It seems the Stewards have finally come to call on us."

Chapter Two

The pair of vampires sat on the couch, leaned back with their legs crossed. From the outside looking in, it seemed just a casual little get-together—all they needed was some tea and finger sandwiches—but inside the room, the discomfort was palpable.

Shufah stood up and gestured toward them. "Allow me to introduce Taos and Jerusa." Her face remained relaxed with a simple smile, but her eyes warned them to follow her lead. "This, my lovelies, is Ralgar and Ming. They have come a great distance to extend to us an invitation to meet with the High Council of the Stewards."

Jerusa wasn't feeling too social this evening, but she managed a nod and a small smile. Taos remained as still as a gargoyle.

The pair on the couch were dressed alike, each with thick, loose-fitting canvas pants, a heavy linen shirt, with a hooded, leather trench coat—sometimes called a duster. The one named Ming was a short, squat, Asian woman that looked to be in her fifties. She had a flat, wide, spade-shaped nose, and salt and pepper hair pulled back into a tight bun. The one named Ralgar was shorter even than Ming, with a friar's bald spot, crooked teeth, fixed in an overbite and beady little eyes.

In the vampire world, for the Stewards to allow you to live, you had to be either beautiful or powerful. Ralgar and Ming were not even attractive by human standards, so . . .

"You're Hunters, aren't you?" Jerusa asked.

Ming stood to her feet. "Yes. We are members of the Crimson Storm, the fiercest group of savage-slayers in the world."

"Why are you here?"

This time Ralgar answered. "Your presence has been requested by the High Council."

Jerusa gave an exaggerated nod. These two had the conversational skills of a grizzly bear. "Yes, I understand that. But why did the Stewards send *you*. Do the Stewards not know about email?"

Ming and Ralgar looked at one another, as if trying to decide if Jerusa was mocking them or not. It was clear they were not unintelligent creatures, not blunt and mindless weapons, but more that they were not used to having their motives questioned.

Shufah placed her hand on Jerusa's shoulder. "The Stewards honor us by sending members of the Crimson Storm to meet with us. That they sent two such elite Hunters is a sign of respect to our modest little coven."

Shufah's soft words eschewed the Hunters' brewing anger while, at the same time, warning Jerusa to tread lightly. Jerusa didn't mean to come off so haughty. Her thirst and the frequent battles with Alicia had given her emotions a hair-trigger. She considered apologizing to the Hunters, but thought better of it. Best not to admit she was mocking them and let them accept Shufah's praise.

"What is it that you want from us?" Taos asked.

Ming looked up into the chiseled face of Taos and smiled. "Please, sit with us. We are here as ambassadors. Let us commune as such. A man wielding such a defensive stance is not apt to hear the words of peace."

Jerusa and Taos each took a chair on either side of Shufah. The Hunters returned to their place on the couch.

"The Stewards of Life didn't summon us to attack you," Ming continued. "Nor are we here to apprehend you."

"If we were," Ralgar said in a gruff voice, "we would not have blessed you with a warning." He stared into Taos's eyes, seemingly daring him to make an aggressive move. Taos held his gaze, but said nothing.

Ming put her hand on Ralgar's knee as though she meant to

calm his ire, but Jerusa read a certain pleasure in her eyes. She liked this game they were playing. Enjoyed passively lording their power over them. Jerusa wondered just how old and powerful they really were. It was impossible to tell.

Ming smiled, flashing her fangs. "We are here to escort you to the High Council. There is much they would like to discuss with you."

"And just what would that be?" Taos asked.

"We don't presume to know the mind of the Stewards," Ralgar answered. "We act only as their hands. Nothing more."

"Where will you be escorting us to?" Jerusa asked.

Ming and Ralgar looked to Shufah.

"The Council is awaiting us in Rome," Shufah said, with the same pleasant face she held through the entire conversation.

"Rome?" Jerusa asked in a gasp. "As in Italy?" Her mind spun at the thought. She had never been much of a traveler. Her mom saw to that. She had only been out of the state a few times, all for medical reasons and never once had her feet crossed over onto foreign soil. She had always wanted to travel the world and now that she was a vampire, with an endless supply of nights, she figured she had time to do so. The only thing holding her back was her mother.

A near uncontainable storm of emotions rushed through her. On one hand, she was excited to set off on an unplanned adventure, to see a place she had only experienced in books and movies. But, on the other hand, she felt crippled with fear. This was no vacation. No sight-seeing expedition. She was being called before the Stewards' High Council to be judged. If they deemed her unworthy to be a vampire . . . well, she and Alicia would soon have a lot more in common.

Shufah flashed Jerusa a concerned glance. "We leave tomorrow night, just after dusk. And Thad must come with us as well."

A knot rose in Jerusa's throat. Though she hadn't been able to be alone with Thad since the blood thirst had come upon her, they still chatted every night, mostly through email and texts. They were careful to keep their conversations vague and cryptic—never know who might be eavesdropping—but one topic that came up over and over, was Thad's fear of this event.

Thad had been infected with the vampire spirit from Taos's bite. Though Thad wasn't yet a vampire, the virus or whatever it really was, now lay dormant in his cells, waiting to become active upon his death.

Infected humans are given few choices by the Stewards. If the human does not meet the Stewards' standards, they are either killed outright or shipped off to a quarantine town, a commune of sorts, peopled solely by the infected.

Thad was tall and athletic, handsome, almost to a fault, with a boyish grin and kind eyes. Shufah and Taos both assured him that the Stewards would find nothing unworthy in him and Jerusa had no doubt he would make a stunning vampire. Though they often skirted away from this subject, she had once asked him what his choice would be. His answer had frightened her.

"I don't know," he had said. "When I think about the options, being a vampire or quarantined away the rest of my natural life, I sometimes think I'd just rather choose death."

Jerusa hadn't asked him again.

"You've known about us this whole time, haven't you?" Taos asked.

Ming shifted in her seat to better see Taos. "Us personally? No. The Crimson Storm only recently became aware of your situation. We've been on assignment and were called back to escort you in."

"Yes. Fine," Taos said, annoyed with the evasion of his question. "But the Stewards were aware of us, right?"

Ming and Ralgar glanced at each other, as if unsure of what they should and shouldn't say. "Yes, the Stewards are aware," Ming said. "The augurs of the Watchtower have been keeping close tabs on you, ever since Kole turned savage."

"I must say, I'm impressed." Ralgar's face looked anything but impressed, however. "A savage born of a fledgling is hard enough for an untrained vampire to dispatch." His nose crinkled at the word *untrained* as though he detected a foul stench. "But Kole was over a thousand years old. He must have been a nightmare for you and yet, somehow, you managed to destroy him. How did you do that, might I ask?"

"I'm sure that if the Stewards wanted you to know that, they would have told you," Shufah said.

The truth was, Kole *had* been a nightmare. Savage vampires were little more than flesh-eating zombies, but not the slow, mindless ones of the movies. The mind of the savage is controlled by the once-symbiotic vampire spirit, which becomes parasitic and rabid upon the vampire's death. Kole was fast and powerful, retaining his pyro-kinesis, motivated by only his fear of the sun and an instinctual need for survival.

Jerusa, with the help of Alicia, had tracked Kole to an abandoned air-conditioner factory, but it had been Silvanus who had killed him. It was unclear how much of this the Stewards actually knew. Shufah had told them that she hoped to keep both Jerusa's gift and Silvanus (who she believed to be a mythical Divine Vampire) out of the Stewards' scope of vision.

Jerusa didn't see how that was going to be possible, but she trusted Shufah.

Ming kept her smile, though it didn't translate to her eyes, making her look strained. Ralgar had a harder time hiding his emotions, scowling at them each in turn.

"That's fine," Ralgar said. "We can discuss something else. Like why hasn't your fledgling been feeding?"

Jerusa's face blushed hot as all eyes fell upon her. She grew uncomfortably aware of her full red lips and blood-ringed irises. Her skin went clammy and she couldn't decide what to do with her hands. The awkward moment of silence seemed to stretch on like the black eternity of space. She opened her mouth to speak—she felt she should say *something*—but the words wouldn't come and she only managed to babble, which made her feel more awkward, which in turn made her babble all the more.

They all looked at her as though her head was changing shape. Even Alicia stood with her arms crossed, shaking her head with pity. Some vampire Jerusa had turned out to be. So much for the image of the graceful and alluring undead. She was Jerry Lewis with fangs.

Thankfully, Shufah came to her rescue.

"These are matters to be discussed with the Stewards in person, not with their slave soldiers." Shufah's face remained soft and beautiful—not a sign of anger anywhere in her visage, except maybe for her fierce eyes.

Ming's mock smile fell away, as though it had been slapped from her face.

Ralgar clenched his teeth together with an audible clack. He stood to his feet, prompting Taos to step in front of Jerusa. "How dare you speak to the Crimson Storm in such a way."

Shufah rose to her feet, and though she was the shortest and youngest looking person in the room, the danger emanating from her permeated the air. She reminded Jerusa of a honey badger: small, beautiful and an absolute terror when provoked.

"How dare you enter into my home and insult my coven," Shufah said. "You are mere servants, yet you presume to question us, as though you rule. You are the hand and foot, not the head. Do not veer from your station."

"And what are you?" Ralgar shot back. "Nothing but an outcast. A worthless parasite, feeding and never contributing to the survival of our species. We are the ones putting our lives on the line, hunting the savages you create, while you live in luxury. You may have age and beauty on your side, but when the veil is pulled back, you are as powerless as a human. Mock me or any of my fellow Hunters again and I will turn you to ash." Ralgar's eyes bulged as he spoke, making his face even more troll-like than before. He stood squared up with Shufah, so fixed on his venomous threats that he didn't see Taos come at him, until it was too late.

Taos shot forward in a soundless blur, catching Ralgar in the side of the head with an immense left-handed punch that sent him cartwheeling over the back of the couch. The blow sounded like a hammer cracking stone, yet it wasn't enough to keep Ralgar down. He rolled to his feet without missing a step, turned and vaulted over the couch, catching Taos in the chest with a powerful kick.

Taos stumbled backward several feet, but managed to stay standing. His ice-blue eyes burned with anger. He let out a roar, then rushed to meet his foe. Taos stood a good two feet over Ralgar and outweighed him by more than a hundred pounds. Had this been a fight between humans, the odds would have been with Taos. But in a battle of vampires, size and muscles don't give the advantage.

Taos and Ralgar came together in the center of the room and the rest of them scattered backward, out of their path. They attacked each other with a speed that would have been too fast for human eyes. Taos sent a barrage of fists flying, like blasts from a canon, but he was unable to connect with Ralgar.

Ralgar danced around the strikes like a matador with a clumsy bull. Jerusa watched in awe as he parried or blocked each of Taos's punches and kicks with the grace of a master martial artist. She had only ever seen such movements in the movies. Witnessing it live sent a blast of cold chills down her back.

A great smile spread across Ralgar's face. He seemed more to be playing than fighting, relishing the frustration seeping from Taos. Ralgar hit Taos with three strong blows—two to the gut and one to the face—that sent him crashing backward into the kitchen.

Taos regained his feet and leaned against the counter, a bit stunned. He shook his head and the anger came back upon him, like a suffocating fire taking in a deep draught of air. He reached over and snatched up a meat cleaver from a set of knives that Shufah had purchased to give the home a more "human" quality. He started out from the kitchen fully intending to hack Ralgar into cubes.

Before Taos could advance, Ralgar reached behind his back, beneath his leather duster and pulled out what looked to be an ornate staff, four foot long. It was hard to tell if it was made of wood or metal, but it looked both beautiful and deadly. But then Ralgar gripped the staff in both hands, gave a twist and from both ends sprang a long thin blade, each with a four-pronged claw fixed near the ends of the staff.

Ralgar spun the double bladed staff over his head and before his chest as though warning Taos to stand down. Taos didn't seem to get that message and rushed in with the cleaver drawn up over his head.

Ralgar blocked Taos's downward swing, smashing the staff upward into his wrist. Then, in what looked to be a simple spin, he disarmed Taos with the tip of one blade, while slashing his thighs with the other blade. The wounds were not deep, mere warnings, and spilled only a few trickles of blood before the cuts zippered shut again.

Taos growled with rage, faked to the left, then rushed in from the right, catching Ralgar by the throat. He landed one strong punch to the side of Ralgar's head, but as he drew back for another, Ralgar twisted Taos's hand away from his neck. Ralgar spun around, flipping Taos through the air, as if he were a pillow on a string. Taos crashed into the wall, jumped to his feet and made another rush for Ralgar.

Ralgar spun his dangerous double bladed weapon before him like a fan and in one quick movement thrust it forward like a spear. The thin blade caught Taos just under his right collar bone and exited his back. Taos's momentum carried him down to the four-pronged claw. Ralgar twisted the handle and another claw opened near the tip of the blade.

Taos thrashed like a caged tiger, but he couldn't get free from the blade. Ralgar held tight to his staff, staying just out of Taos's reach.

"Fight all you want," Ralgar mocked. "I've skewered a

legion of savages with this blade. None have escaped. Neither will you."

An eerie calm fell over Taos's face. He brought his hands up to his chest. A small orb of fire appeared between his palms.

"Well, well, the giant is a pyromancer. I am touched with fire, too." Ralgar let loose of the staff with one hand and held it up before him. A large fire ignited from nowhere and stood licking the air above his palm. He glanced over at the inferno blazing between his fingers. He handled it carefully, as though it might drop and turn its fiery rage against its master. Ralgar smiled at Taos. "Looks like mine is bigger."

Jerusa stood transfixed, unable to flee or even speak.

Alicia appeared next to her and took her arm. Jerusa flinched at the touch. Alicia tugged at her arm, her eyes wide with panic, as she silently pled for Jerusa to escape. There were only a few injuries deadly to a vampire. Massive damage to the heart or brain would cause the vampire to go savage, but fire was the only means to a true death. If Taos and Ralgar weren't bluffing and decided to duel with fire, the resulting conflagration might very well consume them all before any had a chance to flee the house.

Without warning both Taos and Ralgar went ridged as though hit with a great electrical current and the fire in their hands vanished, without even a puff of smoke. Jerusa gasped as both men rose into the air and hovered near the ceiling.

"We can't have this, now can we?" Ming asked. She stood with her eyes closed, her hands out before her, cupped as though she held something in each. She pulled her hands apart and Taos and Ralgar drifted apart. Ralgar released his grip on his skewer, leaving it in Taos's chest as they floated to opposite ends of the room. Ming lowered her hand just a bit and the two men drifted down to the floor.

"This can't continue." Ming's eyes were still closed, but Jerusa got the impression that she could still see. "You two are acting like petulant children and you're going to bring the wrath of the Stewards down upon us all."

Ming squeezed her hands a small bit, bringing a groan of pain from both Taos and Ralgar, then opened her fingers, releasing the men from her mental hold. Ming opened her eyes and regarded both men with a pleasant smile.

"You're a telekinetic," Jerusa said without meaning to. It was an obvious statement and she felt instantly embarrassed, but she couldn't help it. The words just fell out. Shufah had told her much about the gifts of the vampire spirit. She had witnessed the pyro-kinesis first with Taos and later with Silvanus, but this was her first sight of true telekinesis.

Ming smiled at Jerusa as though she were simple. "Every Hunter tribe is armed with two telekinetics, two pyrokinetics and an augur—that's a seer—but you won't find a stronger telekinetic in the entire world than me."

Jerusa knew what an augur was. Shufah seemed especially bitter toward these telepathic vampires that the Stewards used to keep tabs on the rest of them. The most powerful augurs were housed together in a secret location, known only to the High Council. Jerusa thought about saying as much, if only to knock the smug look from Ming's face, but a warning glance from Shufah held back the words.

Ming might be the most powerful telekinetic in the world, but Jerusa wondered how well she would fair against Silvanus. A small smile touched the corners of her mouth. Ming raised an eyebrow, but didn't ask.

Ming turned to Shufah. "My apologies. Barbarians and their fire. We will return tomorrow night to escort you and your coven to the airport. Please make sure the human is with you."

"Thad will be with us," Shufah assured her.

Ming nodded. "Come, Ralgar, let us leave."

Ralgar walked over to Taos and grabbed the staff. He twisted the handle and the two blades, along with the claws, retracted with hardly a sound. Ralgar retuned the staff to its place beneath his duster, held Taos's eyes for a moment and then rejoined Ming. Shufah walked them to the door, made a pleasant good-bye, as though they had just finished a fine dinner together and watched as the pair vanished into the predawn darkness.

Jerusa picked up her cell phone and was half way through dialing Thad's number when Shufah placed her hand over the screen.

"Do not call Thad about what has happened."

"Why not?"

"If you tell him now, Thad will run. We will go get him together tomorrow night." Shufah sighed then returned to her seat.

"What's the matter?" Taos asked, looking at the already-healing wound in his chest.

"I don't know," Shufah said. "But something is amiss. Why have the Stewards waited six months to seek us out? Why now? And why send their most deadly tribe of Hunters as escorts? I don't know what this means, but I know it isn't good."

Alicia stood in the corner with her arms crossed. For once she agreed with Shufah.

Chapter Three

Silvanus sat in the tall grass, legs crossed, eyes closed. He lifted his chin to catch the remaining rays of the Serengeti sun before it dipped below the horizon. The heat of this place was astounding, pouring up from the ground like a kiln, but he didn't mind. A gentle breeze tickled the grass, causing the golden tops to ripple like water. It carried with it the scent of ancient, unspoiled dirt, of wild animals. It whispered of a land where man had lightly tread and much of its form from creation remained intact.

Silvanus looked to be in deep meditation to the casual observer (had there been anyone around to observe), but he remained acutely aware of his surroundings. A smile crept onto his face as he heard the faintest crunch of the soft grass behind him.

He was being hunted.

The hunter moved closer, inching forward on her belly, watching with a trained eye for any indication that she had been discovered. Silvanus remained still. He was waiting for the sun to set, which wasn't for another hour or so, and he hoped this little game might help pass the time.

She must have come upon him by happenchance, spotting him walking through the tall grass, for he gave off no scent to track. She had circled around behind him to stay downwind, never realizing that he could smell the mustiness of her coat nevertheless. Her heart rolled in slow, heavy thumps. Silvanus reached out with his mind, groping for her thoughts, but all he could find was a hunger for raw, bloody meat and a deep instinct to survive.

She crept as far as she dared to go without giving herself away, yet she didn't pounce. She hesitated, watching him. Perhaps she had met with the wiles of man before and suspected a trap. Or maybe she was now close enough to sense that Silvanus wasn't human. It might have been that the sun was in her eyes. Whatever the reason, she didn't wait long.

She exploded from her hiding spot, her powerful legs pumping like great pistons. She covered the ground between them in mere seconds. She leapt into the air, her mouth opened for his throat, but when she hit the ground Silvanus was gone.

The lioness looked around, unable to comprehend how her prey had escaped. Silvanus stood behind the great cat, watching her powerful muscles work beneath her beautiful tawny hide. She sniffed the ground and he startled her with a whistle.

The lioness spun on the spot, then lunged at him. Again Silvanus vanished and reappeared behind her, slapping her on the hind quarter. She came at him again. This time he used his preternatural speed to evade her sharp claws and deadly fangs.

The large cat refused to give up, striking at him again and again. Silvanus broke into laughter. It was a good feeling. He had never laughed before—at least not in the six months since he had awakened in the fortress hidden in the mountains, known only to a few as Purgatory. Whatever his life had been before that day, he could not remember.

That's why he was here. To reclaim the life lost to him.

Silvanus let the lioness take hold of him. She threw her colossal weight into him, but he only stumbled back a step. She raked at him with her claws, but could produce no lasting wounds. She bit down on his shoulder, near his neck, but her fangs couldn't pierce his skin. Silvanus wrestled with the lioness for a moment longer then wrapped his arms around her neck. A jolt of power surged through his body as he fed on her life-force. The lioness made a low growl and fell limp in his arms. Silvanus set her on the ground and backed away.

He didn't want to kill the majestic beast any more than he wanted to kill a human, but he needed to feed and this brought him slightly less guilt. He had only killed five people—that he could remember—since awakening. Four had been humans working in Purgatory, which he had drained in a fit of ravenous hunger. The other had been the savage vampire Kole, which he destroyed with a blast of hellfire to save Jerusa Phoenix.

His heart still ached with the guilt of the four human deaths. Sure he had been disoriented, awakened in a strange place with no memory of his existence, wounded in an effort to keep him from escaping, but the four that he killed had been hiding in a freezer. Their minds told him of their less-than-benevolent intentions toward him, but still that was no excuse. They were scared and weak. Undeserving of the end he had given them. Since then, he swore that no other death would be on account of his lustful hunger.

That turned out to be no easy oath.

He had been violently ill after ingesting the poisoned blood that had threatened to turn Jerusa into a savage. He was no vampire, at least not the kind that drinks blood; his system couldn't handle it and he was further weakened when he had replaced Jerusa's blood with his own.

Silvanus sat in the circle of flattened grass created by his scuffle with the lioness. He looked up at the fresh dusting of stars appearing in the darkening canopy. As most nights, he thought of Jerusa.

So much had befallen her, much of it his fault. She had been the first kind person he had ever met. She brought him clothes and had offered to feed him, without asking anything in return. He imagined her long auburn hair, her pale, almost porcelain skin, her emerald green eyes, so much like his own, all of which were enhanced by the infusion of his blood.

Her inner beauty, however, outweighed her outer beauty by leaps and bounds. There was a gentle meekness about her, a quiet humbleness that one only purchases through great trials. Yet, she was not weak by any means. Even as a human she had a certain fire within. As a vampire she was something to see, that was for sure. His blood had given her incredible speed and strength, something that seemed to both amaze and disconcert the other vampires she was with. Jerusa also retained her ability to see spirits, which according to Shufah—who had lived several millennia—was an unheard of gift among vampires.

Despite all the gifts his blood had bestowed upon Jerusa, she was still a blood drinker. Why? He had traded blood with Jerusa after watching Shufah turn her ill-fated love, Foster, into a vampire in just the same way. Shouldn't his blood have changed Jerusa to be like him? But she wasn't like him. She couldn't bear the sunlight. She had fangs and desired to feast upon living blood. She couldn't teleport or make the hellfire like he could.

His search for answers had only led him to more questions and heaps of frustration. He wanted to know who and what he was, but more so, he needed to know if he had made a mistake in giving Jerusa his blood. Had he saved her or condemned her? Could he still make her like himself? Could he return her to the sunlight?

He wanted to go to her, right then, to vanish from this land and reappear at her side. It would be as easy as a thought to him, yet he knew he must stay. He couldn't face her until he knew how to help her.

The sun vanished beneath the horizon, pulling the thick blanket of night over this part of the world. Silvanus could see why they called it the Dark Continent. A waning crescent moon hung low in the eastern sky, doing very little to dispel the inky darkness that seemed almost tangible. He pitied the humans of this region, who lacking the enhanced eyes of the immortals, felt the true weight of night's obliterating hand.

The world seemed to come alive with the setting of the sun. Lions roared to one another over the long miles. Wildebeests grunted back and forth. Even the lowliest of insects appeared, as if from nowhere, to sing a song to the night.

Though the whole symphony of nature was a masterpiece on the grandest of scales, Silvanus didn't have the luxury of playing audience to it this evening. Other nocturnal creatures, ones far more deadly than the roaring lions, would be stirring soon, escaping their daylight refuge to hunt the few humans that inhabited this ancient land.

Silvanus's lip curled back in a sneer. He understood the hypocrisy of his thoughts. Whether divine or not, he was still a vampire of sorts. He fed from the energy of other living creatures, did he not? Though he had killed, he took no pleasure in it. But the blood drinkers, they seemed to relish in the death of the mortals they fed from or at best looked upon the act with a sort of tired apathy. He didn't really care for any of them, even those in Jerusa's coven.

With just a thought, Silvanus vanished from his spot within the tall grass, reappearing several miles away atop a large outcropping of boulders. The massive round stones were clustered in such a way that it looked as if an army of giants were clawing their way free of the underworld. The granite boulders were hot to the touch, charged by the heat of the intense African sun. Silvanus squatted down in a broken cleft in the top of the highest boulder, his eyes trained on a heavy, flat, slab of stone resting in the scree at the bottom of the hill.

After a long moment, the scree began to dance around as though a tremor moved the ground. The flat slab, which must have weighed a ton or more, rose several inches, sending the loose stones bouncing down the hill. The slab slid to the side revealing a hole at the base of the boulders and out from the belly of the earth, emerged three of the undead.

All three vampires were women. One had skin so dark she seemed to be formed from onyx. Her hair was cropped short, like a man's. She was tall, with long, thin arms and legs, moving with the nimbleness of a gazelle. The second woman was shorter, with long, red hair and skin the color of milk. The third woman had olive skin, much like Silvanus did, but her shoulder length hair was as white as snow.

All three women looked young and were seductively beautiful in their own way, yet they seemed somewhat out of place in the faded and tattered tunics they wore.

They crept from the hole in silence, searching the night with their preternatural senses. The woman with the white hair went to the massive stone slab, sliding it back into place with hardly a grunt. They didn't speak, but seemed to communicate with mere facial expressions. They left their daylight den, moving down the hill and through the tall grass, like three apparitions bent on mischief.

Silvanus watched undetected, wondering how best to proceed. He was sure these were the three vampires described to him by Shufah. She had warned him they would not be easy to approach. If he jumped down and started after them, they would likely disperse when they realized they were being followed. According to Shufah, the three spoke as one or not at all.

Perhaps he should just let them feed and wait for their return. He didn't feel much like watching them glut themselves on human blood, but what if they chose not to take refuge from the sun in the same spot? Considering how difficult it had been to track them down, the odds were good that they wouldn't. He couldn't risk losing them again. It had taken him months to find their trail. He had stumbled upon them in a moment of serendipity and had followed them back to their lair beneath the boulders. He couldn't count on such luck again.

Silvanus vanished from the cleft in the boulder and reappeared in the tall grass. He couldn't see the three women, but he could hear their light footfalls several yards ahead of him. They stopped for just a moment, as if they sensed his presence. They didn't speak their concerns aloud. Instead they continued on in widening paths, fanning out from one another.

Silvanus knew they wouldn't stray far from each other so he decided to follow the woman with the white hair. He listened until her footfalls were almost too distant for even his powerful ears to detect, then he would "skip" over and appear just a bit behind her. Eventually they left the tall grass of the hilly ground and entered into the open plains.

Silvanus spotted a fire off in the distance. It was a large campfire used to ward off the predators hunting the land. Unfortunately for the men sleeping nearby, the predators that were approaching would not be spooked so easily.

Silvanus moved as close to the fire as he could without being detected by either the men or the vampires. He thought of warning the men. He didn't want them to die, least of all at the hands of blood drinkers, but the three women might have some of the answers he desired. If he interrupted their feeding, he doubted they would be in the mood for a chat. Besides, even if he saved these men today, eventually, in one way or another, death would find them. It was a mortal's inheritance, was it not?

There were five men in total around the fire. Three were asleep while two manned the fire and watched for danger. The three women circled around the men, staying just outside of the firelight. There was something odd about their movements, not exactly synchronized, but orchestrated as though each had been carefully thought out ahead of time.

The three women continued to swim the darkness in silence, yet Silvanus sensed it was only silent to the outside world. The trio was communicating every bit as fluently as a shoal of fish or a flock of birds. He could hear the thoughts of mortals as easily as he could hear his own, but the blood drinkers' minds were closed to him.

The three women stopped just outside the ring of firelight, standing in a triangle formation. The two men that were awake seemed to pick up on some subtle clue that they were not alone. They stood with their backs to the fire, scanning the inky world beyond their fire. Without any warning or signal, the attack began.

The dark-skinned woman was the first to strike. She sprang from the shadows with a speed that spoke volumes about her true age and power. She caught one of the men in the chest, knocking the wind from him and preventing him from screaming. The pale redhead moved mere seconds later, taking the other man much in the same way, snatching him up and carrying him off like an owl with a rabbit. The olive-skinned vampire with the white hair remained as a statue, her back to Silvanus, just beyond the rim of firelight.

Silvanus had come across many blood drinkers since his awakening. Some sought out victims of the lowest dregs of humanity: the child molester, the murderer, the terrorist. They channeled the guilt of their own murderous thirsts into a sort of vigilante justice. They were the predators that thinned the mortal herd of the sick, weak and undesirable. Other vampires yielded to their own nature, deeming themselves the top of the food chain and saw no need to discriminate one victim from the next. Mortals were born to die. The vampire was simply a tool of a greater order. Some vampires relished the hunt. They took great pleasure in stalking their prey and when caught, indulged in all manner of physical and psychological torment before allowing their victims to die.

The three vampire women seemed to be none of the above. They killed with speed and mercy and fed with the rapid binging of an animal that feared it may be caught while its head was down. With the men now dead, the two vampires joined their white-haired counterpart within the circle of firelight.

The vampires fell upon the three remaining men without hesitation. The men woke with a start, but died before they could sort out whether or not their terror was real or just a nightmare. The women rose from the corpses of the men, nearly swooning from the fresh blood.

The three women came together near the fire and stood in a tight huddle. Without a word they each extended their left arm to the woman beside them. In another synchronized movement they grasped each other's arms with their right hands, pulled it up to their mouth and sank their fangs into the soft flesh of the other's wrist.

Silvanus watched with amazement. He had witnessed coupling between two before, but only as a means to change a mortal into a vampire. In fact, this was how he had turned Jerusa. It was a called being *born of the blood* and ensured that the fledgling would inherit a great deal of their creator's strength. But these women were already vampires and powerful ones at that.

The three women continued their circuit of giving and taking for a few minutes, then broke off all at once. Again, as if in one mind, they turned their attention to the dead. In a ghastly scene they decapitated each corpse with their bare hands, making sure to crush the skulls before tossing them, along with the bodies, into the fire.

The air filled with the reek of burning flesh. The women left the fire to its business, striking out across the land in the direction opposite their boulder sanctuary. They crossed the land at a rapid pace. They were running from something. Hiding from someone. Only fugitives kept patterns like these.

Near to dawn and close to a hundred miles away from where they started, the women approached a series of caves. The musk of animal fur told that the caves were currently occupied by a pride of lions. Whether the women meant to displace the lions or bunk with them, Silvanus couldn't say. He didn't have time to wait and find out, either. The vampires were fed and the sun would not better their mood. He had to make his move now.

Silvanus appeared in the doorway of the cave. The women topped the hill, saw him standing there and bristled like a trio of startled cats. Without a word to him or each other, the trio attacked.

Their speed and power was matched only by the wordless synchronization of their ferocious assault. At first, they came at him hands outstretched, fangs exposed, perhaps thinking he was a mere human. Silvanus evaded their attack, leaping back with a blast of tremendous speed.

"I mean you no harm," he said.

"Peddle your lies elsewhere, Hunter," the red headed vampire said.

Silvanus took this moment to assess the vampires before him. This was the first time he had been face to face with them. There was something odd about the trio that he couldn't quite grasp. The red head and the tall dark skinned vampires both clenched their eyes shut; only the olive skinned vampire looked upon him. Also, only the red headed vampire spoke, yet to Silvanus it felt as if the words were being spoken by all three.

"I am no Hunter. I seek your wisdom."

"You are a lapdog of the Stewards," the red-haired woman screamed.

The blood drinkers came at him again, their attack more brutal than ever. It was all Silvanus could do to dodge and parry the barrage of punches and kicks coming at him from all directions. Once again, he couldn't shake the overwhelming sense that the three were moving and thinking as one.

Their battle raged in a wide circle, kicking up a great cloud of dust and shattering the rocks on the face of the caves. The lions observed the struggle from the shadow of their den, at one point roaring in warning, but never coming out to challenge the raucous invaders.

Silvanus tried, several times, to explain his case, but the sound of his voice seemed to only antagonize the women more. They continued to attack him, the red-head cursing him, the other two silent; their eyes clenched shut. They were growing frustrated with their inability to land a solid strike and the fact that Silvanus refused to fight back only served to fuel their rage, as though he were mocking them.

He was getting nowhere. He needed their help, but he would never get it unless he could speak. Silvanus vanished from their midst, reappearing twenty yards away.

A look of shock passed over their faces—even the two with their eyes clenched shut. Silvanus stood his ground, expecting another attack, but instead the three women backed away from him.

"You are One Who Has Regained the Sun." The red-head's voice was awestruck and hushed. "Be gone. Trouble us no more. Have we not paid enough?" They turned to go.

"Wait," he called after them, but they continued to walk away, slowly, heads bowed, as though in prayer. "Are you the Erinyes? The Furies?" The women stopped.

"Only one has called us that and not for many centuries," the red-head said. The three kept their backs to him.

A rush of hope flowed through him. "I am Silvanus, sent by the vampire Shufah to seek the wisdom of the Erinyes."

The women turned to face him. The vampire with the white hair stood in the middle of the other two. She searched his eyes.

"We are known by many names," said the vampire with red hair. "Shufah called us the Erinyes, after the mythical Furies of old. We call her friend. Ask what you will. We will give you all that we have."

Chapter Four

Jerusa didn't sleep at all during the daylight hours. Vampires can sleep if they wish, to aid in healing, but it isn't a requirement, as it is with mortals.

She spent the whole day reading books and scouring the internet for any bit of trivia she could find about Rome. She tried to focus on the exotic locales and rich history, but her mind always rolled back to the Stewards.

It made sense that they would use Rome as their home. Shufah described the Stewards as a group of elitist, hypocritical, corrupt serpents who cared not for justice or peace or any of the more nobler pursuits, but instead hoarded power, craved authority and wielded some skewed standard of beauty as a scale for who lived and who died. It all sounded so Roman to Jerusa and gave her very little hope for the future.

But then again, Jerusa wasn't sure she should take Shufah's opinion too much to heart. Something had happened between her and the Stewards, some act of betrayal that lingered with her, even after thousands of years. Shufah wouldn't talk about it, but whatever had occurred, it had not only driven a schism between her and the Stewards, and eventually between her and her twin brother, as well.

Taos stepped up behind her and peered over her shoulder at the computer screen. "I've been to Rome, several times, but never as a human. I wonder if it's as beautiful in the sunlight as the pictures make it out to be."

Jerusa flashed him a small smile. "I guess we'll never know."

"Are you excited?"

"Yes. And no." She turned in her seat to better see his face. "It'll be nice to finally get out of this town, but—"

"You fear the Stewards' judgment."

Jerusa nodded. She knew that she was beautiful, though the awkwardness of growing up as both a "sick kid" and one that sees ghosts had made that fact very hard to admit sometimes. And she was powerful. Silvanus's blood had seen to that. But would it be enough to trump the scar on her chest? If the stories were true, the Stewards had condemned other vampires for less.

Taos reached out and touched the top of her scar sticking out over the V-neck collar of her shirt. "Try not to worry," he said in a soft voice so unlike his usual gruff tenor. "Shufah knows the Stewards well. She won her case with Foster, remember?"

Foster appeared beside them. He smiled down at her, but sadness filled his eyes. Foster had been one of Jerusa's only true friends in the world. She had confided in him about being able to see lingering spirits and he had believed her without question. Shufah and Foster had fallen in love and she had been determined to make him an immortal, though he didn't rise to the standards of the Stewards. Somehow, she had won her case and made Foster a vampire on the same night that Jerusa had been turned. Foster had only lived two nights as a vampire. He sacrificed his life to save Jerusa's, taking on the savage Kole, all alone.

Jerusa glanced over at Shufah, who was deep in some secret research on her laptop. Her bright, bronze eyes flitted side to side as she quickly read the text on the screen. Her fingers flashed in a series of blurs across the keyboard and Jerusa wondered how many computers she had broken that way. Shufah was searching for something important, but her business was her own and no one asked.

Jerusa thought about the timeless grudge Shufah held against the Stewards. How could she not harbor the same feelings for Jerusa? If only Jerusa hadn't been throwing a tantrum at her mother's overbearing hand, had she only stayed home that night, then Shufah wouldn't have lost Foster or her twin brother.

"Are you all right?" Taos asked.

"Yes, I'm fine." But she wasn't. She wasn't fine at all. The cancer of guilt was devouring her from the inside out. Not just for the pain she had caused Shufah, but Thad, and her mother as well.

She stood from her desk, brushed past Taos and approached Shufah, who looked up at Jerusa with a tiny smile. She had been only fourteen when she had been made a vampire and though she had weathered nearly six millennia, her dark face remained as youthful as ever. Only her eyes hinted at the ancient mind within.

"You look upset."

If there was any spite or hatred dwelling within her, she hid it well. "I'm sorry to bother you. I just wanted you to know that Foster is here. Just in case, y'know, you'd like to see him."

Shufah retained her smile, but her eyes glazed over with the promise of tears. "I would like that very much."

Jerusa outstretched her hand and Shufah took it. Foster's spiritual form took on a dim luminescence, a slight blue aura. Shufah searched the room and after a few seconds located him. Her smile broadened, as did the pain in her eyes. Foster came closer, stood before her and caressed her cheek. Shufah closed her eyes and tilted her head as though she could feel his touch, though in truth she couldn't. She couldn't feel him or hear him. She could only see him with Jerusa's aid and even then it was not much more than a gossamer image.

Shufah opened her eyes and stared up into Foster's face. "My love," she said, then slid her hand out of Jerusa's. She swallowed hard, as though her heart was making an escape, then turned back to her laptop.

"I'm sorry," Jerusa said. "Maybe I shouldn't do that anymore."

"Why do you say that?"

"All it does is cause you pain."

Shufah's fingers paused on her keyboard. "Yes. Yes it does. But it also brings me comfort to know he is so near. That he is watching over us. My pain is not of your doing. I wish you would believe that. Your apology is unnecessary."

Jerusa didn't know what to say. Shufah had told her the same thing several times, but it didn't ease the guilt. She glanced around, hoping to find something to talk about, but there was nothing. Finally she pointed at Shufah's laptop.

"You've been on this thing day and night for the past two weeks. You gonna fill the rest of us in on what you're looking for?"

Shufah kept her eyes on the screen and continued to type. "I'm looking for help," she said after a moment.

"Help for what? The Stewards? Who could help us against them?"

"You're not thinking of searching out the Zealots, are you?" Taos asked. "They're too unpredictable to trust."

"Not the Zealots," Shufah said. "They would do us more damage than good. If you must know, I'm searching for someone to help us with Alicia."

At the sound of her name Alicia materialized within the room. She stood with her arms folded over her chest and a scowl on her face.

"Alicia? What do you mean? Why do we need someone to help us with her?"

Shufah turned to face Jerusa. "You can't go on like this. It is imperative that you feed and soon, even if it is only animal blood. It's not just that your thirst is growing, making you more prone to uninhibited attacks. We have the Stewards to worry about. If they learn you are unable or unwilling to feed, they will destroy you without even a moment's hesitation to consider why. And even if they don't destroy you, The Gargoyle's Scales will."

"The Gargoyle's Scales. The Gray Death. The Gray Cloak. The Obsidian Curse. That's all you people seem to want to talk about. Alicia wouldn't do anything to harm me," Jerusa assured Shufah. "Whatever her reason is for stopping me, I'm sure it's a good one."

Shufah scanned the room as though she expected to see

Alicia hiding in the corner. "I hope you're right."

"But you think I'm wrong?"

"You can't trust ghosts. I've told you that before. They are not motivated by the same desires as the living. Though they seem kind, they can be quite bitter and cruel."

"Does that include Foster?" Immediately Jerusa regretted her words. "I'm sorry. I didn't mean to be so harsh."

Shufah flashed a patient smile. "I know you didn't."

"Why don't you trust ghosts? Sure, there are the angry ones, but surely when you were mortal you came across a kind one now and then."

"Oh, yes. When I still had the sight, I met many ghosts. Some angry, some sad. Others were violent. And I too had a few that I called friends. But kindness and friendship are powerful tools to lead one into betrayal."

Jerusa's stomach fluttered. She felt dangerously close to overstepping her bounds with Shufah, but she had never opened up to Jerusa like this before. "A ghost betrayed you? How?"

"Not just me, but my whole family. My brother, Suhail, and I were quite gifted, though my father commanded our silence concerning our gift. In those days, we likely would have been stoned to death or burned as witches." A tiny, sad smile flashed across Shufah's face at some distant memory. "This ghost led me and Suhail to a man named Marjek."

"Marjek of the High Council?" Taos asked in surprise.

"Is Marjek your maker?"

Shufah nodded. "Yes. He turned Suhail and me."

"You were turned by Marjek?" Taos asked again. A look of awe passed over his face. "That explains a lot."

Jerusa wasn't sure what that meant, but she didn't feel right asking about it. "I still don't see the betrayal. Had the ghost not led you to Marjek, you would have died thousands of years ago."

Shufah shook her head. "The ghost didn't lead us to Marjek to be turned. He led us there to die and Marjek would have killed us had he not been so enamored with our beauty. Instead, he sought to make us his pets."

"Why did the ghost want you to die?" Taos asked.

"Suhail and I always believed it was to punish our father. The ghost may have been a man my father wronged in life, perhaps competition for our mother or even a man my father killed in battle. We never found out for sure. Once we were turned, we never saw another spirit again. If the ghost was out for vengeance against our father, he got his wish."

Jerusa wasn't sure she wanted to know, but the question came unbidden. "How?"

"Marjek carried us far away, keeping us as his slaves. After a while, we were able to convince him to take us home, if only for a visit. Once back, we discovered that our mother, thinking her children had died, had plunged a blade into her own breast. Our father still lived, though by then he was quite old and close to passing."

Jerusa could almost see the ancient tragedy playing out in her mind. "You turned your father. You made him a vampire."

Shufah nodded. "Suhail and I took turns feeding on him then letting him feed from us, just as Marjek had done with us. Father was so frail and weak. We were terrified he wouldn't survive. But he did. He became a vampire, too. For that brief moment, we were happy again."

Jerusa swallowed the knot rising in her throat. "Where is your father now?"

"He didn't live to see the next moon rise. When Marjek returned to collect us, he was furious at what we had done. Father's youth had been spent long ago and all that Marjek could see was a vampire locked eternally in the body of an old man. He would not have such ugliness walking the earth."

"Marjek killed your father?"

"He staked my father to a tree and left him for the sun. We were hidden from the daylight, but not so far away that we couldn't hear our father's screams. Not long after that, Suhail and I escaped Marjek. He stalked us for a while, but soon we became too powerful for him to control, so he let us be."

A fire of righteous indignation burned in Jerusa's bones. She wanted to hear a story of vengeance. A tale of Marjek's pain-filled death and of Shufah standing victoriously over his remains. But she knew no such tale existed. Marjek was a Steward, on the High Council and there were no happy endings.

The house's alarm system rang out, snapping Jerusa from her thoughts. The noise was barely audible to humans, but not to the vampires. Shufah turned back to her laptop and pulled up the surveillance cameras. She checked around the outside of the house and when all was clear she switched to the cameras around the perimeter of the property.

The cameras were equipped with UV filtering lenses which made the daylight world outside seem perpetually steeped in shadows. After searching for a moment, Shufah pointed to the screen. Two men stood just inside the edge of the forest, watching the house.

It was hard to determine the men's heights through the monitor, but both were of stocky build. Each man was dressed in dark clothes that helped them blend into the forest, but would also pass as casual wear on the streets.

"Who are they?" Jerusa asked. "They look like cops or maybe FBI."

"No, I don't think so," Shufah said. "Though, they may be military."

Taos leaned over Shufah's shoulder. "I recognize those two. It's hard to forget faces that ugly. They've been snooping around town for the past couple of nights. I don't think they are military, though."

"Then who are they?" Jerusa looked at the men again, checking to see if there was a detail that she had missed. There didn't seem to be anything conspicuous about them at all.

"I think they are Light Bearers," Taos said. "They are the only ones that would know how to track us."

"I thought you said the Light Bearers were passive. That they stayed on the fringes, gathering little observations to add to their musty old libraries. Showing up to a vampire's home, during daylight hours, seems pretty aggressive to me."

Taos looked at Jerusa and shrugged. "I don't know. Maybe they've defected and want us to turn them. It happens from time to time. I can't keep track of humans and their motivations. All I can say is at least they are smart enough not to try this after dark. I'd make a quick meal of them."

"What do you think?" Jerusa asked Shufah.

"I think Taos is wrong."

Taos's face curled in skepticism. "What do you mean I'm wrong? If those two aren't members of the Light Bearers, then I'm a mosquito."

"No, I mean, I don't think they are human." Shufah typed something on her keyboard and the screen changed to a thermal image.

The background color was a spray of blues and greens and the computer showed the outside temperature to be fifty-seven degrees. The two men, however, were amorphous blobs of bright red and orange, which wasn't unusual for living creatures, except that their core temperatures averaged one-hundred and fifteen degrees.

"Well," Taos said in a slow, dry voice, "those two might want to go to the hospital. They have quite the fever going."

"They're out in daylight, so it's obvious they aren't vampires." Jerusa was mostly speaking to herself. "Do you think they are Divine Vampires, maybe come to look for Silvanus?"

Shufah shook her head. "I don't think so. A Divine Vampire mimics a human so closely it is near impossible to tell the difference, which is what makes them so difficult to find and why the Stewards maintain they don't exist."

Taos stood straight as if the view on the monitor gave him

the creeps. "If they aren't human and they're not vampires, then what are they?"

Again Shufah shook her head. "I don't know. It seems the Light Bearers are no longer passive observer. It looks like they've been up to something naughty. Whatever the case, I'm putting the house on lock down."

Shufah typed another command on her computer and the mechanical buzz of steel shutters, descending from the ceiling to cover all exterior windows and doors, filled the house. The band of workers from the community town down south had done a thorough job turning this house into a vampire sanctuary. Jerusa had made friends with several of them and she often wondered how they were doing.

Shufah switched the monitor back to standard view just in time to see the two men—or whatever they were—stand up and strike out through the forest.

"That was strange," Taos said. "Do you suppose they heard the shutters falling?"

"I believe they did," Shufah said. "Incredible hearing, wouldn't you say."

Taos nodded.

The bigger question for Jerusa, however, was would the two men have tried to enter the house had Shufah not dropped the steel shutters? And had they entered, would they have come as friend or foe? Jerusa felt she knew the answer to both and neither one filled her with warm, cuddly thoughts.

Shufah turned to face Jerusa and Taos. "Let's keep this matter to ourselves for now. Ming, Ralgar and the other Hunters need not know of it. Nor do the Stewards, at least until we know what the Light Bearers are up to."

"Can we tell Thad?" Jerusa asked.

Taos barked out a short, dry laugh. "I wouldn't. That boy takes everything too hard. He's been moping about the past few months like the world's coming to an end."

What Taos didn't understand was that to Thad his world *was* coming to an end. He didn't want to be a vampire, despite all of the benefits, which meant his only choice was death or quarantine. And for Taos to just laugh it off, like it was a trivial matter, felt like no less than a slap in the face, especially since it was his bite that had infected Thad.

"Well, since I've been commanded not to see Thad, I wouldn't know anything about that, would I?" Jerusa went back to her computer, but she wasn't in the mood to surf the net. Instead she pulled up her email.

Despite Shufah's warning, Jerusa decided to tell Thad everything, about the Hunters coming to escort them, about the meeting with the Stewards and even about the two men hiding in the trees. He was a part of this, wasn't he? He deserved to know the truth. He deserved to make the choice.

Jerusa typed fast and hit send before Taos or Shufah saw her. Before she changed her mind.

Chapter Five

General Starnes sat relaxed in his chair, his face calm and unreadable, as the man on his computer screen all but foamed at the mouth. Starnes was video messaging with his "superior", Four Star General Zacharias Pleasant. The man didn't live up to his name.

"So you're telling me project Light Bearer is a bust?" Pleasant asked, though it sounded more like a threat.

"Not a bust, sir. We are still rebuilding after the fire."

"Rebuilding? It's been six months. How much more rebuilding do you have to do?"

"We are nearly complete, sir." Starnes kept his voice even and emotionless. "The fire was extensive and much of our research was destroyed. It takes time to get up and running again."

"Don't talk to me about time. Do you know how many other governments are attempting projects like this one?"

"No, sir." That was a lie. There were four countries with Enhanced Combatant programs running: Russia, Israel, China and of course the US. Starnes knew this because the Light Bearer Society had infiltrated all of them. It sickened Starnes that he had dedicated his life to playing the role of the good soldier, following the orders of a deceptive government and its corrupt leaders, but in order to bring the light of truth to the world, you sometimes had to tread through dark places.

"You may have sold your little 'X-Files' program to the joint chiefs, but not me," Pleasant continued. "Promises were made. If there is no delivery, it'll be your skin in the fryer, not mine."

"I understand, sir." Someone entered the room to his right, but Starnes kept his eyes fixed to the computer screen.

"I don't think you do. This is one of our most important

missions. We cannot afford to come in second in this race. If you fail, a court martial will be the least of your worries. Do you understand me? The clock is ticking."

"I understand, sir."

"We'll see." Pleasant reached over, out of the camera's view and the screen went dark.

Starnes made sure the secure link was severed before turning to the tiny man, in the white lab coat, standing in the doorway.

"What is it Willis?"

Willis Goodalle—the top scientist in Purgatory—was tiny, mousy and as frail as a blade of grass, but he was a brilliant geneticist. He wasn't a true believer, not a member of the Light Bearers, but he was, as most scientists are, easily motivated by the research and money.

Goodalle stepped into the room. "Sir, Shadow Team has made contact."

Starnes turned in his chair, which seemed to startle Goodalle for some reason. "Have they located Lazarus, yet?"

Goodalle fidgeted in place. He opened his mouth, but it seemed to take an extra-long time for the words to get past his teeth. "No, sir. They have searched the town, but they say Lazarus is not there."

Starnes clenched his jaw, reining in the scream of frustration brewing inside. The being, designated with the code name Lazarus, had escaped from Purgatory six months ago. He had somehow reanimated, or maybe hatched was a better word, from one of the rock-oddities the order had collected from around the world. To Starnes's knowledge, this was a first. Lazarus had destroyed the lab—and several well-armed soldiers—in a great conflagration, before killing four scientists and vanishing into thin air. Through a painfully detailed search, they had tracked him to a small Midwestern town, where a small coven of vampires had taken up residence. But as before, he vanished before they could get to him.

"If they have not located Lazarus, then why are you

bothering me?"

Goodalle cleared his throat. "Shadow Team is requesting to feed, sir."

Starnes looked at the digital calendar on his computer. "What? Already? They fed less than a week ago."

"I know, sir, but their monitors are reading a high level of blood toxicity. They need another transfusion. They are requesting to feed on the vampires."

"Negative," Starnes snapped back. "They are our only link to Lazarus at the moment. Tell them to seek out a human transfusions. But not in town. I don't want to tip off the vampires to our presence."

"With all due respect, sir," Goodalle said in a timid voice. "Vampire blood may sustain them for a much longer duration."

"Can you say, without a doubt, what effect vampire blood will have on them? Will it make them stronger? Maybe uncontrollable? Or is it possible that it could kill them?" Starnes sat back and crossed his legs, enjoying the look of discomfort on Goodalle's face. He was worse than a whipped dog.

"No, sir, I can't say *without a doubt* what will happen to them."

"Then the subject is closed."

"Was it wise for us to send them out without finishing our tests, sir? We have no idea the long term effects of the process."

"Willis," Starnes said, with all the condescension he could muster. "Fortune favors the brave." Goodalle didn't seem convinced. Starnes stood up and placed his arm around his shoulders, smiling a bit when the little man flinched. "Let's take a walk, shall we?"

Goodalle gave a reluctant nod. "All right. Where to?"

"The incubators."

Goodalle's face tightened in disgust. "Do we have to?"

"Don't you want to see your children?"

"I hate when you call them that." Goodalle shivered as though a snake had slithered across his feet.

Starnes clapped him on the back, then led him back out into the hallway. Purgatory was a busy place these days, despite what he had told General Pleasant. Scientist, soldiers and other personnel scurried from place to place, never stopping to make chit-chat, or even eye contact, with Starnes and Goodalle. Near ninety percent of the Purgatory staff belonged to the Light Bearers and the other ten percent were either too scared or well-paid to step out of line. Starnes would have preferred a hundred percent fealty, but he had to work with what he had.

"So, tell me about your children."

Goodalle squirmed. "Please sir, don't call them that."

"Oh, fine. Tell me about the umbilicus. What are the stats?"

"Out of twenty, five have either perished of massive organ failure or we've had to euthanize them, due to uncontrollable mutations."

"And of the others?" Starnes stopped in front of an elevator, took the key fastened to his wrist and inserted in the lock near the buttons.

"Of the thirteen left in stasis, I'd wager we'll lose another five to ten."

The elevator doors opened. They stepped inside the car and Starnes pressed the button for sub-level three. "I don't like what I'm hearing, Willis."

Goodalle seemed to shrivel in his lab coat. "I'm sorry, sir. It's impossible to predict just how the gene therapy will react with any given subject. The two umbilicus in Shadow Team may just be flukes. They could fall ill to any number of maladies in the field. Mutations, tumors, they could even create some sort of global pandemic."

"You said they couldn't reproduce."

The elevator doors opened and they stepped out into the brightly lit hall. Just a few steps brought them to the observation windows looking down onto the clean room.

"So far they seem unable to affect others, as the vampires do, but that doesn't mean it will stay that way." Goodalle's voice seemed to gain strength. Perhaps it was because in this level of Purgatory he was the lord and master. "This is why I strongly urge you to call Shadow Team home. We need more testing."

Starnes leaned in and looked down upon the twenty incubation pods. Seven were empty, but the other thirteen were filled with an amber liquid, so thick you could barely make out the bodies resting within. The amber liquid was some sort of amniotic fluid used to introduce the umbilicus gene to the human "volunteers". It was all very technical, which is why it was best left in Goodalle's hands.

In one of the pods, a pair of wrinkled hands pressed against the glass. A face swam to the surface, its dark eyes fixed on Starnes. The mouth opened as if to scream, but was silenced by the amber fluid and thick glass. In defeat, the face vanished in the murky depth. A thick rope-like appendage slammed against the glass hard enough to be heard in the observation deck. It slithered against the glass like an eel seeking escape. Starnes took a step back, repulsed by the sight.

Goodalle smiled at him. "It knows you're watching. Enhanced senses and strength are present, though not in the levels seen in the older vampires. They possess incredible regenerative abilities, as well." He paused for a moment. "That is, once they have a transfusion."

"Yet, they aren't true vampires. Nor are they like Lazarus. Why?"

Goodalle shrugged. "The blood sample Lazarus left in the lab was already dissipating when we collected it, so it wasn't a true sample. We had to do a lot of guess work. You know, genetic fill-in-the-blanks. Now that the sample is gone, this is all we have to work with."

"That's why we need Shadow Team out in the field. When they locate Lazarus then we'll have our pure sample. How long until the others are up and running?"

"Three out of the remaining thirteen are showing promise. I'd say they'll be up to par with Shadow Team in another three months."

"Three months?"

"Please, sir, don't push the process. If we hatch them too early, they could die. Or worse yet, they could live, but the compliance data chip might not take hold. You don't want them running loose without a leash."

Starnes nodded, but deep down he didn't believe they had three months. General Pleasant suspected something. Starnes could see it in his eyes. Sooner or later Pleasant would stop by, with a few well-armed friends and want to know what the taxpayers' money was being spent on. Starnes couldn't allow that to happen, not when the Light Bearers were so close to the answers they had sought, so diligently for, throughout the centuries. The vampires had hoarded their secrets like spoiled dragons, but soon the Light Bearers would have the power to take what they wanted, to slay the old dragons in their lairs and retrieve the treasure for the good of mankind.

"Sir," Goodalle said, drawing Starnes out of his thoughts. "Maybe there is another way to advance the program."

Starnes turned his attention to the scientist, though he felt oddly uncomfortable turning his back on the incubator pods. "I'm listening."

"Just because we don't have Lazarus doesn't mean we can't benefit from what we do have."

"And just what do we have?"

"We have the location of a small vampire coven, with Shadow Team within walking distance of their sanctuary."

"I thought we discussed this. I don't want the umbilicus feeding from vampires until we know what it will do to them."

Goodalle shook his head. "That's not what I meant. Why not apprehend one of the vampires? Bring it back here to Purgatory. True it isn't Lazarus, but just think about it. An endless supply of vampire blood, to do with what we please."

"We've made attempts to capture vampires, many times. All

have failed. They are too strong and fast."

Goodalle smiled. "But that was before you had two umbilicus at your disposal."

Chapter Six

"I'm going," Jerusa said.

"No, you're not," Shufah answered back.

Jerusa forced herself to breathe while trying to keep her emotions under control. She had never spoken harshly to Shufah before and right now she was on the verge of screaming her head off. "You can't stop me. I'm not a prisoner here."

Jerusa looked to Taos for support. The hulking blond was the eternal scoundrel, who considered rules and boundaries to be as irritating as a rash. He'd take her side in this.

Much to her chagrin, Taos shrugged his shoulders. "I have to agree with Shufah. It's foolish and unnecessary. What do you hope to gain from it?"

Jerusa stood silent for a moment, fixed in an indignant awe. When the words finally came, they rose up out of her like volcanic bile. She shook her head. "I should have known better than to expect any help from you. You play the great warrior—the vampire that answers to no one. But the truth is, you're nothing but a mindless drone, doing the bidding of whatever master you serve. First it was Kole. Now Shufah."

Taos squared his stance. His jaw jutted forward in defiance. "I am my own master, no one else's. Not Kole. Not Shufah. No one."

Jerusa spat a derisive laugh at him. She didn't know why she was being so hateful, but she couldn't stop it. "It was you and your master that caused all of this. If it wasn't for you, I'd still be human. The least you could do is take my side."

A glimmer of regret flickered in his cold blue eyes, but it was quickly devoured by anger. "Kole was not my master," he yelled, taking a step toward Jerusa.

Jerusa lowered her stance, preparing for Taos's attack, almost craving it. But before the battle could begin, Shufah stepped between them.

"Easy," she whispered to Taos, who turned away with knotted fists and a clenched jaw. "It is the hunger that maddens her." Shufah looked to Jerusa with eyes soft and full of love. Jerusa hated how those eyes somehow changed her anger into guilt. "I know it's important. I do. I'm not so old that I've forgotten. But is it worth the risk?"

Jerusa found it hard to press the words past the knot in her throat. When she spoke, her voice sounded shaky and frail to her own ears. "She's my mom. I know she's just another human to you, maybe not even worth feeding on, but she's mine." She turned away, unable to look at either of them. "Let's be honest here. I'm not going to make it back. The Stewards are going to take one look at my scar and order the Hunters to turn me into a pile of ash. I can accept that. I'm not afraid to die. But I can't leave without saying goodbye to my mother. You want to know what there is to gain, Taos? Nothing. Nothing at all. Life is about the comfort you give to others, not yourself."

She glanced at Taos over her shoulder, but he remained silent with his back to her.

Shufah placed her hand on Jerusa's neck, a gesture so soft and kind that she wanted to cry. "All right. If you want to see your mother, we won't stand in the way. But know the risk. In your state, you may attack her. Alicia may stop you, this is true, but if she's too slow . . . The guilt of killing your own blood is overwhelming. Believe me, I know."

Shufah would know. She had risen up against her own brother to save Jerusa's life.

"I won't attack her. I promise."

"Just the same, Taos and I will be close by, watching. Don't be tempted to tell your mother the truth of your situation. It could drive her mad."

"I understand. I won't."

Shufah sighed. She looked over Jerusa's face with careful scrutiny. "Well, you can't go see your mother looking like that."

Jerusa turned to the decorative mirror on the wall. Shufah was right. Jerusa could pass off the deep red of her lips as lipstick. Her mother wouldn't approve, but it wouldn't draw her suspicion. Jerusa's eyes were a whole other story. The rings of blood surrounding her irises were ghastly and inhuman.

"I see what you mean. Maybe I can wear sunglasses. Tell my mom my eyes are irritated."

"That may work for you mother, but the Stewards will see you for what you are."

"And what is that?" Jerusa didn't mean for the question to come out so harsh.

"All I'm saying is that the Stewards will see you as a vampire that has not fed. For the Stewards that's an offense worse than the scar you bear."

"Oh, sorry."

Shufah smiled. "I understand. Let me teach you a trick that may help us with our tasks ahead."

Shufah brought her hand to her mouth and used one of her fangs to draw a drop of blood from her thumb. Jerusa caught the scent and her body tensed. Alicia appeared beside her and placed her hand on Jerusa's chest. It was warm to the touch, as real as any living person's, but there was warning in that embrace.

"Alicia won't let me drink from you, either." The smell of blood, though slight, sent a shudder through her body. Every muscle burned, urging her to abandon reason and pounce on Shufah. Her mouth filled with saliva, to the point of nearly slobbering, yet her throat remained as parched as the desert.

"I figured as much," Shufah said, her deep voice soft and calming. "I'm not offering you to drink from me, though I would if Alicia would allow it."

Jerusa glanced at Alicia and the ghost shook her head.

"She says no."

Shufah stepped forward. "Then let me place a few drops in your eyes."

Alicia's hand tightened on Jerusa's chest and a bolt of pain flashed throughout her body. "Stop," she said throwing out her hand. "Back up. Please."

Shufah sighed, then sucked the blood from her thumb. When she removed her thumb from her mouth the tiny wound was gone.

"I told you," Shufah said. "Ghosts cannot be trusted." Jerusa had never heard such disgust in her voice before. It pained her to know that she was angry with Alicia. "If not my blood," she continued, "then what about your own?"

Alicia glanced over her shoulder at Foster. The two ghosts exchanged a silent conversation using only their eyes. Alicia turned back to Jerusa and nodded.

"She says yes."

"Wonderful," Shufah said sarcastically. "Do just as I did. Pierce your thumb with your fang and draw out a little blood."

Jerusa did as she was told, gasping a bit at the sharpness of her fangs. She had never used them before and though she had run her tongue across them many times, she never realized just how deadly they were, until now. In movies, vampires always looked like some sort of saber-toothed monster, with fangs longer than her pinky fingers. Those movie creatures were so wholly inhuman that they shocked their prey with fear and repulsion. But true vampires weren't meant to drive humans away, but to mimic them, draw them into their clutches by beauty and mystique.

No, those long grotesque fangs were not the dangerous ones. The tiny fangs, the ones you don't notice until they have opened your veins, they were the substance of nightmares.

Jerusa pulled her hand away from her mouth and stared at the tiny crimson drop tenuously balancing upon the curve of her thumb. It seemed so powerful, so volatile, like a drop of nitroglycerin.

"Place a couple of drops of blood in your eyes," Shufah said. Jerusa hesitated, more than a bit mortified. "Go on. Trust me."

Jerusa tilted her head back and brought her hand over her face. The wound in her thumb was already starting to heal. Jerusa had to squeeze hard to get the drops to fall. There was a fraction of a second when the blood caused her eyes to burn, but that quickly gave way to a cooling sensation, so refreshing that a small moan of relief fell from her mouth.

She looked up, amazed at how much better her eyes felt. Until now, she hadn't even realized how irritated they had become.

"Now smear some blood on your lips," Shufah said.

Jerusa reopened her thumb and rubbed on a thick layer of blood.

"Did it work?"

Taos made a tiny, impressed smirk. Shufah smiled and pointed toward the mirror.

Jerusa stared at her reflection in awe. She understood that her body would reabsorb her own blood, but that knowledge couldn't replace eighteen years of human rational thinking. With the amount of blood that she dropped into her eyes and smeared on her lips, her face should have been a macabre mask. Yet, her pale skin was clean and flawless. Not only that, but the rings of blood around her irises were gone and her lips no were longer crimson.

Shufah stepped up beside her and ran her fingers though Jerusa's hair. "It will hide the signs of your hunger for a couple of hours. Long enough for you to meet with your mother. I want you to do this as often as you can while we are in the company of other vampires and especially when we stand before the Stewards. The more secrets you keep from them, the better off you will be. Understand?"

"Yes," Jerusa said. She turned back to the mirror. "Thank you."

The last remaining rays of sunlight bled into the purple twilight. Jerusa knew this, not because of the clock on the wall, or the security monitors, but because she could sense it. Shufah typed in the security code to lower the steel shutters and unlock the sanctuary door. They moved upstairs where the lights, set on timers, were brightly glowing.

"Ming and Ralgar will be here to collect us in a bit," Shufah said. "We haven't much time. Jerusa, we'll go to your mother's first, then go get Thad." She caught the look of concern that flashed in Jerusa's eye and cocked her head with intrigue. "Is something the matter?"

"No," Jerusa said, a little too quick to be convincing. "I'm just worried about Thad. I don't think he's going to be too happy to see us."

"I suspect not."

Taos stepped out of his bedroom, dressed in dark blue jeans, expensive leather boots, a button-down shirt and a sports coat that made his broad shoulders seem as wide as Jerusa was tall. He pulled his long blond hair back into a tight ponytail, checked himself in the hallway mirror and then turned to the group. "That boy needs to stop being a bleating little sheep and let me finish the job I started on him."

"You mean to kill him?" Jerusa asked, a slight edge to her voice. "Cause that was your original intent, wasn't it?"

Taos looked at her with one raised eyebrow. "Don't get sassy. You know what I meant."

"Thad has some tough choices to make," said Shufah. "But he must decide for himself. Come, we must go."

"All right," Taos said. "But I'm driving. I can't stand to ride shotgun to Jerusa any longer. You know, for a fledgling vampire, you sure drive like an elderly human." Taos turned and stepped out the front door before Jerusa could respond.

A small smile flashed across Shufah's face before she turned and followed Taos. Jerusa, the last to step outside, closed the door and reactivated the security system. It was a short walk from the house to the garage, but the three of them took it slowly, scanning the darkness with their enhanced senses for any sign of danger. The area was clear, but the two men from the Light Bearer's Society were still out there somewhere and Jerusa didn't like that thought at all.

Taos parked down the street from Jerusa's old home.

"Are you sure you want to do this?" Taos asked. "We can come in with you."

Jerusa touched his arm and smiled. She couldn't quite figure Taos out. When they had first met, he had been a nightmare, a hulking vampire with a short temper and a bad attitude. And though he sometimes slipped back into his misanthropic, sullen persona, there were times when a light of kindness would spring forth. She sometimes caught him watching her and the look in his eyes both disturbed and fascinated her at the same time. And there were times when he spoke so harshly to her that she would gladly set him ablaze just to shut him up. But other times, he treated her with such thoughtful compassion, like now, that it made her want to weep. She wished that he would just pick one mood or the other so that she could stop feeling confused.

"No. You both should stay here. For better or worse, she's my mother. This may be the last time we ever see each other."

"We'll be here if you need us," Shufah said.

Jerusa nodded, then slipped out of the car and made her way toward the house. The downstairs lights were on. The curtains were open, giving her a clear view of the living room, but she didn't see her mother.

The house, which seemed so large to her as a child, yet so tight and constricting as a teenager, looked practically miniscule to her now. It wasn't that living in the lavish house Foster had bequeathed to her had given her a haughty spirit toward her mother's home. But sometimes places become cluttered, not with physical items, like in a hoarder's den, but with memories. In open spaces, those memories might drift to you like the subtle scent of a sweet perfume. But when those memories collect in a small space, they can choke you.

Or maybe she was being melodramatic.

Jerusa glanced in the window of her mother's car as she passed by. The keys were still in the ignition. She gave a tiny laugh, but the sight of the keys made her heart hurt. When she was gone, who would take care of her mother? Who would make sure she locked the doors at night and remind her to check the car for her lost keys?

Jerusa pulled the keys from the ignition. She opened the front door of the house, which was of course unlocked, and knocked as to not startle her mother. "Mom," she called. "It's me. Are you home?" She knew her mother was home. She could hear her heart beating, but asking seemed like the human thing to do.

"Jerusa? Is that you?" Debra Phoenix poked her head out of the kitchen, as timid as a rabbit emerging from its burrow. She glanced about as though the room was dim, then locked on to Jerusa. A great smile broke across her face and she shuffled out of the kitchen with her arms outstretched.

Debra hugged her tight, saying her name over and over as though Jerusa had been lost to her for years. Jerusa tried to return the hug, but her mother's frail form felt alien to her now. Debra had always been skinny, but now her mother felt like a loose bundle of sticks hiding within a thin leather bag. Her heart roared in Jerusa's ears and she struggled to tune out the sound of the rushing blood.

"Okay, okay, I missed you too, mom." Jerusa gently pushed her mother back. She wanted to breathe through her mouth to keep from smelling her mother's human scent, but she was afraid of revealing her fangs if she did so. "Let's go sit down. I have something I need to talk to you about."

"Oh, okay." Her mother looked around the room as though she were unsure where she was, then turned and shuffled off toward the kitchen.

"Why are you dressed like that?" Jerusa asked, pointing out her mother's bathrobe and slippers. "It's only seven o'clock."

Debra Phoenix flashed a sheepish smile as she sat at the kitchen table. "I don't have anyone to talk to or be with, so I usually get ready for bed as soon as I get home from work."

And the guilt trip begins, Jerusa thought.

"Why don't you get a hobby? Sewing club. Bowling. Anything is better than just hanging around the house all night. You need to get out and make some friends."

Debra pursed her lips as though Jerusa's advice was sour to the taste. "I'm too old to make friends. Besides, no one wants to hang around an old, crazy woman like me. I could get some cats, though. That would be nice. There's a lot more room now that you've left me."

Jerusa suppressed a deep sigh. It was an act, all of it. The frazzled expressions, the lonely spinster routine, even the weight loss was just a conscious act to seem more lost without Jerusa around to take care of her.

"Mom, you can't be like this," Jerusa said as soft as she could. "I'm not moving back in." Her mother's eyes became slits. "I'm just saying, you need to take care of yourself. You spent your whole life taking care of me, but I'm okay now. I can take care of myself."

"I did just take care of you." That spiteful edge started to creep into her mother's voice. "For eighteen years I gave you everything I had. Sacrificed everything. My marriage. My life."

"Don't put that on me. I understand what you gave up for me and I'm thankful, but you can't expect me to shut down my life and lock myself away with you here."

"No, but you don't have to abandon me, either."

Jerusa covered her eyes with her hands. "I'm not abandoning you."

Her mother pushed away from the table and went to the sink to finish hand-washing some pots. "What do you want to talk to me about?"

Her wall was up. Anything short of Jerusa begging to move

back in would not be welcomed.

Jerusa swallowed hard.

"I'm going away for a while."

The words fell like a hammer's blow. Debra stood motionless for a moment, as though she couldn't quite process what she had heard. Jerusa considered repeating herself, but before she could, her mother slammed the pot on the counter with a thunderous clang.

"Not abandoning me, huh? What a nice little liar you've become."

"Don't be that way."

She turned around. "Is it that boy?"

"Thad?"

Her mother nodded. "Yeah, him. You've been different ever since you met him."

"Don't bring him into this."

"Are you running away with him?"

"We're not running away."

Her mother pointed an accusatory finger at her. "You are running off with him. What? Are you getting married or something?"

Jerusa's cheeks blushed hot. "No, we're not getting married."

Alicia and Foster appeared in the room, one on either side of Debra. Alicia crossed her arms and rolled her eyes as she always did. Foster, who in life, had only heard the stories Jerusa had told him, seemed aghast by the actual woman of the tales.

"So, where are you going?"

Jerusa hesitated, considering whether she should lie or not. Her mother was on the verge of a full tilt tantrum. Jerusa wanted to tell her the truth, all of it, but Shufah was right. Her mother would never be able to process the whole story. Either she'd think it was some cruel jape or she'd go mad with the knowledge that the world wasn't flat.

"I'm going to Rome," Jerusa said, just above a whisper. She closed her eyes and awaited the explosion.

But it didn't come.

She opened her eyes. Across the room Debra Phoenix stood as stiff as a tree, her face a twisted scowl of rage. "Get out," she said and Jerusa nearly flinched at the venom in her voice.

"Mom," she implored.

"Don't call me that. Don't ever call me that again. Go on. Leave. Run off with your boyfriend and leave me here to die."

"Don't talk like that."

Her mother's lips pulled back from her teeth like a snarling dog. "You're sick. Have you looked in the mirror? You look terrible, all pale. You've not been taking your rejection medicine. Don't deny it. I've checked on it. And now you want to run off to Rome. What for? To die? Well, I won't let you. I'll have you committed if I have to."

She turned side to side, mumbling and raving to herself. Jerusa rushed to her side, a little too quickly judging from Debra's panicked expression. She looked into Jerusa's face and gasped. It was then that Jerusa noticed the tiny wet trickles tickling her cheeks.

Jerusa wiped her face and looked down upon the blood-tears glistening on her fingertips before they reabsorbed into her skin. She hadn't realized that she had been crying. She looked into her mother's frightened face, searching for a way to explain this away.

Debra's eyes fluttered down to Jerusa's mouth, to her fangs. Her ragged breath seized in her chest. She reached behind her, grabbing a steak knife from the sink full of dirty dishes and held it high in front of her face with both hands.

"Who are you? What's going on? What have you done to my daughter?" Her hands trembled almost as much as her voice.

"Mom, it's me. Calm down. I can explain this, but not until you relax."

Jerusa took a slow step forward. Her mother slashed at her with the knife. Jerusa avoided the knife with ease, but her speed only rattled her mother more. The front door opened and then closed. Jerusa glanced over her shoulder, expecting to see Taos and Shufah coming to her aid.

But the two forms darkening the doorway were not her friends. Jerusa had seen these men earlier in the day, in the security monitors at home.

Chapter Seven

Silvanus sat inside the lion's den. The three female vampires—sometimes called the Erinyes, sometimes the Furies—had led him down into the deepest part of the cavern where the piercing rays of the sun could not find them. The lions had let them pass without so much as a sideways glance, as though the four of them were part of the pride.

The Erinyes started a small fire with dried brush and a few chips of coal. The fire flashed to life from nowhere. At least one of the three possessed the gift of fire. Silvanus suspected it was the woman with the olive skin and white hair. She regarded him with a look of curiosity, as one who has found something in the open that was previously thought lost.

The black vampire and the red-headed vampire sat on either side of her, their legs crossed, close enough that their knees touched the one beside them. Flickering shadows waged a silent and bloody war upon their faces. The three sat motionless, awaiting him to speak.

"Can you help me?"

"What manner of help do you seek?" the red-headed vampire asked. So far she was the only one of the three to speak.

"I seek knowledge."

"What would you like to know?"

"What am I?"

The red-head and the black vampire looked toward the olive-skinned vampire, though their eyes remained closed. They were communicating, but Silvanus couldn't hear their thoughts.

"You are a Divine Vampire," the red-head said. "One Who Has Regained the Sun. Not a drinker of blood, as we are, but a drinker of life just the same. Shufah should have told you this."

"She did. But how did I become this? Why am I different from you? I gave a dying girl my blood to save her. I had hoped she would be like me, but—"

"She became a blood drinker?"

"Yes. I don't understand."

"I'm sorry. The secrets of how a blood drinker becomes divine is lost or maybe just hidden."

"Hidden by whom?"

"The other Divines."

Silvanus's spirit leapt within him. "So there are others? I'm not alone?"

"There are others. Or there *were* others. We haven't come across a Divine in centuries."

"How do I find the others?"

"We don't know."

Silvanus stared down into the tiny flames. "There must be a way."

"When the savage wars threatened extinction for mortal and immortal alike, the Divines appeared like moonlight through the clouds. We don't know where they came from or where they vanished to."

Silvanus sat in silence for a long time. Why had Shufah sent him to find these women if they didn't have any of the answers he needed. Maybe he was asking the wrong questions.

"Who are you?"

"We are the Furies. Why do you ask questions that you already know the answer to?"

Silvanus sighed. This was going nowhere. "Who were you before Shufah named you the Furies?"

"We no longer remember our true names. A torment we suppose you understand. But Shufah, our friend, named us after the Erinyes on the day she saved us from the wrath of the Stewards." She gestured toward the black vampire. "This is Megaera." Then to the olive-skinned vampire. "This is Alecto. And I am Tisiphone. What name do you take?"

"I am called Silvanus."

"Welcome Silvanus the Divine," Tisiphone said. "We hope we are well met. We are honored to be in the presence of one such as you."

He felt humbled and unworthy of their awe. "Why do you alone speak while the others remain silent?" he asked Tisiphone, but he couldn't help but glance at Alecto. Her eyes were so expressive and he once again felt as though he were in the presence of one, instead of three. "And why do you alone open your eyes, Alecto?"

"I speak for us because I am the only one that can," Tisiphone said. Silvanus furrowed his brow and she smiled as though she could see his confusion. "The Stewards have many cruel punishments in their arsenal. They took my eyes and my ears, but left my tongue so that they could hear my cries." She opened her eyelids revealing empty voids beyond. She pulled her thick red hair back from the side of her face showing him the puckered scars where the Stewards had dug out her ears.

Silvanus wanted to turn away from the horror, but he kept his eyes fastened on her.

"The Stewards stole Megaera's eyes and tongue, leaving her with ears to hear the screams of those she loves," Tisiphone said in a flat tone.

"And from you, Alecto, they took your ears and your tongue?" Silvanus asked.

The olive-skinned beauty nodded.

"But if you have no eyes or ears, how is it that you seem to see and hear me, Tisiphone?"

"Because I can," she answered. "Megaera is our ears. Alecto is our eyes. And I am our tongue. We long ago ceased to be three. Now, we are only one."

"Is that why you feed from one another?"

Tisiphone and Megaera both made startled faces, but Alecto

smiled. "You Divines hide rather well," Tisiphone said. "No wonder you are impossible to find. Yes, that is why we feed from each other, daily, in fact. We share one blood, one mind, one purpose. Alone, we would be doomed, easy prey for the Stewards and their little army of Hunters."

"Why did the Stewards do this to you? What could you have done to deserve such torment?"

Tisiphone turned her face toward Alecto, silently asking permission to speak. Alecto fastened her unblinking eyes on Silvanus for a long moment. He could feel the weight of her scrutiny, the power of her mistrust. She gave a subtle nod of consent, then looked into the tiny fire as though through its flames she could see the distant past.

Tisiphone turned back to Silvanus. "There have been many wars between blood drinking vampires and flesh eating savages throughout the ages. Many have been recorded by humans as plagues or pandemics. The worst of these battles hit in the early 1300s. The humans called it the Black Death. We called it the Great Savage War."

"Shufah told me of this," Silvanus said.

"At that time, there was no rule over the vampire nation, not like today. The eldest of the blood drinkers had formed the Stewards of Life centuries before, but had yet to establish any true authority. Many careless vampires fed without killing, leaving their victims infected. There were many things that a human could die from in those days, but the onslaught of Bubonic Plague created countless weak fledglings that were born of the bite."

Tisiphone paused a moment, lost in her thoughts.

"It didn't take much to tip the scales," she continued. "Imagine hundreds of fledglings, born of the bite, weak, confused, starving. Make no mistake, humans are not helpless, especially in large numbers."

"The humans tried to kill the fledglings and the fledglings turned savage."

A somber and pained look passed over the three women's faces. "By the time we realized what was happening and gathered our numbers for battle," Tisiphone said, "it was too late. One savage can create hundreds more within a week."

"I thought that a savage devoured the brain of its victim. Those without brains didn't change, did they?"

"No, you're right. The younger savages were mindless animals, devouring like a swarm of locust. But the older savages, the ones that were well-fed, became smart. Just as a savage will devour an arm to replace one that they have lost, they will devour a brain in order to replace the brain cells damaged during death.

"Those savages, that had regained a measure of conscious thought, began to form strategies. They no longer killed their victims but merely bit them and moved on to the next village. We lost many of the ancient vampires during those times. Many were turned."

Tisiphone stopped. She, along with Alecto and Megaera, seemed to be on the verge of tears. Silvanus wondered how long it had been since they had spoken to someone outside their tiny circle. Had they ever shared this story with another? He didn't believe so and he understood why not. The savage, Kole, had been an abomination to behold. To have the countryside overridden with savages would be hell on earth. Who would want to remember such a time?

"Is that when the Divine Vampires appeared?"

"No. First, the Stewards elected the High Council, the oldest and most powerful vampires that had survived the battles. The High Council began scouring the vampire ranks, pulling out any that showed a talent useful for war. The mind-movers and the fire-makers were the most common enlisted. The augurs—the seers— were collected as well. This was the beginning of the Hunters and of the Watchtower."

Silvanus wanted to ask about the Watchtower, but he didn't want to disrupt their tale.

"At the time it was a great honor to be chosen as a Hunter, to take on the savage horde face to face and drive them into extinction."

"But the Hunters were not successful."

"No. Though they were ideal warriors to dispatch the savages, the horde was too great, growing every day. Thousands died at the hands of the Hunters. And many more, left without shelter, were destroyed by the sun. Yet, our losses were greater than theirs. The savages could replenish their numbers much faster than we could.

"The vampire ranks, which had started in the hundred-thousands, were whittled down to mere hundreds. But the human loss was far worse. Millions were dead or turned savage. The war stretched across Europe and Asia. There seemed to be no hope for any of us, human or vampire. But then, from nowhere, the Divines appeared. And I mean that literally.

"We were seeking refuge from the sun in an underground fortress when ten individuals appeared in our midst—exactly as you did during our battle. That's how we knew you were Divine."

Silvanus looked away from their faces, fidgeting in place. "I wish you wouldn't call me that. To be divine is to be a god. I am no god."

"It is simply a title of respect, which is why the Stewards refuse to use it."

Alecto smiled at him. Her warm eyes beckoned to him like a song. He wished that she could speak, that he could hear her voice. A flash of rage burned in his bones at the injuries delivered to these three. He swore a silent oath that he would repay their wounds on those that delivered them. Alecto tilted her head, questioning, with her eyes, the look upon his face.

He buried his anger and stilled his face. "The Stewards have no love for my kind then?"

"In the beginning they did. They hailed Those That Have Regained the Sun as heroes."

"What changed?"

"We never saw any Divines other than those ten. If more exist, they didn't join the fight. But those ten were all that were needed. Their powers were extraordinary, as I'm sure you understand. Their strength and speed were unmatched, not to mention their ability to skip from place to place. Some could conjure great storms of fire or lightning, some could command the waters. Others could ride the wind or cause the earth to quake. The bite of the savage didn't cause them to turn. Is it any wonder why we called them Divine?"

Silvanus nodded, but he still didn't like the title.

"They made short work of the savages," Tisiphone continued. "The war ended faster than it had begun. It was then, with the savages no longer a threat that the Stewards' true fear came to light."

"What do they fear?"

"The same that all those in power fear. To lose that which they have, to become subjugated, obsolete. It was clear that the blood drinkers and the Divine were in some way related. The Stewards sought the secrets of the Divines' power."

"Did they obtain these secrets?"

The faces of all three women became grave all at once. "We don't know," Tisiphone said. "If they found what they were looking for, then the truth didn't please them. The High Council devised plans to capture the Divines."

Silvanus sat up straight. "How is that possible? To capture us, I mean? We can vanish, at will, like a ghost. How can you capture a ghost?"

Alecto's eyes lit up. She seemed to have caught something, but it was hidden to Silvanus. He couldn't read the minds of vampires as he could humans. The three turned toward each other, silently sharing that which Alecto had detected.

"There are ways to detain the Divine," Tisiphone said. "If we three were to take hold of you and you tried to vanish, we would travel with you wherever you went. But let a large group take hold of you, say twenty or thirty, it seems to be too much for the Divine to move and they become locked in place. We are surprised that you do not know this."

"Don't be. There is very little that I know."

"Interesting," she said. "Nevertheless, the High Council's plan became moot. The Divines were warned of the betrayal and they vanished with the wind, never to be seen again . . . until now."

Silvanus sat silent, watching the Erinyes across the fire. "How do you know so much of this tale? You were members of the High Council, weren't you?"

The three nodded in unison.

"And it was you three that warned the Divines of the plan to take them."

Again they nodded.

"That is why the other Stewards punished you."

"Yes," Tisiphone said. "For our treachery, for what we saw and heard and spoke, we were made to suffer greatly. We were cast into a pit, left to feed on rats to stave off the Gray Death. But it was more than that. You see, blood drinkers cannot regenerate a limb that is taken from them. It can be returned and will heal, but another will not grow in its place. They placed us together for a reason. If one of us chose to steal from the other two, or even go savage, we could regain our lost senses. It was the mental torment that the Stewards enjoyed the most. They checked on us nightly, taunting us to give in."

"Monstrous," Silvanus whispered to the fire. "How did you escape?"

"It is a long tale. Let us just say that we soon discovered that by feeding from each other, we could combine our remaining senses. It didn't help us escape the pit, but it did drive away the madness. There was another vampire that shared our hatred of the Stewards. It was she that set us free."

"Shufah," Silvanus said.

The three nodded in unison.

"Shufah released us and her twin, Suhail, hid us away. That was centuries ago. We have been on the run ever since, moving from place to place, hiding in holes and hovels, waiting for our chance for revenge."

The sound of Tisiphone's voice reverberated off of the close walls of the cavern. The lions above roared in protest. The silence afterwards was deep and consuming. Silvanus hated to break it, but a question gnawed at him.

"Tell me, was I one of the ten Divines that fought off the savages?"

"No," Tisiphone said. "We don't know who you are."

Silvanus's heart fell just a bit.

"Why does it matter who you were?" Tisiphone asked the question, but it was in Alecto's eyes that he saw the puzzlement. "We no longer remember our true names. The pit stole it from us. But it no longer matters. All that is important is who we are now."

Silvanus nodded. He couldn't help but feel that they were hiding something from him. It may have been the disorienting effect of addressing three as though they were only one, but he didn't think so. Tisiphone talked around his questions and Alecto's eyes betrayed her. Megaera, the ears of the three, could not speak and had no eyes to read, but her facial expressions were like a whisper in a quiet room.

"You're afraid of me, aren't you?" The directness of his question caught them off guard. All three slid back from the fire in unison, giving him his answer. "You know something that you aren't telling me. You hide it because you think that once I have all I need that I will either turn you over to the Stewards or kill you myself. Tell me I am wrong."

Tisiphone and Megaera leaned into Alecto as they had one of their silent psychic conversations. Alecto kept her soft brown eyes tethered to Silvanus, a mix of fear and distrust swimming in her expressions. With their conversation finished, Tisiphone and Megaera turned their blind faces toward him as well.

"Why do you fear me?" Silvanus asked. His frustration with their silence bubbled to the surface of his emotions. "I came to you in peace. It was you that attacked me. I came for answers and all I get are stories and riddles."

Alecto watched him, her intense eyes peeling back the layers of his existence as one who searches a tome for the secrets of life. She gave a quick glace toward Tisiphone.

"We were truthful when we said that we have never seen you before. You were not among the ten. You are correct. We do fear you, as we feared them."

"Why?"

"Though the ten Divine Vampires vanquished the savage horde, it was not for the sake of blood drinkers. It was the humans they fought to save. They looked upon us as though we were a disease. The High Council believed that when the savages were destroyed that the Divine would turn their wrath upon us. This is why they moved to overtake the Divine before it was too late."

"If you thought this, why did you warn them?"

"To gain their favor, of course. To show them that not all blood drinkers were without redemption. When we were punished and thrown into the pit, none of the ten came back to save us. It was within their power, but they abandoned us to our fate. How are we to know if you will do the same once you have what you desire?"

"If you cannot trust me, then trust in the judgment of your friend, Shufah. It is she that sent me in search of you."

The three Erinyes sighed in unison.

"We do not know you, but we do know this. You were once a blood drinker as we are now. You were not born Divine. You became Divine."

"How?"

"What is your first memory?"

"I remember waking up in a laboratory hidden in the mountains. I was naked, surrounded by black glass, as though I had been born from some strange egg."

Alecto raised her eyebrows, letting him know he was close to the answer.

Chapter Eight

Jerusa stepped in between her mother and the two strange men.

"What do you want?" her mother asked in a frail, squeaking voice. "Why are you in my house? Get out before I call the police."

The men cocked their heads as though the concept escaped them. Both were large and well-muscled. Their heads and faces were bald. Not shaved, but hairless, as if they lacked the follicles to grow hair. Even their eyebrows and eyelashes were missing. Long, dark veins, grayish-green in color, ran down the sides of their faces, made even more visible by their pale, almost translucent, skin. They had no teeth, which caused their lips to pucker inward. Jerusa couldn't decide if they looked like the world's oldest men or a pair of oversized mutant babies.

"I thought Light Bearers just stood on the sidelines and watched." If they were surprised that Jerusa knew who they were, they didn't show it and she began to wonder if Taos had been wrong. "If you boys are looking for dates, you're in the wrong house. The Phoenix girls aren't interested." The men cocked their heads again, confused by her snarky babble.

She didn't know what else to do but stall for time. She couldn't engage them in front of her mother, yet as the seconds passed, she felt more and more threatened. The men were repulsive to look at. She could feel the heat of their flesh, hear the rapid stuttering of their hearts. The scent of their blood seemed tainted and alien somehow. They had been in the sunlight when she had witnessed them on the security monitor, so she knew they weren't vampires. But they weren't human, either. She hoped that Shufah and Taos were on their way to help.

"We're looking for Lazarus. Where is he?" one of the men asked. From the rattling of his voice he either had a terrible sore throat or his larynx had been crushed. His jaundiced eyes were piercing and Jerusa felt a bit dizzy, as if he were attempting to enter her mind.

"We know he has been here," the other man said, his voice just as raspy. "Is he hidden or has he teleported elsewhere?"

A jolt of shock knocked the wind from her. The only person she knew that had that talent was Silvanus.

Jerusa shrugged her shoulders. "Sorry. Never heard of him."

"You must come with us."

"I'm sorry, but I'll have to decline. You two don't seem so well. Maybe you should go see a doctor."

Both men were sweating heavily, giving off the sickly-sweet aroma of rotting meat. The sweat dripped down their foreheads and off their noses, but neither man moved to wipe his face. One of them looked down to a watch-like device strapped to his wrist, but instead of a clock-face there was a digital readout flashing the number 92.6% in bright red.

The one checking his watch looked to the other. "We should feed on them."

The other man shook his head. "Our orders are clear. We can feed on the human, but the vampire must be returned to base."

The man touched the back of his head and Jerusa thought she caught the high, whining sound of an electrical device. "Father has changed our parameters. We won't be able to subdue the vampire unless we have replenished our blood. Let's feed on these two, then apprehend one of the other vampires."

"True," the other said. "I get to feed on the vampire."

"That's not fair."

"We can't split her. You can feed on one of the other vampires."

The man's face puckered in a grotesque way as he considered this. "I guess I could. We were only ordered to bring in one."

It was disturbing watching this discussion. They were like petulant children fighting over a stash of candy and felt neither the need to hide their agenda, nor the fear that they could be stopped.

Jerusa heard what they were saying, she understood what it meant, but she didn't feel as concerned as she knew she should be. An inexplicable warmth spread throughout her body, tingling her fingers and toes. She let her sleepy gaze fall on her mother. Debra Phoenix's eyes were glassed over and a broad smile covered her face.

Alicia and Foster appeared in the room. The faces of the ghosts were stricken with fear, but Jerusa couldn't help but find them comical. She waved at them and laughed.

The men looked to see who Jerusa was addressing, saw no one, then turned their attention back to Jerusa and her mother. The men were sweating so much now that the collars of their shirts were wet and the room was choked with the cloying sweet scent of their perspiration.

Jerusa could feel the muddy eyes of the men fastened to them, though she was unable to hold her head up straight to look at them. She felt drawn to them, as though an invisible tether were around her waist and the men were towing her in. She started to move forward, but Alicia held her back.

Jerusa's mother stumbled forward, as if drunk. Foster tried to hold her back as Alicia had with Jerusa, but she passed right through him with only a slight shiver.

Jerusa brought her head up, but it teetered on her neck like an unstable boulder. She tried to walk toward the men again, but Alicia held her in place. The ghost-girl's hands felt like slabs of ice against her skin. The scar on Jerusa's chest began to ache, as though her borrowed heart was trying to leap through the old wound.

"She's not coming to me," said the man in front of Jerusa. The ridges above his eyes, where the brows should have been, furrowed with displeasure. "How is she resisting?"

"How should I know," the other said. Jerusa's mother

stumbled into his arms and he caught her so that she wouldn't fall. "You wanted the vampire. Go get her. Unless you want to trade."

Jerusa's head felt full and light, her eyes were heavy. A strange, almost pleasant burning filled her muscles, compelling her forward. Somewhere, deep inside, she felt horror grasp her heart when the man holding her mother opened his mouth and a long pointed tongue snaked out between his pink, glistening gums. He leaned in closer and with a quick flick, the tip of his tongue pierced the delicate skin on Debra's neck.

The man made a wet, gulping sound and his vile tongue swelled and contracted as he siphoned the blood from Debra's carotid artery. Jerusa went cold all over, but then the shirt around the area of his stomach started to writhe and spasm, and she managed to eek out a tiny scream. Out from the space between shirt buttons slithered a long, slender, serpentine appendage composed of sinew and veins with a sharp, dangerous barb on the end.

The appendage snaked its way upward, nuzzling against its master like a faithful pet, then turned toward Debra. With the speed of a striking cobra it pierced her chest above the heart.

Her mother gave a pain-filled gasp. She searched the room with wide, panicked eyes, but she seemed unable to move otherwise. She locked onto Jerusa's face, silently imploring her to do something—anything—to save her. Tears streamed down both cheeks. Debra's mouth hung open in a silent scream. She had no idea what was happening to her, but Jerusa's enhanced senses painted an all-too-clear picture.

The creature was making a transfusion, drawing Debra's clean blood out through his syringe-like tongue and replacing it with his own vile blood through the umbilical cord. Jerusa listened to the thundering of their synchronized hearts. She watched as the dark veins receded from the beast's flesh only to resurface in her mother's.

Alicia shook her by the shoulders, but Jerusa still couldn't move. The other creature approached with caution at first, but his steps grew bolder the closer he came. He placed his hot, tacky hands on her shoulders. His serpentine tongue slithered out from between his lips just as the umbilical cord slipped out from under his shirt.

The beast moved in for the strike, but halted when a bright light exploded to his left. His unnatural, child-like face lit with surprise and he stared in awe at Foster, who glowed like the sun. He tilted his head as he tried to understand what he was seeing, but he didn't release Jerusa from his grip. After a moment, when Foster didn't attack, the man turned his attention back to his prey. Alicia's spectral body erupted into light, but this time the creature seemed neither impressed nor concerned.

Alicia looked at Jerusa, her eyes apologetic. Before Jerusa had time to ponder Alicia's look, the ghost reached down and placed both hands over Jerusa's scar. The fiery lightning exploded throughout Jerusa's body, filling her with a level of pain she had never felt before. Her senses were devoured by a vicious, consuming force, causing the entire world around her to melt into a bright white void, a bottomless pit in which the only substance that existed was excruciating pain.

She didn't know how long she existed in this hellish limbo, but it was long enough to beg for death. Death did not oblige her request, however. When the white pain subsided, Jerusa found herself on the floor, on her hands and knees. The creature that attacked her lay on his back not far away, writhing and screaming.

Jerusa staggered to her feet, once again in full control of her body.

The beast on the floor rose to his feet. The other, now finished with the transfusion, dropped Debra Phoenix on the floor in a heap. Their umbilical cords retracted back into their shirts. The men, one now pink and human-looking, the other still jaundiced and sickly, stood poised for attack.

"What did she do to you?" asked the one.

"I don't know, but it was painful. There are others with her."

"Others?"

"We cannot feed on her. She must be taken back to Purgatory."

Droplets of sweat formed on the tops of their heads and once again Jerusa felt the nauseating swoon threatening to overtake her, as the air in the kitchen filled with that sickly-sweet aroma.

Jerusa spun in a tight circle, snatching a butcher's knife from the block as she passed and sent the blade flying at the beasts with all of her strength. The creatures' reflexes were every bit as fast as her own. The jaundiced one brought his hands up in an attempt to catch the blade and succeeded, just not in the way he had hoped.

Jerusa had been aiming for his throat, but instead the knife buried itself up to the handle in his forearm. The creature clutched his arm as a teeth-rattling screech poured from his mouth.

Jerusa didn't wait around to see what was going to happen next. Continuing in the momentum of her spin she flipped up onto the counter and jumped feet-first out of the tiny kitchen window above the sink.

Jerusa rolled to her feet and took a deep breath. The crisp autumn air quickly cleared her senses.

The beasts barreled head-first out the window with impressive agility. They hit the ground like jungle cats and came at her without hesitation. Jerusa turned and fled, pressing her vampiric speed to the limit. She had to get clear of the neighboring houses, find an isolated place where she could make her stand. She would not allow her actions to put any more people in danger.

Jerusa ran for the deep forest, nestled around the abandoned train tracks. The place where she had first met Silvanus and this strange new life of hers had begun. She darted between houses, just a blur in the night.

She was fast, but the creatures were faster still. No sooner had Jerusa cleared the trees than the men were upon her. One swiped low, snatching her ankle. The other tackled her around the waist and the three of them tumbled through the dead foliage and crashed into the thick trunk of a beach tree.

Jerusa fought to her feet, dodging punches and blocking kicks. She tried her best to break free of them, but whenever she knocked one back the other came at her again. They were as ferocious as a pair of savages, yet focused in their purpose. One of them caught her across the jaw with a hammering fist and for a moment the world was filled with stars.

A vision of her mother lying on the kitchen floor like discarded trash filled her mind and a burst of hatred flashed within her. Jerusa sprang to her feet, thrusting an uppercut into the face of the beast that attacked her mother and driving him backward. She then turned on the other man. He lashed out at her, but she caught his wounded arm, wrenched the butcher's knife free and slashed at his throat.

He sprawled backward, but not soon enough. Jerusa managed to open two deep gashes in his throat, spilling out a foul smelling dark blood. She smiled, but it was short lived. The two neck wounds zippered shut almost immediately.

The other man rushed in from the side and smashed the knife from her hand with a downward blow. She spun to face him with the intent of tearing open his chest with her bare hands, but the jaundiced man snatched her from behind in a hug so tight that she felt her ribs crack.

The man holding her turned his eyes away from Alicia and Foster, as if the sight of the glowing specters unnerved him. Alicia rushed in, arms outstretched, preparing to deliver another bolt of her ghost-lightning.

"No," Jerusa cried out to Alicia. "Don't." She couldn't stand another blast of white pain.

"Stop fighting us," the man in front of her said. "Come with us to Purgatory. Help us dispel the ink of ignorance and bring the light of truth unto the world."

"And what truth is that?" Jerusa asked, struggling to speak.

"That there is more to the world than mortality," the man said with a glass-eyed expression. "That the failed reign of man is at an end."

Jerusa didn't know how to answer that. The lunacy of his face, the brainwashed look of a devoted acolyte, drove any response from her mind. He took her silence as dissidence and his eyes went cold and blank.

"Very well."

His shirt pulsated and out from the bottom came the vile umbilical cord. It bobbed back and forth, the sharp barb waving before her eyes.

"You can't," the jaundiced man said. She struggled against his grip, but he squeezed her all the tighter. "We must take her back. Besides, I'm the one that needs fresh blood."

"Just a quick sting to make her compliant," he said. "Once she's secured then you can find a donor."

Jerusa dug her feet into the ground, pushing back with all her strength, but she only managed to drive the one holding her back a foot or so. She glanced at Alicia, who was standing at the ready. Jerusa considered unleashing her ghost friend, but the attack would only affect her and the jaundiced man. The other wasn't touching her and wouldn't receive the shock. He'd be free to attack her while she was down. She needed to get a hold of the other man, but he was staying out of her reach as though he anticipated her plan.

"Maybe you should sting her," he said to the jaundiced one.

She kicked at his legs, drove her head back into his face, but no matter what she did the creature wouldn't release her. A deep and primal panic flushed through her, igniting her into a wild frenzy. The very touch of these creatures was hideous enough. She couldn't bear the thought of being stung, as her mother had.

Something shiny glinted in the darkness, off in the distance, traveling toward her at incredible speed. It came silent as the darkness and before Jerusa could even register that she had seen it, the jaundiced creature fell away from her, shrieking in pain. She spun around to find him writhing on the ground, with a long spear penetrating his eye and exiting the back of his head.

Jerusa recognized the spear sticking out of the beast's head. It was the same one that Ralgar had used on Taos. He had called it his skewer.

They came out of the night like a storm prepared to lay waste to the land. Shufah and Taos grabbed her by her arms and dragged her away from the creature still standing. Ralgar rushed in, flipping through the air like an acrobat and snatched his skewer from the still squirming beast on the ground. Ming stood poised to attack, though she held no weapon in her hand. Three other vampires appeared that Jerusa had never laid eyes on.

The injured creature stood to his feet. His wounded eye healed almost immediately.

Ralgar cocked his head in mild surprise. "That's different. Why aren't you going savage?"

"They aren't vampires," Jerusa said. She replayed the attack on her mother over in her mind and had to fight back the urge to vomit.

"What are they then?" Ming asked.

The beast that had attacked her mother stepped forward. "We are the umbilicus. The new kings of this world. Feel free to bow anytime."

Ming raised her hands, as did one of the other vampires—a tall skinny man with a large Adam's Apple and long, stringy hair falling back from a bald spot. The umbilicus rose from the ground with a cry of shock and slammed into each other midair. They remained floating in the air, reaching for the ground as though they could claw their way back to the earth.

"Ralgar. Quinn," Ming said, her eyes still fastened to the umbilicus. "Burn them."

Jerusa looked up at the two creatures—beasts that were neither human nor vampire. She wanted to watch them burn. A dark and consuming hatred filled her. They had attacked her mother. She hoped they burned slow. Though she was no longer a human, Jerusa still considered herself a member of the natural world. She continued to think, her heart kept on pumping blood, she hungered, she tired, she felt joy and pain, but these abominations were not natural. How the Light Bearer's Society had created them, she didn't know, but every facet of her being told her they didn't belong in this world, or any other for that matter. Even the savages were not as alien as this pair. They needed to die. Not just die, but be erased.

The air around Ralgar and the vampire Quinn (a short, stalky man with a thick, black beard and matching eyebrows) became distorted with heat waves. Orbs of fire danced between their open palms. The umbilicus regarded the flames with defiant hisses. The orbs grew, pulsating almost as though they were alive. Ralgar and Quinn thrust their hands forward in unison and a gushing fountain of flame erupted forward, blanketing the umbilicus.

Jerusa pulled away from Taos's grip and stepped closer. She wanted to relish this moment. The umbilicus shrieked in horrible agony and she forced her hands away from her ears. It was a heart-wrenching sound, but she told herself it would be salve for her aching soul. Their clothes turned to ash, their skin blackened, yet they didn't die. Pity rose into Jerusa's throat, threating to choke off her rage and she had to fight off the urge to beg for mercy on their behalf.

Ralgar and Quinn flashed a concerned look at each other, then looked to Ming.

Ming's eyes were wide, glistening in the firelight like jewels. Jerusa's stomach twisted into a knot. Something was wrong. This band of assassins, killers of humans, vampires and savages, had finally come across something their training and preternatural gifts had not prepared them for. And they were frightened.

"Stop toying with them," Taos said. "Just get on with it and kill them. That noise is just going to attract unwanted eyes."

Shufah touched his shoulder, staying his rage for the moment. "They are trying to kill them."

Taos stepped forward, summoned his own fire and thrust it at the umbilicus. Their black skin cracked like desert clay, yet the fire didn't consume them. Their shrieking gave way to fits of guttural coughs, as though they were choking on their own boiling guts.

Jerusa felt a spark of hope that their end would soon come, but that didn't last long.

Both of the burning umbilicus turned their attention to Ming and the tall vampire. Their eyes glowed like hot coals. Jerusa tried to convince herself it was only a reflection of the light, but she was not so sure. The umbilicus opened their mouths and from their long pointed tongues they vomited out a thick, oily liquid. The liquid ignited as it came through the flames and rained down upon them like a cloud of napalm.

The fiery liquid burned their arms and lit their clothes on fire. Ming and the tall vampire reeled back in pain. The moment their concentration broke, the umbilicus dropped to the ground like wayward comets, sizzling against the wet, muddy earth. They sprang to their feet and fled, with great speed, into the darkness of the forest.

Ralgar, Quinn and Taos extinguished their fires and the world returned to darkness.

The fifth member of the Crimson Storm, a petite beauty with a pixie-style hairdo and bright blue eyes, attended to Ming and the tall vampire, whom she called Mikael. Taos came over to Jerusa and tried to search her for injuries, but she shrugged him off.

She caught a subtle noise drifting through the night, like the rustling of leaves in a great wind, and her breath caught in her chest. It was a voice—her mother's voice—alive and calling out for Jerusa.

Chapter Nine

Jerusa scooped her mother up from the floor. Her skin had turned to the color of old newspaper, except for her lips which were pale and dry. Her eyes rolled listlessly in their sockets and she uttered a raspy moan. Jerusa carried her mother to the couch and laid her down as though the woman was made of glass.

Debra reached out and Jerusa snatched her hand. She had the urge to hold it tight, but she knew if she wasn't careful that she could crush every bone in her mother's hand. It had been less than fifteen minutes since the attack, but already Debra's body was on fire with a deep fever.

The other vampires entered the house, lining up behind Jerusa. No one spoke, or even made a sound, but she knew they were there. Debra's roaming eyes flickered, startled, toward the undead visitors abiding in the shadows.

"I see terrible things," her mother said in a wispy voice between shallow breaths. "Are they here for me? Am I dying?"

"No," Jerusa said, a bit too harsh. She smoothed her mother's hair back away from her face. "They won't hurt you. And you're not dying." She hoped her voice sounded more convincing to her mother than it did to her own ears.

"What happened?" her mother asked. "I had a terrible dream. Are you all right?"

Jerusa nodded, forcing back tears. It would do her mother no good to see drops of blood running from her eyes. "Everything is fine. We're both going to be just fine."

A great, wet cough erupted out of her mother like an angry volcano belching sulfer. A non-stop roll of thunder welled up from her lungs, shaking the tiny woman mercilessly until she fell back against the cushions, her eyes closed, struggling to catch her breath.

"What happened to her?" Shufah asked.

Jerusa wiped away the welling blood-tears from her eyes and watched as it reabsorbed back into her own skin. "We were arguing, about me leaving for Rome." She caught something change in Ming's eyes—an almost imperceptible twitch—but it was gone before Jerusa could evaluate it. Her heart hurt too much to care. "I didn't hear them come in the house. Maybe they were already inside. I don't know."

"How could you not know?" Ralgar asked, his words shooting out like spurts of venom. "You didn't hear their hearts or smell their flesh? Are your senses so dulled?"

Ming held up her hand, demanding Ralgar's silence. He closed his mouth like a chastised child, but retained his irritated scowl. Ming motioned for Jerusa to continue.

"They made no sound or smell unless they wanted to."

"What do you mean?" Taos asked.

"Just what I said. They made no sound, not even a heartbeat, until I noticed them. And they had no scent, until they began to sweat." Jerusa looked down on her mother who was still unconscious. She wished that she would wake up, would help her tell the story. It all seemed like a dream now, the kind of nightmare that vanishes with the daylight, but still leaves you with a film of dread even if you can't remember why.

"It was some kind of pheromone," Jerusa said looking up at them. "Something in their sweat caused us to become docile. Compliant. Mom walked right into one of their arms without hesitating. I would have to if not for—" She almost said *Alicia* but a stern look from Shufah told her to omit any mention of her ghost friend. That wouldn't be easy. The two shared one heart, literally in a way, and there could be no tale of Jerusa, the vampire, without Alicia, the ghost.

"Go on," Ming insisted. "If not for what?"

Jerusa averted her eyes from Ming's probing glare. She

glanced at the pretty vampire with the pixie hairdo. She watched Jerusa with an intensity that made her uncomfortable. A tiny smile curled at the corners of her mouth making her look more human than the other vampires. She nodded and Jerusa couldn't help but feel that the gesture meant that it was all right to lie to Ming. Not just all right, but necessary.

"I guess it didn't affect me like it did my mother. I came to myself just in time. I attacked him with a knife, then jumped out the window so that the fresh air could clear my head."

"What did it do to your mother?" Ming asked. "Describe everything."

"It fed off of her, except they don't seem to have any teeth. It pierced her neck with its tongue." She gently turned her mother's head so that they could see the tiny wound, no larger than the circumference of a pencil. "There's something hidden within their stomachs. It was hidden by their shirts, but it looked like an umbilical cord, except with a stinger."

"Makes sense," Taos said. "They referred to themselves as the umbilicus. I guess coming up with clever names isn't one of their strong suits."

Jerusa would have laughed had she not been on the verge of falling apart. She swallowed the lump in her throat and it went down like shards of glass. "It stabbed her in the chest—in the heart—with its umbilical cord. It used it to replace my mother's blood with its own. I can't explain why, but I got the sense that it wasn't feeding, not like we do." She felt weird saying we since she had never fed before. Nevertheless, she was still a vampire.

"Why do you say that?" Ming asked.

"It didn't seem to take any pleasure in drinking blood. It seemed more like a tedious act to it."

"Anything else?"

Jerusa tried to think if she had missed anything important, but she felt dizzy and she couldn't focus. "There is one thing. They wore some kind of device on their wrists. I'm not sure, but I think it had something to do with blood toxicity."

"We need to burn her," Ralgar said to Ming. His words came so fast and unexpected that they were like a slap across Jerusa's face.

"Wait. What? What are you talking about?" For a moment Jerusa thought that Ralgar had been referring to her, but a sickening heat flushed throughout her body when she realized he had meant her mother. "No. No. I won't let you. Come near her and I'll kill you!"

Shufah and Taos immediately positioned themselves between Jerusa and Ralgar.

"She must be burned," Ralgar insisted to Ming. "She has the blood of that umbilicus inside her now. She could turn any moment. You saw how resistant they were to my fire. We must burn her before it's too late."

Jerusa stood to her feet. Taos caught her by the shoulders, in an attempt to halt her, but she shoved him off, as though he were a child. Shufah reached out and pressed a gentle hand upon her chest where her scar lay hidden beneath her shirt. No one had ever touched her scar before, not even her mother. The anger drained from Jerusa, from her head down to her feet, leaving her feeling oddly hollow inside. Shufah's eyes once again warned her to tread lightly and to let her handle the Hunters.

"It is not your place to make this decision, Ming." Shufah's low, melodic voice seemed almost like a song instead of a warning. "Jerusa is part of my coven and this is her mother, therefore she is also of my coven. You cannot violate the sanctity of my coven without cause or direct order from the Stewards. To do so is to forfeit you own life."

"Don't quote us the laws," Ralgar spat back at her. "We have cause. And even if we don't, it is but a simple matter of contacting the High Council." He looked to the vampire with the pixie hairdo. "Contact the Watchtower, Celeste. Have them inform the Stewards of the situation."

Celeste turned her doe-brown eyes to Ming, her eyebrows

raised, awaiting confirmation. A dull throb pulsed throughout Jerusa's body. A deep weariness, the kind only brought on by terrible sadness, overshadowed her mind. The world seemed strange all of a sudden, as though she had slipped into a rambling nightmare where all the edges were fuzzy and the Earth no longer spins east to west.

"No, Celeste, that won't be necessary," Ming said.

Ralgar started to protest, but she shut him up with a snap of her fingers. Mikael and Quinn watched in silence. Celeste retained her upbeat and cheery little grin. On any other face that smile would have seemed pretentious or even mocking, but from Celeste it looked pure and angelic, as though no matter what circumstance happened upon her, she simply enjoyed being alive.

"We'll take the human with us," Ming said.

"Her name is Debra," Jerusa said, nearly shouting. Her emotions were boiling beneath her skin like a kraken preparing to breach the surface of the ocean. "Debra Phoenix. She's a person, not some vermin to wrinkle your nose at." A soothing hand touched her shoulder. Jerusa looked back to find Alicia standing behind her. The ghost's eyes radiated sympathy, her mouth pressed into a tight, lipless line.

"We will take her with us," Ming continued. "The Stewards will decide her fate, though I can't imagine it will be any different than what Ralgar proposes. Nevertheless, we will honor your coven, Shufah. But know this, if she changes, if she becomes one of those things, we will protect our own and leave you to deal with the mess. It is only because of Marjek that we extend you such hospitalities."

Shufah flinched at the mention of her maker. She nodded without retort, then turned toward Taos. "Will you please carry Debra to the car? We need to collect Thad."

Taos moved to pick up Jerusa's mother, but she shouldered past him. "Don't touch her. I'll get her." Taos seemed hurt by this and the look on his face stabbed her with shame. She wanted to apologize. For better or worse, Taos was her friend. He deserved better from her than to be treated like this. Yet, she couldn't force the words past the hole in her chest.

Jerusa pulled her mother into her arms, holding her like a baby. The reversal of roles brought a bitter smile to her face. For the first time in her life she understood just how her mother had felt all those years, sitting there helpless, watching with baited breath, wondering everyday if this would be the day that Jerusa's heart would take her away. It had been the fear of loneliness that brought out that overbearing monster in her mother.

Jerusa could feel that same ill spirit struggling to rise within her. She stood fixated on her mother's breathing. The shallow, inconsistent rise and fall of her chest was maddening to behold, and though Jerusa no longer needed to breathe, she couldn't help but feel suffocated by the sight.

Debra's eyes opened for a moment, rolling fast as though she were dizzy, and then another wet cough ripped its way out of her lungs. Jerusa held her close, squeezing her as tight to her chest as she could without crushing her. The coughing subsided and she fell limp once more. Her head lulled to the side, exposing the wound on her neck. A tiny trickle of blood, dark, almost blue-green, oozed from the hole, and a blow of utter hopelessness hit Jerusa in the stomach.

"I want to turn her," Jerusa said. Everyone stopped and turned to look at her. They seemed to be moving in slow motion, but whether that was real or only a fabrication of her weary mind, Jerusa couldn't tell. The weight of their eyes was unnerving. "I want to turn her," she repeated. "My blood could save her."

"Absolutely not," Ming said, her voice echoing through the empty halls. Her broad nostrils flared like a raging bull's. "I will not allow it."

"It's not your decision," Jerusa fired back.

Ralgar, Quinn and Mikael stepped up behind Ming. The lust of battle burned in their eyes. Celeste, however, stood in the corner, away from the confrontation, her deep eyes flitting around the room in anticipation. She seemed neither invested nor concerned, as though this was all a movie playing out on TV, instead of unfolding before her eyes.

Shufah once again placed herself in the void between Jerusa and Ming. Taos stood just off to the side of her, his broad shoulders back, his fists clenched. As always, he looked prepared for battle, like some angry Nordic god. Thor sans Mjolnir. His lip drew back in a sneering smile and he tested the sharpness of his fangs with the tip of his tongue. Taos thirsted for battle, almost as much as he did blood. Jerusa had spent the better part of six months trying to temper his aggression, but now she wanted to unleash him, to feed his fury.

"You know it is forbidden, Shufah," Ming said. A calm demeanor now replaced her furious visage. "If we take her with us to the Stewards, they may spare her, if for no other reason than curiosity. But if you allow your fledgling to turn her, you will bring down the wrath of the Stewards, not just on the human, but on your whole coven."

Shufah held up her hand, as though she expected the Crimson Storm to rush in on them, before turning her back to Ming. Her brows furrowed together and her mouth pressed into a thin line. She didn't speak. She didn't need to.

"You can't stop me, either," Jerusa said, though there was no conviction in her voice. "You have to let me do this."

"You can't help her, child." Shufah's voice quivered. "I know you want to. Believe me, if anyone understands, it's me."

Jerusa remembered the story of Shufah's father, turned a vampire by his twin children, only to be staked out in the sun, left to perish by the vampire Marjek. Shufah did understand, perhaps even better than Jerusa. She had lost her father, her twin brother, her great love Foster and innumerable others over the millennia. Jerusa had considered the pain of immortality many times since becoming a vampire, but this was the first time she felt its sting.

"You can't turn her," Shufah said. "It's impossible."

"No, it's not. I'll just swap her blood. Like Silvanus did for me."

Shufah gave a subtle wince. Ming's eyes sparkled with interest.

"You are not him," Shufah said. "The umbilicus's blood is poison. If you take it into your body you will only suffer the same fate as your mother."

Jerusa looked from face to face. Shufah, Taos and Celeste seemed almost angelic, their individual beauty enhanced by the vampire spirit. Ming, Ralgar, Quinn and Mikael had not been so fortunate, though they were far from hideous, disfigured monsters. Debra Phoenix wouldn't approve of either group being in her home.

"What if you all helped me," Jerusa pleaded with them. She hated the sound of her own voice, so weak and timid. "We could cut her wrists to drain her, then each of us can give her a little blood. That way—"

Shufah cut her off. "We don't know if that will make any difference. The umbilicus blood is already infiltrating her cells."

"I have to try something! I can't let her stay like this!" A few loose strands of hair fell into Jerusa's eyes. Shufah reached to brush them away and though Jerusa didn't feel like being touched, she allowed her to do so.

"I'm sorry, child. Ming is right. Even if we all band together, flush out the poisonous blood and refresh her on our own, even if she turns and rises a vampire, the Stewards will not allow her to live. They will exterminate her, and most likely you as well, if for no other reason than to make an example."

"Then what am I supposed to do?"

Shufah caressed her cheek. "Steel yourself, child. Whatever happens, you must be strong. You have many trials before you. This is only the beginning."

Jerusa looked down at her mother cradled in her arms. If not for the yellowish-gray skin and the dark veins popping out like night-crawlers after a heavy rain, she might've just been lost in a restless sleep.

"She could get better." Jerusa said it for her own benefit, as though if the words were spoken aloud they would come true. "She could pull through this. She's strong, always has been. It could still be all right."

"Of course it could," Shufah said. "Take your mother to the car. We need to go get Thad."

"Okay, but I don't think he'll be at home."

"Why do you say that?" Ming asked.

"Because I warned him you were coming. He's probably long gone by now." Jerusa enjoyed the looks of anger that filled the room. She didn't care anymore. She was in the mood for another fight.

Chapter Ten

For a split, second Celeste thought that Ming might explode into a fit of violent rage. She had witnessed Ming's temper many times before and it was never a pretty sight. From the outside looking in, it would seem that Ralgar was the unstable one, but in truth his ferocity was only a byproduct of Ming's.

One time, almost a century ago, the Crimson Storm had captured a small group of humans that had fled one of the quarantine communities. Ralgar raged in their faces, all slobber and fangs, demanding that they give their fealty to the Stewards. To their credit, the humans were quite brave . . . or foolish. It's hard to tell where one begins and the other ends.

Despite Ralgar's terrifying display (he even incinerated a roaming cow), the humans would not buckle. The Stewards had denied them eternal life, and the humans refused to be slaves any longer.

Celeste understood. Though she had passed the Stewards standard of beauty and was granted the vampire spirit, when the High Council discovered she was an augur, she found herself an obligated member to their cause.

Had she known, all those years ago, that she could just lie, that her beauty alone would be her saving grace, that the other augurs could not wrench the truth from her mind, she would be free today. Unfortunately, she had learned this lesson the hard way.

She thought again of that group of humans, the way they had refused to yield. Ming had placed a hand on Ralgar's shoulder and he ceased his barking, like the faithful dog he is. Ming had squatted down to be at eye level with the kneeling men. Her voice had been calm and reasoning, as it so often is with her. One of the men spat in

Ming's face. He had smiled defiantly at her, even when her eyes turned wild and her face twisted in anger. Celeste thought Ming might feed from the man. She sometimes did that to dissidents—drain them until their hearts fell silent within their chests. Then she would wait for them to rise, vampires born of the bite. Sometimes she would stake them to the ground and leave them for the sun. Other times she would let Ralgar and Quinn work on them with fire, slowly roasting the poor creatures.

But the man that had spit in her face, he died in the most terrible way. Ming had used her telekinesis to explode the man from the inside out, but not quickly. She had taken her time on all of them. And Celeste had been the one to lead the Crimson Storm to the men, as she had countless others before . . . and after.

Celeste understood servitude. She was a slave to the Stewards. But that didn't wash the blood from her hands. Perhaps that is why she spoke up.

"Ming, the human has not gone far."

"Are you sure?" Ming asked. "You can find him?"

"Yes, I'm sure." Celeste tilted her head back a bit and allowed her vision to drift. Her face tingled as blood filled her eyes. The room dimmed as shadowy figures began to pass before her. She pressed through the crowd of shadows, searching for the human named Thad. When she found him, she pulled his form closer with her mind. "He's still in town. He is saying goodbye to his parents. He will be leaving his home soon and will drive to the coven house."

"How sweet," Ming mocked. "When can we expect him?"

Celeste searched her vision for a clock. "He'll be there within the hour."

"Then so will we."

Celeste pulled back from the vision. The blood drained from her eyes, leaving them dry and irritated. Her face felt as though she had been out in an artic breeze. The shadow crowd vanished and she looked around, squinting at the light. She couldn't stand the looks of betrayal and disgust emanating from the eyes of the small coven.

The blond giant's cold eyes were full of murder. He wasn't very old, perhaps a few centuries, but he did have the touch of fire. She would be safe as long as she stayed in the company of the other Hunters, but she tried not to think what would happen if he caught her alone.

Shufah's face remained unreadable to the rest of the room, but as an augur Celeste could feel the utter loathing hiding just below the surface. Celeste had heard tales of Shufah the Defiant, the one who time and again had taken a stand against the Stewards and somehow lived. Rumors floated here and there that her survival was due only to the love of her creator, Marjek. Celeste didn't know about all that, but one thing she did know: she had never sensed hatred more powerful than that which Shufah held for the Stewards.

Shufah was highly intelligent, wise and had the strength of several millennia resting within her tiny form. Celeste didn't want to be Shufah's enemy. To the contrary, she had great respect for her. She had to find a way to make friends with Shufah. Explain that her interference with Thad was to dispel Ming's wrath. They had, after all, in a sense, spat in her face, just as that infected human had all those years ago.

It was the fledgling, however, that scared Celeste the most.

Jerusa's eyes were wide with grief and clouded with a hint of madness. She was unpredictable. Uncontrollable. It wasn't just what had happened to her mother tonight. Jerusa hadn't been feeding. Celeste couldn't understand why she was abstaining from blood or why her coven-mates were allowing it, but she could feel the twisting knot of thirst tearing at Jerusa's insides.

There was something else amiss about Jerusa, though Celeste couldn't quite place what it was. Something strange set her apart from the others. An aura of sorts; a dark shadow looming over her. There was something they were all trying desperately to conceal.

"I'm sorry," Celeste said. She glanced from Jerusa to Taos to Shufah, hoping they could read the sincerity in her eyes. If they did, they didn't seem to care. "There's nowhere Thad can go that they won't find him. If he runs, they'll hunt him."

"If he's going back to our house, then it doesn't look like he plans to run," Shufah said. Her tone was flat, almost accusatory, as if Celeste was some school-yard tattle-tell stirring up strife for the fun of it.

"You're right," Celeste said. All eyes in the room were upon her, none of them friendly. She served a purpose with the Crimson Storm, they needed her sight, but she wasn't really one of them, any more than she was a member of Shufah's coven. She lacked the hatred and lust of killing, which was a birthright for most Hunters. She wished they would stop watching her. She couldn't stand the pinpricks of their disapproval.

"We should leave soon, so that we can meet Thad at your house." Celeste needed something to break their hateful glares. Mentioning Thad didn't work, but only threw gas on the fire of their anger. Faces tensed, eyes narrowed, jaws clenched tight. Even those of her own group looked at her as though she had blasphemed by calling the human by name. "We don't want him to be alone there, just in case those things return."

Shufah gave a slight nod of agreement. Jerusa, still holding her mother like a sleeping child, was the first to leave the house, stepping out into the chill autumn air without a word. The blond giant and Shufah followed her out like a pair of faithful guards, which Celeste supposed they were. Ming motioned, with her head, for the others to follow. Ralgar, Quinn and Mikael exited the house, but when Celeste made to join them, Ming stopped her.

Ming put her hand on Celeste's chest and pushed her back away from the door. It wasn't a harsh action, but not gentle either. "Do you trust me?"

An icy chill slid down Celeste's spine. Such a poisonous question. "Yes, Ming. Of course, I do."

"That's good. Trust is a good thing." Ming's face was so close that her breath tickled Celeste's eyelashes. She whispered so that the others couldn't eavesdrop. "We've been together a long time, seen each other through many perils. We hold each other's lives, wouldn't you agree?"

Celeste nodded.

"You know, as well as I, that savages are not the only threat to our lives," Ming said. "If we begin to doubt one another, if our inner circle is compromised, the Crimson Storm will fall."

"I understand." Celeste wanted to step away from Ming, but she knew better. Ming thrummed her fingers on Celeste's collar bone. A playful warning. It wasn't the strength in Ming's fingers—though she was old enough in the blood to crush Celeste's throat with one squeeze—but the power of her twisted mind. With just a thought, Ming could cause Celeste's heart to implode or her brain to evacuate her skull through the eye sockets. She tried hard to hide the fear in her eyes, but deception had never been her strong suit.

Ming smiled. "I don't trust Shufah and her coven, especially the fledgling. Marjek only asked us to deliver Shufah. If you sense anything strange, anything that could be a threat to us, you will tell me, right?"

Celeste's throat constricted. Was Ming going to crush her windpipe as a warning? Such an injury would not cause her to go savage, but the pain would be intense until she healed. Could she read the truth in Celeste's eyes?

Celeste buried the knowledge of Jerusa's fasting, though she didn't know why. The fledgling was nothing to her, no friend or even acquaintance. In fact, the look in Jerusa's eyes, when Celeste had revealed Thad's whereabouts, bordered on threatening. Celeste couldn't call Ming and the rest of the Crimson Storm friends, but they were allies. She had saved their lives many times, they had saved hers. Yet, she held tight to Jerusa's secret.

"You know you can count on me," Celeste said, forcing a small smile. "If I sense anything, you will be the first to know."

Ming's sour eyes scanned her face for lies and once more Celeste felt the rush of anxiety as she awaited her head to be crushed or her limbs to be snapped in half. Pain can draw the truth from even the strongest of souls. Celeste was neither strong nor sure she even possessed a soul. Ming could draw the truth from her as easily as she drew blood from her victims.

"I don't believe they will be any trouble, though," Celeste said. "I mean, I don't sense any desire for strife. They will go before the Stewards willingly. Even the human."

"Perhaps," Ming said. "But we will see how compliant they are when the Stewards render their judgment."

Ming turned to leave the house, but Celeste stopped her.

"What about the umbilicus? What should we tell the Stewards?"

"Nothing," Ming said. "As of right now, they do not exist."

"Is that wise?"

"Would you rather have the Stewards think us incapable of dispatching a threat? The High Council is in a state of agitation. Why, I don't know, but until we discover how best to deal with the umbilicus, they remain a figment of our imaginations."

"And if Shufah and her coven reveal the umbilicus?"

Ming's eyes formed spiteful little slits. "I will convince them to remain silent and if they do not, all we saw were shadows. These are dangerous times, Celeste. We must play the game with wisdom, both with our enemies and those who have rule over us. Do you understand?"

Celeste nodded. She understood better than most.

Chapter Eleven

Jerusa sat in the back seat, Debra's head resting in her lap. She caressed her mother's hair, brushing her fingers through the short wispy strands, which seemed to grow more gossamer as the minutes passed. Taos whipped the car around the curvy road with the talent of a European road racer. With every toss or bump of the car, Debra Phoenix groaned and flinched, as if caught in some terrible nightmare.

"They are going to kill her, aren't they?"

Shufah turned in her seat and looked back, but Jerusa kept her eyes on her mother.

"If she doesn't die from the transfusion," Jerusa continued, "Ming will kill her before we even get to the Stewards. Won't she?"

"No, I won't let her." Shufah's deep voice seemed in tune with the car's engine, a soft purring melody that caused Jerusa's bones to ache with weariness. "We have invoked the right to judgment. As long as your mother doesn't become hostile, then we reserve the right to stand before the Stewards."

"Ming won't let that happen."

"Why do you think that?"

"I don't know. It doesn't matter. Even if we get her to the Stewards, they can't help her. They *won't* help her."

"I won't lie to you. There's little chance she will survive the Stewards' judgment."

Though Jerusa expected that answer, it still felt like a cleaver to the chest. "If she is going to die anyway, maybe I should just kill her now." Her voice shook, making it almost impossible to say those words. "Maybe I should spare her this pain. If she is going to die, it should be by the hand of someone that loved her. Not some remorseless Hunter."

Shufah stared at her, saying nothing.

Jerusa looked up into Shufah's eternally youthful beauty—something her mother would never have. "What does the wisdom of the ages have to say? Do I kill my own mother or let her be butchered, like your father."

Jerusa immediately regretted her words. She hadn't intended for them to be so harsh. She honestly wanted to know. She felt so lost. Just a spec of sand amidst the dust storm. If her words stung Shufah, she didn't show it. Instead, her resplendent features knitted together a mask of pity so pure Jerusa had to look away or be consumed by its power.

"One truth you must understand, dear child, is that immortality—or perpetual life, if you prefer—doesn't bring you any closer to the answers of great mysteries than it does for the humans that spend their few short breaths trapped on this rock. I have lived for thousands of years, yet I continue to make the same mistakes and ponder the same questions that I always have.

"Sometimes I envy the dead. Before the vampire spirit stole them from me, I always sought answers from the spirits, searching their silent expressions for the meaning of life, believing they had attained a greater perspective of the world. But now, I no longer know what I believe."

Jerusa knew she should say something in response to Shufah's revelation of lost faith, but she couldn't manifest anything of substance, so she remained quiet. Taos continued to drive as though he were lost in his own thoughts and hadn't heard any of the conversation. It was strange to see him so reserved, this blond giant who normally belched out loud pedantic opinions without regret or apology. It was almost as if he was grieving. Whether it was for Debra Phoenix or her misfit vampire daughter, Jerusa couldn't tell.

Taos pulled the car into a sharp turn, jostling them all and brining a yelp of fear from Debra. She gazed about the darkened cab with glassy, unfocused eyes, then sank back into the bog of her dreams. Gravel skipped beneath the tires telling Jerusa that they were home, churning up the long driveway cutting through the forest like a scar.

"Oh, this isn't good," Taos said as they cleared the last of the trees.

The timbre of his voice caused Jerusa's borrowed heart to skip a beat. She craned to the side, peering between the bucket seats. Thad's Jeep (this new one neon green instead of the old candy-apple red) was parked in front of the garage, surrounded by Ming and the other Hunters. An intense blue light danced around inside the cab of the Jeep, sending demonic shadows crawling up over the garage and across the lawn.

Taos spat out a phrase in some ancient tongue that sounded both beautiful and vile. He stomped the accelerator and the Charger's engine roared like a lion. The instant g-force sent her flying back against the seat, then the sudden stop bolted her forward again. The doors sprang open; Taos and Shufah vanished like wisps of smoke. Jerusa eased her mother down, then slid out from behind the seat.

A white plume of gravel dust, kicked up by the Charger, swirled in the beams of the headlights. The blue light continued to dart this way and that, even though the Crimson Storm no longer encircled the Jeep, but instead stood toe to toe with Taos and Shufah. The group of vampires had moved their confrontation around the corner of the garage, out of the blue light's line of sight.

Why are they hiding from the light? she wondered. Then she stepped within its range and caught the beam full in the face.

Instantly Jerusa's legs went weak, though from the pain or the nausea she couldn't say. An intense burning erupted behind her eyes. At the same time, a deep sickness writhed in her guts as though a nest of dragons had been disturbed. Her muscles betrayed her, quaking and spasming, trying to dislodge themselves from her bones.

The dreaded blue light passed by, dancing its erratic pirouette around the Jeep. The pain and nausea oozed out of her, sinking into the soft cool dirt. Jerusa remained on the ground, smelling the slight fungal scent of the decaying leaves and sharp, almost sterile, smell of the crushed limestone gravel. She kept her eyes closed, afraid that they had been vaporized within their sockets.

"Thad," Taos shouted, "will you turn that damn thing off."

"They attacked me," Thad answered back.

"We did no such thing," Ralgar said. "We approached you and you blasted poor Quinn in the face."

Jerusa ventured a glance around and was happy to find her eyes intact. Thad stood above the roll bar of his Jeep, clutching a spot light in both hands as if it were a gun. Thad had replaced the halogen bulb with a UV bulb, which explained why she felt like she had been trampled by an elephant.

The hard top of Thad's Jeep had been wrenched off and lay twenty yards away. Jerusa couldn't tell whether that had happened before or after Quinn had been blasted in the face by the UV light. She liked to imagine that the Hunters had hoped to take Thad by force and that he had sent them scattering like startled fish.

"Thad, turn the light off," Shufah said. "You hit Jerusa."

Thad made a panicked scan of the grounds, noticed Jerusa lying next to the Charger, then fumbled to extinguish the light. As soon as the UV light went out, Ralgar and Quinn made a run for the Jeep. Thad tried to relight the UV lamp, but he couldn't outmatch their vampiric speed. Ralgar reached in, snatched the spotlight and crushed it, as though it were made of paper. Quinn grabbed Thad by the throat and yanked him over the roll bar.

Jerusa sprang to her feet and rushed for Quinn. She had every intention of driving her fist through his chest and plucking out his heart, but before she could reach him a brutal blow blindsided her. Jerusa slammed into the side of the Jeep, hard enough to rock it up on two wheels. The Jeep slammed back down, but Jerusa remained pinned against the door. She shifted her stance, preparing to unleash an assault on whoever held her, but no one was there.

Mikael stood facing her with his hands upraised. She wrenched from side to side, but could not dislodge herself from the grip of his telekinetic hands.

Taos appeared so fast that the dead leaves formed a wake behind him and the gravel dust, drifting in the headlights, swirled away in a frightened vortex. He snatched Quinn by the back of the neck with one hand and raised the other above his head. A small nest of fire ignited in his open palm.

"Drop him," Taos said. His tone was calm and the surety in his voice was more menacing than if he had screamed it.

A bright light exploded near the corner of the garage. Ralgar stood with an even greater fire dancing in his hands. Shufah stepped into the gap between Ralgar and Taos, an open hand pointed at each of them.

"Ming, call off your team." There was no anger or fear in Shufah's voice. She might have been requesting a small favor from a friend. "Taos, let go of Quinn. Extinguish your fire."

"Not until he lets go of Thad."

Ming strolled into the light, a little amused smile playing upon her face. "Drop him, Quinn."

"But he sunned my face," Quinn said, almost whining. "Look at me."

Quinn's face, from his forehead to his neck, was covered in tiny, oozing blisters. It was then that Jerusa noticed her own face stinging, as the cool autumn breeze washed over her skin. She raised her hand and found her own face covered with soft, wet bumps the size of marbles. One of the blisters ruptured and it was as if someone stabbed her in the cheek with an icepick.

Quinn glanced over his shoulder at Ming, decided she was in no mood for any more whining and released Thad with a bit of a shove. Taos let go of Quinn, extinguishing the fire in his hand. Ralgar squashed his fire with a clap. And Mikael released Jerusa from his telekinetic grip.

Thad ran up to Jerusa, but stopped short of hugging her. She wasn't sure if it was the hideous blisters on her face or the fact that Taos and Shufah had simultaneously moved to intercept him.

Thad's boyishly handsome face was pinched with dismay. Jerusa flashed him a smile that faltered when the blisters on her cheeks popped, spilling warm liquid over the corners of her mouth.

"I'm so sorry." Thad's hand crept up to his mouth, though she doubted he realized it. "I didn't mean to hurt you. I just got startled. I . . ."

"It's all right. It was an accident."

"It is *not* all right," Quinn said. "Do you know how bad this hurts? I ought to cook your pretty little face off. Let you know how it feels."

"Shut up, Quinn," Ming said.

Thad looked to Shufah. "Will this go away? It's not permanent, is it?" His eyes fluttered to the scar hidden beneath Jerusa's shirt and she felt her face flush hot.

"I'm okay," she said, before Thad accidentally blabbed about her scar to the Hunters. "Really. I'll be fine."

"They'll both be fine," Ming said. She seemed insulted that Quinn wasn't part of Thad's concern. "The blisters will be gone by tomorrow night. Faster if they feed." She kept her eyes tethered to Jerusa's, searching them for misplaced secrets.

"We don't have time for that," Shufah said. Ming reluctantly pulled her eyes away from Jerusa and it felt as though a splinter had been removed from Jerusa's flesh. "The sun will be upon us soon. Unless you want to shelter for another night and risk the umbilicus storming our sanctuary, I suggest we make for whatever transportation you have prepared for us."

Ming looked out at the darkened forest as if she expected the still-smoldering creatures to burst from the trees. "No. You're right. We shouldn't delay. The Stewards are expecting us. There is a private jet waiting for us at the airport outside of town."

"We're taking off from here?" Jerusa asked. "Will a small jet get us all the way to Rome? I mean, don't we need a larger plane?"

She caught another strange twinkle in Ming's eyes, as though she was locking a door inside her mind.

"The jet will get us to our destination. It is specially designed for our needs. It's not as if we can fly coach on any old airline." Ming gestured at Jerusa's blistered face. "Unless you wish to be caught out in the daylight while locked in a tube full of panicky humans." When Jerusa didn't answer, Ming shot her a condescending smile. "I didn't think so."

"We'll meet you at the airport in half an hour," Shufah said. Ming's face pursed in protest. "We cannot go by foot. We have Thad and Debra to think about."

Thad leaned over to Jerusa. "Your mom is coming with us?"

Jerusa just nodded. She didn't have the strength to explain right now. She decided to change the subject. She looked down at the shattered remains of the spotlight. "What's with the UV light?"

Thad's eyes moved over her face, going from blister to blister.

Jerusa turned away. "I'm fine. They don't even hurt." That was a lie. They did hurt. Bad. Like she had caught a face full of sulfuric acid.

This was her first taste of UV light since becoming a vampire. She winced as another blister popped and dribbled a wet mess down her cheek that instantly turned cold in the breeze. She appreciated, now, all the precautions they had gone through to hide from the sun. Her blisters had come from a mere few seconds of UV exposure. Quinn, who suffered a fifteen second blast at most, had fared far worse than she had. Jerusa couldn't imagine—or maybe she didn't want to—what an hour's worth of sunlight could do. Or a whole day's worth.

The story of Shufah's father rose to her mind, how poor Shufah and her brother, Suhail had had to listen as the sun melted her father away. That had been Marjek's doing. Marjek of the High Council, who now held Jerusa's life in his hands. A shudder rose in her that came not of the cold, nor of the wind.

Thad stepped just behind her and placed his hands on her shoulders. "Are you all right?"

Jerusa wanted to answer that she was, that she was neither in pain, nor afraid, but she found she couldn't speak. The warmth of Thad's body intoxicated her, rushing through her like a magic elixir. His heart pumped strong and steady. The blood roared through his veins. An emptiness opened up within her, a black hole where her soul used to be, an immense and ravenous nothing drawn forth by the rhythmic thrumming of that heart.

Alicia stood before her, Foster not far behind. The pair of ghosts looked not at Jerusa but at Thad, their grim faces full of warning. Jerusa felt Thad's hands slip from her shoulders, but still his heart, his blood, called out to her. Her tongue lulled in her mouth, as if it were a sea creature, beached and dehydrating in the open air. A deep ache settled into her tiny fangs, a dull but maddening itch that could only be quenched by the piercing of flesh.

Alicia stepped forward, placing her hand on Jerusa's scar. Jerusa gasped, preparing for the jolt of pain, but it didn't come. The ghost put her other hand on Jerusa's cheek and it felt as real as any living person's. If the ghost would brush the hair from Jerusa's eyes, would it move? Would the others see it move? Would the Crimson Storm mistake it for an act of the wind or understand it for what it really was?

Alicia willed Jerusa's eyes to her own. The ghost's chest inflated and deflated as she mimicked breathing. Ghosts don't need to breathe, neither do vampires—though the action is involuntary and feels strange when stopped—but Jerusa got the message. She needed to relax, clear her mind, get control of that base desire to feed. Though Jerusa didn't want to kill anyone, she did want to feed, not just to curb the pain of the thirst, but to move on and lend herself wholly to who she was now. But in this case, she agreed with Alicia. Thad was not on the menu, nor would he ever be.

Jerusa took several deep breaths, her eyes closed, as she willed the thirst to leave her. It didn't vanish like water from a broken pitcher, but after a while the storm within calmed and went back to sleep. She opened her eyes and turned back toward the group. From the concerned look on her friends' faces and the derisive smirks on the Hunters' faces, she came to understand that her little breathing exercise had lasted far longer than she had thought.

"I'm sorry about that." She combed the loose strands of hair from her face with her fingers. She gave an awkward little smile to Thad, who now stood behind Taos. She didn't remember Taos stepping between them, which caused the moment to seem all that more surreal and detached, like the misty remnants of a dream.

"Are we famished, my dear?" Ralgar asked, with a short laugh.

"If you wish to feed upon the human," Quinn said, touching the blisters on his face, "feel free. You'll hear no complaints from me."

Ming silenced her team with a single stern glare. "It is dangerous to travel with a hungry vampire, Shufah. You know this. She could put us all at risk."

"She's fine," Shufah said. She was calm and sure, her voice even, as though she was discussing a trivial matter. "Jerusa is still but a babe in the blood. You forget what it is like to be a fledgling. It takes time to temper your thirst. Even we aged vampires are sometimes swept away by the presence of a human. Please, don't make more of this than it is."

Ming flashed a flaying look at Jerusa and she could almost feel that invisible hand, borne of Ming's mind, crawling across her throat. A moment of frisson overtook Jerusa, which seemed to be what Ming was hoping for, because her face broke in a menacing smile. Ming turned to her team. "Let's go."

Ming led the way, darting off into the darkness, a demon of the shadows off to do hell's bidding. The rest of the Crimson Storm followed—all except Celeste. The pixie-haired beauty hesitated a moment, her large eyes fastened on Jerusa. She chewed on her bottom lip, as if biting back a question, to the point that her fang drew a tiny trickle of blood.

She licked away the blood, her eyes sheepishly scanning the dark forest where her team had gone. She was waiting for something.

Celeste had something to say. Something she didn't want Ming or the other Hunters to hear.

"The plane awaiting us . . ." she said, letting the sound trail off.

"Yes," Shufah said, with all the patience of a mountain.

"It's not taking us to Rome."

A moment of shock hit Jerusa like a punch in the gut. It was like holding a great treasure in your hands, only to watch it snatched away by a greedy dragon. From the look on his face, Taos was just as shocked. But not Shufah. As always, she viewed the world with a calm demeanor.

"Not to Rome, huh?" she asked. "Then to where?

Celeste traded nervous glances between the forest and Shufah. She needed to go. To catch up to Ming and the others. "I don't know. Honestly, I don't."

"Ming didn't tell you?"

Celeste shook her head vigorously—an almost childlike gesture. "Ming never tells me anything. Maybe she doesn't know we're not going to Rome. I don't know. I just know that's not where the plane will be landing."

Jerusa felt dizzied by Celeste's confession and a dull pulse rose from the base of her skull and nestled in behind her dry eyes. "What does that even mean? How can you know, but not know?"

"She's an augur," Shufah said. Her expression changed. She now studied Celeste as though she were the most interesting of trinkets. "Augurs are seers. They have visions, sometimes of the past, sometimes of the future. They have highly tuned instincts and empathy. But Celeste is not with the Watchtower, but runs with the Crimson Storm."

"Which means?" Jerusa asked.

"Which means, though her special vision is strong, it is not accurate enough to make her one of the elite, one of the eyes of the Stewards."

"Which means?" Jerusa asked again. It was more than a bit annoying to always have to draw answers out of people.

Shufah kept her eyes on Celeste, who was now dancing from foot to foot, as though she needed a bathroom break. "It means she could be wrong—misreading the vision."

"But I'm not," Celeste said.

"Then why are you telling us?" Shufah's question wasn't rude, but almost concerned that Celeste would risk being on Ming's bad side to divulge such a trivial detail.

"I don't know that, either." Celeste looked at Jerusa, but her mind seemed to be somewhere else, somewhere far away. "I just feel that you should know. That you would understand what it means."

Celeste opened her mouth as if she had more to say and Jerusa had the strangest feeling that it had something to do with her. But in the end, Celeste closed her mouth, a sad little shadow passing over the light of her eyes, then turned and vanished into the night.

Jerusa glanced over at her ghost companions to see what they made of all of this. Alicia ran a finger around her ear, making it clear that she thought Celeste was cuckoo-bananas. Foster's face seemed chiseled out of stone, jaw tight, eyes narrowed. He knew something . . . or at least suspected something. But there was no use asking his opinion. He couldn't share it if he wanted to. Ghosts are annoying like that.

"What was that all about?" Taos asked.

A tiny smile crept onto Shufah's face. "I think we may have found an ally."

Taos rolled his eyes. He wasn't much for friends. "Yeah, but what was she blabbing on about?"

"If she's right, then the Stewards—or at least the High Council—have fled the Roman sanctuary."

"Why would they do that?" Thad asked.

"That's a good question," Shufah said. "I don't believe we will have to wait long for the answer. I think our summons is about more than Thad and Jerusa, or even Kole." Her voice took on the slow pondering tone of one lost in a dream. She shook herself and blinked away her thoughts. "Let's go. We mustn't keep our escorts waiting."

Thad parked his Jeep in the garage, while Taos hid the ruined hard top in the woods. Then, they climbed into Taos's Charger—Thad awkwardly pulling Debra Phoenix's limp legs into his lap—and off they sped to the tiny airport outside of town.

Chapter Twelve

Silvanus spent the daylight hours discussing many things with the Furies. He was moved by their story of being wronged by not only the brutal Stewards—who didn't flinch at killing, even when it came to their own kind—but also the powerful Divine Vampires.

Unfortunately, where to find the other Divines was just as unknown to him now as before he met the Furies. All they held were rumors and vague mysteries they didn't quite understand themselves. But it was their theory on how a blood drinker becomes a Divine Vampire that vexed him the most. The Furies believed the Stewards suspected the method, but had not yet perfected it.

"Can you imagine the calamity that would befall the world if the High Council of the Stewards were able to be reborn as Divine Vampires," Tisiphone said. Alecto and Megaera nodded, their faces grave. "They fancy themselves gods already. I shudder to think what would happen if they actually became gods."

The three looked on Silvanus with a kind of muted reverence (though Alecto held the only eyes to perceive him with).

"I told you, I'm not a god," Silvanus said. "Neither are those that abandoned you to the cruelty of the Stewards."

They spoke no more for a long time and when the sun vanished beneath the horizon the four of them walked out of the cave, passing amidst the lion pride, without even a growl of warning.

"Why are the lions so docile toward us?" Silvanus asked as they stepped out into the fresh night air.

The three smiled at him in unison and even after a whole day of witnessing their synchronized movements, it still caught him off guard.

"We don't know," Tisiphone said. "Normally we have to force our way in and out of the dens of beasts. They don't much like the presence of other predators. It must be you."

Silvanus didn't argue. He turned and looked at the lionesses exiting the mouth of the cave to go on their nightly hunt. To his surprise, the large female that had stalked him—the one he had fed from—passed beside him, brushing against him with the flirtatiousness of a house cat. He had thought that he killed her, but it seemed he had only taken a taste of her life. How strange that he should end up in her daytime sanctuary.

A thought occurred to him just then. It was an epiphany of such simplicity that he felt foolish to admit that he never realized it before. He turned his head up, looking into the black canvas, speckled with the diamonds of the Milky Way, at the vastness of the universe, realizing his own minuteness and a laugh escaped him. He sensed the three watching him through Alecto's eyes, listening to him through Megaera's ears and it made him laugh all the more. A god, indeed. Would a god miss such an obvious detail?

It hadn't just happened with the lioness. It had happened in the beginning, when he had first met Jerusa.

"Why do you laugh," Tisiphone asked. "Is it for joy or madness?"

"Perhaps both." He turned to face them. The beauty of the three and the tragedy of their story combined to make a potent elixir, intoxicating and sickening all at once.

"Has our wisdom brought you hope?"

"Indeed it has." He felt almost giddy. "Know this, my dear Furies, you can count me forever as your friend. I will not abandon you in your time of need, as my kin have. And I vow to set right the pain brought upon you."

The three smiled at him, though it seemed only to humor his kind words. It was alright if they didn't believe his vow. It was true nonetheless.

"Where will you go from here?" he asked.

"Where the wind will take us." It was Tisiphone that spoke, as always, but the words seemed to come from Alecto. "We will feed, then we will flee. We dare not linger, for the Watchtower of the Stewards perpetually seek us out."

His heart reached out to them. Such a terrible life had been thrust upon them.

"Will you feed from me?" The question was such a natural impulse that Silvanus asked it before he knew it had formed on his tongue.

The three flinched in shock and stood with their mouths gaping. For a moment, he couldn't tell if they were flattered or offended. Silvanus had the strangest sensation that the Erinyes would flee at any moment, taking to the darkness, scurrying into far flung caves. But they stood their ground, breathless as statues, watching him, measuring him through Alecto's eyes.

"Why would you make such an offer?" Tisiphone asked.

"Is it such a terrible thing? Is it not a custom of the blood drinkers to share of themselves with those closest to them?"

The trio's faces pursed. "You know that it is," Tisiphone said. "But it is so much the more for us. To us, it is our survival."

"Then I wish to contribute to your survival."

The three of them smiled, their white fangs glittering like jewels in the darkness.

"If we accept your offer, what will happen to us?"

Silvanus shrugged his shoulders. "Very little, I suspect. You won't burst into flames and rise from the ashes as a Divine Vampire, if that's your thinking. My own fledgling is a blood drinker, just as you, though I must admit her abilities from the start are not to be winked at. I can only imagine what time will give her."

The three stepped forward, tantalized by this revelation. "So, you wish to better arm us with your blood? Give us strength and power that centuries of blood have not already bestowed upon us?"

Silvanus threw up his hands in frustration. "Have you been so long alone that friendship has become an alien concept to you?

~ 117 ~

All that I offer is myself. I have made this clear time and again. If you do not want what I offer, then I will thank you for your wisdom and be gone to finish my quest."

"No, wait." Tisiphone that spoke, but it was Alecto that threw up her hands in protest. "If we accept your offer of blood, then you must feed from us as well."

"I must decline. I'm not much for blood. I tried it once and it nearly killed me."

"To be part of our circle you must give as well as take. If you do not take from us, then you are our victim, not our friend. If we feed from you, you must feed from us."

He thought of the little taste of life he had taken from the lioness. Could he do it again? Take just a bit of life from each of the women without hurting them? "What if I can't control it? What if I kill one of you?"

"That risk is always present," Tisiphone said. "In all matters of love, is it not? It is the balance of give and take that binds beings together. It is not the passing of blood that join us three together, allowing one to use the senses of the other two. It is an act of love, of trust. Only by these intangible rungs can we hope to climb to a higher plane. To merge the natural with the divine."

Silvanus wanted to rush to the women, take them in his arm and kiss them all. At the same time, the tiny ember burning within his heart, that spark of desire to avenge their injuries, burned as hot as the sun. He would restore these women, somehow give them back all that they had lost.

Silvanus nodded and the Erinyes stepped in close to him. Megaera stood to his left. Her dark skin smelled of the earth and the wind. He leaned in and kissed the short, rough hair atop her head. Tisiphone stood to his right. Her alabaster skin was as soft as silk. The wind whipped her red hair about, until she seemed to be wreathed by fire. He leaned in and kissed her forehead. Alecto stood before him. Her white hair cascaded over her shoulders, like the snow that blankets the great mountains. Her skin was so much like his own that he wondered if they had perhaps known one another in the distant, ancient days of their mortal lives. Alecto caressed his cheeks with her fingertips before pulling his face down so that her lips could touch his. The kiss, though long and tender, didn't carry with it any semblance of love. Silvanus looked deep into Alecto's eyes and realized she had not meant the kiss as an act of seduction, but as a token of his union with the three.

Silvanus felt lightheaded, drunk by the heat of the Erinyes surrounding him and almost laughed. He closed his eyes, imagining another kiss. One full of passion and love. A kiss powerful enough to bind two souls together. A kiss with Jerusa.

The earth beneath his feet, charged by the sun's scouring light, emanated with a pulsing heat, rising and falling as though singing to the stars above. The wind, dry and brittle, buffeted them with dust and grit, as it chased itself through the tall, undulating grass and around the ancient boulders. The partial moon, already nestled deep in the inky night, tugged at them with invisible hands too weak to fend off earth's gravity. The lionesses cut the night with a series of roars that echoed far over the open ground, bringing a heavy silence afterward, as all other lesser beings scrambled to hide.

Silvanus, still with his eyes closed, felt the turning of the planet as one might feel the churning of a vessel tossed on the sea. No place was hidden to him. It was all laid open like a map resting before him. With a thought, he could whisk himself to any point in the world. But where to go? Having unlimited choices was just as binding as having no choice at all. He longed to see Jerusa again. So strong did this urge surge through him that he had to force it away lest he vanish from the midst of the Furies and not fulfill his promise to them.

Silvanus placed his arms around the women, drawing them in even closer. Megaera and Tisiphone took him by his arms and placed their mouths on the crooks of his elbows. Their tiny, but sharp fangs pierced his skin. He flinched at the sensation, not because of the pain, but because of the acute rapture it brought. Alecto leaned in close, nuzzling his neck like a lover. Her hot breath prickled his skin with goose-bumps. She clamped her mouth down tight upon his neck, her fangs sliding through with little resistance.

He wondered in drowsy half-thoughts whether they had the power to kill him. If he didn't resist, allowed them to take all of his blood, would his soul fly free of its eternal prison, or would he blink out of existence like a flash of lightning? It was a tantalizing thought, to die, to search out what was beyond, but he didn't believe it would be so simple for him to escape this life.

The vampires pulled the blood from him in slow, measured drinks, as though they were savoring every drop. They clutched him tight, their powerful fingertips kneading him as clay. Rolling groans, like the chuffing of tigers, rolled up from their throats. The wounds in his neck and arms kept trying to heal shut, but he willed them to stay open, to give all that the women desired.

An emptiness, a pang so much more that hunger, opened up within him. He thought of the day he had awakened in Purgatory, that cold, sterile fortress under the mountain. How that emptiness, that black hole had consumed him. He had taken four lives before he had come to himself.

He had promised the three that he would feed, too. A black and crippling fear rose up in him. What if he couldn't stop? What if he killed all three of them? Silvanus thought of the lioness again, thought of Jerusa. He hadn't killed them. He wouldn't kill the Erinyes, either.

Silvanus concentrated on their heartbeats, not the least surprised to find the three pumping in perfect time, joined in a single percussive melody. He reached out and touched them, not with is flesh, for they were already in contact, but with the gnawing pang within his bones. The three gasped in unison as if surprised by a sharp electrical current, but not one relinquished her bite. A rush of power flowed into him and it was all he could do to not take a gulping drink of their collective life-force. He reined back the greedy black hole, but it was like holding a great, wriggling sea serpent.

Silvanus focused the dark hunger toward Megaera instead of allowing it to drink from all three. He gave it only a heartbeat's worth of time then forced it over to Tisiphone. Another pulse and he pushed it over to Alecto. On and on he did this, cycling one, two, three then back again, moving with the rhythmic cadence of their unified heartbeat. After a time it became no more than a reflex, a product of muscle memory.

Though his eyes were closed, Silvanus could see the aura of life, a resplendent river of sentient light, as it cycled from each of the women into him, then back out through his blood. It was a perpetual circle of energy, giving and taking in equal quantities and he wondered if it might truly go on forever. But no sooner had the thought filled his mind, the Furies dropped away from him with a collective gasp.

Silvanus rocked back on his heels, swooning from the sudden break in contact. He managed to keep his feet, but the Furies were splayed about him on their backs, staring wide-eyed—two with black, empty sockets—up into the night as the dry breeze fluttered their tattered garments.

The wounds in Silvanus's arms and neck healed immediately, not even a drop of blood spilled. He was all at once weak and energized. He could feel his mysterious body working rapidly to replace the blood the women had taken and within seconds the swoon was gone.

He smiled in the darkness, both amazed and a bit embarrassed at what he had discovered. He could feed without killing. It didn't have to be all or nothing.

More than that, though, it pointed to why he hadn't yet found the other Divine Vampires.

For six months he had been searching the most solitary places of earth. The Divine Vampires hadn't been seen in centuries and Silvanus had assumed that they were in hiding, much like the Erinyes were.

The Divine Vampires were not in hiding, but moving about

in plain sight, living among the mortals.

Silvanus thought to expound his epiphany to the Erinyes but the three crept toward one another in a silent, dreamlike trance. Without a word or a glance toward him, they formed their tight triangle and began feeding from each other.

Silvanus couldn't help but feel a little sting of rejection. He couldn't see through Alecto's eyes, nor hear through Megaera's ears, nor express his thoughts through Tisiphone's mouth. But his blood would make them strong, more so than they already were. If it gave them the power to avenge their eyes and ears and tongues, then Silvanus would not mourn the blood he gave.

Silvanus turned his thoughts toward the other Divine Vampires. There were ten, at least, scattered somewhere around the globe. On the night he had awakened, while the agents of Purgatory attacked him upon the deserted cliffs, he had focused his mind on finding another like himself. He had skipped through time and space landing in a small town, where he had found the two blood drinkers, Kole and Taos. He had always thought his gift had brought him to the blood drinkers because they were the closest thing to what he was. But now he wondered if he hadn't just missed the mark a bit. Maybe there had been someone else close by that night. Someone he had mistaken for a human.

Silvanus closed his eyes. He focused his thoughts on finding another Divine Vampire, specifically on the one that had been hiding in Jerusa's town. There he left the Furies feeding upon each other and vanished without even stirring the dust.

Chapter Thirteen

A wave of nausea hit Jerusa as they pulled into the tiny airport parking lot. They drove through a gate marked *restricted* and out onto the runway. The private jet sat alone on the tarmac, waiting for them like a hungry dragon. She had never flown before—Debra Phoenix wouldn't allow such a dangerous mode of travel, even if it was statistically better than driving. She didn't allow much driving, either, which was why Jerusa hadn't seen much more than a walking tour of her own small town and maybe a few of the more ritzy hospitals.

Jerusa thought that becoming a vampire would drive out most of the phobia's her mother had selectively placed inside her head over the years, but it turned out that flying was still a tender spot for her.

"Isn't this a bad idea?" she asked Shufah.

It was Taos that answered: "I guess that depends." He flashed her one of his mischievous smiles, the kind that not only showcased his perfect set of teeth, but also filled his eyes with a pale glow.

Thad made a not-too-subtle *huffing* noise, shifted under the weight of Debra's legs and turned his gaze out the side window. Thad hated that smile, really wasn't much of a Taos fan, truth be told. He had his reasons. Being infected by Taos's bite was one, but not the only one.

Jerusa wasn't really in the mood for whatever joke Taos had in store, but she needed something to break the awkward level of testosterone building up between Thad and Taos.

"Depends on what?"

"Well, on a lot of things," Taos said. "Like whether we crash during the day or the night. If it's the daytime . . . *fugedaboudit*."

His switch into a perfect New England accent was jarring. "That sun will make short work of us. Unless of course we can dig ourselves into the ground or crawl in some dark hole." He eyed the blisters on Jerusa's face and seemed, for a moment, to doubt the hilarity of his taunt. "But even the dark of night won't do us much good if the plane explodes. Fire is not our friend. Really our best option would be to hit the water at night. Plane sinks, we stay underwater until it's safe to come out." He pointed at Thad. "Of course, that won't do chuckles here much good. But don't worry, kid, if it comes to that, I've made sure you won't stay down long."

Thad whipped around so hard that Debra's legs fell from his lap and she uttered a sharp cry, as if startled by the devil. Thad's eyes were wide with fury. Taos's smile bordered on maniacal. Over the past six months, Jerusa had become accustomed to the domesticated Taos, but now, in the glimmer of his eyes, she saw traces of the beast he once was.

"Enough," Shufah shouted. "This will not do. You two must put aside your quarrels and competitions. Like it or not, we need each other, now more than ever. The Stewards are the craftiest serpents to slither the earth. Don't think for a moment that they wish us anything but harm. They will do what they can to twist our union, pit us against each other, for their own gain. We must be wise. We must be strong. Something is amiss. Can you not feel it? If we lose our wits, we may lose our freedoms or even our lives."

"If they hate us so much, why don't the Stewards just have us killed?" Thad asked. "Why all the pomp and circumstance? I'd rather they just get it over with."

"Because they are kings and queens of a glass kingdom," Shufah said. She wrinkled her nose, as if the very mention of the Stewards brought a rank odor to the air. "Though they are each powerful in their own right, they know that they cannot withstand an uprising. They hoard the most powerful vampires to their cause, brainwashing the Hunters on the belief that they are saving the world, keeping it clean of undesirables that would easily go savage.

If there is no pomp and circumstance, if there are no mock trials, no sifting the powerful from the weak, the beautiful from the ordinary, then there would be no veil to hide their ravenous hunger for control."

"Why don't you tell this to other vampires?" Thad asked. "Why not warn them before they fall into the Stewards hands?"

Shufah turned to look at him. "I have been, for thousands of years. But you'll find, soon enough, I'm afraid, that it is easier to kneel with the crowd than stand alone."

A door opened in the side of the jet, dropping to the ground, to provide a staircase to the inside. Ming stood in the opening, motioning for them to hurry up. Though the sky was still dark Jerusa could feel the approaching sunrise.

They slid out of the car and stood for a moment in the cool autumn breeze. Taos and Thad each offered to carry Debra, but Jerusa waved them off. She didn't know what was going to happen once they boarded the plane and she wanted as much close contact with her mother as she could get, no matter how brief.

Jerusa pulled her mother out of the back seat, cupping her under the armpits, then scooped her up like a sleeping child. Debra's eyes snapped open—the whites stained pink from countless burst capillaries—and glared about in panic, for a second or two, before drifting back down into the murky depths of fitful sleep.

No one exited the control building asking to see passports or even to question what they were doing. Vampires may thirst for blood, but humans thirst for money. Something the Hunters had provided well in advance, it seemed.

Ming stood to the side and allowed them to climb the stairs. Jerusa came up last, clutching her mother's shivering body close to her chest. She hesitated in the doorway a moment, turned and looked out into the night. The wind plucked the remaining leaves from the trees at the far end of the airfield, leaving only skeletal branches scratching at the starry sky. She had a sudden fear that the umbilicus would burst from the forest like a pair of smoldering demons. They would rush forward with all the speed of the damned, rip open the jet like a bloated fish and ignite the jet fuel with their boiling blood.

Nothing stirred in the tree line, however.

"Are you coming?" Ming asked, with an irritated little sigh. "Or do you wish to catch the sunrise?" She flashed a smile that looked more like a silent snarl. Jerusa stepped away from the door, wondering what she would see when it opened again and Ming pulled it shut.

The cabin of the jet was simple, yet still luxurious. A double row of cushy armchairs, made of pale, supple leather, lined both sides, enough to seat all of them plus ten more. The walls were painted a soft pink and were without windows. Dim light emanated from indirect-lamps recessed in the ceiling, giving the cabin a mellow, evening-at-home feel to it. Jerusa moved to a set of empty seats, lifted the arm rest between them to form a short couch and gently eased her mother down onto the plush cushions.

The engines roared to life and the jet shuddered as if chilled by the prospect of flight. An ear-popping hiss echoed through the room as the cabin became sealed and pressurized. It was then that Jerusa became acutely aware of the humans piloting the jet.

She listened as they spoke pilot-jargon, both to each other and to the people in the tower. She could hear their hungry lungs pulling in breath after breath, the drumming of their hearts—one man seemed to have an irregular beat—until they seemed to blend with the rumble of the jet. The scent of their skin, of their breath, wafted to her, even through the sealed door of the cockpit and there came that terrible pulling within her. That maddening, insatiable itch that crawled beneath her skin, that called in a singsong voice to her humanity, lulling it to sleep as it drew forth the beast within. Her fangs burned as though the nerves within had become tiny threads of molten steel.

A soft hand fell upon her shoulder. Jerusa turned, expecting it to be Shufah, but instead there stood Alicia. Jerusa flinched for fear that a jolt of electricity was about to fry her synapsis, but the ghost simply looked her over with a doctor's interest, nodded, then faded into nothing.

With Alicia gone, Jerusa was free to see the room full of questioning eyes staring back at her. A bark of dry laughter erupted from her chest. The quizzical glances turned toward one another, seeking out an answer to her sudden hysteria. Jerusa laughed all the harder.

It really wasn't funny, but it was better to laugh than cry. Jerusa feared that if the blood-tears started falling from her eyes that they wouldn't stop until she had become a desiccated, dry husk.

So Jerusa laughed. She laughed because, in one way or another, those same quizzical, pity-filled eyes had daunted her every day of her life. If it wasn't Debra Phoenix and her coworkers staring down at the poor little girl with the heart condition, then it was Jerusa's classmates watching her from the corner of their eyes, as if she might drop dead at any moment. The way they unconsciously wrinkled their noses when they caught a glimpse of her scar, how they wiped their hands after touching her, as though she were infectious. The way she stared off at nothing or sometimes talked to herself. Yes, the lingering dead, along with her malformed heart, had conspired to make her an ignominy.

And now she was a vampire. Wasn't this the dream of every lonely, awkward teen? To rise above the social sheep bleating to each other about cell phones, video games, fashion and all other mortal nonsense. To inspire awe with your beauty or strike fear with your power. To be everlasting. But the stares of concern, of pity, were not so easily shaken. They had followed Jerusa into immortality. Would most likely follow her into the afterlife when the Stewards saw fit to send her there.

She felt dizzy, queasy, on the verge of hysterics. She was also hungry, or thirsty, whichever best described her all-consuming need for blood. If she didn't get ahold of herself she might burst through the cockpit door and gorge herself on the pilots' blood, or worse, turn her fangs on Thad. Alicia would try to stop her. She would pump Jerusa full of that inexplicable spectral electricity. Maybe that would halt her attack again, maybe it wouldn't.

Jerusa choked back her laughter. It was like wrestling a swarm of angry bees into a burlap sack, but somehow she managed. It wasn't until she noticed Thad bent over, his hand pressed to his ears, as though he were trying to keep his skull intact, that she realized her vampiric voice had been a sonic assault booming off the walls of the tiny cabin. Even her mother, still lost in fevered dreams, had cast her hands up to her face in search of her ears, though they seemed lost to her. The banter of the pilots had ceased as well.

"I'm sorry," Jerusa said.

No one answered her.

Jerusa turned to go to her mother. At that moment, the jet shifted as it started to taxi down the runway and Jerusa, still dizzy, stumbled. Celeste reached out to steady her. She caught Jerusa by the shoulder and her other hand drifted down to Jerusa's wrist. Celeste gasped when her fingertips touched Jerusa's bare skin. She looked to the left, startled by Foster. Jerusa jerked her arm away.

"Are you all right?" Ming asked Celeste.

Celeste recovered her composure with practiced simplicity, casting a bright smile to counter Ming's shovel-nosed scowl. "I'm fine, thank you."

The jet sprinted down the runway. It made the great leap into the air, pinning them all back in their seats momentarily. The jet evened out and soon it was impossible to tell they were skirting miles above the ground at several hundred miles per hour. In fact, without any windows to glance out of, Jerusa found it easy to imagine they were in a car or even a train, churning through some enchanted forest.

Jerusa sensed the strength of the sun, a kind of menacing hum, lift up over them. It droned in her ear like a large, angry hornet. The blisters on her face tingled and several burst, coating her cheeks in a briny lacquer. She absently wondered how Quinn was doing with his own blistered face. He was seated somewhere behind her and she thought of turning around to have a look, but decided to stay put. A warm numbness filled her limbs, like being drunk, only she had never had a drink of alcohol in her life, thanks to her mother and now she would never know the taste of alcohol or being buzzed or outright drunk, thanks to Silvanus.

She didn't know when her eyes closed, but at some point her eyelids eased their way down. She listened for a while to the pilots chit-chatting in the cockpit, nothing interesting except for a piece about a change in the flight plan. But Celeste had warned them about that. Jerusa's breathing slowed, may have even stopped completely. Turbulence rocked the plane from side to side and she indulged in a light dream of being adrift on the ocean. Just her, alone on a raft, staring into a red sunset as the water ebbed and flowed, glittering with millions of red, glowing rubies. The sunlight didn't blister her skin, didn't rupture her cells, reducing her to a boiling, churning puddle. The dozing star warmed her with the last of its tender light and she felt sublimely happy. No fear. No anxiety. No one to judge her or hate her. Just her and the sea.

The plane jostled her from sleep. Shufah stood near her, a hand on her shoulder.

"We've landed for a moment. Just to refuel. Then we'll be off again."

Jerusa nodded, but to be honest, she didn't understand what Shufah was talking about. Landed? What did that even mean? She had been in the middle of the ocean just a moment ago and hadn't seen even a hint of land in any direction. Her face still felt hot from the rays of the setting sun. She closed her eyes again. The conversations surrounding her melted into mumblings, then into silence. Then she was in a great, sticky darkness, where no sun could ever shine.

When Jerusa next opened her eyes, she exploded out of oblivion with a start. Shufah, who was kneeling beside her seat, gripped Jerusa by the shoulder and shushed her before she could cry out. The room was almost in total darkness, only the glow of an exit light illuminated the cabin. They were no longer moving. Jerusa could feel the jet at rest upon the earth. The sun was still up, not far from setting, but Jerusa could not say if this was the sun setting on the same day they had left or not.

She started to ask Shufah what day it was and where they were at, but Shufah pressed her fingertips to Jerusa's lips, silencing her once more. Shufah pulled her hand away, stuck her thumb in her mouth and then pretended to press it to her left fang. She pulled the thumb out and held it first to her left eye, then to her right, then proceeded to run the tip around her lips.

Jerusa nodded that she understood. Shufah glanced about the cab of the tiny jet, seemed satisfied by what she saw and then motioned for her to go ahead. There was an urgency about that motion, though. Jerusa could feel it prickle on her skin like an icy drizzle.

Without thinking too much about it—she still felt a bit squeamish about tearing into her own flesh—Jerusa jabbed her thumb into her mouth and bit down hard. Her fangs were as sharp as a razor blade and slid through skin and muscle, clicking at last on the thin bone beneath. A yelp rose in her throat, but she choked it off. She hadn't meant to bite down that hard, but Shufah's anxiety washed over her, leaving her jittery and clumsy.

The blood gushed from her thumb, falling across her tongue. An involuntary quiver, not unpleasant, rocked her in her seat. A deep ache filled every muscle. Her senses sharpened, carrying to her all the sounds and smells of Thad's human body. Somewhere deep down, maybe even on a cellular level, her body understood that the blood on her tongue would do her no good. It was a dream-feast, a useful diversion, but not at all fulfilling. How wonderful would it be to taste Thad's blood? The urge to find out burned in her bones.

Jerusa closed her eyes and forced herself to concentrate on the task at hand. A firm hand pressed against the scar on her chest and she didn't need to open her eyes to know that Alicia was standing in front of her.

What was the ghost getting from all of this? Jerusa didn't understand why she couldn't just leave well enough alone and allow her to do what was natural to her. The spectral shocks Alicia delivered seemed to hurt her just as much as it did Jerusa. Was it because she has lost her life young and now found all human life precious? Or could it be that she feared that when Jerusa at last yielded to her thirst that that final step would drop an impassible veil between them as it had for Shufah and spirits she once communed with?

Shufah gripped her arm, bringing her out of her thoughts. Jerusa pulled her thumb from her mouth and squeezed a couple drops of blood into each eye.

This time the burn was intense, like pepper spray, nevertheless her corneas lapped up the blood and begged for more. Jerusa pressed another blob of blood from the wound and rubbed it on her lips as though it were balm.

Shufah, still holding onto Jerusa's arm, stared up into Alicia's face. She glanced about and Jerusa knew she was using this moment of contact to search for Foster. He appeared as if bidden and reached out to touch Shufah's cheek. She nuzzled her face against his hand even though she could not feel his touch. Her smile was so happy and wretched at the same time that Jerusa couldn't bear to look at her.

Suddenly, both Alicia and Foster glanced toward the back of the cabin. Ming appeared out of the gloom like a fairy tale monster, hovering over Shufah's shoulder.

Jerusa quickly wrapped her fingers around her wounded thumb and tucked her hand underneath her leg. She didn't know if it was within her power, but she willed the hole in her thumb to close, bending so much of her mind toward that goal that she didn't at first hear what Ming said to her.

"I'm sorry, what?"

Ming's lower jaw protruded, then clicked back with a loud clack. "I asked what you two are over here conspiring about. If your ears are so weak, I pity what the High Council will think of you."

"She heard you just fine," Shufah said, standing to her feet. "And there is no conspiracy. I was simply checking Jerusa's wounds."

Jerusa had forgotten all about the blisters on her face. She reached up with her other hand and caressed the skin of her cheek. The blisters were gone and her skin was once more smooth and flawless.

Shufah looked down on her. "She seems in fine order to me. Beautiful as ever. Don't you think so?"

Ming bristled at this insult and Jerusa couldn't help but enjoy the moment. True it was unfair that Ming's lack of physical beauty—as deemed by the Stewards—had doomed her to eternal servitude, but Jerusa had a feeling Ming's insides were just as hideous as her outsides.

Ming opened her mouth to answer Shufah, but her cell phone buzzed, cutting off her thought. She pulled her phone from a pocket inside her leather trench coat and read the text message.

"Our transport is here. It is time to go."

Ming opened the door. Though it was night, a muted glow filled the cabin from outside. A blustery breeze charged in, howling as it came. Jerusa crossed her arms to fend off the cold. Though the frigid weather had no power to harm her, she felt its sting more now than she ever had as a human. She was disappointed that they had landed somewhere even colder than where they had left. She had hoped for some place tropical.

Two sets of headlights struggled to cut through the wall of blowing snow that had whitewashed the outside world. Jerusa couldn't shake the disconnected feeling the snow storm brought her, as though they had not flown a plane to a different city, but a spacecraft to another planet.

Shufah touched Jerusa's shoulder. "It'll be okay," she said, giving her a reassuring smile. Jerusa tried to return it, but she seemed to have forgotten how to smile.

Ming exited the jet, followed by the rest of the Hunters. Taos and Thad came up and stood near Jerusa. They seemed almost as nervous as she was. Jerusa didn't want to move, but she knew there was no other choice. So she scooped up her mother and pushed her way to the door, wincing at the biting cold as she descended the stairs.

Chapter Fourteen

The jet was parked inside of a large hanger. The lights were dim and the large fixtures, descending from the ceiling, rocked in the harsh wind that charged in through the open doors.

The two pilots (she recognized them by their scents) were busy securing the jet and moved to shut the great sliding doors, set in the front of the hanger. They nodded to Ming and the other Hunters as they passed, careful not to make eye contact, then went back to their work.

Jerusa had felt as though the jet had been parked for days, but it seems they had only been here a short time, just waiting out the daylight, perhaps. The night was fresh, though she only knew this from her heightened senses, for the sky was a bleached violet from the falling snow. Off in the distance were faint lights, what she assumed was the airport tower. She couldn't say why, but she had a feeling this was a very small, private terminal.

They passed through the great sliding doors just as the pilots sealed them shut. In the short space between the hanger and the idling vehicles the wind seemed determined to bury them in a snow drift. Jerusa turned her head away from the wind, letting her hair cover her face like a scarf and only noticed the two vehicles were black Hummers with chains on the tires as she was swept inside to the warmth of the cab.

The five Hunters had taken the Hummer to the rear, filing in quickly and slamming the door, but whether to shut out the cold or issue the point that they wished to keep their own company, Jerusa couldn't tell.

Jerusa slid into the third set of seats, still holding her mother. Thad made to sit next to her, but Shufah changed his direction with a gentle nudge, pushing him into the second row. Taos climbed in next to Thad and Shufah took her place next to Jerusa. When the door was shut, cutting off the cruel wind, Jerusa sighed with relief. The warmth melted the layer of snow blanketing her head and she shivered as cool tendrils of water trickled down her cheek.

The driver, another human, gave a quick glance back at his passengers, then started off through the snow. The Hummer behind followed in tow, but was only visible by its headlights which seemed strange and ethereal in the wall of blowing white.

The ground was flat and they moved along at a good pace, sliding only a bit. They pulled away on a stretch of road that had been recently plowed but was quickly being reclaimed by the snow. Off in the distance, she spied the landing strip, but the lights had been turned off, hiding it from any other passing planes. No unwanted guests.

They trudged on in silence for a long while, neither the driver speaking to them, nor they to each other. Not that Jerusa had much of anything to say.

Soon, the path curved its way into a thick forest. Every branch and bough was layered with snow, lending a muted light to the darkness between the trees. The ground no longer lay flat here and travel slowed even more as they maneuvered up and down each hill. Their chauffeur seemed well practiced at driving in these conditions, handling each slide with an assured calm. Every now and then, Thad and Taos would take turns looking back at Jerusa. She offered them what smiles she could muster, but she soon grew weary of that and instead looked out the window, refusing to meet their glances.

At long last, they emerged from the forest, into another open area. A vast, high wrought iron fence, forged of fierce, deadly spears, ran off in both directions, vanishing into blinding white. A gate of matching ferocity—a piece of work that would be at home at the castle of Vlad Teppish—stood, stabbing at the sky in contempt. Beyond the gate, up atop the hill, stood a colossal mansion, its windows all ablaze with light, yet its deeper features obscured by the snowstorm. Jerusa's heart crept into her throat at the sight of the great house, not so much for the size of it, but the menacing way it seemed to stare down at them.

There was no call box at the stop, to radio up to the house, nor were there any cameras that Jerusa could detect. She looked for a guard patrolling near the gate, either within or without, but there was nothing but the blowing snow. She expected the driver to blow the horn or perhaps make a call on his cell phone, yet he sat silent, unmoving.

Jerusa shifted in her seat, agitated, but by what, she couldn't say. She noticed Taos and Thad stir as well. It was as if a great number of eyes, all placed just outside the Hummer, were peeking through the windows, evaluating her and her friends, whispering to each other in some unknown language. She looked out into the storm again, thinking she might catch a glimpse of some lingering spirit, but there was none. The only ones that seemed unaffected by this strange sensation were the driver and Shufah.

Jerusa turned to Shufah and was about to ask what was happening when the gate swung inward with a loud groan, digging great swipes into the snow drift covering the road. The driver waited for the gate doors to complete their path, then put the Hummer into gear and drove toward the mansion. The Hummer behind them followed close on their rear and just as soon as they passed the swipes in the snow, the gate doors pulled shut.

The sense of being watched passed, flickered away like a candle being snuffed out by the harsh wind and Jerusa sighed, as did Taos and Thad. It was like awakening to find a large spider perched upon your forehead and the relief that comes when it moves on, without biting you.

The driver continued toward the house, pushing the Hummer through the thick snow. The road was marked on both sides by tall, ancient evergreen trees, their boughs drooping under their wintery burdens. The driver moved slowly and steadily up the winding path.

The wind buffeted the Hummer, rocking it so hard it seemed it would tip over, yet the driver continued on without incident.

They pulled beneath a great covered area before a grand stone staircase. Shufah motioned for the others to exit the Hummer. Taos came around and took Debra Phoenix into his arms so that Jerusa could slide out without jostling her too much. The icy breeze tore at Jerusa, gnashing its fierce teeth on her bones. Poor Thad shivered uncontrollably, squinting as the snow pelted his face. The five members of the Crimson Storm climbed from their Hummer and made straight for the stairs, without even a glance at the others.

Shufah waited for them to pass before moving. Jerusa stood a moment longer, despite the cold and took in what she could see of the great house. It was built of large, milled stones, not unlike limestone, but a dark sooty gray as though they had been through a fire. The masonry was superb, with the blocks fitted so tight only the slightest traces of mortar could be seen. The ceiling of the covered pass-through stood thirty feet off of the drive—which from the absence of snow was revealed to be cobblestone. A row of windows burned hot, casting a hearty glow down upon them. The far wall was all but closed off, except for a series of arched windows, open to the night, which reminded Jerusa of gothic cathedrals. Gas torches lined the outer wall, their furious flames flickering in the breeze as if they might go out, but always rising again when the wind settled.

It was as though she had stepped back in time. She wouldn't have been surprised had she turned to see the Hummers had transformed into a pair of horse-drawn carriages.

Jerusa was content to stand there, indulging in this mirage of time, but her friends were already at the top of the stairs watching her. She climbed the stairs, which were made of the most beautiful marble she had ever seen. There were only seven steps, but with each one her hope of enduring past this night diminished. At the top the doors—two thick, darkly stained panels, tall enough to admit a giant—stood open. She crossed the threshold with a sigh, fighting off the urge to bury her face in Shufah's back like a frightened child.

The doors swung shut behind them and only then did Jerusa notice the two vampires standing guard. Both men were well dressed in light, thin button down shirts and slacks. Neither was armed, but Jerusa noticed both men wore rings upon their right hands, embossed with the emblem of the Hunters: two curved swords crossing over one another to form what looked to be fangs. Jerusa had noticed the members of the Crimson Storm wore similar rings, all on their right hands, but on their left they wore rings with the insignia of a deep red thundercloud.

Neither of the Hunters guarding the door regarded them in any fashion, but instead returned to their post and stood as silent as a set of gargoyles. Jerusa didn't want to turn her back on them. It seemed a better idea to back away, keeping eye contact, as one does with an ill-tempered dog, but she didn't want to expose the depth of her fear all at once.

Instead, she turned and took in the grandeur of the room in which they stood. A vast marble floor spread out before her like a perfectly still pond. The marble was polished to a high shine and reflected the cluster of chandeliers floating about the ceiling so that it seemed as if there was a light source buried within the depths of the magnificent stone. The space was so large that it could have housed a thousand, with room to spare. Luxurious, yet comfortable looking, couches were scattered about, though all were empty. The walls were formed of wonderful dark wood with carvings set into the moldings. Several doors were visible on the ground floor and three mammoth staircases—one to the left, one to the right and one directly before them—drifted off into the upper levels.

Jerusa had never seen such extravagance with her own eyes and the fullness of the ostentatiousness was a bit overwhelming. She felt suddenly unworthy to tread these floors, like a bug that has been exposed by the light and must scurry back to the filth behind the walls. Perhaps that was the point.

"Welcome," a deep voice rang out. It echoed from wall to wall, ceiling to floor, making it difficult to know where it came from. A man, tall with the ruddy handsome face of a twenty year old, came sauntering down the center staircase, with his arms spread open wide. "Come forth my friends. Be not shy."

Jerusa noticed Shufah stiffen and she knew without being told that this was Marjek, Shufah's maker.

Marjek rubbed at the tight black beard covering his face and gave a great hearty laugh. The members of the Crimson Storm stepped forward to greet him, but Jerusa and her coven stayed in place.

"You have done well," Marjek said to Ming. "It's no small task convincing my daughter to come home."

Though Shufah's face remained calm, Jerusa could sense the fuming anger brewing within her. This seemed to be Marjek's objective at calling Shufah his daughter for he smiled brightly as though he had told some wonderfully amusing anecdote.

"That's strange," Shufah returned, "for I recall my father as a kind and gentle man, put to death to sooth the jealousy of a brutish monster. I lay no claim to you and beg you bid me the same courtesy."

"Like it or not, fair child, you were borne of my blood, therefore you are mine to claim." Marjek retained his broad smile, but a flicker of sullen anger passed behind his eyes.

Faces began to emerge from doors, some timidly peeking around corners, others marching in grand boldness to the balcony rails. Many were vampires, looking down on them with haughty interest. Yet others were human, bitten and enlisted as servants, just like the drivers that had collected them at the airport.

"Tell me, Marjek," Shufah said, her voice ringing off the high ceilings and bare floors. "Why did you feel it necessary to send your foot soldiers to come collect me and my own? There is a marvelous invention of this day called a telephone. It is an amazing time saver. I know that it is a burden for a mind such as yours to keep up with the ever-changing technologies of the human race. Perhaps one of the fledglings in house could give you a few lessons."

Marjek's eyes narrowed, he squared his broad shoulders, but he managed a smile for the gawking crowd. Marjek was a frightening physical specimen—larger even than Taos—not to mention one of the oldest living vampires. There weren't many who would dare oppose him, let alone insult him, yet Shufah stood fearless.

"You should be flattered that I sent our best Hunters to escort you and your coven," Marjek said. Ming stood straight and stuck her chin out with pride at the praise of her master. "The Crimson Storm were sent not as your prison guards but as your protectors."

Shufah barked a loud, hard laugh. Whispers slithered through the gathering crowd and glowers from the Crimson Storm—except for sweet Celeste—were as venomous as a viper's bite.

"Protection," Shufah said incredulously. "If they are your best then I think I shall soon see your ruination, for which I have long desired. See how well they protected us," she said motioning toward Debra.

He looked at Debra Phoenix cradled in Taos's arms. Ming shriveled when Marjek cast his questioning eyes upon her. "There was an incident," Ming said. "We were going to discuss it with you in private."

Ming was a convincing liar, doling out just the right amount of contrition and confidentiality. In reality, she had hoped to sweep the incident with the umbilicus under the rug, to stash Debra Phoenix away in some unremembered room of the mansion.

"There is no need for secrecy amidst family," Shufah said, turning the word *family* into a sharpened little jab. "Tell me, why have the mighty Stewards taken to hiding in the Northern Sanctuary? And why did you take so long to call us to your court? Is there danger abroad? Are we at war?"

The members of the Crimson Storm—except for Celeste, once again—stood seething, their eyes wide with fury. Jerusa was sure any moment Ming and Mikael would crush them with a blow of their telekinetic powers and that Ralgar and Quinn would finish them off in a rush of fire. Several other vampires, both above and below, stepped forward from the lingering crowd. Jerusa couldn't be sure about all, but several wore the insignia ring of the Hunters.

A woman, with flowing blonde hair, reaching near to the floor, emerged from the crowd and descended the center staircase. She stood beside Marjek with her hands lightly clasped before her and though the stance was meant to exhibit poise, it looked more as if she were restraining madness.

"Temper yourself, Shufah," she said in a singsong voice. "Your wagging tongue endangers your coven." She stood tall, slender, with pale skin, as though she was formed of living alabaster. Her bright, dark blue eyes held a measure of cruelty that could shame a crocodile. She wore a silky white dress and her long hair was braided into seven locks, bound with jeweled silver bands. Her beauty radiated, diminishing all those in the crowd. "There is much to be discussed, but now is not the time."

Shufah gave a mocking little bow. "As you wish. Is there anything you require of us?"

"That is all for now," Marjek said. "We have rooms prepared for you. Shufah, I trust you remember the rules of the house?"

"I trust they are the same tyrannical tripe you enforce at the house in Rome?"

Marjek forced a small smile, but the woman with the long hair stabbed at Shufah with her eyes. "The rules are the same," he said. "Be sure your coven follows them. Does your human require medical assistance? Has she been bitten?"

Shufah glanced at Debra Phoenix lying limp in Taos's arms. "That would be kind, thank you." Her eyes flitted over to Ming before she answered the next question. "No, she hasn't been bitten."

"Very good." Marjek looked to his left and a short, middle-aged man—a human—stepped forward. "Show them the way. And call for the doctor."

The man nodded, then waited patiently for the vampires to

approach him.

The man took them up the staircase to the right. By the time they reached the top, the crowd of vampires was starting to disperse, but many interested eyes followed them down the passageway. They passed by several open doorways that lead to great spacious rooms, some empty, some furnished with plush chairs and couches, where groups of vampires lounged in silence or sometimes danced to blaring rave music.

It was all a bit unnerving to Jerusa. She understood that the world had a large population of vampires, but were they all sheltered in this house?

"Who was the ice queen back there?" Taos asked as they passed down a silent stretch of hallway.

"She once was known as Albeinheide," Shufah answered. "These days she simply goes by Heidi."

"She doesn't look like a Heidi," Thad said. His voice came out hoarse and scratchy, as if he had forgotten how to speak.

"No," Taos agreed. "I would have pegged her as a *Rasputin*. I take it she's one of the Stewards."

"Yes. One of the High Council, actually. She is wicked and spiteful in a way that makes Marjek seem congenial."

Jerusa nodded toward their human guide, who continued to walk at a slow even pace, never venturing to turn or engage in conversation.

"Oh, it's nothing he doesn't already know," Shufah said of the guide. "This poor soul has to attend to her. He should be granted eternal life on those merits alone."

"How many Stewards are there?" Thad asked. "How many are on the High Council?"

"There are over one hundred elders that are considered Stewards," said Shufah. "They are scattered about the globe to enforce the Blood Laws. There are only five in the High Council, however. Marjek and Heidi you have met. Cot, Othella and Mathias will make an appearance soon enough, I'm sure."

Their guide took them up another two flights of stairs and brought them to a collection of rooms at the eastern most part of the house. They each had their own room and though they were small, they were well decorated and comfortable.

"Everything you need is inside," the man said. "If you have need of anything else, please call us." With that the man turned and hurried off.

Jerusa took her mother from Taos. Her skin was damp and cold. Jerusa looked around at their surroundings, trying to keep herself from crying again. "Why did they stash us away, up here? It's so secluded."

"Because of Thad and Debra, I suspect," Shufah said. "Vampires and humans usually keep to their own areas, for many reasons. They are showing us a courtesy by giving our group its privacy." She motioned toward Debra. "You should lay her down on the bed. The doctor that watches over the humans will come by soon. We should all rest and clean up." No one moved toward their rooms. "Go on. We are safe enough, for now."

Jerusa went into her room with her mother. Thad lingered in the doorway to his own room, watching her. She thought of inviting him in—she didn't want to be alone if her mother . . . died. But she knew Shufah wouldn't allow her and Thad too close to each other, so she slid the heavy oak door closed with her foot.

She placed her mother on the bed and covered her with a heavy down-comforter. She explored the room, but there wasn't much to look at, other than an array of clothes in the closet and some dusty books on a shelf. Her room was equipped with a full bathroom, however, so Jerusa decided on a shower.

She ran the water as hot as it would go and slid beneath the steaming spray with a sigh. It seemed centuries since she had been warm. She had discovered since becoming a vampire that dirt and grime didn't adhere to her skin. She didn't sweat, didn't have body odor and didn't have to use the restroom—all perks of being undead. Though the water was enough to make her clean, she used the shampoo and soap anyway, relishing the soft clean scent they produced.

She would have stayed in the shower until the hot water expired, except that her keen ears caught the sound of her door opening. There was a thud on the floor, a soft whimper and the door shut again.

Jerusa, fearing her mother had awakened and fled the room in confused panic, quickly rinsed off and wrapped herself in a terrycloth robe she found hanging on the door. She ran out of the bathroom, looked toward the bed, but her mother still lay beneath the covers.

Tiny puddles formed around Jerusa's feet, dripping from her wet hair, as she pondered the noises. She started to turn toward the door, thinking that Thad or Taos had entered, found her showering, then turned and straightway left, but the soft rustle of someone shuffling across the floor stopped her mid-step.

Jerusa's senses heightened and she became aware of a foreign scent, of human sweat, almost hidden by her mother's own odor. She could hear ragged breathing mixed with tiny, exerted grunts.

Jerusa moved to the center of the room where she found a man near the foot of the bed. His hands and feet bound with zip ties, a ball-gag pressed in his mouth, like an apple in the mouth of a suckling pig.

His heart raged at the sight of her and the sound of his rushing blood lit like a flame in her chest. Alicia appeared next to the man, her pale face drawn tight with dismay. A fury filled Jerusa, a blind instinct, demanding action without thought. She rushed toward the man. Alicia rushed towards her.

Chapter Fifteen

Jerusa collided with Alicia and it was as two comets striking in the cold dead of space. Her bones felt like molten lead and for a moment—before she blacked out—she wondered if she was on fire.

Her legs folded beneath her and she hit the ground next the man, who let out a muffled screech of horror. Galaxies of stars were born in her sight, only to swell and shrink in supernova. Alicia's hand gouged into Jerusa's chest, into her scar and it would've been no less painful had she been branded by a hot iron. Convulsions overtook her body, smashing her violently against the floor.

Then came darkness. Not a blessed, pain-free, restful darkness, but a bottomless pit where she fell, rolling over and over, spinning at terrific speed with no hope of escape.

A pitiful, pleading groan cut through the darkness. Her heart raced, because she thought the noise had come from Alicia. It was impossible, though. The dead have no voice. Then again, she had never been touched by Alicia until six months ago. Nothing was certain anymore. The spinning blackness faded and Jerusa found herself upon the floor, her back set in a deep arch, her head tipped backward to its limit, and realized for the first time that the pleading groan had come from her own mouth.

Her electrified muscles gave way, dropping her to the floor with one last crash. A soft, beautiful face, a mask of perfect youth, hovered over her. "Alicia," Jerusa said in a croaking voice. But there was something wrong with the face before her.

A hand touched her on the shoulder and Jerusa's head lulled to the side. Alicia lay beside her, her round face twisted with spent anguish, her eyes heavy, as if ghosts could grow weary. Soft fingers, not belonging to Alicia, caressed Jerusa's cheek. The owner of the fingers gasped suddenly, as if startled and pulled her hand away. Jerusa's hand shot forth like a striking viper and caught the girl by the wrist. The girl gave a short, muffled cry, but didn't attempt to free her hand.

Jerusa turned her head toward the girl, though it seemed to take a great deal of energy to get the message from her brain to the muscles in her neck. Celeste stared down, not at Jerusa but at Alicia. Foster appeared in the room and Celeste gaped in awe.

"Have you seen enough?" Jerusa asked. Her voice came out like gravel spilling down a mountainside. Her throat felt full of hot ash and had black smoke erupted from between her lips, she wouldn't have thought it strange. "If you were sent to spy out my secrets, you've just discovered a doozy."

Celeste gingerly slipped her wrist from Jerusa's grasp and seemed even more astonished, if that were possible, when Alicia and Foster vanished from her sight. "I didn't come to spy on you," she said, returning her wide, wondering eyes to Jerusa. "I came to warn you."

Jerusa sat up and Celeste scurried away like an abused beast. "Warn me about what?"

"Shufah should have behaved with more discretion." She glanced around the room as if her comment might offend and re-conjure the spirits she had just witnessed. "Ming demanded silence on the issue of the umbilicus, but now she is explaining what happened to the High Council. Shufah shouldn't have lied. The Council will know that your mother has been bitten."

"Not bitten by a vampire," Shufah said from the doorway. Celeste turned on her heels and stepped away. "That was the question they were asking. Had she been bitten by a vampire? Is she infected? So, you see, I didn't lie."

"Nevertheless," Celeste said. "When Ming finishes her account of what happened, they will come for Jerusa's mother."

Jerusa climbed to her feet, but a wave of dizziness overtook her and she stumbled into the wall. Celeste rushed forward to help, but stopped short of touching her. "You aren't well. You should feed." She indicated the bound man still squirming on the floor.

"I can't," Jerusa said.

"You must. The Stewards will see it as a great insult if you refuse the blood they've offered."

"You don't understand," Shufah said. "She cannot feed, nor has she since the day she was born of the blood."

"That's madness." Celeste turned to Jerusa. "The Stewards will destroy you for such an act and even if they don't you will bring the Stone Cloak down upon yourself. Why would you do such a thing?"

Jerusa tried to answer, but found that she didn't have the strength. A deep, lethargic weakness had fallen over her, like a blanket of lead threatening to draw her to the floor and smother her.

"It's outside her power," Shufah said. "The spirit, Alicia—the one you saw when you touched Jerusa—will not allow Jerusa to drink blood. We don't know why, but she is willing to enforce her decision through pain or even death, I suppose."

Celeste looked from Shufah to Jerusa, searching their eyes for the truth. Then she did something that took both of them by surprise.

Celeste went to the man on the floor, scooped him up beneath the arms and without a word plunged her fangs into his neck. The man squealed like a rabbit in the clutches of an eagle. He had over a foot of height on Celeste and kept trying to stand up, but she kept him at her level. He hammered her with his bound hands, wriggled like a fish, but in the end, there was nothing he could do. His eyes fell to the side in a fixed, glassy stare, his hands drooped and his legs no longer fought to stand. Jerusa listened as his heart gave a few more raging beats of protest, then went silent.

Celeste pulled away from his neck with a pleasure-filled gasp. Her pale skin held the warm ruddy glow of someone just in from the cold. Her eyes sparkled as she glanced about the room, almost as if she found herself in some transformed location, a place of magic and whimsy. A faint pink tint coated her white teeth, drawing out the true deadly nature of her fangs. She turned away from Jerusa, as though embarrassed.

Jerusa wasn't sure what look Celeste read on her face, but twin armies of thirst and jealousy waged a bloody coupe within her. She wanted to strike Alicia, hammer her as the dying man had Celeste. Alicia could touch Jerusa. Perhaps she could touch her back. But the look on the ghost's face withered her anger. She was suffering right along with Jerusa, but for what purpose, she couldn't say.

Celeste became suddenly startled by something unseen or unheard to the others in the room. She cast the dead man down at Jerusa's feet just as the door to the room swung open.

In marched Marjek accompanied by Ming and Ralgar. Lusty, childish grins spread across the faces of the Hunters, until they observed Celeste standing sheepishly near the bed.

"Why are you here?" Ming asked.

"I just came to see that our guests didn't need anything." It was a weak response from Celeste, not at all believable. Jerusa felt sorry for her.

"We have human attendants for that," Ralgar said, his face wrinkling with suspicion.

"Enough," Marjek said and the room fell quiet. He glanced down at the dead man. "I'm sorry to interrupt your feeding, young one." Jerusa didn't like the condescending tone that came along with being called *young one*. "Don't worry," he said, mistaking the look on her face, "he was a vile human, I can assure you. It's hard for us to hunt here, so sparse is the population. We pay prisons well to deliver to us those that won't be missed."

Marjek turned to Shufah. "You know why we're here."

"Yes, but your trip is an unnecessary one. There is no danger here."

"You'll forgive me if I don't believe you."

Jerusa stepped over the dead man, placing herself between

Debra and the Hunters. "She's not infected. She's not one of them."

Taos and Thad appeared in the doorway, but neither Marjek nor the Hunters paid them any mind.

"Is it true one of the creatures transfused its blood into her?" Marjek asked Shufah.

"Yes, but they were not vampires. They were—" She hesitated for a moment. "They were something else. Something the Light Bearers have created."

"The Light Bearers?" Marjek said in a near laugh. "That withering clan of librarians would perish if ever they came out from behind their books. They would never make an attack on us."

"Things have changed, it seems," Shufah said. Her tone was soft, not near the acerbic assault she had poured on him earlier. Marjek stepped closer to her, delighted to see her so pleasant. "The librarians are no longer satisfied to just watch us."

Marjek's countenance fell. "We shall have the Watchtower look into it. But for now, we must take the human."

"No," Jerusa shouted. "I won't let you hurt her."

Debra Phoenix shuffled beneath the blankets as if she were trying to wake from a nightmare.

"I'm sorry, but we cannot have this breech in security." Marjek's tone was flat, uncaring, final.

"And what do you mean to do with her?" Shufah asked.

"We cannot risk her becoming one of those creatures. She must be destroyed."

The strength went out of Jerusa's legs and she sat on the edge of the bed. Taos and Thad both rushed to her. Taos stood with his broad chest out, silently daring the men to take Debra without his permission. Thad placed his arm over Jerusa's shoulder to comfort her. She appreciated his gesture, but the sound of the blood rushing beneath his flesh was near maddening.

Shufah placed her hand on Marjek's arm and he became almost giddy at her touch. "Do not be rash in your decisions," she said. "We don't yet know what the Light Bearers have conjured.

Don't destroy what may be our only key to defense. Take the human if you must, but lock her in the secure isolation ward. Let us watch and learn what we may from her."

A dreamy smile washed over Marjek's face. Ming stared at him with muted revulsion.

"Sir," Ming said. "The umbilicus were highly resistant to fire. The human could be growing stronger as we speak. This may be our only chance."

"This is our most secure stronghold," Marjek said, still looking fondly at Shufah. "Surely you are not frightened of one dying human." Ming bristled at the insult, but said nothing. "Yours is not the only team of Hunters within these walls. We are quite safe, I assure you." Ming backed away, as if Marjek might turn and strike her. "Take the human to the observation ward."

"I'll do it," Celeste said. She had been standing so still and quiet that Jerusa had forgotten she was there at all. "I'll take her to the ward, if that is all right." Marjek nodded his approval and Celeste scooped Debra out of the bed and darted out the door.

Jerusa wondered if Celeste could feel the stabbing pains in her back from the angry glares Ming and Ralgar cast at her. She would have laughed, but a sudden and almost debilitating fear that she would never see her mother again swept over her. Still, all things considered, this was the best outcome she could hope for. Her mother was safe, for now and would be looked after. And of all the Hunters to carry her away, Jerusa was glad that it had been Celeste.

"Can I visit her?" Jerusa asked Marjek.

"In time, perhaps. But for now you should entrust her to our hands."

"It might be wise to have one of the augurs from the Watchtower keep their sight on her," Shufah suggested.

Marjek smiled, his fangs glimmering in the light. "Yes. You are right." He turned to Ming and Ralgar. "Go at once and see that it is done." The pair of Hunters bowed low, then hurried off to fulfill their task.

Shufah's eyes were soft, almost flirtatious. A tiny grin tickled her mouth. It was such a change of demeanor from the Shufah at the front door that Jerusa wondered if there might have been a triplet sibling to her and Suhail. Shufah glanced down at the dead man heaped up on the floor. "We thank you for your hospitality, Marjek."

A quick glance at Jerusa told her she needed to reply. "Um, yes. Thank you. It was very kind of you." She tried not to look directly at the dead man. She had an overwhelming urge to ask what his name was and why he deserved to die.

"You're welcome." Marjek's smile broadened, causing his cheeks to dimple in a way visible even through his beard. He was attractive in a rugged, masculine way. Jerusa imagined that in his human life he would not have been found in a great house such at this, but surviving alone in the wilderness. "Make sure that you do not feed on any of the humans in residence. This house serves as a quarantine community for infected humans." He glanced at Thad who became visibly agitated. "It is a high honor to serve out your days here."

"My coven understands the rules," Shufah said.

Marjek glanced down to the dead man. "I will have that removed at once. I wish that I could stay, but I must meet with the Council. We will call upon you soon, but until then, you are free to roam the house, except for the southernmost wing."

"We understand," Shufah said.

Marjek gave her one more appraising look, then left without another word.

Shufah crossed the room and shut the door. Jerusa started to speak, but Shufah shushed her. "Do you hear anything, Taos?"

Taos turned his head from side to side, his eyes closed. "I hear nothing."

"What are you listening for?" Thad asked.

"Electronic devices," Shufah said. She looked at Jerusa. "Can you hear anything? Listen for anything emitting an abnormal frequency."

Jerusa pushed her hearing past Thad's heartbeat, past the wind ravaging the stone façade of the house, down to the bottommost limit, where all noise took on a warbling cry. "No. I can hear the buzz of the light bulbs, but that's it."

"Do you agree?" Shufah asked Taos.

"Yes. I don't think they are listening to us."

"Good," Shufah said. "We have a few moments for discussion."

"Shufah," Jerusa said, not sure she could get the words past the lump in her throat. "Thank you, for what you did for my mom. I know it wasn't easy for you."

"No," Shufah agreed, "not easy at all. I want to roast my own flesh, just to purge it from his lingering touch. But it was necessary to distort his judgment or he would have executed poor Debra right before your eyes. Besides, Marjek's lusty infatuations have given us a great deal of information."

"What kind of information?" Jerusa asked.

"His comment about the community of infected shows that I was right about this house. This is the Ice Sanctuary, a last refuge of sorts for the Stewards. And if they have moved the Watchtower here as well, then something has them terribly frightened."

"What would they be frightened of?"

"I don't know." Shufah pointed to the dead man. "Celeste seems quite eager to please our little coven, especially you, Jerusa."

"What's that supposed to mean?"

"It means be wary of her. Often your most dangerous enemy will come to you with open hands and comforting words. You should distance yourself from her. She knows too much already."

"But if I get close to her, maybe she can help sway the Council to spare me."

"I don't think so. She is just an augur and not even of the Watchtower. I may be able to persuade Marjek, but I'm not hopeful. He sets his distorted sense of righteousness even above his putrid affections for me. Go ahead and befriend Celeste. See just how eager she is to help us. But do not turn your back on her."

They halted their conversation as the soft tread of footsteps—human footsteps—approached their door. Shufah opened the door before the knock and neither man seemed all that surprised. The two men, both middle-aged but healthy looking, nodded to Shufah. "Sorry to disturb you," one said. "We've been ordered to dispose of your feeding."

Shufah stepped to the side, allowing the men access to the room. They went to work without delay, carrying the dead man, between them, out the door. They had no emotion about their work and may have just as easily been taking out a bag of trash or a pile of dirty laundry.

"Do any of the other rooms need cleared?" the second of the pair asked.

"Not at the moment, thank you," Shufah said. "Give us another hour or so and we should be ready for you to come."

The men nodded, then left with the corpse.

Jerusa was happy to see them go, not just because they had taken away the dead body—which had started to take on the most miniscule scent of decomposition—or because of the matter-of-fact way they took to their macabre task. But because their scent, comingling with Thad's, had reignited her thirst. She had hoped that their leaving would bring a release, but it instead brought her focus to Thad.

Jerusa turned toward the wall. "Thad, I think you should go back to your room."

Thad started to protest, but Taos ushered him out the door, a bit too harshly, truth-be-told. Thad lingered in the hallway for a moment. Jerusa could tell from the sound of his heart.

"Go on, Thad," Shufah said softly. "It's dangerous for you to be around Jerusa right now."

Shufah shut the door. Jerusa listened as Thad shuffled—none too quickly—back to his room. His scent still lingered. Soon the roaring tempest of blood thirst fell into a dull ache throughout her body.

"I don't mean to hurt your feelings," Taos said to Jerusa. "I know you're fond of your little ghost friend, but to be honest, she's starting to get on my last nerve."

Jerusa sat on the bed. "Mine too." She glanced over at Alicia who had a sad, but unapologetic look on her face. Foster stood in the corner of the room with a bewildered sort of grimace on his face. In life he had been so learned, so full of wisdom. It was no small torment for him to be struck dumb by death.

"I still have a human tied up in my room," Taos said. "Maybe together we can fight off Alicia long enough for you to feed."

Jerusa barked a humorless, tired laugh. "I appreciate the thought, but I don't think that will work. I can't take another jolt tonight. I'd rather go sunbathing."

Taos shook his head. "It's that bad, huh?"

Jerusa glanced at Shufah who had a strange, thoughtful expression upon her face. "What? What are you thinking about?"

Shufah twitched as if startled. "Huh? Oh, nothing. Just dreaming on my feet, I guess." She turned and started for the door. "Come on, Taos. Let's leave Jerusa to her rest." Then she was out the door.

Taos raised an eyebrow toward Jerusa and shrugged his shoulders. "Good night," he said, then followed Shufah out of the room, closing the door behind him.

Jerusa touched the bed where her mother had been lying. She thought of Silvanus and a stab of anger filled her heart. If not for his interference, none of this would have happened. She shook herself and remembered that had it not been for Silvanus, she would be dead, or worse, savage. Where was he? Why hadn't he come back? If she called his name right now, would he appear?

Jerusa opened her mouth to speak his name, but the sounds died in her throat. Something in the room had changed. A subtle stirring like a change in temperature. Or a brightening of the lights. Or perhaps the beginnings of a new scent. It was all of those things, yet none of them at all. Jerusa looked up expecting to see Alicia and Foster moving through the room (which they were), but she was not prepared to see a third spirit standing by the window, staring at her.

Chapter Sixteen

Thad sat at the table in his room looking down at the meal provided to him. It was wonderful to behold: roast chicken with garlic, new potatoes, green beans and yeast rolls. It was more than he had expected to get from the undead, that's for sure.

He had half believed that as soon as he passed the threshold of the great house that the vampires would either burn him alive or drag him off to be one of the infected human slaves. But now, sitting in this plush room, with a fine meal steaming before him, he could almost imagine that he really *was* on a trip, as he had told his parents. After six months of his moping about and morose attitude, his parents had been all too keen on him getting out of the house and seeing the world. They thought his depression was due to Jerusa and in a way, it was.

Thad's stomach growled, as the mingling scents of the food rose to his face. He wanted to eat, to plunge his face into the plate and feed like a hog at slop, but he held tight to the gnawing knot in his midsection. This was what Jerusa felt, only a thousand times worse. That thing attached to her, that greedy, lonely ghost was somehow keeping her from feeding.

Maybe if Jerusa could feed then it wouldn't be so dangerous for Thad to be around her. He didn't care for the thought of her killing and drinking blood, but that was her nature now and he could accept that.

It wasn't fair. For six months, he had been separated from her, only able to communicate through email, and now she was just a few rooms down from him and he couldn't be with her.

It was stupid to even think about. He was sure she had had feelings for him in the beginning, but that was back when they were both human. Now her eyes, her face, they were unreadable to him. What could he possibly offer her?

Thad's eyes flitted away from the food to the silverware resting on the napkin near the plate. He picked up the knife and tested the edge with his thumb. It wasn't razor-sharp, but had a serrated edge that might do the trick.

A cold sweat broke on his forehead and his stomach knotted, but he figured that was only natural. He was still mortal and the fear of death still inhabited his very DNA.

It was an appealing thought, though, taking matters into his own hands. It wasn't the first time it had crossed his mind. He had considered it more than once, but the thought of his parents finding him dead on the floor, or worse, him reanimating and feeding upon them, stayed his hand every time.

But what reason did he have to stop now? Why wait for the Stewards to hand down judgment? Why not narrow their choices for them? He could either be a vampire with them or they could put him to death. Either option seemed better than forced servitude.

Thad pressed the blade of the knife to his wrist. Would it hurt? Did it matter? Would the Stewards accept a vampire born of the bite, instead of born of the blood? He would be a weak vampire or so said Shufah. Vampires born of blood are always stronger. Taos would still have the advantage.

Thad didn't care. He could teach himself to be strong.

He drew a breath, dug the serrated teeth into his skin, but stopped.

What if his blood brought the other vampires to his room, like a frenzy of sharks to an injured seal? They might fall upon him and tear him to shreds. Or worse, injure him too badly to become a vampire. What if he turned into a savage instead?

Thad shuddered, despite the warmth of the room. He remembered well his encounter with Kole.

He dropped the knife onto the table.

Thad searched through the drawers and closets. He found an

array of clothing and was more than a bit disturbed to find it all his size. Everything from soft flannel pajamas to a crisp, expensive suits were at his disposal. He didn't like to think what such a wardrobe might mean about his pending freedom, so he shut the drawers and closed the closets.

Thad had a sudden thought. He could drown himself. That would bring on the change without drawing any blood. It wasn't the ideal way to go. He didn't like the idea of suffocating to death, wasn't even sure he could manage the pain long enough to get the job done. Maybe he could find a way to weigh himself down.

He stepped into the bathroom and threw up his hands, both disappointed and relieved at the same time. There was no bathtub, only a narrow shower stall. He checked the toilet, almost giggling at the thought of the headstand maneuver he'd have to perform, but even so, it was a modern water-saving model that would barely wet the top of his head.

"Okay, drowning is out."

All this thought of suicide was making him dizzy—though was it really suicide if you rose from the dead? He closed the lid of the toilet and sat down with his head in his hands. He didn't want to kill himself, not really. He was in no rush to die and truth be told, wasn't all that thrilled with the prospect of being some eternal blood-drinking ghoul. But as much as those avenues of choice left a bitter taste in his mouth, the alternative made him feel physically sick.

Thad thought of the two men that came to retrieve the dead body from Jerusa's room. He had guessed both men to be around the age of his father, not old, but past their prime. They weren't ugly or out of shape. They seemed hard working (most people Thad knew wouldn't cart away a dead body by hand), humble, obedient. Shouldn't their service toward the undead be rewarded with immortality?

No, the Stewards, self-proclaimed leaders of the undead, were the ultimate clique. Worse than any high school elitism, or college frat mentality, or religious/political bigotry. The Stewards made no qualms about their admission standards: beauty, which was subjective, or power, which was corrosive.

Thad understood Shufah's disdain of being a member of such a group, but being one of the infected human slaves, whittling away the years in servitude to ungrateful masters until old age crippled you, finding at the end the only gift of retirement is to be burned to ashes so that you won't rise as an embarrassment to the ones you served, seemed all the more abominable.

Though he took no certain pride in it, Thad knew he had the youth and looks to appease the Stewards . . . if he were turned now. Five years from now, ten years, who knew? He should have taken Taos's offer six months ago and let him complete the change. He'd be a vampire, born of the blood and they wouldn't be in any more trouble with the Stewards than they were right now.

Thad glanced over at the belt of the terrycloth robe hanging from the door and wondered if there was any place to hang himself. The shower curtain rod was a no. He didn't think the dowel rod in the closet was all that promising, either. Thad went to the robe and pulled the belt from the loops. Its soft yet sturdy material would make a fine impromptu noose. Maybe he could sneak off to some other part of the house.

He laughed to himself. It was true what his dad always told him. The hardest choices in life were often just choosing a path. Once you focused on one direction, all other steps were easier.

Thad tucked the belt into his back pocket and stepped out of the bathroom. He went to the table where his food sat cooling. The aroma of the chicken filled the room and his stomach roared out. He stood next to the table, shoveling the food into his mouth with his hands, like some starved refugee. He thought perhaps he should slow down, enjoy each morsel of his last meal as a mortal, but he had made his choice to join the undead and he wanted to get on with it before doubt had a chance to sweep in.

Thad stared blankly at the remains of his dinner, licking the grease and salt from his fingers, when a knock came at the door.

His heart lurched at the sound. Were the Stewards sending for them so soon? Would they judge them tonight? Thad crossed the room with weakened legs and opened the door just a crack. An older woman, perhaps in her sixties, stood with a pleasant smile on her face.

What has she got to smile about? Thad wondered. "Yes," he said, opening the door.

She started to speak in Russian, caught herself and said in English, "I'm here for your dishes, dear. Are you finished with your dinner?"

Thad nodded that he was. She came strutting in with a youthful gate, almost joyful. He had expected her to come lumbering in, but instead she seemed happy to have something to do.

"I would ask how dinner was," she said, surveying the wreck of his plate, "but I can see, well enough, you enjoyed it. I'll let the cooks know. They'll be pleased." She gathered up the dirty dishes onto a tray and covered them with a towel. She glanced over her shoulder at him. "I'm not supposed to ask, but will you be joining us here?"

Thad had the urge to smile, not because he found her question funny, but because for the first time he had a clear answer. He held the smile at bay, though. She might misread it. "No. I'm afraid not."

A bit of joy drained from the woman. "That's too bad. We could use some more help around here. It hasn't been this busy in, well, all of my lifetime."

"A lot of visitors, huh?"

"You could say that and not all of them vampires. Humans, from all over, have been shipped here instead of the other communities."

Thad didn't want to talk about the quarantine communities, but the lady had an easy charm about her that made conversation effortless. "Why are they coming here? What's wrong with the other towns?"

"Not sure. Maybe something. Maybe nothing. Hard to tell." She smiled at him in a motherly sort of way, as if to say *he's grown to be such a good lad.* "It's a shame you won't be staying. There are far too few young backs around here and I'm not getting any younger."

"Why don't you leave?" Thad asked. He hadn't meant to, it just fell out. She stood straight, as if he had jabbed her in the side. Thad thought maybe he should apologize, but he didn't. "Why stay here if they are never going to change you? Why not run away and hide? Live your life for yourself."

"Why would I do such a thing?" she asked. Judging from her reaction Thad might have asked why she didn't stomp puppies with cleated boots. "There is nothing for me out there. Here I'm safe. Cared for. Useful."

"No, you're not. You are a slave." Instant regret. "I'm sorry, but it's still the truth."

"To your eyes, maybe, but not to mine." Her words were soft, not at all angry like he had expected.

"Don't you deserve immortality? Don't you deserve to have what they have?"

Her brow furrowed softly, as though she pitied him. "Who says I want that? Not all servitude is forced. Some is born of gratitude."

"Gratitude," he said in exasperation. "Gratitude for what? For kidnapping you? Stealing you away from everyone you love?"

"Gratitude for my life," she said. "When I was very young, only nine years old, I was bitten by a rogue vampire. It was a terrible creature, born of the bite. It had awakened with a terrible thirst. It came upon our home one night. There were ten of us under the roof. I was the only one to make it out alive."

"I'm sorry," Thad said.

She nodded in appreciation. "A group of Hunters had tracked him to our house. They caught him feeding on me. By their hands, my family received swift justice. I was infected. They could have killed me too, but they chose not to. I grew and when I came of age, I hoped that I would be offered the blood, but I didn't pass the tests. I didn't begrudge it, though. I was given my life and a home and a new family. I have no regrets."

The weight and tragedy of her story fell on Thad and he felt as if he should sit down. He leaned against the doorjamb instead. "I'm sorry, but you and I see things very different. Who cares if you didn't meet their beauty standards? Had you been given the chance, you might have become the most powerful vampire to have ever lived. It's not fair. Why should they get to choose?"

Her face grew somber and she rushed forward, forgetting her tray of dirty dishes on the table. "Shhh," she said, placing her soft fingers upon his mouth. "Watch what you say within these walls. The Watchtower is very near and they may be monitoring you." Thad looked around for a hidden camera. The woman shook her head. "They don't watch you like that. They don't need to. The Watchtower is full of fierce and powerful vampires. Their minds are not like our minds and if ever there were slaves that lament their lot, it would be them. Keep your hatred of the Stewards buried within your heart and pray the Watchtower does not find it there."

Thad felt shaken by the woman's visible fear, but more so by how quickly it passed, as if she had taken off a mask and cast it aside.

"Don't worry about my lot," the woman said. "I doubt it will be your own. You will make a stunning vampire." She seemed embarrassed by her compliment, grabbed the tray of dirty dishes and rushed past him into the hallway.

"What's your name?"

She smiled again, a youthful flirty smile. "Dorothy, but everyone around here calls me Dot." She sped off with a chipper little strut.

Thad stepped away from the door, but didn't close it. He sat on the edge of the bed. A lump of something shifted beneath him, tilting him at an uncomfortable angle. He reached back to move the obstruction and found the robe belt still in his back pocket. He pulled it out and coiled it in his lap, like a sleeping snake.

A noise roused him.

Four men passed by his open door in pairs. Each pair carried a dead body between them. None of the men glanced into Thad's room, but kept their eyes straight ahead, as they continued on their grim task in silence.

Thad figured the dead bodies were the prisoners cast into Shufah's and Taos's rooms. He tried to feel some remorse for them, but found a great vacuous space where his empathy should be. He should be appalled that his *friends* had killed the men to feast on their blood, but he wasn't. Shufah and Taos were vampires. Vampires fed on blood. Jerusa was a vampire, too and if she ever found a way around her annoying ghost groupie, she would feed on blood as well.

But it was more than that. He could feel no sorrow or disgust over the slaying of the prisoners because Thad now knew that one day he would feed on the blood, too.

A gnawing curiosity crept over him. What did they do with the dead bodies? Where were the four infected men going and what would they do afterward?

Thad stood to his feet before he realized what he was doing. He crossed the room quickly and poked his head out the door in time to see the pallbearers turn the corner at the far end of the hall. He waited for them to vanish, checked the hall to make sure no one else was watching, then shut his door and followed them.

It was slow going. The men were older, packing a decent bit of dead weight between them. Thad was young and swift. More than once her turned a corner and had to jump back as to not collide with them. If they knew he was following them, they made no mention of it, keeping on their chosen path for this lonely funeral march.

Thad watched every closed door he passed, as if it might spring open suddenly and the grasping hands of one of the many vampires in the house would take hold of him. But no door opened and he never crossed paths with anyone, vampire or human.

Finally, the pallbearers came to a set of elevators. They set the dead men on the floor, with no more care than if they were bags of flour and stretched their backs as they waited for the door to open. One of the pallbearers flinched, perhaps catching a glimpse of Thad from his peripherals. Thad pulled his head back around the corner and stood with his back pressed against the wall, fearful that his breathing was as loud to them as it was to him.

No one said anything and Thad didn't hear anyone approaching. Still, he couldn't muster the courage to glance around the corner again until he heard the ding of the elevator car announcing its arrival to the floor.

Thad chanced a peek. The men were gone. He moved to the elevators, which were old but not the most ancient set he'd ever seen. Over top each of the doors was a semicircle of numbers with a brushed copper arrow indicating the floor the car was on.

Thad watched, in fascination, as the arrow fell farther and farther, until it landed on the floor marked B3. It thrilled him to think this house had almost as many floors below ground as it had above. He reached over and pressed the button between the doors and the arrow that had been still came to life. The door to his left slid open. Thad took a deep breath and stepped inside. His hand trembled so much he almost tapped the button for the wrong floor. His finger hovered over B3. He took a deep breath and pushed the button.

The doors pulled shut and the elevator dropped slowly, as if it were still contemplating its decision to allow Thad a ride. The elevator passed through all of the floors without stopping and coughing him out. Three floors below ground, the elevator doors opened to darkness.

Chapter Seventeen

Jerusa was almost as surprised to see the ghost as he was to be seen. He looked around and noticed Alicia and Foster. He came close to them and the trio exchanged some silent communication that brought a frown to the new ghost's face. Jerusa wondered if the man realized he was dead. From his fangs, she could tell that he had been a vampire when he had died.

The new ghost was not much taller than Alicia. He had a piebald set of eyes, one brown, one blue, which didn't seem to line up symmetrically. His hair was a mess of thinning tangles, giving him the look of someone long on the run. He might as well have had UNACCEPTBLE branded on his forehead.

After a bit of time, another ghost appeared inside the room. This one was an elderly woman, toothless, except for her fangs, with a long hoary shock of hair running down her back like a silver waterfall. More and more ghosts began to appear and before long the room was full. The restless spirits of countless vampires milled around each other, shoulder to shoulder, prattling on in silent voices. Jerusa could feel the weight of their raucous conversations, but couldn't detect even a whisper. Several times she had to close her eyes to shake off the sensation that she had gone deaf.

She breathed a sigh of relief when she caught the sound of the men coming to remove the dead bodies from Shufah and Taos's rooms.

She glanced around at the mob of murdered vampires and felt a deep stitch of pity for them. Why had they all lingered here, in the place of their execution? Did they not know they could leave, that they were free? Or had they been confined in darkness, afraid to venture out, but were now drawn to her like hordes of insects to a solitary candle flame?

The crowd of ghosts stopped suddenly, like a herd of spooked deer. They stood still, watching the far wall of the bedroom. Jerusa stood on her bed to get a better look over their heads, but couldn't see what had caused such a strange reaction.

Something entered the room—several somethings—passing through the wall as though it wasn't there. At first, Jerusa thought it was just another group of vampire ghosts, but when the crowd of spirits began to rush away, she caught a glance of what was frightening them.

Four, five, six, a dozen came into the room, all slumped and bewildered, eyes burning with hatred and unfettered hunger. These were not the ghosts of blood-drinking vampires, but of flesh-eating savages.

The savage spirits were more gossamer, less defined than the vampire ghosts, sometimes flickering in and out of existence. Several were missing limbs, but not in the sense of an injury. Legs and arms were not hacked off, leaving gory stubs. They were just gone, as if these demonic apparitions were not complete souls.

The crowd of ghosts rushed about the room in a panic and had they been corporeal, they would have trampled Jerusa into a fine paste. Instead they passed through her body without disturbance, bringing only a slight chill to her skin. They moved about, like a great shoal of frightened fish, incapable of fleeing too far from the light that Jerusa gave them.

The savages chased the vampires, catching more than a few and tried to feast on flesh that was no longer there. The savages didn't seem to understand why they were unable to devour the vampires they caught, just as the vampires didn't realize they were safe from the savages' bites.

It was a macabre production spilling out before her. Jerusa stood fascinated and appalled. She called out to several ghosts, trying to explain that they were safe, but none listened.

Jerusa hopped down from the bed, rushed to the aid of a child vampire being mauled. She reached down, knowing she could not touch the child ghost and the savage turned his wrath on Jerusa.

Jerusa was thrust backward, not by any physical touch, but by a blast of frigid malevolency such as she had never felt before. The other savage ghosts, seeing Jerusa on her back and flailing, gave up the assault on their spiritual victims and rushed to join the attack on a living creature.

The world filled with dead eyes and the gnashing of festering teeth. Jerusa swatted at the snapping jaws, but her hands passed through without impact. They tore at her with their mouths, their hands, their feet and though they caused no physical damage to her, each blow pressed her soul deeper into black, icy waters. And though they took no flesh from her, it was clear the ghostly savages were feeding on her nonetheless, for they grew clearer, more defined and their missing limbs were coming into focus.

A bright light erupted over Jerusa's head, spilling the savages backward. They shielded their eyes, as if the sun itself rushed upon them to melt the flesh from their bones. In the light that should have brought clarity to their form, they instead bled away like silt settling to the bottom of a still pond.

Jerusa looked up, not at all surprised to find Alicia with her arms stretched wide, her body aflame with spectral light.

With the savage ghosts gone, the spirits of the vampires filtered back into the room. Their movements were slow, their faces full of awe. They circled around Alicia, forgetting Jerusa on the floor and seemed, for the first time, to notice the young ghost in the prom dress was somehow different than they were.

The light emanating from Alicia faded away and she regarded the crowd of spirits with a stern look. Her eyes conveyed some message of authority to them that they recognized. One by one the vampire ghosts vanished, slipping from Jerusa's sight like mist in the moonlight, yet she sensed they were all still there watching her.

Alicia extended her hand and helped her up from the floor. Jerusa wondered if she would ever get used to it. "Thanks." Alicia smiled. "Well, that was new."

Alicia swatted at the air, her way of saying "don't worry."

Foster caught Jerusa's attention then pointed to the back corner of the room. The vampire ghost with the piebald eyes, stood kneading his hands together, shuffling his feet from side to side. He watched Jerusa with his brown eye and Alicia with his blue eye. The sight made Jerusa's head hurt. She thought to ask him to stop, but didn't want to seem rude.

The ghost moved to the door, passed partway through the solid oak door, then leaned his upper torso back into the room and motioned for Jerusa to follow. Jerusa looked at Alicia and Foster. They seemed unsure, but both nodded.

The ghost vanished through the door and Jerusa followed him. The heavy door slid silently on its hinges. Thad's scent hung heavy in the air. He had left his room not too long before. A stab of panic wriggled through her midsection at the thought of him happening upon the wrong group of vampires. Was this where the ghost was leading her? Was Thad in danger?

The thought of being lead to Thad was dispelled when his scent turned a corner going in the direction of a set of elevators and the ghost motioned for her to continue straight on. She stood in place for a moment, glancing between the ghost and the elevators. The urge to follow Thad boiled in her blood, but it was not just a desire to make sure he was safe that pulled at her. She recognized the low fires of the thirst hiding just below the surface.

She turned away from Thad's scent and followed the ghost.

With the ghost leading on, Jerusa maneuvered a series of hallways, some broad with many unmarked doors, others narrow and dark. He moved fast, causing Jerusa to run to keep up. They came to a staircase, though not the one they had used to get to their suites. This one was made of dark stone that seemed out of place in this bright and lavishly decorated house and more at home in a long forgotten castle. They moved down two flights before the ghost continued down another narrow hallway ending in a plain looking metal door. The ghost passed through the door. Jerusa followed at a run and found herself in a large utility closet where a group of humans stood talking.

The humans stood frozen with shock, gawking at her as if she had appeared in a burst of flame and smoke. Jerusa glanced back at the door she had come through and watched as it pulled closed, seamlessly blending with the wall. She thought to apologize for her intrusion, but the roar of their hearts, the aroma of their blood, caused her to rush from the room before it could fuel the blaze of her thirst.

Jerusa fled the utility closet by the regular door, slamming it behind her. The ghost glanced back at her, his duel colored eyes begging her to hurry. He passed through an adjacent door. Jerusa followed the ghost as he once again maneuvered through a series of halls and down another flight of stairs, this one not so deserted.

Several vampires were milling around this part of the house as though it were the lobby of some common hotel. They watched with gossiping interest as Jerusa rushed down the stairs. She reined back her speed, taking to a gentle walk, as though she was just taking in the sights and in no rush at all. This had the opposite effect making the gawking vampires all the more interested in her.

The ghost urged her on, but she maintained her casual stroll. The others couldn't see the spirit with the piebald eyes, nor could they see Alicia and Foster trailing behind Jerusa. All they could see was the panic stricken fledgling running through the halls as though she was looking for a way to escape. She didn't care for their greedy eyes or the way they whispered to each other in languages she couldn't understand.

Whatever the ghost had to show her must be important, but Jerusa couldn't bring herself to run with the crowd watching her. She had given them enough to gossip about for one night. She could only hope that word of this didn't reach the Stewards. She had a feeling the ghost was leading her someplace that she would not want the Hunters to find her.

She continued down to the first floor where the ghost led her to a door beneath the stairway. A set of spiral stairs made of that same dark stone descended into the murky gloom. The air felt cool and musty, ancient as the stones forming the walls and stairs, as if the levels below ground had been sealed away for centuries.

She rushed after the ghost down the spiral steps so fast that when she reached the landing at the bottom she nearly spilled face-first onto the floor.

The room she now stood in was round, with doors circling all about her. Candles burned in sconces near each door and a war of shadows waged upon the walls. The ghost motioned her toward one of the doors, but she couldn't tell one from the other nor what direction she was heading.

She stepped inside the room, cringing at the loud squall of the hinges and pulled it shut behind her. It was another circular room, except that there were no other doors and the floor cascaded down, creating a miniature coliseum. The room stank of soot and char. Opposite the door was a small stage, built of wood, that overlooked the lowest part of the floor. The wood of the stage looked old but sturdy and all around the edges was a great, colorful curtain, embossed with the symbol of the Stewards, which reached from the platform to the floor.

The ghost motioned for Jerusa to hurry to the stage. She circled around the room instead of going down and through the middle. There was something about the lowest part of the floor that she didn't like. It was the blackest part of the room. The stones looked brittle and well-worn and it just felt wrong to tread upon them.

She came to the stage and the ghost motioned for her to climb beneath the curtain.

"What? In there? I don't think that's a good idea. Maybe I should just go back to my room." Her voice echoed around the room.

The ghost looked at the door in a panic, then dove beneath the stage, as though he wasn't invisible to everyone except Jerusa.

She was about to point this out to him when she caught the sound of approaching footsteps.

Jerusa stood frozen with fear, her heart racing and might have stayed that way had Alicia not given her a hard shove to the back. Jerusa scrambled forward on hands and knees searching the curtain for a seam she might slip through. When she could not find one, she gave up and crawled beneath the heavy fabric on her stomach, snaking her way between the beams of the stage. The hinges of the door cried out in alarm just as she pulled her feet beneath the curtain.

"I offer my deepest apologies to the Council." It was Ming's voice. "I didn't mean to hide anything from you. I only thought—"

"We don't care what you think," said a male voice Jerusa didn't recognize. "It's not your duty to think. Yours is to obey. If this is too much for you and your little scrabble of hideous misfits, then I shall gladly see you and your team standing in the pit of judgment."

"Calm yourself, Cot," said a voice Jerusa recognized as Marjek. "The human is confined to the observation ward, just as I said. She shows no sign of regeneration. Ming and her team have been warned. There is nothing to worry about."

Jerusa's heart leapt into her throat at the mention of her mother. She slithered her way to a crack of light breaking through the curtain and watched as Marjek and the other four members of the High Council marched around the outer wall toward the stage. Ming and the Crimson Storm followed along behind, like hungry, yet timid dogs.

"We shall see," said the vampire, Cot. He was a tall, thin vampire with a youthful face, full lips and a shock of black hair hanging loose upon his collar. His features were handsome, yet cruel, as though he had been chiseled from ice and all warmth disgusted him. "I still say they should be excused from this session, as punishment."

"I disagree," Marjek said. "They did well. It was no easy task bringing Shufah to us."

"Your infatuation with that woman will be your undoing," said a female vampire, though her tone was light, almost mocking. "I don't see why she is so important. We should just be done with her small coven and send her on her way."

"Because, Othella," said a voice Jerusa recognized as Heidi's. "She may be able to root out her brother. If you destroy her coven, do you think she will aid in his destruction?"

"We've been over this at length," Marjek said, the finality in his voice falling like a gavel. "The decision has been made. Now let us get on with the judgments. Bring in the first."

Celeste sprang up as if startled by Marjek's voice. Jerusa wasn't sure, but she thought Celeste had been staring at the crack in the curtain that she was spying from. Jerusa's mind reeled at the mention of Shufah's twin brother. Suhail was still alive? True he had escaped that night they had battled Kole, but when Jerusa later asked what had become of him, Shufah assured her that Suhail was dead.

Did Shufah know her twin brother was still alive? And if so, why would she have lied about it? Was it because of Suhail that the Stewards had fled to the Ice Sanctuary? These questions, and more, swirled within her and the more she thought about it, the more she dreaded their true purpose for being here.

Heidi had said something about needing Shufah's assistance, hadn't she? That destroying their coven was not an option? For the first time in months, Jerusa felt the flicker of hope. Perhaps she, Thad and Taos would escape judgment after all. If they couldn't rely on the mercy of the High Council, maybe they could barter out a treaty.

Jerusa was so engrossed in this train of thought that she almost didn't notice when Celeste returned, marching a human girl down into the sooty pit.

Chapter Eighteen

Thad stepped out of the elevator, glancing about the room. Not much could be seen outside the spray of light spilling from the elevator doors, but he could tell the room was large and open, with high ceilings. He couldn't see the walls, but the floor was made of large, ancient-looking stones. Every instinct in him said to flee back into the elevator, and he might have, but before he could turn, the doors closed, pinching off the light.

Thad spun toward the elevator, clawing at the doors, but it was too late. They were sealed shut and the sound of the car ascending to the upper floors echoed all around him. He groped along the wall for the call button, but there didn't seem to be one. The sound of his frightened breathing and the slap of his hand against the elevator doors seemed magnified, but whether that was due to the cavernous room or his ears compensating for his blinded eyes, he couldn't say.

He pressed his back against the elevator. He clenched his eyes shut. Thad had never been prone to fear. He had always been taller than others, athletic, well liked. He had never known the sting of a bully or abuse of any kind. He was the perfect extrovert, leaping into any situation with both feet, rushing headlong into adventure with the faith that no matter what, it would work out for him.

In retrospect, this old version of him seemed prissy and sheltered. That world vanished in the blink of an eye the moment Taos had bitten him. Now his life was off course, washed out to sea by an unimaginable storm. He drifted alone in an uncharted part of the map. The place where the inscription read *here, there be monsters*.

And there truly were monsters in the world. Not vague and

metaphoric. No, there were real monsters, hidden away in the dark places of the world, places like the dungeon in which he stood. What other ignominies lurked below this house?

He tried to keep the image of Kole from rising in his mind. Vampires were frightening enough when you looked at them, really looked at them. Past the eternal youth and beauty, past the enchanting eyes and pretense of civility, they were still blood drinkers. But peal all that back, dig down to the center of the beast and what comes forth is truly horrific.

Thad shivered against the cool metal of the elevator door. In his mind's eye, he could see them, a horde of savages creeping through the darkness toward him. He swatted at the void before him, but he didn't know what he hoped this would accomplish. His hand came down, brushing something hanging at his side. He reached back and pulled the terrycloth belt from his back pocket.

Strange as it sounds, the belt calmed him, like some mystical talisman.

"And Death shall have no dominion," he whispered to the darkness, remembering the first line of some poem he had read in English class a lifetime ago.

Thad opened his eyes and found that the darkness was not as impenetrable as he had first thought. Now that his eyes had adjusted, he could make out the far walls and a glimmer of light coming from a door at the end of a long corridor.

Thad pushed toward the thin strip of light at the back of the corridor. There were doors on both sides. Now and then he heard what he thought was a murmur of conversation behind them, but he kept walking toward the door at the back.

The door was unlocked, so he eased it open, just enough to peek through. The light from the next room seemed dazzling compared to the murky dungeon he was coming from, but he could see it was only a few bare light bulbs attached to the stone ceiling. The room was stifling hot and he could hear what he thought was the sound of movement within.

Clutching the belt tight in his hand (as if it could ward off danger), he eased the door open further, squeezed through, then pushed it almost shut again. The room was large and square with thick stone columns holding up the ceiling. Thad hurried away from the door and hid behind the nearest column just in time to see a long shadow slide across the floor.

A man called out and though he spoke in what sounded to be Russian, Thad could tell from the tone that he was asking if anyone was there. Thad held his breath. Another man spoke, again in Russian and the two engaged in a bit of small talk, before returning to their task.

There came a loud clank of metal and the screech of old hinges, then the room filled with bright light, dancing shadows and a gust of heat, as though the door to Hell had just been opened.

Thad chanced a glance around the column. Two men stood before a great open furnace, its intense flames lapping at the air within the belly of the large metal beast. Thad had never seen the men before, but he did recognize the two dead bodies—the men Shufah and Taos had fed upon—lying naked on a table, not too far away.

Rivers of sweat poured from the men's heads, pooling in a swampy mess at the tops of their shirts. They took hold of one of the dead men, one man grasping him under the armpits, the other man hooking him beneath the knees. With a collective grunt they hoisted the corpse from the table and in a synchronized swing, tossed it into the flames. They repeated this method with the second corpse, tossing him in on top of the other dead man.

With their gruesome task completed, they closed the furnace doors, choking off the heat spewing forth and ending the dance of shadows upon the walls. They rubbed the sweat from their faces, then left the room without speaking.

Thad remained pinned against the column. His knees were weak and his stomach wrenched tight. He had known what the men were going to do with the dead bodies when he saw them slink past the door to his room, but seeing it first-hand made his head reel.

The corpses in the furnace had to be cremated. It was the only way to ensure they wouldn't rise from their deaths as vampires born of the bite, the only way to know they wouldn't turn savage.

Thad thought the stench of burning flesh would drive him from the room, but he could detect no scent at all, other than the earthy smell of the stone column. The heat of the room zapped his energy and he felt as though he could fall down on the floor and sleep for years. He watched the furnace and wondered if he would someday be pitched in among the flames, naked and unremembered.

One of the doors in the corridor slammed open and the crashing noise brought him out of his stupor. Several voices echoed through the empty passage. Thad moved to the door and pulled it open only a fraction of an inch.

Far down the corridor, close to the open room with the elevator, one of the doors to the left stood open. A pair of vampires waited on either side, each wearing a long black cloak with the symbol of the Hunters on the back. Though neither was a large man, their eyes—even at this distance—spoke of cruelty.

Were they sent to search for him? He looked back into the room in which he stood, searching for a place to hide. He had used the columns to escape the human workers, but that wouldn't cloak him from the enhanced senses of the vampires.

Again the sound of voices caught his attention. In the corridor, from the open door, came a line of humans shambling out single file. There were men and women in the line, all dirty and disheveled.

Thad's first thought was that these were the prisoners Marjek had spoken of. The poor souls condemned to death by their governments, purchased by the vampires to be food for the undead. This turned out to be untrue, as least for some of the humans in line, for a woman near the end of the line, speaking in a British accent boasted to her captors that she was to be judged now and would soon join their ranks. One of the Hunters silenced her with a slap that sent her to her knees. She climbed to her feet, massaging her jaw and wiping tears from her eyes, then followed along with the group.

Thad's stomach twisted and he felt as though he might get sick. He choked back his nausea knowing that the Hunters would sniff him out in an instant if he vomited. That poor woman wasn't a condemned criminal. She was one of the infected. But why was she being housed in this dungeon? Were the others infected, too?

He shouldn't have left his room. That had been a terrible mistake, he realized now. He twisted the belt in his hands, hoping to wring some courage from it, as he had earlier, but it had lost its enchantments and felt no more pleasant to him than a dead snake. Thad tried to chase away his despair for the woman and her group, thinking that the Stewards would judge them worthy—the woman, after all, was very pretty despite the filth clinging to her from untold days within this dungeon—yet in his heart he didn't really believe it. Thad had a feeling that if he lingered in this room long enough he would see the infected servants carrying the British girl and her companions back down to feed to the furnace.

The Hunters marched away, one before the line of humans, the other behind. He started to pull the door to the furnace room open, but leapt back, startled, when one of the other doors on the right side of the corridor opened with a loud bang.

Another set of Hunters stepped into the hallway. They were dressed just as the other two, except that this pair each held a long, sharp spear—the weapon Ralgar had called a skewer. They gripped their skewers tight, holding them at the ready before their chests. One of them pointed the dangerous tip into the room and motioned with it for someone to come out. Neither spoke, but it was clear that disobedience would not be tolerated.

Another line of wretched souls filed out of the room, but these were not humans.

Thad counted half a dozen vampires, each shackled wrist and ankle, with heavy fetters. He could tell they were vampires, not by their fangs (he was too far away to see those, thank goodness), but by the way their skin remained pristinely clean without even a smudge of dirt. He had seen this with Jerusa, Shufah and Taos as well. Even mud and soot wiped right away without any additional cleaning. Also, the eyes of the group were not the eyes of mortals, but the gleaming jewels of predators, searching the darkness unimpeded.

They looked about the corridor, sniffing the air like a pack of hungry dogs. One vampire caught the scent of something missed by the others, even the Hunters. He stiffened, straightened his posture, looking almost gentlemen-like despite his tattered rags and chains. He turned his gaze slowly to the left, his yellow eyes glimmering in the light cast from the small crack of the furnace door.

Thad wanted to push away from the door, wanted to curl up in a darkened corner and hide, but he stood transfixed by the vampire's stare. For a brief moment, he feared the vampire would call out to him or shout his location to the Hunters, but instead, he simply winked, then turned his face back toward his captors.

Thad did push away from the door this time, hard enough to ram his back into the column he had hidden behind. He stifled a grunt, which was from surprise as much as it was pain. The long moment of silence afterwards was terrible, each second stretching into an hour as he awaited the Hunters to burst in and take him. Or kill him.

But the furnace door never moved and after a time, Thad thought he heard the mechanical swish of the elevator doors. It took him a few more minutes before he could approach the door. His legs had become like rubber and when he did manage to push away from the column, a blast of pins and needles rose from his soles up into his calves.

Thad pressed his face to the door and peered out the crack. He detected no movement in the darkened hall, so he slowly pulled the door open, just enough to slip out. He pulled the door shut and waited for his eyes to adjust to the dark. When he could see well enough, he crept to the first door on his left.

The door was dense wood, inlaid with heavy brass hinges. There was a keyhole below the knob and a sliding latch near the top that wasn't engaged. Thad reached out for the knob. It was cool, fixed firmly in its mount and yet turned without complaint. Thad had expected the door to be locked, but it drifted silently inward an inch. The stench of human waste belched forth and Thad stepped back shielding his face with his arm.

He pushed the door open to its fullest and found a long room, dimly lit, with what looked to be medieval prison cells lining both walls. Faces pressed against the bars, sometimes as many as ten in a cell. They looked at Thad, moaning in desperation or speaking to him in languages he didn't understand. Arms extended through the tiny squares formed from the crossing bars, waving at him, compelling him closer.

"Please," a voice said in English. "Don't go." It was a woman that spoke, though her voice was hoarse and gruff.

Thad stepped into the room looking for the woman that had called out to him. The extended hands swiped at him, almost in reverence, as though being on the outside of the bars had given him power to heal their wounds.

At the far end of the room, in the cell to the left, Thad found the woman that had called out to him. He gasped when he saw her. For a moment he thought it had been Jerusa. The girl had the same height and build as Jerusa, though her hair was blonde and she was still a human.

"Help me," the girl said. The others in her cell were crowding her out, reaching through the bars toward Thad, jabbering to him in unknown tongues. "Please, help me."

Thad wasn't sure he'd be able to speak through the knot in his throat, but he managed to squeak out, "I can't."

The girl eased her way to the bars. "Yes you can. Just open the door and let me go."

"I can't," Thad repeated. "There's nowhere to go. Even if you get out of here, they are everywhere. Even if you made it outside, you'd freeze to death within an hour."

"Why am I here?" the girl asked, her eyes stabbing at Thad as if he was the one that brought her here.

"Were you bitten?"

Her eyes widened. "Yes. I was on spring break with friends in Mexico. I got separated from the group. Someone grabbed me from behind. All I remember is him biting me on the neck."

"How long have you been here?"

Tears welled in her eyes, spilled down her cheeks, leaving track marks in the grime of her face. "I don't know." She tried counting on her fingers, became unsure of her figure, tried again, but then just gave up. "Let me out. You have to let me out."

"If I do, they'll kill you."

"They're gonna kill me anyway. Let me out!"

Her shout quickened the others, who began to shuffle around their cells, shrieking, sometimes pitching themselves against the bars. The noise echoed off the stone until it grew to a mild roar. Thad glanced at the door, sure at any moment one of the Hunters would burst through to see what had agitated the prisoners.

"Okay," Thad said, motioning for the group to be quiet. "I'll get you out, but you have to shut up."

He rushed out of the room, shutting the door to dampen the sound of their moans. He needed something, a pipe, a crowbar, anything, to pry open the door. Or maybe a knife would be better. He could use it to pick the lock. Thad went to the next door on the left side and made the mistake of rushing in. It was a twin room to the first, with cells full of human prisoners. They too began to call out to him, begging in different languages to be freed, but there was nothing in this room for Thad to use.

He continued down the left side of the corridor. Every door led to the same sight and had Thad not been able to see the large room with the elevators growing ever closer he would have believed he was stuck in some sort of temporal loop. By the time he reached the last door on the left, the cries of the prisoners were deafening.

Thad felt time slipping away. He ran across to the opposite side of the hall to the door nearest the elevator. He wrenched it open, preparing himself for the added cries of the prisoners inside, but instead he found quite a different group.

This room had no cells, but many prisoners. They were fastened to the stone walls by the wrist, waist and ankles with the thickest fetters Thad had ever seen. Piercing eyes caught the dim light and reflected it back with luminous fire, as they searched him with greedy delight.

Thad stood frozen in the doorway like a mouse in an open field, hoping the passing hawk didn't see him. None of the vampires spoke to him, none pleaded to be released, but several did thrash within their shackles like feral beasts.

Thad backed out of the room and shut the door. He slid the locking bar into the thick eyelet, but it did little to make him feel safe. If one of the vampires managed to wrench their fetters from the wall, the locks on the door would do little to keep them from getting out.

Thad checked the rest of the doors on that side of the corridor, only easing them open a crack. They were all the same, full of vampire prisoners, until he came to the door closest to the furnace room.

This door opened unto blackness so dense the light spilling from the furnace room did little to penetrate it. Thad started to step over the threshold when he kicked a loose pebble and felt the floor disappear beneath his foot. He snatched back his foot and gripped the door as if it were a lifeline. Seconds passed before the pebble hit bottom and the sound echoed back up. Thad started to close the door on the pit when a noise, almost lost in the roaring cries of the human prisoners, caught his attention.

It started low, just a single growl, but soon others joined in. Thad couldn't tell how many were down in the pit, but it sounded like a lot. He didn't need a light to tell him what was below. He had heard those growls before, from Kole after he had gone savage.

Thad closed the door and sat on the cold stone floor. He felt so useless. All those people were going to die. He tried to tell himself that the girl in the cell, the one that looked like Jerusa with blonde hair, would be turned. The Stewards would see her beauty and give her the blood. Yet, he didn't really believe that.

He twisted his hands together and found he was still holding the belt to the terrycloth robe. An idea, a dangerous, stupid idea began to form.

Thad jumped up and ran into the furnace room. He searched the ceiling until he found what he was looking for. A thick black pipe was anchored to the stone wall, delivering fuel to the furnace.

Thad moved one of the tables directly under the pipe and climbed up. He tied one end of the belt around the pipe and tested the strength of his knot with a hard yank. It cinched tight and held firm.

With the other end of the belt Thad began to form a makeshift noose.

Chapter Nineteen

The boards of the platform creaked as the five members of the High Council approached the edge. "What is your name child?" Marjek said to the human girl standing in the pit.

"Bethany," she said. She clutched her arms about her and shivered uncontrollably. She spoke English, but her accent wasn't American. British, perhaps, but her hoarse, quaking voice made it difficult to tell.

"Bethany," Marjek repeated, almost as it were something savory rolling across his tongue. "Do you know why you are here?"

"No," Bethany said. "Please, let me go home. I've done nothing wrong." She looked as though she might start crying, but no tears fell. Jerusa had the feeling the girl had cried herself out long ago.

"I'm sorry. We can't do that. You have been bitten by an immortal. You're too dangerous to set free." Though Jerusa couldn't see Marjek's face, she imagined him smiling when he spoke those words.

Bethany remained standing, but her eyes were on the floor as though she considered falling to her knees and begging. She was a pretty girl, despite the grimy skin and knotted hair. She held all the requirements the Stewards had set forth: youth and beauty. Marjek and the rest of the Council were just having a bit of fun before they decided to change her.

Ming stepped down into the pit and stood next to Bethany. Celeste turned without a word, her face still and emotionless, and walked away. Ming looked upward toward the Council on the platform, a despicable little smile curled on her lips. Jerusa pulled back from the curtain just a bit, fearful that Ming would look down and notice her.

The soot and ashy smell of the room permeated everything, making it impossible for Jerusa to catch Bethany's scent even though she stood so close. She hoped the same held true for her own scent.

"To be one of us," Heidi said in haughty voice, "you must be perfect. Immortality is only given to those that deserve it." Bethany seemed to whither at those words. "Strip her."

Ming immediately began ripping Bethany's clothes from her. The poor girl screamed, tears welled in her eyes, but she didn't resist. Within moments she stood naked, her arms wrapped across her chest. Ming circled her like a hungry wolf, scanning every exposed piece of flesh.

Jerusa wanted to scream out, rush from beneath the curtain and smash that arrogant smile off of Ming's face. Alicia must have sensed this in her, because she appeared beside Jerusa and placed a hand on her shoulder. Foster lay prone beside her, shaking his head with a firm no. The other ghost, the man with the mismatched eyes, just looked at her in a kind of wonderment.

Jerusa, uncomfortable with the man's look of awe, turned her focus back to Bethany. She sobbed quietly, flinching every time Ming's face came close to her own. It was just an act. Just a method of humiliation to show fledgling vampires the authority of the Stewards. In her heart, Jerusa rooted for Bethany. She was a fine girl, not only in looks, but in courage to endure such an ordeal. She would make a great vampire. It was almost over now.

Ming made one more pass then stopped behind Bethany. She glanced up at the High Council, a perverted sort of amusement burning in her eyes.

"What is your opinion, Ming?" Marjek asked. "Is she worthy to join us?"

Ming shook her head no and Jerusa felt the wind go out of her.

"She is not worthy," Ming said. Poor Bethany nearly crumpled to the floor and would have, had Ming not caught her and spun her around. Ming pointed to Bethany's back, where amidst the pale flesh was a series of four moles, none larger than a pencil eraser. "The Council asks my opinion and I say she is blemished."

"Does the Council agree with Ming's observation?" Marjek asked.

"Yes," Heidi said.

"I agree," said Cot.

"Agreed," said Othella.

"She is unworthy," said Mathias.

"I agree with the decision of the Council," Marjek said. "You have been found unworthy and are condemned to die."

Jerusa flinched at Marjek's words. Surely she had heard him wrong. Even if Bethany's small moles were reason enough not to make her a vampire, they wouldn't kill her. Not for that. They would just ship her off to one of the quarantine communities. There was no reason to kill her.

Before Jerusa had a chance to spin the words over in her mind, Ming snatched Bethany by her shoulders and plunged her fangs into the girl's neck. Bethany tried to scream, but the sound fled from her. She clenched her eyes in pain, reaching back for Ming's face, but could not muster the strength to form an attack. Bethany's legs gave out and Ming followed her to the floor. Ming finished the act quickly, killing the poor girl within seconds. She stood up, swooning from Bethany's blood and almost tripped on the poor girl's corpse.

"Take her away," Marjek said.

Celeste darted back down into the pit, knelt down to scoop up Bethany, but halted for a moment as if something caught her attention. Jerusa's vision was blurred with red tears, but she could have sworn that Celeste was looking at her. She backed away from the curtain.

"What is it?" Heidi asked.

Celeste flinched as if stung. "Nothing, ma'am. I was just making sure the girl is dead."

"Do you hear that, Ming," Heidi said with a laugh. "Your augur doubts your ability to kill a mortal."

Ming's eyes narrowed into spiteful little slits.

"No," Celeste protested. "That is not what I meant. I only thought I felt the presence of life lingering in her, but I was wrong. The girl is dead."

"It's lucky for you," Othella said in an annoyed tone, "that you are such an accomplished augur, for your incompetence as a vampire is astounding. In the future, be careful what you say or you may end up a victim of the Crimson Storm, instead of a member."

Ming took great pleasure in Celeste's chastisement, but she remained quiet.

"Yes, ma'am," Celeste said. She scooped Bethany's body into her arms and carried her out of the room. Not long after, she returned leading another prisoner, a man this time, down into the pit.

Celeste left the man in the pit and returned to her place. This time Ralgar came and stood next to the man. The process was repeated, the mockery, the false hope, the stripping and the searching. Just as Bethany, the man was found unworthy. The High Council unanimously agreed with Ralgar's observation and the man was sentenced to death. Ralgar fed from him, then tossed his corpse to the side like a sack of trash. Celeste gathered up the man, leaving his clothes mingled on the floor with Bethany's and carried him out the door.

This repeated until each of the Crimson Storm, Celeste included, had fed from two human prisoners. None of the ten humans were found worthy. None was granted a pardon and sent to a quarantine community.

After the last human corpse was carried away, Celeste escorted in a female vampire to be judged. She was in her late forties, early fifties when turned, but the vampire spirit had smoothed out her age lines and given the few grey streaks in her hair a glow of polished silver. The only flaw Jerusa could find in her was the rosy lips and crimson rings around her irises that indicated an underfed vampire.

Jerusa touched her own lips, caressed her own silky eyelids, wondering if she should apply some more of her own blood soon. She didn't dare do it here, not now, where the Stewards and Hunters might detect her.

"Welcome," Marjek said. "What is your name?"

The woman looked around like a cat cornered by angry dogs. Had she not been shackled, wrist and ankle, with a heavy band pinning her arms to her midsection, she might have chanced a run for freedom.

But there was no freedom from this house, not from the judgment of the Stewards. Jerusa realized that now. She touched the scar on her chest. The line of bubbled flesh tingled with electricity and she felt Alicia's grip tighten on her shoulder.

"My name is Chloe," she said in defeat.

"How long since you were turned?" Heidi asked.

"I'm not sure," Chloe said. She appeared to try to remember, but looked confused. "A few months, maybe. I don't know how long I've been here."

The Stewards didn't answer her.

"Were you born of the bite or of the blood?" Mathias asked. She didn't seem to understand so he added, "Were you just bitten or did you drink the blood of the one that made you?"

Chloe looked horrified to have to answer the question, but a rough nudge from Ming's telekinetic hand loosened her tongue. "I didn't drink anyone's blood," she said. "At least, not until I woke up in the morgue. I couldn't help myself." Her voice grew frantic. "It was like fire inside me. I didn't know what was happening until it was over. I didn't mean to kill those people. I'm sorry."

Marjek shushed her. "Be calm. Tell me, Chloe, do you know why you have been brought before us?"

She glanced around, unsure. "No. I don't understand any of this."

"Do you understand what you have become?"

Chloe gave a timid nod. "A vampire?" She seemed embarrassed to admit something that she had been taught her whole life was an impossibility.

"That's right," Marjek said. "I know you have many questions, but they will have to wait a bit longer. First there are some things I need to know. You see, normally when our Hunters come across one born of the bite, they will just dispose of that vampire and move on. But the vampire that made you seems to have bitten several others. Tell me, Chloe, who bit you?"

"I don't know who he was. He said his name was Samuel. He was tall with red hair. He had a Scottish brogue. Very handsome. I only talked with him for a few minutes at a party, but that was years ago, when I was a teenager. He caught me outside and bit me." Chloe looked down, unable to hold the gaze of the Stewards above her. "I never told anyone about what happened. The bite was gone by the next day. Does that help?"

"Yes, Chloe, that does help. Thank you. None of the others could give us such a positive description. I believe we know just who you are talking about."

Chloe chanced a look up. "So, can I go now?"

"No, I'm afraid not." Marjek spoke in a jovial tone, as though he were giving her a tour of the great house. "You are a weak specimen, not deserving of the perpetual life you have stolen. You are not Samuel's first mistake, nor his last, but you can rest assure that we will punish him for what he has done."

Chloe started to argue, but before she could utter a word, Mathias sprang from the stage in a blur of speed, snatched Chloe around the waist and bit into her neck.

Jerusa turned away, revolted at the sight. Shufah once told her that it was forbidden for a vampire to feed from another vampire, except when turning a mortal. The Stewards claimed it was to keep vampires from killing each other in confrontations over hunting grounds, but Shufah said it was to keep any one vampire from growing too powerful. Apparently the High Council didn't follow their own laws.

It took much longer for Mathias to drain Chloe than it did the Hunters to kill their mortal victims. Chloe screamed as she writhed in her chains, snapping at Mathias with her powerful jaws. She soon weakened, though and after that, went still. Her eyes whitened, her skin grayed. Mathias, perhaps caught in a moment of blood rapture, squeezed Chloe so hard that her chest imploded. A spurt of blood shot from her mouth and it was then that he pulled away with a gasp. He dropped her to the floor, then returned to his place on the stage.

Jerusa held her breath and willed her raging heart to slow. No one moved, no one spoke. The silence filled the room like a thick smoke. A terrible anxiousness overcame Jerusa and she had to stifle the urge to rush from under the stage and run for the door.

Chloe's foot suddenly twitched, rattling her chains. The noise seemed so loud, compared to the deep silence, that it startled Jerusa. Chloe's spider-like fingers curled and stretched. She blinked her eyes, which were now the color of clotted blood. She opened her mouth, releasing a gurgling groan that morphed into a growl. She sat up, her lips withered and curled back, exposing dangerous teeth that now looked poisonous and festering.

The savage Chloe climbed to her feet, struggling to break free of her chains. She lunged for Ming, but staggered in her ankle shackles and fell on her face. The Hunters laughed, except for Celeste who seemed disgusted by this whole process. Chloe inched forward on her stomach like a snake, unfazed by the fall, biting at the air in loud ravenous chomps. She pulled hard and managed to free one of her hands from the shackles, but not without a great loss of flesh.

"Ming," Marjek said and without another word Ming extended her hands toward the growling savage.

Using her telekinetic abilities, Ming lifted Chloe a couple of feet from the ground. The savage wrenched her left foot free, skinning it to the bone. She tried to run toward Ming, but her feet couldn't reach the floor.

Ralgar stepped forward, conjured fire within his hands and sent a spray of flame arching through the air. Chloe ignited like a shock of dry grass. She kicked and pawed at air while belting out a high pitch scream. Ralgar intensified the fire to the point that Jerusa could feel the heat baking her face through the heavy curtain. The smell of Chloe's cooking flesh made her want to retch.

Soon Chloe stopped fighting, stopped screaming, yet Ralgar didn't rein in his fire. He continued to burn the poor girl, until even her bones sizzled away to ash. When he finally did halt his conflagration and Ming released the grip of her mind, the metal shackles, now glowing red, fell to the soot covered stone in a spray of sparks.

Poor Chloe was gone in body, but Jerusa thought she saw a dark phantom, the incomplete spirit of a savage, spiral around the room before rushing through the wall.

"Did you have to crush her heart, Mathias?" Heidi asked. "Don't we have enough vile savages to deal with?" There was no real rebuke in her words. More of a friendly jab.

"My apologies. She was delightfully tasteful. I merely wanted to get all of her that I could. I will be more careful in the future."

They marched in three other vampires, one by one, condemning them all to death for various reasons. One had been too lax in the rules, not killing all of his victims and allowing some to be infected. Cot fed on him and this time Quinn burned the body. Another had killed a rival vampire. Othella fed from this one and again the body was burned. The third was a vampire accused of sedition against the Stewards. Heidi fed upon him. He must have been an ancient and powerful vampire, because it took both Ralgar and Quinn to cremate him.

Jerusa wondered why the Hunters had burned the vampires that had been killed, yet not the bodies of the mortals. She wasn't sure just how long these judgments had gone on, but by the time Celeste marched in the fifth vampire, she felt stiff and numb, as though all her bones had turned to ice.

The fifth vampire stood silent in his bindings, staring, without fear, up at the High Council. He had a handsome face with a strong jawline and bright blue eyes. Though he was of average stature, he had a well-toned physique.

"What is your name?" Marjek asked.

"Does it matter?" the vampire answered.

Marjek laughed. "Not to me, it doesn't. Tell me, are you born of the bite or of the blood?"

"The one that made me gave me all of his blood that I could ask for."

"Do you know the name of the one that created you?"

The nameless vampire shook his head. "He has no name. And neither do I."

"No name at all?" Marjek asked. "I find that hard to believe. We all have names."

"It may be that he has so many names that he cannot settle on any certain one."

"He has many names then?"

The vampire shrugged. "It's possible. I didn't ask him. I suppose if he took the name of every one of your Hunters that he has used to improve himself, then that would be many names indeed."

A chilling silence fell over the room. Though Jerusa didn't quite understand what the nameless vampire meant by this, it was clear from their reaction that the High Council and the Hunters did.

The nameless vampire smiled at their stunned shock. "He did give me a message to pass on to you, in the event that I was taken."

"And that message is?" Marjek's voice was cold and distant.

"He told me to tell you that the Monster will have his vengeance." His eyes flickered towards the tiny opening in the curtain. Though his gaze had only lingered there a fraction of a second, Jerusa was sure that he saw her.

Marjek leapt from the stage, landing silently before the nameless vampire. They glared into each other's eyes, each refusing to blink. "Celeste," Marjek said, without looking away. "Can you verify this vile worm's story?"

Celeste drifted to the man's side like a timid shadow. She reached over, her hand hovering as though not sure whether she should touch the man or not. She placed her fingertips upon his face and the man sighed as though he enjoyed her touch. Celeste pulled her hand away, not near as pleased with this contact.

"He is telling the truth," Celeste said, looking neither at the man nor at Marjek. "His creator is the Monster."

A devilish smile curled upon the nameless vampire's face. Celeste backed away, but Marjek straightened his stance, pushing out his chin.

"The Monster is a heretic," Marjek said. "And we will not suffer his children to live."

With blinding speed, Marjek reached out and twisted the nameless vampire's head nearly all the way around. The man twitched, but made no move to run or fight. Marjek yanked the man's head from his body and tossed it to the ground. The head rolled across the floor, coming to rest near the base of the stage. His body collapsed and his blood pooled around him.

Marjek stepped away, wiping the blood from his hands with a handkerchief. "Burn him."

Quinn and Ralgar stepped forward and doused the man's head, torso and pooling blood in a rain of fire. When the nameless vampire was nothing more than a pile of black ash, the High Council dismissed the Crimson Storm.

"Is it possible the Monster still lives?" Cot asked.

"Don't be a fool," Heidi answered.

Marjek left the room without a word. The rest of the Council soon followed. Jerusa remained beneath the stage, blanketed by the scent of smoke and ash, the grime of soot clinging to her clothes. She glanced around her darkened surroundings. Alicia and Foster were there, as was the ghost with the piebald eyes. She sensed a crowd of spirits surrounding her, though they chose to remain invisible. The only other spirit to appear to her was the nameless vampire.

He watched her with an intense fascination, as though he could see something hidden. Jerusa didn't like the way he looked at her. It made her feel awkward and out of place. She turned away from him and started to crawl out from under the stage when the door across from her opened.

Jerusa pulled back and stilled the motion of the curtain. She closed her eyes and held her breath, hoping that whoever had entered the room had not noticed the movement.

"Jerusa Phoenix."

Jerusa felt as though the floor vanished beneath her.

"Jerusa, it's okay. They are gone now. You can come out."

She remained still for a moment, not sure she had heard right. Timidly, she poked her head through the slit in the curtain. Celeste stood in the doorway, looking even more frightened than Jerusa felt. A girlish smile, easy and unbidden, appeared on Celeste's face and she beckoned for Jerusa to hurry.

"Come on. Let's get you out of here and back to your room before the daylight lockdown."

Chapter Twenty

Silvanus stood in the shade of the trees, far enough inside the forest where he wouldn't be noticed by human eyes, watching the home that Jerusa shared with Shufah and Taos.

Dusk was still a few hours away. He had planned to wait until dark before visiting Jerusa, but he could sense that she and the other vampires were not home. The daylight defenses had not been activated, the blackout shutters had not been drawn, the alarm wasn't activated and an unmistakable stillness settled over the house.

He had many reasons to make the journey back. He needed to retrace his steps, to figure out the piece to the puzzle he had missed the first night he had appeared here. He also wanted to thank Shufah for leading him to the Erinyes. Alecto, Megaera and Tisiphone had helped him to better understand his origins, though, if they were right, it meant that Jerusa could never be like him. But now that he was back, he realized that most of all, he just wanted to see Jerusa.

Silvanus took a step and with just a thought, traveled from the shadow-soaked forest to the interior of the garage. One of the spaces was filled with Thad Campbell's Jeep, which looked to have taken some damage and not from another car.

With another step, Silvanus appeared inside the house. He moved from room to room, mulling over every detail. Nothing seemed to be disturbed, yet he felt that the house had been abandoned in urgency. He worked his way down to the basement and then into the emergency vault they kept hidden. He was right. The house was deserted.

His blood had changed Jerusa into a powerful vampire. She was with Shufah who was ancient and wise, and Taos who had brute strength and the fire gift. Wherever Jerusa was, Silvanus was sure she was okay. Yet, he couldn't help but worry. He considered using his strange teleportation to guide him to her, but that didn't seem to work so well. Who knew where he might end up?

He thought back to the first time he had tried to locate someone. He had just escaped the Purgatory facility and had pressed his gift to take him to another like himself. Instead he found himself in this town, following a pair of vampires.

He pondered further, the night he had discovered Kole and Taos feeding on a group of hobos. He hadn't actually appeared before the vampires, but had discovered them traveling the abandoned train tracks. When he first materialized in this town, naked and confused, he found himself standing before a mortal woman.

At least he had believed her to be mortal.

The woman had been pretty, young, perhaps in her early twenties. She had been wearing a hooded sweatshirt, shorts and tennis shoes, which seemed appropriate for hiking down a wooded trail at night during the summer. When he had appeared before her unannounced, she seemed genuinely shocked. She didn't scream or call out for help, but it was obvious his sudden manifestation had jumbled her wits. She had turned, ran back down the path and vanished.

She had behaved, more or less, how any other mortal would have to such an odd occurrence. Humans are an unpredictable breed. Whereas some might have fled, others might have tried to attack him, so hers wasn't out of the scope of normal reactions. Yet there had been something strange about her.

On a whim, Silvanus decided to check one more place, before moving on to the abandoned train tracks cutting through the forest that had been restructured as a walking trail. He took a step, leaving Jerusa's house and arriving outside of Debra Phoenix's house.

He appeared across the street, around the corner of a neighboring house. A couple of police cars were parked in Debra

Phoenix's driveway. A loose collection of neighbors stood just off the property, whispering to each other, as though they had important secrets to discuss.

Silvanus reached out for their minds, gently probing their thoughts, so as to not be detected. From what he could gather, there had been a disturbance late last night. The neighbor to the south had heard the commotion, but chalked it up to another fight between the controlling Debra and her strange, sickly daughter. Some of the others claimed to have heard the same thing, though most were lying.

The neighbors didn't seem to have high opinions of Debra or Jerusa. Most of those in the gossiping crowd believed Debra to be unstable, capable of all kinds of deranged acts. There was a running rumor that her husband had never really left, but that she had murdered him and stuffed him in the crawlspace or behind one of the walls. They joked that she abused Jerusa, tying the poor girl to her bed at night or beating her when she didn't clean the house. Some believed that Debra suffered from Munchausen-by-proxy Syndrome and was poisoning poor Jerusa. Why else would the child have spent so much time in and out of hospitals? It was only a matter of time before it came to violence. Most in the crowd were surprised that the police hadn't become involved sooner.

Silvanus left the minds of the neighbors and turned instead to the police officers who had discovered signs of a struggle and were now entering the house.

Though the disturbance had happened sometime last night, it wasn't until about an hour ago that a neighbor, walking her dog, noticed a broken window and decided to call the police.

Silvanus searched the house through the eyes and minds of the police officers. Most of the house was undisturbed, except for the kitchen and nothing seemed to be missing. Neither Debra nor Jerusa was home and there was no sign of foul play.

The window had been broken from the inside out, meaning Jerusa or one of the other vampires had had to make a fast escape.

But escape from what? And the fact that Debra was missing brought a chill over him.

Silvanus's lip curled in disgust as he watched one of the officers discover an envelope of money in a kitchen drawer, then swiftly tuck it into his pocket. He justified the theft by the fact that the family was either dead or he could blame the loss on one of their neighbors.

The other officer's thoughts were no better. He moved from room to room, disappointed that there were no dead bodies to report. He had been on the force for a long time and he longed to come across some murder/suicide scene. Something gritty and perverse enough to get him interviewed on TV.

Silvanus withdrew from the minds of the police officers, feeling dirty and saddened by what he had witnessed. He hated being able to hear thoughts, though it had come in handy, helping him integrate into the mortal world with great speed. He did his best to stay out of mortal minds, only venturing in if he needed some vital piece of information. He did, however, wish he could read the minds of vampires, but they were locked to him.

Something jostled within Silvanus's mind. A thought, just out of reach of his mental grasp, a fossil buried deep underground with only the tip breaking the surface.

He remembered the night he had first appeared in this town, when he had willed himself to find others that shared his rare gifts. The woman, shocked and frightened by the naked stranger appearing before her. How, for the briefest of moments, she seemed to recognize him—perhaps not *who* he was but *what* he was.

And then it hit him, what had made the woman seem so strange. He hadn't been able to read her thoughts.

When Silvanus had first appeared in this town and found the pair of vampires hunting in the forest, he had assumed that he had teleported to them because they were the closest thing to himself. But now he saw the foolishness in that theory. He had spanned a great distance from Purgatory and America had no shortage of vampires. Why wouldn't he have just transported to the closest vampire?

What if he had been wrong all along? What if his gift had given him just what he desired? What if the startled woman had been a Divine Vampire?

Everything about the woman, from her scent, to the sounds of her body, to her movement, seemed so utterly human that he had never before questioned it. He had been so new to this life, so unaware of his own abilities that he never questioned why he could hear the thoughts of other humans, but not hers.

Had not the three Furies, with their combined senses, mistaken him for human at first?

Silvanus stepped out from his hiding spot, catching the eyes of several onlookers. He scanned their minds. They thought him extraordinarily handsome, but none questioned whether or not he was a human.

"Hey," one of the police officers called. "Hey you, come here." He had stepped out of the house and noticed some of the female neighbors staring at Silvanus. His suspicions were up, but not about Silvanus's humanity. "I want to talk to you."

Silvanus started around the corner of the house. The cop took off at a run to pursue him. His shoes kicked up the gravel from the driveway, his breathing tightened. He unclasped his gun and drew it from the holster.

Silvanus focused his thoughts on the woman he had met six months ago. In his mind's eye he traced every line of her face, every feature. As he did this, he thought of the other Divine Vampires— ten more if the Erinyes were correct. Was this woman one of the ten? If she was truly one of the Divines, why hadn't she revealed herself to Silvanus? There was no way she could have mistaken him for a human. Not the way he had appeared before her out of thin air.

The cop was getting closer. He crossed the street and was almost around the front corner. Silvanus was in the back yard now, treading in slow, even steps, allowing the desire to find another

Divine Vampire to flood his mind, as he had that night outside of Purgatory. He didn't concern himself with a location. All that mattered was finding that woman.

As the cop turned the rear corner of the house, preparing to call out or maybe even fire his gun, he caught one brief glimpse of Silvanus and then in the next step he was gone.

The roar of many voices filled Silvanus's ears. He opened his eyes to find hundreds of people moving up and down the sidewalk behind him. Traffic in the street, the majority being cabs, seemed almost at a standstill and the drivers made full use of their horns. Tall buildings—masterpieces of metal, concrete and glass—rose high into the air, leaving only a small strip of blue sky visible. He plucked from the mind of a passing man the name of the city: New York. He stood before the outdoor patio of a restaurant, where people dined despite the cool autumn breeze. No one had noticed him appear out of nowhere, or if they did, they weren't impressed. Only one set of eyes were upon him and this time they were neither frightened nor surprised.

"I was wondering when you would figure it out," she said. She leaned back, holding a steaming mug of coffee in her hands. "I was hoping you wouldn't. That you'd just go on doing your own thing, but I guess it's inevitable." Silvanus was at a loss for words. She motioned for him to sit. "Don't just stand there like some crazed stalker. C'mon, let's get this over with."

Silvanus pulled the chair out and sat, never once taking his eyes off of the woman, for fear that she might be gone when he glanced back. He reached for her mind and found it inaccessible.

"Don't do that," she said. He frowned as though he didn't understand, but she didn't buy it. "Don't try to read my mind. First, you can't and second, it's rude."

"I'm sorry," he said, not sure what else to say. "I didn't mean to be rude."

"It's okay," she said with a shrug. "Save it for the humans. But if you'd like some free advice, limit the time you spend in their heads. Most of what you'll find there isn't pretty."

"I believe you."

A waitress came to the table and placed a decadent looking piece of dark chocolate cake before the woman. "Anything for you?" she asked Silvanus.

Silvanus looked from the cake to the woman to the waitress. He didn't know what to say. He had never hidden himself among so many humans. The woman took pity on him and asked the waitress to bring him the same. She sped off with a fake smile plastered to her face.

At first, Silvanus thought she had ordered the cake to better blend with the humans around her, but then she picked up her fork, cut a piece and put it in her mouth. She chewed the cake slowly, then swallowed with a tiny shudder of pleasure. Silvanus watched, mesmerized by this.

She smiled at him. "You've never tasted food, have you?"

"I didn't know I could." He felt giddy at the thought of eating and drinking like a mortal. "I assumed we were like the blood drinkers."

She laughed as though this was the most absurd concept she had ever heard. "Oh no. Not at all. We have our similarities, sure, but we evolved past those barbarians long ago, didn't we?"

"I don't understand. They call us Divine Vampires. Is there a connection between us and the blood drinkers?"

She took another bite of cake. "As I said, we evolved. We moved past the need for blood and climbed to a higher station."

"How did we do that?"

The waitress returned with his chocolate cake before the woman could answer. Silvanus stared down at the dessert, fascinated and full of anticipation. He picked up his fork, cut off a large bite and shoveled it in his mouth. His breath caught in his chest at the rush of flavor. Never had he imagined something so sweet, so delicious. It was all he could do not to plunge his face down to the plate and feast like a pig. He forced himself to use the fork, devouring the large piece in five bites. The woman didn't seem appalled by his table manners, in fact she matched him fork for fork.

"Wonderful, isn't it?"

Silvanus smiled at her. He longed for more, yet felt happy and content. "And it won't harm us?"

"Of course not," she said furrowing her brows. "It would sicken the blood drinkers, but we do not drink blood."

Silvanus thought back to the one and only time he had tasted blood—when he had replaced Jerusa's savage-infected blood with his own. It had nearly killed him, if that was even possible. Just the thought of those days, hiding in darkness, alone, waiting for that festering sickness to leave him, made his flesh go cold.

"And we can eat anything we like?"

"Yes. Anything and everything, though you'll find that you won't get much more out of it other than the taste."

"So, we cannot survive on it?"

"I'm afraid not. Your body will consume every part of it, yet it cannot give you the power to sustain life. Only feeding can do that."

"So, we are like the blood drinkers. Taking a life to prolong our own."

"Life demands life," she said. "But we and we alone have the ability to feed from our prey without causing harm. The blood drinkers can feed without killing, but they risk passing on their vile disease."

Once again Silvanus's mind ran back to the four he fed upon in Purgatory and a dagger of guilt twisted in his gut. "You're talking about taking just a small bit from several humans, aren't you?"

"Why yes." She seemed surprised by his revelation. "Why do you think we hide among the mortals? In a place like this city, I can stroll down the street gathering all that I need and never harm a single person. You didn't know this?"

"I guess I had my suspicions."

"How long have you been awake?"

"Six months. I woke up in a laboratory hidden in the mountains. I had been encased in some black shell."

"Strange," she said, drifting off into her own thoughts. "Where did they find you?"

"I'm not sure. They weren't exactly forthcoming with the information."

"What did the shell look like?"

"It was black, like obsidian glass."

That wasn't the description she was looking for and it annoyed her to have to explain. "Was it thick or thin?"

Silvanus thought back. His birth into the world had been traumatic, as most are he supposed, and he had been consumed with hunger pangs, confused and eager to escape. "Thick. I could see the impression of my body within, but the outside held no markings. Why? What does that mean?"

She looked at him for a long moment over the table. "It means that you took on the change a very long time ago. What do you remember? I mean, from your life before."

"Nothing before waking up in the mountains. What do you mean by *took on the change*? Changed from what?"

She eyed him as though she weren't sure if he was mocking her or not. "Changed from being a blood drinker, of course. I said we evolved past those barbarians. What did you think I meant?"

"So, it's true then. We are descended from the blood drinkers."

"Descended? No. We are perfected."

"I met a trio of vampires, hiding and on the run from the Stewards. They told me of a rumor that a Divine Vampire is born when a blood drinker denies his nature. That if they can purge themselves of their thirst that they will become like us. Is this true?"

She rolled her eyes. "Ah, the Stewards of Life. Such a bunch of arrogant tyrants. They have been trying to gain our secrets for millennia. They believe they hold the key, but there is more than one lock."

"I'm confused again."

"The Stewards believe that, to become Divine, a vampire must refuse blood and bring about that terrible disease they call the Stone Cloak. That is why they will destroy any vampire that refuses to feed on blood."

"So, the shell that I broke free of, that is the Stone Cloak?"

"Yes. I believe that you wore it a long time and must have suffered terribly in whatever dark depth you were cast in. That is why we cannot remember our lives before. Or at least that is the consensus among the ten of us. Eleven now that you are here."

"You can't remember who you were before, either? Not your name, your family, where you came from?"

The woman shrugged again. "I'm afraid not. But names are easily given and changed whenever necessary. I have had many names over the years. Right now I call myself Laura. What do you call yourself?"

"Silvanus."

Laura wrinkled up her nose. "That is a terrible name. Who gave it to you?"

"A friend."

"You should consider changing it if you want to blend in with the humans."

Silvanus smiled at that thought. He was elated to be sitting here with Laura, one of his own, but the idea of living his life as a human, to integrate himself into their history, seemed almost too wonderful to believe.

"If the Stewards want to become Divine, why don't they stop feeding and allow the change to come? You said there was another lock. What did you mean?"

"Over the centuries, the Stewards have often sentenced one of their own to some deep pit, some inescapable hole, under the pretense of punishment. But in truth, they were watching, experimenting, weighing the cost." She took a sip of her coffee and suddenly Silvanus wished he had ordered a cup. "You see, of all the blood drinkers, legions I should think, that have ever taken on the Stone Cloak, only ten—now eleven—have ever broken free of the shell and arisen Divine."

"Why so few? What makes us different from the rest?"

Laura motioned for him to lean in closer. She cupped her hand to the side of her mouth as though she feared someone might read the words on her lips. "The truth is, we don't know. The Stewards believe we hold some great secret, but none of us can remember who we were before and so the key to this mystery is lost." She leaned back in her seat. "But we let on like we know the answers, if for no other reason than to drive the Stewards crazy. It's a fun little game."

"A game?" Silvanus couldn't believe the flippant attitude she held. "The Stewards order the deaths of humans and blood drinkers alike, and you tease them as though they were spoiled children."

"Long ago, we tried to make a treaty with the blood drinkers and came to their aid before they destroyed the world. They repaid us with betrayal. Now we don't trouble ourselves with their business." She took another sip of her coffee. "Why do you care what the blood drinkers do? The Stewards hold no authority over you. They fear your power. Put them out of your mind."

"I would, but the only friends I know are vampires and one is a fledgling from my own blood."

Laura slammed her mug onto the table, shattering it and splashing coffee across the floor. "You created a blood drinker?"

"Yes. Her name is Jerusa. She was dying from the bite of a savage."

Laura jumped up, sending her chair skipping out into the crowded sidewalk. Silvanus stood to his feet, unsure if she was about to scream or strike him. Her eyes were wide and wild and her beautiful features were pulled into a sneer.

Silvanus reached out to her. He was about to ask why she was so angry, but before he could voice his question, Laura vanished from his sight.

Chapter Twenty-One

Jerusa climbed out from beneath the stage and Celeste rushed around the perimeter of the room to meet her. Jerusa wiped the dust and cobwebs out of her face, but her clothes were stained with black, sooty smears.

"How did you know I was beneath there?" Jerusa asked. A sudden fear arose in her. If Celeste and the nameless vampire had sensed her beneath the stage, did that mean that Marjek and the others knew as well? "Could you see me? Or smell me?"

"No, I just felt that you were close by. Beneath the stage is the only place to hide." When Jerusa looked at her questioningly, Celeste said, "I'm an augur. I feel things sometimes. I can't explain it."

Jerusa understood. There were things about herself that she couldn't explain. "Why did you come back here for me?"

"We are under a daylight curfew. You need to get back to your room. You don't want to be caught out after sunup."

She started to turn for the door, but Jerusa touched her arm. "No, why are you helping me?"

"Does it matter?"

"I like to think that it does."

Celeste looked over her shoulder. "It's just another augur thing. I just have a feeling . . ." She started to say more, but thought better of it. "Look, I'm trying to keep you alive. That's all that should matter right now."

"Why should I trust you? You're a Hunter. All you know is death."

"You're one to talk." Celeste's eyes drifted all around the room. "You're the one surrounded by ghosts."

Jerusa snatched her hand back from Celeste's arm. "I didn't make them ghosts. They just follow me."

"I didn't ask for an explanation. Will you just please follow me, before it's too late?"

Jerusa nodded. Celeste moved up the risers and around the edge of the room, avoiding the center ring with its pile of ash and heat-scarred chains, and that was all right with Jerusa. When they left the room it was like bathing in clean waters. The air was cool, a bit stale, but at least it didn't smell of fire, death and judgment.

"What exactly was going on in there?" Jerusa asked. "Why did the High Council kill everyone? I thought they judged on beauty and power. But none of the humans were allowed to go to any of the quarantine communities."

"I'm afraid those days are gone." Celeste kept her voice low as she moved through the halls, listening for any noise out of place. "I'm not sure what has changed, but the High Council has declared that no more infected humans are to be given refuge."

Jerusa thought of Thad and her heart stuck in her throat. "But why did they kill all of the vampires? Not all of them were guilty of breaking the Stewards' laws."

"The laws change on a whim. The Stewards have grown paranoid."

Jerusa looked over at the train of spirits following behind her and her eyes fell upon the nameless vampire. "Who is the Monster? Why did it make Marjek so angry when that vampire mentioned him?"

Celeste stopped. She glanced around nervously, as though her words might conjure some demon from the shadows. "He's a myth. That's all. A hunter of Hunters, deformed, crazy, bent on revenge for some wrong dealt to him by the Stewards. He doesn't exist."

Jerusa wanted to point out that Marjek wouldn't have reacted in such a way if he believed that the Monster was a myth, but she decided to drop the subject. She felt as though she had stepped through a portal into another dimension, one where reality was caught in the swift current of a whirlpool. She felt as though she might suddenly wake up—the nightmare of her vampiric existence dissipating, like smoke in the wind—and find herself still at her mother's house, in her own bed.

A wave of sadness overtook Jerusa and she had to stop. Somewhere in this wretched house her mother was sick, maybe dying, surrounded by creatures who cared nothing for her and wouldn't think twice about burning her alive. She looked around at the dim tunnels. The great house covered a good sized piece of ground, but the labyrinth below it could very well go on for miles. Was her mother close by? Perhaps just around the next bend, behind the next door? Jerusa wanted to go to her, to hold her. If she was going to die, didn't she deserve for it to be in the arms of the only person that loved her? Jerusa wished that she had told her mother the truth, all of it. Even if she hadn't believed her, thought her mad and banished her forever, at least Jerusa would have explained why she had left, why she had to abandon her mother.

Celeste noticed Jerusa had stopped and came back to her. "What is it? Are you all right? Is it the thirst? Is one of the ghosts attacking you?"

Jerusa smiled despite the gaping hole she had raging in her soul. Celeste was like a sleep-deprived chipmunk on caffeine. Had she started bouncing up and down in agitated anticipation, Jerusa would not have been surprised.

"I'm fine," Jerusa said, motioning for Celeste to calm down. "Is the observation ward near? Y'know, the place they took my mom."

Celeste hesitated a moment, unsure if she should answer. "No, sorry. It's in another wing of the house. Near the Watchtower." She whispered the last word, but whether from fear or reverence, Jerusa couldn't tell.

"Can you take me there? I want to check on her."

"No," she said firmly and left Jerusa standing there.

Jerusa ran after her. "Please. I just want to make sure she's all right. She's all alone. I'm all she has."

"I can't." She looked around a corner. "It's too dangerous. It's forbidden to go so near the Watchtower. They'll know we're there. There is no way to hide from them."

Jerusa touched her shoulder and gently turned her around. "I don't want her to die alone in this place. Please take me to her."

Celeste had trouble keeping eye contact with Jerusa. She could feel the conflict raging within her. "Okay," she said, brushing Jerusa's hand away. "I may be able to cloak our presence for a short time. But not tonight. Daylight is almost here. It'll have to be tomorrow night."

"Thank you."

"Don't thank me yet. You might not like what you see." She motioned for Jerusa to follow. "C'mon, the elevators are just ahead."

They made their way back to the elevators without encountering anyone, but just as they passed, heading for secret passage in the utility room, the doors opened and out stepped an elderly woman.

Jerusa recognized her as one of the infected humans who served the house. The woman stood startled for a moment at the sight of the two vampires skulking through the dark. Her gray hair was disheveled and she was panting, as though she had been running. She took a few steps forward, limping. She clutched her chest, pulled in a series of deep breaths and braced herself against the wall.

Jerusa caught the scent of the woman and the thirst churned within her. The woman was so weak, so helpless, Jerusa could take her before she even had a chance to register that she had been attacked. All she needed was the first few drops of her blood. If she could get her fangs into the woman, even Alicia couldn't pry her away.

Alicia anticipated this move and placed her hand on Jerusa's shoulder. She tried to shrug away, but the ghost only tightened her grip.

"Oh, thank goodness it's you," the woman said after catching her breath. She stepped forward, grasping for Jerusa's arm, but she took a step back with the help from Alicia's gentle tug. "You have to come. Please hurry."

"What's wrong?" Celeste asked, her voice both concerned and reluctant at the same time.

"The boy," she said, keeping her eyes on Jerusa. "The boy that came with you."

"Thad?" Jerusa forgot for a moment the nagging thirst brewing within her.

"Yes, Thad. He needs your help. Come quickly."

Celeste and Jerusa followed the woman into the elevator. Jerusa backed in the corner farthest from the woman and made sure that Celeste was between them. The woman eyed Jerusa, suspecting something, but she showed no fear of being attacked. Perhaps she had been so long in the company of vampires that she had grown lax in her vigilance or maybe she had just lived long enough not to care how her life would end. Either way, Jerusa found her demeanor comforting. Fear and panic made the thirst worse.

The elevator descended two floors and opened upon a large spherical room. A thunderous roar of voices echoed throughout the room, bouncing off of the stone, swirling together until they formed the sound of a great rushing river. The clamor originated from a corridor across from the elevators, seeping through the thick oak of many doors. The doors were all closed, except for one at the very end of the corridor. Through the open door came the soft, ruddy light of a muted fire.

The woman led them down the corridor into the open room where a large furnace sat purring like a slumbering dragon, exhaling its dry, superheated breath at them. A table was overturned beneath a large black gas pipe. Tied to the pipe was a flat piece of cloth. Thad lay on the floor beneath it, the other half of the rope around his neck, his head resting on a pillow of blood.

Jerusa called out his name, but turned from the sight. The blood sent a shockwave through her and it was all she could do not to fall on the ground and lap it up like a dog.

"What happened to him?" Jerusa asked.

"I found him hanging from the pipes. He tried to kill himself. I cut him down, but when he fell he cracked his head on the stone. Please, we must move him before anyone else finds him here."

Jerusa moved further away. "I can't." She clutched her stomach. "Celeste, you have to do something."

Celeste looked up at the woman. "Dot, the blood."

Dot understood what was needed without any further instructions. She ran to the furnace and opened a panel near the bottom. She grabbed a metal bucket resting nearby and scooped up a pile of glowing embers. Celeste hoisted Thad into a sitting position and Dot dumped the embers over the puddle of blood.

The blood still dripped from the back of Thad's head. Celeste looked the wound over with a calm and steady hand. "It's just a scalp laceration." She put her thumb into her mouth, ripped open the skin with her fang and let a few droplets fall down upon Thad's head. Immediately the wound closed. "The bleeding has stopped. Will you be okay or should I take him alone?"

"I can still smell the blood," Jerusa said. "I don't think I can be near him right now."

"If you take him," Dot said to Celeste, "I will make sure she gets back to her room before sunrise. But we must hurry. They will be bringing the dead humans down from the judgment hall any time now."

"Thank you, Dot." Celeste scooped Thad into her arms and rushed down the corridor.

With the scent of Thad's blood now fading, the thirst began to ebb. Dot approached her, but Jerusa stopped her. "Not too close, please. It's not safe."

Dot nodded. "We should go."

She led Jerusa back down the corridor. The howling started

to wane or at least had grown hoarse. Most of the noise came from the doors on her left. They were human voices, talking in languages she didn't understand. It was the noises on the right—particularly the ones coming from the door closest to the furnace room—that concerned her.

"Are those savages in there?" Jerusa approached the door and pressed her ear against the polished wood. She could hear them growling and chattering, but it sounded far away.

Dot came to her side, reached out, but stopped short of taking her by the hand. "Please, we need to go. There are more important things to worry about right now."

"Why are the Stewards keeping savages? Isn't that dangerous?"

Dot could see that Jerusa would not move until she had her answer. She glanced about in panicked jerks. "All right. I'll tell you what I know. This house is very old. There are a few secret ways in and out. The Stewards have placed a group of savages at each of the three secret exits to keep out any intruders."

"Or to keep anyone from escaping."

"Exactly. Can we please go now?"

"Where does this door lead to? Where does the secret exit come out, I mean?"

Dot sighed in frustration. "Through that door you'll find a deep pit with slick, walls not easily climbed, even for a vampire. At the bottom there is an iron portcullis that keeps the savages from entering a network of caves. I have never been down there, but I've heard talk from the Hunters that it is a series of dead ends and roundabouts, but if you are able to find your way through, it will take you to an opening hidden behind a cascade several miles to the west. That's all I know."

Jerusa stepped away from the door. "The Stewards just trust that the savages will never get out?"

"There are surveillance cameras in the pit," Dot said. "And a patrol of Hunters come by now and then to check. That is why we need to hurry."

As they approached the elevator a light between the two doors clicked on with a ding. The needle of the floor indicator began to drop.

"Damn," Dot said in a hiss. "Come on, hurry."

She hobbled around the left side of the elevator shaft at a pace slower than a walk. At the corner where the elevator shaft met the wall, Dot frantically searched the grout edge of several blocks. She mumbled to herself, sometimes in what sounded to be Russian and Jerusa worried the woman's heart might explode from her anxiety. At last, she found what she was looking for. She pressed the corner of a block at eye level and a section of the grout gave way. Moments later a door, seamlessly hidden within the block wall, swung open.

"Who built this house?" Jerusa asked as she followed Dot inside. "Batman?"

"I don't know who that is," Dot said, closing the door. "Now, hush, if you value your life and the lives of your friends."

With the hidden door closed, the room they were in was tarred in darkness. Even Jerusa's vampiric eyes could detect no light. She could, however, hear the elevator car come to a halt on the other side of the stone wall. From the sound of the footsteps two had exited the elevator. They spoke to each other, but their voices were muffled by the thick stone—Jerusa thought they were speaking another language anyhow. She vowed to herself, that if she survived her judgment, that she would dedicate the first part of eternity to learning all the languages of the world.

Dot touched her arm and Jerusa quickly pulled away, not just because of the thirst, but because enough people had learned of her spectral gift already.

"We need to hurry," Dot whispered. "Daylight is coming. I can't see anything, but we should be able to follow the wall for a ways."

And that is how they traveled for a time. Dot groped her way in the darkness, one hand always against the stone. Jerusa followed behind Dot, tracking her movement by the sounds of her body and her scent trail. The floor began to ascend in a gentle slope and from time to time made a sharp turn. It felt like an eternity in that dark tunnel. Dot hobbled slower and slower and it was all Jerusa could do not to rush ahead to see what awaited them.

At long last, they came to a dead end with a metal ladder fastened to the wall. They were just about to start their climb when a voice, deep and raspy, spoke out in the darkness.

"I wouldn't go up there if I were you," the voice said. "Sunrise is upon us and the lockdown will commence any moment now. You'd best just stay down here with me."

A light, resplendent and blinding after so long in the blackness, filled the chamber. Jerusa pushed Dot behind her and stood ready to face the one holding the light. When her eyes adjusted, she saw it was a battery operated lantern and the one holding it stood no more than three feet tall.

The dwarf smiled, showcasing his fangs and said, "I think we're going to have to wait this one out."

Chapter Twenty-Two

Dot stepped to the side of Jerusa and dropped (with a bit of difficulty) to one knee. "Master Sebastian," she said with humble reverence.

The dwarf laughed. "Please, Dot, get up before you break your hip. You've been such a good worker all these years. It'd be a shame to put you out of your misery like some lame animal."

Jerusa helped Dot to her feet, though the feel of her tissue-paper skin disturbed her. She pulled her hand away hoping Dot hadn't noticed the group of spirits in the room with them.

Jerusa kept her eyes on the dwarf and he held her gaze with a mocking little smile perched upon his face. His eyes were set at different positions in his bulbous skull and large, crooked teeth filled his mouth. He stood pigeon-toed in a pair of brown, canvas pants that were fitted perfectly to his size. His legs seemed like a pair of twisted tree roots springing from the floor. His arms were too long with his fingers almost touching the floor. His only non-deformed feature was the set of perfect vampire fangs.

Though Jerusa thought herself better than those that judged on appearances, she couldn't help but be repulsed by the dwarf. He looked at her lovingly, as though he meant to court her, but had he turned and scurried up the wall like a spider, she wouldn't have been surprised.

"Sebastian," Jerusa said, forcing the thought from her mind. "Or should I call you master?"

The dwarf chuckled, waving her off. "Call me what you will. Dot here is just a creature of habit. The others demand such respect, but no matter how much I beg of her to refer to me common, she just can't find it within herself to do so."

"If you don't mind me asking, why are you here?"

"Why, waiting for you, of course."

"Waiting for me?"

He nodded. "I knew you would linger too long at the pit, asking questions about the hidden entrance. You're a very bull-headed and curious girl." When he saw that Jerusa took offense, he put up his stubby hands. "Meant as a compliment of course. In this house, all you see is blind fealty. You and your coven are a fresh spring breeze, which I must say I haven't felt rush across my cheeks in millennia."

"I don't understand. How did you know I'd end up in here?"

"Master Sebastian is an augur," Dot said with her eyes pointed reverently at the floor. "He is the oldest and most powerful augur of the Watchtower."

"Oh, Dot, you forgot to add most crafty, witty and good-looking augur in the Watchtower."

Jerusa laughed, but quickly clapped her hands over her mouth. "I'm so sorry. That was rude."

Sebastian smiled, his large overbite seemingly reaching out for her. "It's quite all right, child. I'm well aware of my hideous form. Not a day goes by that the Stewards don't remind me and in crueler ways than you could ever muster. As all who are born into this world disadvantaged and different, I found myself faced with two choices. Either succumb to the scoffing hatred of the *beautiful* or mock them by loving myself enough not to care what they think." He pointed at Jerusa and she had a feeling he could see the scar hidden beneath her shirt. "You might well remember that."

"I will. So . . . what now?"

"As much as I'd love to stand in this dank little tunnel, I think we should move to more comfortable quarters. This passageway is well known to the Hunters." He glanced up at Dot. "You should go back to your duties, child. Celeste has returned the boy to his room. You should tend to him. I suggest a swat to the head and a reminder that such foolishness will not gain him immortality."

"Yes, Master Sebastian." She started for the ladder, but he stopped her.

"You know you are in no condition to climb that. Go back the way you came. The Hunters are busy in the dungeons. If you go straight into the elevator they will not even detect your scent when they return."

Dot did as she was instructed, traveling back down the long tunnel as fast as her withered body would take her. She opened the secret door and crept back out into the large room. When they heard the door click shut Jerusa pointed toward the ladder. "You lead the way."

Sebastian puckered up his face, which made him even more hideous than before. "I think not," he said, waving his gangly arms. "I try to avoid ladders if I can keep from them. You would think that after being a vampire for as long as I have that something as common as a ladder wouldn't befuddle me, but alas, they are the bane of my existence."

His comical charisma put her at ease. She wondered how much he had suffered at the Stewards hands over the long years. Looking as he did, Jerusa marveled that the Stewards allowed him to live at all. Just how powerful of an augur was the dwarf to have been judged worthy of eternal life?

"I can carry you on my back, if you like."

Sebastian shook his head. "I don't like. I am no monkey to be carted around. Besides, that way will only lead us to trouble. I prefer to go this way." He squatted down and worked his fingers into the mortar joint of a loose stone in the floor. He lifted one corner then let the stone drop back into place. A door, hidden in the wall behind the ladder, slid open with a hissing gush of air. "You'll find this path a bit more private."

Jerusa glanced into the darkness behind the ladder then back to the dwarf. He wobbled up to her, handed her the lantern and then motioned for her to enter.

"Hurry now," he said. "It won't stay open for long."

She stepped behind the ladder, the dwarf following on her heels. No sooner had they crossed the threshold than the door slid shut. Jerusa held the lantern high, surveying the long hallway spilling out before them.

"And where does this one lead?"

"To my quarters in the northern wing of the house."

"And no one else knows about this?"

"No one left alive." His eyes twinkled as though he had shared an inside joke with her, but the meaning was lost on her.

"How do you know about it?"

"I have a wanderer's heart, a philosopher's inquisitive mind and the eternal boredom of the devil." He started down the hall and motioned for her to follow. "Join me, blood witch and bring your entourage of spirits with you. We have much to discuss before nightfall."

Jerusa stood shocked, her feet rooted to the stone. She couldn't decide whether to follow the dwarf or look for a way back to the ladder. He turned the corner without looking back at her. The light dimmed and darkness covered her before she decided to follow.

They continued for a long time in silence. The floor kept rising as it zigzagged its way back and forth like a steep mountain pass. Soon they came to a place where the stone of the walls and floor ended and gave way to wood and plaster.

She started to ask him how much further it would be, but he shushed her. "No sound from here until I say," he said in a whisper only a vampire could have heard. "Cliché or not, these walls truly have ears. We do not want to be discovered on the move."

"Why?" Jerusa whispered back. The thrill of the secret passageways had worn off and now she was feeling tired and annoyed.

"If we are found, the Stewards will block up my favorite escape route and they will have you burned where you stand, as an example to the others."

That shut her up. Jerusa followed behind the dwarf through another series of halls and rooms hidden within the inner walls of the great house. She knew that the sun had risen high and though she could not feel its heat, she could, nonetheless, sense the weight of its power pushing down on the Earth.

Sebastian glanced back at her several times, eyeing her as though she might collapse. He seemed to want to ask her something, but obeyed his own rules for silence. After climbing two more sets of narrow stairs and passing through one last dust-filled crawlspace, they came to a plain looking door without a knob. The dwarf picked up a length of copper tubing resting in the corner and nudged a switch a few feet above his head. The door popped open just an inch. Sebastian stepped out, without scanning the surroundings for unwanted eyes and motioned for Jerusa to follow.

The battery in the lantern had begun to fizzle and now only emitted the faintest glow. Though the room was steeped in darkness, Jerusa's vampiric eyes told her they were now in some kind of parlor, full of comfortable couches, artwork and books.

"The first time I explored this passage," Sebastian said, placing the copper tube back in the corner and closing the door, which vanished behind a large wardrobe, "and I found this room, I knew it had to be mine." He flipped the light switch and several lamps came to life.

"The room belonged to someone else?"

"Oh yes. An augur named Philippe lived here once, many years ago. It took me quite a while, but I finally convinced the High Council that Philippe was plotting to escape from the Watchtower." Sebastian turned, picked up a book from an end table and returned it to one of the lower shelves.

"What happened to Philippe?"

The dwarf flashed a sinister smile. "Let's just say the room became vacant not long after."

Jerusa's lip curled in disgust. "You had a man killed so that you could have his room?"

He looked at her with pity. "Oh, don't think me too evil. Philippe was a vile creature. If he were still here, he would have exposed all your little secrets to the High Council and then begged to feed upon you . . . not that I blame him on that account. You look delicious."

Jerusa turned away, not liking the look in the dwarf's eyes. "I don't have any secrets."

"Hmm," he said, with a look of over expressed doubt. "If that were true, then I would have left you in the tunnel with Dot to be discovered by the Hunters. Don't be coy. It doesn't become you. Embrace the mysteries surrounding you. They just may be your saving grace."

"You said Philippe would have told my secrets. So what keeps you or one of the other augurs from spilling the truth to the Stewards?"

"You need not fear the other augurs of the Watchtower," he said, hopping up onto one of the couches. He patted the seat next to him, but Jerusa shook her head. He shrugged. "They see only what they are told to see. Boring, I know."

"What are they told to see, exactly? You'll have to excuse me, but—"

"But you've only had your fangs half a year. I know. I know." He *tsked* in disapproval, in a way that reminded Jerusa too much of her mother. He either didn't notice the pain etched into her face or he chose to ignore it. "You really need to search out the limits of your powers if you hope to survive very long. Study to show thyself approved, as they say. And please don't give me your sob story about how your little ghost friend won't let you feed."

Jerusa turned, shocked and prepared to play dumb, but Sebastian's little smirk told her she could not outwit him. "How do you know that?"

"I'm an augur. A rather powerful one, if I may be permitted to brag. I see things, feel things and understand things others can't comprehend." He smiled and pointed a stubby little finger at her face. "Besides, your eyes have the most wonderful rings of blood and your lips are the color of an apple."

Jerusa touched her face. She could have kicked herself. She put her thumb in her mouth, preparing to bite down, but Sebastian stopped her.

"That's not necessary," he said. "Save it for the Stewards. I don't care that you haven't been feeding. If anything, it makes you more interesting. That's good for you. I hate to be bored."

Jerusa bit into her thumb anyway, wincing at the pain and dripped two drops of blood into each eyes and smeared some over her lips. She couldn't contain her shivering as the blood reabsorbed into her body. "Is that a threat?"

"Those who are threatened, often hear threats, even in the most mundane of conversations." The dwarf flashed a bemused glare. "That little trick may buy you some time, but eventually the thirst will betray you."

"So I'm told. Any suggestions?"

Sebastian sighed. "The best way I know to quench a vampire's thirst is with blood. You should try it some time. It's wonderful. Better than sex. Before the Stewards decided to grace this house with their congenial company, I would sometimes feed on two or three humans a night. Now I'm lucky to feed once in a month." He giggled at the disdain in her face. "Oh, please spare me the 'sanctity of human life' speech. You'll live much longer if you concern yourself with the sanctity of your own life."

This conversation was going nowhere. He would just talk in circles if she allowed him to. She moved to the couch and sat down beside him. He turned to face her, delighted that she had joined him. She wondered if he had ever had a willing guest in all his long life.

"You said we had much to discuss. What do you want to talk about?"

Sebastian pretended to think on this for a moment. "Tell me about your ghost friends."

"First, tell me how you know about them."

"I watched you the night you were made. I found you when Kole bit you and I watched as that stunning creature pulled the savage blood from you and replaced it with his own. When you opened your eyes as a vampire, for one brief moment, I saw the dead girl standing beside you."

"What do you mean 'found me'? How did you see me?"

"You silly girl. Are you truly this dimwitted or is it just an act? The Watchtower are the eyes of the Stewards. We are the elite augurs, gifted with distant sight and visions of things that may or may not come to pass. When we are close to each other our powers grow exponentially, hence the reason for our incarceration here. Whenever a vampire feeds, we can sense it, lock on to it and peek through the veil of space for a brief glimpse."

"So you're spies. The Stewards use you keep tabs on the other vampires, make sure everyone is following the rules. Is that right?"

"An oversimplification, but not incorrect. Why do you think we are called the Watchtower? We report any transgressions of the law. As you know, all vampires are required to kill their prey. If they fail to, we send the Hunters for both the vampire and the human."

"And if a vampire is not feeding at all?"

"We can tell that, too, by the lack of contact with that vampire. It is a far more serious offense to the Stewards, but not as easy to track. We have to be specifically watching for a certain vampire to know whether or not they have been feeding."

"And you have been watching me?"

"Yes, but don't worry. As far as the Stewards know, you are a voracious little predator."

"You lied to them? Why?"

"Because they bore me. And I'm curious to see how this will all play out."

"I don't understand."

He shrugged. "Nevermind."

"Why have you been watching me?"

"In the beginning it was because of your unique birth. No one has ever survived a bite from a savage, yet you did. I was kind enough to hide that little fact from the Stewards. They believe you were created by a regular blood drinker, but I know the truth. The one that made you was no blood drinker, but to speak of that is heresy and I think the High Council might even put little ol' me to death for speaking it."

He reached for her hand, but stopped just short of touching her. "May I?" he asked. "I just want to see with my own eyes."

Jerusa nodded. Sebastian placed his tiny hand upon hers and gasped as he took in the sights that moments ago were invisible to him. He let his eyes drift slowly from one side of the room to the next, examining each of the lingering dead as though he was their final judge.

"Amazing," he said in a breathless whisper. Jerusa pulled her hand from beneath his and he looked at her in awe. "You really are a Blood Witch."

"I don't know that I like being called that."

Sebastian laughed. "Oh, but you should. You should love that title. Wear it as a shield. If you play your cards right, you may be able to use that little talent of yours to strike fear into some hearts. Including that wretched High Council."

"Shufah says that I should keep my powers a secret from the Council."

"Ah, lovely Shufah," Sebastian said. "She is strong and wise. Such beauty in that one, though I never quite cared for her brother. Troublesome, that one is." He stared off as though lost in thought. "I know you trust Shufah," he said regarding her again. "And though I love her rebellious spirit and share her hatred for the Stewards, in this instance she is wrong. If you could stand on your beauty and mystique alone, then I should say her advice is spot on. But tomorrow night when you are judged, they will see the scar on your chest and deem you unworthy."

"They would really kill me because I have a scar?"

"Oh yes, my dear. Perfection is the sword they hold at our throats. But there is more at play here than a typical judgment. Marjek has long been obsessed with Shufah and her deep hatred of him only drives his dark desires to new depths. He has used you to bring her here. Now that he has her under this roof, he no longer needs the rest of you."

"What are you saying? Marjek is going to have Taos and Thad killed, too?"

"Yes." The lack of empathy in the dwarf's eyes brought a chill to Jerusa's soul. "If, however, you keep your wits about you, things may still work out."

"What do you suggest?" She clenched her fists to keep her hands from shaking. Was there no justice with immortals?

"Reveal your gift to the High Council. Swear your fealty to them and ask to join the Hunters."

"The Hunters? No! Never. I won't be a butcher."

"Just because you swear fealty doesn't mean you are bound to it. Becoming a Hunter is your only way out of this house. After that, you can escape. The Watchtower will not be able to track you because you do not feed. You will be invisible to us."

"What about my friends? How will this save them?"

"I never said it would save them. Shufah will be fine. Marjek will not suffer her to be harmed, no matter what laws she breaks. Taos is strong and has the fire gift. I'm sure he will be a welcomed asset on the Crimson Storm's next mission. The human, however, is on his own. The Stewards have suspended the changing of any infected human and the quarantine communities worldwide are on lockdown. There is nothing that can be done. I'm sorry."

"Why?" Jerusa's blood burned beneath her chilled skin. The moisture in her throat vanished, making it hard to speak or even breathe. "Why won't they turn him? He's more than handsome enough to pass their stupid test. He would make an incredible vampire." Her voice trembled. "He's innocent in this. Why would they kill him? Why have they closed the towns?"

"Because infected humans have become too great a liability and because the Stewards are frightened." Sebastian's words were slow and calm. He watched her as though he expected any moment for her to lose control.

"What are they so afraid of?"

For the first time, caution flashed in the dwarf's eyes. "They are afraid of Suhail and his army of savages."

Chapter Twenty-Three

"Suhail?" Jerusa questioned. She was glad she was sitting down because all of the strength went out of her legs. "That's impossible. Suhail is dead. Shufah told us he's dead."

"She's wrong," Sebastian said, a deviant little smile playing on his face. "Or maybe she just lied." Jerusa looked down on him, a slow-growing fury burning within her. The dwarf touched his chest as if to apologize. "Don't look so surprised. You know the rules. When a mortal dies he sometimes rises as the undead. When the undead perish, they sometimes rise as something much worse. It's the price of immortality. Did you think that Suhail was exempt from that? That you or I are exempt from it?"

"No, of course not. I . . . just, well . . . did you say he had an army of savages?"

"That's the rumor, if you can trust what you hear being whispered while scurrying behind the walls like a rat."

"Why hasn't there been any news of attacks? From the human world, I mean." Jerusa thought of the tales Shufah had told her of the last savage army. "It's been six months. If it were true, then Suhail and the other savages would be rushing across the US like a plague."

"Ah, that is the question, now isn't it? Why indeed? I suspect when you discover the answer you'll understand why the Stewards now cower in this ice fortress. Know this, though. There has never been a savage born from a vampire as old as Suhail. If he has devoured enough gray matter to regenerate his own brain, then he may be something terrific to behold.

"There is a war coming. The last time it came the savages were like a mindless swarm of angry bees. I sense this army is more advanced, better equipped and in full understanding of their purpose."

"What is their purpose?"

"Control," he said with a smile. "No different than our friends here." He glanced at the door just as it burst open. Marjek stepped inside flanked on both sides by a vampire wearing the Hunters' insignia.

Jerusa jumped to her feet, but Sebastian remained seated. He clapped his tiny hands together and held them outstretched toward Marjek.

"To what do I owe the honor," he said. "I cannot recall the last time one of the High Council has graced me with their presence."

"Silence you disgusting little gnome," Marjek said. "I'm in no mood for your insolence. Please, explain to me why the fledgling is not confined to her room and why you are harboring her in yours."

"Well," Sebastian said, rubbing his chin, "that will be difficult to do without the insolence. I know you're not a fan of heavy words so I will try to be as to the point as possible. She is my guest. Is that now a crime, too?"

Marjek kicked Sebastian hard enough to send him flying across the room. The dwarf smashed into a table and fell onto his face in a pile of broken wood. "I already have two tongues as trophies. Speak to me out of turn again, troll and I'll add a third."

Jerusa rushed over to Sebastian. She pulled him to his feet and knelt down to make sure he was all right. He grunted, swaying on his feet, but there were no wounds that she could see. He reached out and touched her face. Hidden within the deformities of his face, his eyes sparkled with genuine gratitude. Jerusa wondered once again if she was the first to show him any kindness at all. It was sad to think he had lived such a long life surrounded by only cruelty.

He moved his hand from her face down to her chest. She gasped, uncomfortable with this action, but he merely tapped the top of her scar. "Don't worry about me. You're the one in danger, my dear. Please take my advice. I would find this world even more boring if you were no longer in it."

Powerful hands gripped Jerusa by the shoulders, hard enough to bring a yelp of pain and turned her to face Marjek. The Hunters still remained where they had been. No one held her. She had been turned by a telekinetic hand and she could tell from the look on Marjek's face that the pain she felt was only a taste of what he wanted to give her.

"Night is coming," Marjek said to Sebastian. "Shouldn't you be getting back to the Watchtower?"

"It's good to be needed," he said, dusting off his clothes.

"Come with me, fledgling."

The invisible hand jerked Jerusa forward, almost taking her off of her feet. She walked forward, to keep from being yanked again, but it took all that she had not to rush Marjek and rip his eyes from their sockets. She doubted that she would get close enough to even scratch him before the Hunters smashed her to the ground and set her on fire, but it seemed better than marching to her death like some condemned prisoner. She glanced back at the dwarf. He urged her with a stern look to obey, to take the pain and humiliation that was about to come and endure.

Marjek started out the door. Jerusa fell behind him with the two Hunters standing at her shoulders. They passed through the halls of the great house without speaking another word. Though the sun was still up, Jerusa could sense that it wasn't far from setting. Other vampires—at least the ones not confined to their rooms—were stirring about. They watched in silence as Jerusa and her escorts passed and as soon as they went by, turned to each other in little gossiping huddles.

When they finally made it back to Jerusa's room, Shufah and Taos rushed to meet her. Marjek held out his hand, stopping them in their tracks.

"What is the meaning of this?" Shufah asked. Her honey badger fierceness had resurfaced. Her eyes blazed like molten bronze as she met Marjek's haughty gaze.

"Your fledgling is a bit of a roamer," Marjek said. "And much like you, has a problem with the laws of our people."

"Your laws," Taos said. "Not ours." He stood with his shoulders squared and his fists clenched. His pale eyes kept flickering to Jerusa. If she gave the word he would attack. It didn't matter that they had no hope of escaping this house. He would battle any that stood before him without fear of death.

Jerusa didn't give the word though. She turned her eyes to the floor. If she was condemned to death, she would accept that, but she would not allow her friends to die for her.

"We found your fledgling in the north wing," Marjek said. "I thought that I made it clear that it is off limits."

"I was invited by Sebastian." The strong telekinetic hand tightened around her neck, silencing her.

Marjek laughed. "The dwarf thinks he is above the rules, just like the rest of you. No one is above the laws."

Yeah, unless it's the High Council feeding on other vampires, Jerusa thought. She kept this to herself, though.

"It's forbidden for anyone but a Steward to commune with a member of the Watchtower. And someone was down in the dungeons stirring up trouble." Marjek turned to Jerusa and forced her to look up at him. "Would you know anything about that?"

Thad poked his head out of his room. His face was pale and a faint pink ligature mark curled around his neck. Marjek looked at him as if he was an insect and though Thad seemed shaken by this he stepped out of the room. He opened his mouth to speak and in that moment Jerusa knew he was going to confess.

"I was down in the dungeon," Jerusa said, before Thad could speak. His eyes became as large as saucers and he seemed stunned into silence for a moment. "I was looking around and got lost. I somehow found my way downstairs, but I didn't mean to stir up any trouble. I was just trying to find my way back up here. Sebastian found me downstairs and invited me to his room."

The looks of jealousy that passed over the faces of Thad and Taos when Jerusa mentioned Sebastian was almost comical. The look on Marjek's face, not so much.

"And what was the little gnome doing lurking around in the dungeons?"

"He said he was looking for me." She didn't think Marjek believed this, but he said nothing to contest it.

"I brought your coven into my house in peace," he said to Shufah. "I gave you comfort and nourishment when by all rights I should have confined you all to the dungeons. And in one night's time you have spat on our customs. I know you have no love for our laws, but they are for our protection and not just ours, but the humans as well."

"Spare me the speech. I have heard it before. We were not forced to come here for comfort and nourishment. We were brought here to be judged by the all-wise High Council."

"True," Marjek said. "But is it so wrong to want to show kindness to you first? The rest of the Council would have judged you the moment you came through the door. They are most disturbed by the death of Kole and the creation of your fledgling. And your human pet angers them even more. But I fought for time. Time for you to gain their trust."

"I don't want their trust," Jerusa said, shocked at the anger she heard in her own voice. "You don't want time for us. You want time with Shufah. Taos, Thad and I are just a means to an end. I've spent the last six months dreading this day. If you are going to judge me, then judge me now." She stepped away from Marjek and the Hunters, expecting at any minute to be dragged back by a telekinetic hand, but they let her rejoin her friends.

Marjek's handsome face pursed tight. Had he clenched his jaw any tighter his teeth would have shattered. "Do you both feel the same?" he asked Thad and Taos.

"Wait," Jerusa said. "I only meant my own judgment."

"The giant must answer for infecting the human instead of

killing him. And the human must be judged worthy to bear the vampire spirit."

Jerusa started to argue but Taos cut her off.

"I am ready to be judged. I don't fear my destiny."

"I'm ready, too," Thad said. "Let's get this over with."

"No, wait," Jerusa said. "You don't understand." She wanted to explain about the judgments she had witnessed from beneath the stage. She wanted to tell them what Sebastian had told her. But how could she without getting Celeste and Sebastian into trouble.

"Do you consent, Shufah?"

Shufah searched Jerusa's eyes, but offered up no advice out of this predicament. "If there must be judgment, let it come sooner, rather than later."

Marjek's face was somber. "If that's your wish, so be it. You are all confined to your rooms until we call for you. Break this commandment and you will be sentenced to death. The fledgling and the human must be inspected to be deemed worthy." Jerusa's scar burned. "Yield yourselves or the penalty is death."

"We understand." Shufah motioned for them to return to their rooms. Jerusa tried to argue, but Shufah's stern eyes told her the time for debate was over. The others did as they were told, but Jerusa remained in her doorway.

"Whatever you may think of me," she said, "Taos and Thad have done nothing wrong."

Marjek gave her a mocking smile. "I really don't care." With that, he turned and left, but the Hunters remained.

Jerusa went back into her room and closed the door behind her. She found it strange that she could feel so alone when there were so many spirits moving around her. Foster stood close to her side. The concern on his face made her want to cry. What she wouldn't give to be able to hear his voice again. She needed his advice more now than ever.

"I'm so stupid," she said to him. "Why couldn't I just keep my mouth shut? It's bad enough that I'm gonna die, but now Taos and Thad are gonna die, too. Maybe if we had taken our time, we could have made friends with the Stewards. If I could have explained to Shufah what I saw in that pit, maybe she could've convinced Marjek to spare them."

A hand touched her shoulder. Alicia pulled her in and hugged her tight. Jerusa knew the ghost wasn't really there. Alicia's corporeal body had been in the ground for more than two years, yet somehow Jerusa felt her touch nevertheless. A tickle of the thirst rose from deep within, but the absurdity of trying to draw blood from a restless spirit was a level of insanity she had not reached yet.

She held onto Alicia until the sun finished its trek across the sky and the blanket of night fell heavy over the great house. A knock came to the door. Two female vampires stepped inside, without being invited.

The two women, both turned in their youth and astoundingly beautiful, paused in the doorway watching Jerusa with puzzled looks upon their faces. For a brief moment, Jerusa couldn't grasp what had confused the pair, but then Alicia vanished from within her embrace and Jerusa's arms fell limp in her lap. The rest of the spirits followed Alicia's example, though she once again felt they hadn't gone far.

"What?" Jerusa asked them, making sure they caught the full force of her disdain. "You never see anyone hugging the air before?"

The women kept their eyes focused on Jerusa, but she could tell they were uncomfortable with her strange actions. They were both clad in long red dresses—simple, elegant coverings that looked both modern and ancient at the same time. The women gained their composure, their faces falling placid and unreadable. One of the women—her hair much the same color as Jerusa's—stepped forward.

"We come in the name of the High Council of the Stewards of Life," she said as though reading a royal proclamation. "You have been called to judgment and must be inspected to deem your form worthy of immortality."

"Why don't you just say you've come to make sure I'm not

too ugly to be a vampire?" Jerusa spat back at them. "Do you talk like this on purpose or have you forgotten what century it is?"

The women looked shocked that someone had spoken so harshly to them. Maybe it was their first time.

The thirst was rising in her again, burning in her bones, slithering in her skin. Her fangs ached to be used. The events of her short life raged in her mind like an uncontrollable tempest. She not only wanted to kill, she wanted to bring pain.

Jerusa started up off the bed with every intention of ripping out the throats of the two women, but before she made her feet, Alicia was there to push her back on the mattress.

This time the women did glance at each other. A cloud of fear passed over their faces, but they quickly buried their emotions. The other woman (this one a blonde) took a step forward, perhaps to assert her authority over Jerusa, or to prove to herself that she was not afraid.

"You must be searched," she said. "Please remove your clothes."

Jerusa stood to her feet, bulling past Alicia, but stopping out of reach of the women. She leaned over, pulling her shirt collar down so that they could see her scar. "Here, are you satisfied? I'm a deformed mutant not worthy of the vampire spirit. Go tell your masters what you found."

A moment of tenderness flickered in the eyes of both women. Though it was fleeting, they seemed genuinely sad for Jerusa.

"That being so," the vampire with the dark hair said. "We still must inspect you. I'm sorry."

It wasn't enough to condemn her for a simple scar, the Stewards wanted to demean her in the process. It was just one more weapon of control wielded by the Stewards. Demean, deface, abuse and destroy. Repeat often enough and those that would oppose their rule become too afraid to speak up.

Jerusa turned her back on the women and undressed.

The women did a fast, yet thorough job. Alicia remained in

the room, but the other spirits remained hidden. Jerusa kept her eyes fixed on Alicia, willing herself not to cry. Not while the women were in the room.

When the inspection was over, one of the women—Jerusa wasn't sure which one—placed the terrycloth robe from the bathroom over her shoulders. They turned to leave the room without word.

"Well," Jerusa said stopping them. "Am I worthy?"

"If it was in our hands?" asked the blonde. "Then yes, you are worthy."

"But it's not in your hands."

"No. I'm sorry. I can find no flaw in you, but . . ."

"But my scar," Jerusa finished for her.

"Yes. I'm sorry."

Jerusa wanted to curse them, to spit on them. She hated them for their flawless beauty. She despised the long lives they would be permitted to live. Yet when she opened her mouth to scream at them, she found she had nothing to say.

"If the vampire spirit has given you any talents, you should show them," the dark haired vampire said. "Beauty is Marjek's standard for immortality, but Heidi will choose power every time. And if you have Heidi's vote you will gain the votes of the others."

The two women left the room and as soon as the door latched behind them, Jerusa's bloody tears burst forth. She went into the bathroom and took a shower, allowing the water to drive out the deep chill that had settled in her flesh ever since she had crossed the threshold of this house.

When she was finished showering she searched the room and found a beautiful ball gown in the closet, entombed in a plastic bag. It was a sleek, azure dress that looked like a more expensive version of Alicia's prom dress. Jerusa slipped into the dress—just to see how she would look. No piece of clothing had ever fit her better. It was as if the dress had been made just for her. The only thing she didn't care for was the plunging neckline, which revealed the scar on her chest. But as she stood swaying from side to side, examining the dress from every angle, rubbing the raised line of flesh upon her chest, she decided that maybe this dress was just the thing to be condemned to die in. And so what if her scar was showing. Let it show.

Alicia appeared next to her. Jerusa reached out and took her hand. Foster and the rest of the lingering spirits appeared within the room. They looked upon her in awe, as though she was something resplendent and miraculous.

Jerusa had to admit, it felt nice to be looked upon that way. The only other person that had looked at her with such adoration had been Silvanus.

"I wish he was here," she said to Alicia. "I wish he would appear right now and take me out of this place."

Alicia looked at Foster. He questioned her with his eyes and she nodded. There was no other form of communication. Foster turned and walked away. Within two steps he had vanished from the room.

Foster had not just become invisible to her. He had actually left this time. Jerusa could feel the absence of his spirit. She turned to Alicia to ask where Foster had gone, but before she could speak, the door to her room opened and in walked Ming and Ralgar.

They stared at Jerusa for a moment—Ming with a look of hatred, Ralgar with a look of twisted desire—but whether it was the dress or the scar on her chest, Jerusa couldn't say.

"It's time," Ming said. "Come with us."

Chapter Twenty-Four

Silvanus passed down the crowded New York sidewalks with his hands down at his sides, outstretched just a bit so that he could brush his fingers against every human he passed. He walked against the current of people, ensuring that he could touch as many as possible. Though the crowd moved in a surly, disconnected flow they didn't attempt to avoid his touch—in fact they seemed almost unaware that he was touching them at all.

With just the swipe of his fingers he pulled a tiny spark of life from each human, but more than that, he was able to pass something back. The life he took was so small that it would never affect any of them, yet when they moved on from his touch they walked away with a dreamlike contentment, as if all was right in their worlds.

Silvanus didn't know if he could keep feeding like this indefinitely, but he decided to stop when the wake of happy wanders, drifting along behind him, began to draw attention. He turned down the next street.

It was a magnificent city. Beyond anything he could have ever imagined. He marveled at the humans' gift for creation. The glass windows of the skyscrapers glittered in the afternoon light. Silvanus purposed in his heart that he would stand atop each one. The autumn air was comfortably cool with a fresh breeze to blow away the smell of the city. He didn't know where he was. He could have pulled the information from countless minds, but to be honest, he liked searching the city first hand. It was a place always in motion, as if it were a giant creature itself. No wonder Laura hid here among the mortals.

Silvanus passed by a group of mingling teenagers loitering

outside of a bodega. The conversations stopped as he passed. The young girls followed him with enraptured eyes. The guys (not happy about losing the attention of the girls) puffed up like a flock of angry peacocks. He thought it funny that the girls found him attractive—or that the guys were jealous—but he remembered that in their eyes he probably looked no older than seventeen.

How old am I really?

Did it matter? Time held no meaning for him.

A wave of excitement fell over him at the thought of living among the humans. Suddenly it all seemed so possible. He could get a job, buy a home, make friends, create a life. He wouldn't be alone anymore. Sure he wasn't really a part of the human race, would be an imposter, but they would never know, so what difference did it make.

Silvanus's mind went to Jerusa. She would like a place like this. But she couldn't see it the way he saw it, with the sunlight pulling out every vibrant color. She would be confined to the night. And even then, with the humans all around, she couldn't be here. He had made her an outcast, a hunter, a nightmare of the human race. But maybe there was hope yet. According to the Furies and Laura, a vampire can become Divine. Too bad she had disappeared, yesterday, before explaining how to bring about such a change. It had something to do with the Stone Cloak, or whatever you wanted to call that horrible vampire disease, but Laura had been holding something back. He was sure of it.

The light dimmed all around him. Silvanus looked up and realized that during his deep thought of Jerusa he had turned down an alley where the tall buildings blocked out the sunlight. For a moment, he thought he had teleported without meaning to. It seemed a different city now. All was steeped in shadows. The air was stale and foul, choked with the noxious fumes of car exhaust and human waste. Windows didn't glitter but were instead painted with graffiti or smudged over with filth.

A man approached him from the far end of the alley, which

was strange because according to Silvanus's powerful senses, there were no other living beings close by.

Silvanus stood still, watching the man approach him without a trace of fear in his eyes. He tried to touch the man's mind and found he was not able. There was something strange about the man's walk, as though he were walking on a thin cushion of air and the imperfections of the road didn't unbalance him. He looked at Silvanus with a fierce determination. Nothing good ever came from such a look. There was something familiar about the man, but Silvanus couldn't see him well. He looked to be shrouded in thick fog, but the air around him was clear. It wasn't until the man came to a large trash bin and passed through the solid metal unhindered that Silvanus realized who the man was.

Silvanus ran to meet the man. "You are one of Jerusa's spirits, aren't you? Your name is Foster."

The man nodded. Though he stood directly in front of Silvanus, he still was hard to see. Sometimes his form was opaque, others it was as gossamer as spider silk. Occasionally he would flicker out of sight, like a light bulb preparing to burn out.

"Why are you here?" Silvanus asked. "Is Jerusa here, too?"

Foster shook his head.

"Where is she? Is she all right?"

Again, Foster shook his head no.

"Tell me where she is at."

Foster pointed to his mouth and shook his head. He couldn't speak. Or at least Silvanus couldn't hear what he had to say. Foster made a series of signs with his hands, trying his best to pantomime what he needed to say.

"I don't understand what any of that means. Jerusa's in trouble, am I right?"

The ghost nodded.

"Is she close by? Can you lead me to her?"

The ghost shook his head no. Foster looked at Silvanus with strained exasperation. It was clear the ghost thought Silvanus could just will himself to Jerusa's side. "I can't go to her if I don't know where she is. I can only find my own kind that way."

The look of fear on Foster's face caused a stone of dread to fall into Silvanus's stomach. When he gave her his blood he made her an outcast, not just from the human race but from the other blood drinkers.

"Do the Stewards have her?"

Foster nodded, excited that they were finally getting somewhere.

"Is she somewhere close?"

Foster shook his head.

"Is she still in America?"

Foster shook his head.

Silvanus sighed in frustration. This was taking too long. Foster's spiritual body was beginning to fade and the aura surrounding him grew dimmer by the second. Whatever gift Silvanus had gained from Jerusa's blood, it was fast losing its potency. Even if Foster didn't vanish into thin air, by the time Silvanus finished playing the guessing-game with the ghost, Jerusa might already be dead.

"If I find a map, can you show me where she's at?"

Foster shook his head yes.

"Can you follow me if I jump from place to place?"

The ghost nodded that he could, but Silvanus thought he saw doubt swimming in his eyes.

"Then follow me to a map and let's hope we're not too late."

Silvanus searched his understanding of the city for the best place to find a map. He had gained much from the human minds he had searched, but in a way he still felt lost and confused. A stranger in a strange land. He needed a place of books, a temple of information. The New York Public Library popped into his mind. He didn't know if it would be the most efficient place to find a map, but he didn't have time to think of a better place.

He closed his eyes, concentrating on the name of the library, on his knowledge of the topography of New York. He didn't know where in the building he would appear or if the humans there would be astonished or be blind to his arrival as they so often seemed to be. All he knew was he had to get to Jerusa.

Silvanus prepared to take a step out of that alley and into the library when a strange sensation covered him from head to toe. His skin tingled as though he stood in the midst of a great ball of static electricity. But this was no natural phenomenon for the static had a weighted feel as though a net had been cast over top of him. Silvanus tried to ignore the static and attempted to jump from the alley to the library, but when he placed his foot down and opened his eyes he remained right where he had been before.

Foster glanced about in nervous agitation. Could he feel the net surrounding them? Or did he see something Silvanus couldn't see. Suddenly, without a sound, Laura appeared in the alley standing no more than ten feet from Silvanus. Her arms were outstretched as though she were awaiting an embrace. Silvanus started to ask her what was happening, but before he could form the words, nine others appeared, all of them holding hands, forming a locked circle around him.

Silvanus turned in place, searching the faces of the ten besieging him. They were young, handsome men and beautiful women, all of them, yet their eyes were grim and filled with inhuman indignation. He turned once again to face Laura. The look of anger upon her face startled him.

"Hello, Laura. Why do you seem so angry with me?" She didn't answer him. "I thought that I would see you again, but had I known you were going to bring the other Divine Vampires with you I'd have chosen a more congenial meeting spot. As it is, I don't have time to talk right now. A friend of mine needs my help."

Silvanus tried once again to leap from the area and found that he was unable to do so. "Are you holding me here?" he asked Laura.

"Yes," she said, without much emotion. She seemed to be in deep concentration. "I'm sorry, but we can't let you leave."

"And why is that? I have done nothing wrong. Release me and let me go to my friend."

"And to whom do you wish to visit?" asked one of the men. He was tall with thick blond hair and a defined cleft in his chin. "Off to see your fledgling, are you?"

Silvanus turned to the man. "As a matter of fact I am. Her name is Jerusa and she is in grave peril. So, if you don't mind, let me go on my way."

"We can't do that," said a flaxen-haired beauty with pale green eyes. "We have much to discuss, Silvanus."

"Believe me, there is much I would love to discuss with you. I have been searching for you for many months, but now is not the time. My friend needs me. I must go to her."

"She is a blood drinker," said another of the ten. This one was a black man, shorter with a muscular build. "Blood drinkers are no concern to us. They are vile parasites. Deceitful and conniving. Why should it matter to us if they destroy each other?"

Silvanus's limbs felt light and detached from his body. His face flushed hot and he clenched his jaw to keep the magma of anger stirring in his chest from erupting. "Jerusa may be a blood drinker, but she is neither vile nor a parasite. She is one of the few beings in this world that has shown me kindness. And that includes the ten of you. Are we not the same? Why do you treat me as an enemy?"

The tall man with the cleft chin spoke again. "We are the true immortals. We have not witnessed another of our kind in many thousands of years, but you have broken our one covenant . . . the only law by which we live."

"And what law is that?"

The black man spoke up. "We are forbidden to give or take the life's blood of any creature. It is this that defines us. It is this that made us what we are. To partake in the blood rituals is to blaspheme against our very nature."

"I was unaware of any such law," Silvanus shouted at the group. "If you wished me to live by your law then Laura should have revealed herself to me when I appeared before her. All I have done since awakening is to search for the truth of who I am. She could have given that to me on the first night. But she chose to flee from me. She chose to keep me blind."

"I recognized you for what you were," Laura said, "but I could not be sure from whom you were sent. I feared that the Stewards had finally learned how to regain the light."

"So I am to be condemned because of your fear?"

"We haven't condemned you," said the flaxen haired woman. "The law has never been broken and we're not yet sure what to do with you."

"But I didn't know. How can you judge me for something beyond my understanding?"

"Your ignorance is no excuse," said the cleft-chin man. "You are Divine. Your very nature told you that it was an abomination."

"If you wish to judge me, fine," Silvanus said. "But, please, let me go and save my friend. Give me this one mercy." He dropped his hands to his sides, willing the fire to kindle in his palms.

"I'm afraid that's impossible. You must come with us."

Silvanus dropped his head, nodding as though he conceded defeat. He waited a moment for the besieging circle to let down their guard, then he sprang forward with a shout, fire flowing from his hands as though they were the mouths of twin dragons.

The fire rushed toward Laura, but she neither seemed surprised nor attempted to move out of the way. Just inches before the fire engulfed her it met with a curved wall of resistance made visible only by the deflected flow of the flames.

Silvanus turned, dowsing the others with the fire, but they all were protected by the same invisible net that was keeping him from teleporting. He focused his thoughts, intensifying the heat of the flames until they burned white as lightning. The air shimmered from the intense heat, revealing the dimensions of the invisible dome covering him. Soon, there was no oxygen left for the fire to breathe and it began to smother shortly after leaving his hands.

Silvanus quenched the fire in his palms. His skin was baked from the heat. His clothes were singed. The soles of his shoes were melted to the scorched pavement, leaving tacky prints as he stepped forward.

"Let me go," he shouted. He looked into the faces of his ten captors and found no mercy. How had it come to this? All he had dreamed of since awakening in the mountain lab was to find others like himself to learn from, commune with and now that he had found them they were treating him as though he were the most evil of criminals. "It doesn't have to be this way. Let me go to Jerusa and I vow that I will return to you."

A look of doubt passed over the faces of a few, but none answered him. Instead they stepped in closer, tightening the circles. They stood shoulder to shoulder now, their clasped hands down at their hips. They closed their eyes and lowered their heads.

Silvanus rushed them, pushing all of his speed and power into the attack. If he couldn't teleport through their invisible net, perhaps he could bull his way through. He dropped his shoulder fully expecting to burst through their ranks, but instead he met a solid wall of blinding pain that sent him tumbling backward.

He pushed to his knees. His head filled with the roaring bustle of the whole city. The ground shifted beneath him in rolling waves. A bright ball of light appeared before each of the ten Divines. Tendrils of lightning reached out from the orbs, fanning in all directions, overlapping and intertwining until the entire invisible dome was filled with their resplendence. The orbs pulsed with slow but bright strobes. They buzzed and vibrated like enormous angry bees. Silvanus's body began to turn clockwise against his will. He tried to plant his feet, to stop the spinning, but found he was now several inches off of the ground. The ring of Divine Vampires was turning too, counter-clockwise, their feet lifting above the pavement and the orbs of light dancing before their chests.

Faster and faster the opposing circles turned, until the ten Divines became a grayish backdrop and their orbs of light melted into a ring of searing emptiness. Silvanus was falling, tumbling, uncontrolled, down a bottomless pit. He tried to reach out for the white ring that followed him down into the pit, but he could not grasp it.

"Let me go," he said. Or maybe he only thought it. "Let me save her."

The glowing ring of light swelled, brightened beyond what he thought possible. Then, without warning, the spinning stopped and Silvanus felt as though he had fallen from the moon and crashed into the earth. The ten looked up in unison and their orbs shot forth, hitting him all at once.

The pain was immense, but short. He sank into a frigid darkness and just before he yielded to its grasp, he thought he saw Foster reaching out for him.

Chapter Twenty-Five

Jerusa followed Ming down a familiar path. They were heading to the room with the stage she had hidden under yesterday. The Judgment Room. She slowed her pace, glancing over her shoulder, hoping that Shufah, Taos and Thad would be following close behind. The only one behind her, though, was Ralgar who greeted her with a sneer and a hard shove to the back.

"Stop wasting time," he said. "The Council does not like to be kept waiting."

"Where are my friends?" she asked, trying to hide the desperation of her voice. "They should be here with me." A terrible thought occurred to her. What if they had already gone before the Council? What if they were already dead?

She shook the thought from her mind. They were still alive. They had to be. If she believed anything otherwise she wouldn't be able to hold her composure before the Council. And she didn't want to give them any more satisfaction in her death than she had to.

Alicia remained by her side, holding her hand. She gave Jerusa a reassuring smile, but whether that meant Jerusa would be all right or that her troubles would soon be over, it was hard to tell. Ralgar watched Jerusa with suspicious fascination, but didn't question her strange actions.

The other vampires of the house gathered in the halls, poked their heads out of their rooms and gawked at Jerusa over the balconies. Normally she didn't like being the center of attention. A lifetime of being an outsider had given her a certain craving for blending into the background. But now she marched down the halls with her shoulders back, her head held high. The scar on her chest burned hot, as though it too was proud to finally be displayed. The crowds of vampires pointed and whispered, but it no longer bothered her. The scar was part of her, as was the borrowed heart behind it. Without it, she would not be who she was today. Without it, she would not have Alicia.

They came to the place where the fancy carpets stopped and the hewn stone floors began. They were cold to the touch, as though incapable of being heated and Jerusa realized that she had left the room without any shoes. She and Alicia were quite the matched pair.

They descended down to the lower level, past the elevators. Jerusa stopped breathing, stopped feeling the cold stone beneath her bare feet. The silence of the hallway became a droning buzz in her ears. She could smell the ash and soot of the judgment room up ahead. Alicia squeezed her hand, but she couldn't find the strength to squeeze back.

Jerusa kept her eyes forward, locked onto Ming's back, but from her periphery she could see her new entourage of spirits following along. Heads and bodies popped out of the walls as they fought with one another for the position closest to Jerusa. The sight reminded her of a pod of dolphins, playfully leaping from the ocean, before the bow of a great ship. She laughed at the thought.

Ming stopped and looked at Jerusa, which only made her laugh the harder, but to be honest, Jerusa felt no humor at all. Ming started to speak, changed her mind, then turned and continued on. When she opened the door to the judgment room the laugh died in Jerusa's throat. This brought a smile to Ming's face.

They stepped inside the room and Ralgar closed the door behind them. The crowd of spirits passed through the walls and filled the room. The High Council sat upon the stage, motionless as stones. Near the bottom of the sloping room stood the rest of the Crimson Storm. Mikael and Quinn looked at her as though she smelled terrible. Celeste did her best to mask the pain on her face.

Jerusa wanted to ask Marjek if he had any other dogs attend his executions. The words were on the tip of her tongue, but she choked them back. To admit she had been hiding beneath the stage yesterday, might lead to the question of how she had escaped. Celeste, Dot and even Sebastian had gone out of their way to help her. She couldn't repay their kindness like that.

Ming led her to the bottom most level of the room. The scorched floor was still covered with the ashes of the poor condemned souls from yesterday, but at least the melted shackles had been removed.

Jerusa stared at the curtain surrounding the stage, at the small tear that she had peeked through and she wondered if there was someone under there right now, spying on her execution.

"Jerusa Phoenix," Marjek said, stepping to the front of the stage. "You have been inspected and found unworthy of the vampire spirit."

"Way to let me down easy," she said.

He continued as though he had not heard her. "Vampires must be beautiful and while you still hold the treasures of youth—"

"Why don't you just say that you hate my scar?"

"I'm sorry, but the one that made you must have known that we could not accept you."

"The one the made me doesn't abide by your rules," Jerusa said, struggling to keep her composure. "What he did, he did to save my life."

"And today you will lose that life," said Heidi. She stepped forward and for a moment Jerusa thought she might spit on her. "His mercy was an act in futility."

"No mercy is ever futile."

A strange look of hurt and respect passed over Celeste's face. She quickly squelched any sign of emotion, but Jerusa could still see it swimming just below the surface. She hated this more for Celeste than she did for herself. Jerusa never had many friends, but she thought, in another time and place, she and Celeste would have made a great pair. If only there was some way to break her free of the Hunters.

"Tell us of the one that made you," said the vampire whose

voice she recognized as Cot. "The Watchtower has had a bit of trouble locating him. Why is that? Does he still live?"

The last time Jerusa had seen Silvanus he had still been weak from the poisonous blood he had pulled from her veins. In six months, he hadn't come back to see her. It hadn't occurred to her until just now that maybe he *couldn't* come back.

"He's still alive," she said.

"Then why can't we track him?"

"Please, Cot," Marjek said. "Is this really important? Let us make an end of this and be done with it."

"No," Heidi said. "I want to hear her answer."

"The Watchtower cannot track him because—"

Suddenly the door burst open, cutting her off. Jerusa turned and almost cried out from joy when she saw Shufah standing in the doorway. She stepped forward, her dark eyes burning in anger. Taos entered the room behind her, followed by Thad. Dot hovered just outside the door like a lost shadow, hoping not to be noticed.

"What is the meaning of this?" Marjek asked.

"I should ask you the same thing, Marjek," Shufah said. "Is Jerusa a criminal? Why does the Council presume to judge a member of my coven without my consent?"

Marjek didn't answer her, but instead looked at poor Dot hovering in the shadows. "You, human," he said harsh enough to make her flinch. "Why did you bring them here? Where are their guards?"

Dot stepped inside, her eyes pointed toward the floor. "I'm not sure where the guards are, sir. I received an order from the Watchtower to escort them here at this exact time."

"The Watchtower?" Marjek's voice echoed around the room. "Who gave the order? Was it the dwarf?"

Dot trembled so hard that Jerusa thought the old lady's knees would give out. "I don't know, sir," she said, her voice hardly above a whisper. "I was sent a written message. It had a wax seal on it . . . the Watchtower crest."

A demented and murderous fire burned in Marjek's eyes. "It was the dwarf. I know that it was." He turned his attention to Jerusa. "You put him up to this, didn't you? Beguiled his twisted little heart." Jerusa shook her head, but he didn't give her a chance to answer. "Don't think for one moment that you have made a friend in that little beast. He would stake you to the ground and leave you to the sun if it would slake his boredom for a few minutes."

"What does it matter," Heidi said. "The decision has been made. If her coven wishes to be witness to her death, so be it."

"You will not harm her," Shufah said. The power in her voice brought chills to Jerusa.

"You dare to command us?" Heidi asked with a mocking laugh.

Shufah ignored her, keeping her eyes fixed on Marjek. "If you kill Jerusa then you will have to kill me as well."

"What?" Marjek and Jerusa said at the same time.

"If Jerusa dies by your hands, then so do I."

"No," Marjek said. "That will not happen."

But Heidi put a hand on his shoulder. The rest of the council stepped forward. "If she wishes to die with her fledgling, I say let her die."

"I will not allow it." Marjek pushed Heidi's hand from his shoulder.

"Shufah has plagued our steps for thousands of years, challenging our rule, poisoning the minds of countless vampires. We have endured her, at your request, but I say no more." Heidi turned to the other council members. "Shufah has betrayed us for the last time. We have her now in our grasp. If we allow her to leave, she will continue to sow insurrection. I say we kill them all."

"No," Marjek said again. "Shufah is a child of the ages, older than most on this council. By all rights she should be a Steward."

"She mocks our ways," Heidi said. "She seeks to dismantle our rule. We cannot allow her to live, not when she is so willing to lay down her life."

"I forbid it."

"It is not your decision alone, Marjek. The Council will put it to a vote. We know which way you are leaning. And I have made my choice clear." She turned to the others. "What say you, High Council of the Stewards of Life? Does Shufah the Traitor live or die?"

"Die," Cot said, without hesitation.

Jerusa's pulse raced, throbbing in her ears. Her mouth went dry and a warm, heavy weight settled into her stomach.

"I vote for death," said Othella.

This wasn't happening. It couldn't be real. It was Jerusa that was supposed to die, not Shufah. Jerusa had already mapped it all out in her mind. The Stewards would execute her for nothing more than the scar on her chest and that would satisfy their lust for death and power. When Shufah heard of her death, she would leave with Taos and Thad. She had survived for thousands of years. She couldn't die now, not like this, not for her.

"Shufah," Jerusa said, but Shufah hushed her. Jerusa wouldn't be silenced, though. "No, listen to me. Don't do this. It's all right. I'll be all right."

"Quiet child."

"No, Shufah. Just go. Take Taos and Thad and leave."

"They will never let that happen, child. You know that. If you die, we all die." Her eyes were still upon Marjek. There wasn't a bit of fear in her. She stood with her head held high, as did Taos and Thad.

How could they be so calm?

"What say you, Mathias?" Heidi asked. "Live or die?"

"Let the traitor die," Mathias said. "Let them all die."

The strength went out of Jerusa's legs and she dropped to the ground. The soot and ash marred her gown, painting her legs and hands black. The room had gone strangely silent. Marjek's mouth worked in quick, chopping movements as he raged against his own Council, yet she couldn't hear a thing he said. Alicia stood close by and the room became crowded with the ghosts of vampires. The lingering dead jostled and pushed, fighting for a spot close to her, though they seemed afraid to step within Alicia's reach. Shufah and Taos stood like stone soldiers, unmoved by the verdict, but Jerusa could smell the fear coming from Thad.

Sebastian's words rang out in her mind. She wasn't sure if it was just the strange deafness that had overtaken her or whether the dwarf was able to speak to her mind like a telepath, but she heard him the same, either way.

Tell them of your gifts. It is the only way to save yourself. And your friends.

"I can help you," Jerusa called out. She wasn't sure if she had shouted it or if it had squeaked out as a hoarse whisper, for it all sounded muffled to her own ears. "I can find him for you."

The heated conversation between Marjek and the Council halted. Shufah, Taos and Thad looked down upon her in horror.

Jerusa stepped forward and looked up at the Council. "I wish to join the Hunters. If you spare my friends, I will help you find him."

"What do you think you are doing?" Shufah asked. She took Jerusa by the arm and pulled her close, but Jerusa pulled away.

"I can help you, but only if you help me."

Marjek watched her with silent distrust. Heidi, however, seemed fascinated.

"And whom would you help us find?" she asked.

"Suhail." Jerusa could see from the corner of her eye the look of shock that passed over Shufah's face.

"Suhail lives?" she asked. "That's impossible."

"I'm afraid not," Heidi said. Though she didn't come right out and say it, from the tone of her voice and the look on her face, it was clear she didn't believe Shufah's reaction.

"It can't be. I severed his hand with a pair of shears. The blades were covered in savage blood."

"So it was you that turned your brother," Mathias said. His sharp, accusatory voice echoed off of the stone walls. "Do you know what you have done? It is trouble enough when a fledgling becomes a savage. Suhail was older than many of the Stewards. He held great physical strength and a formidable mind. Thanks to you, he has become a nightmare."

"No," Shufah said shaking her head. "I don't accept this. Suhail would never allow the change to happen. He would have walked into the morning light rather than accept the change."

Heidi laughed. "It seems you underestimated your brother, Shufah."

"Never mind that right now," Marjek said. He swatted at the air as if the conversation of Suhail was an annoying insect buzzing about his face. "Tell me how you know of Suhail. Did the dwarf tell you?"

Sebastian had told her of Suhail, as had Celeste and to a lesser degree Dot. Jerusa forced the truth deep down and wiped the emotion from her face. "No, Sebastian said nothing to me. I know because of my gift. A gift I will use to help you if you will spare my friends."

"Jerusa," Shufah said in a stern voice. "Do not do this. I beg you."

"You wish to join the Hunters?" Heidi asked, ignoring Shufah's pleading. "Are you an augur? Is that how you know of Suhail? Did you see him in a vision? You must be very powerful. Even the Watchtower hasn't been able to locate him."

"I'm not an augur."

"Can you conjure fire? Are you a telekinetic?"

"No," Jerusa said.

"Then what use would we have for you?" Othella asked. "Only the most skilled and powerful vampires are admitted into the Hunters. We have heard that you are an especially fast and strong fledgling, but that is not enough. What gifts could you possibly possess that would deem you worthy of the Hunters?"

Jerusa took a deep breath and let the air slide out of her mouth in a hiss. "I can see the spirits of the lingering dead."

"You're a blood witch?" Marjek said. He crossed his arms over his chest and gave a dismissive laugh. "You lie. That power is beyond the reach of a vampire."

"I'm not lying," Jerusa said. "I have always been able to see ghosts. First, it was the ghosts of humans, but now all I see are the spirits of vampires." She turned to Shufah. "Tell them I'm not lying."

But Shufah wouldn't answer.

"Shufah knows better than anyone that the stories of the blood witch are mere myths," Marjek said. "She and her brother both lost their gift of sight when they were given the vampire spirit. We cannot see ghosts for we are beyond death. And you cannot see the spirits of vampires because we have no souls to linger on."

"You're wrong and I can prove it to you."

"How?" Heidi asked, her intrigue matching Marjek's irritation.

"I can show them to you." Jerusa approached the stage and raised her hand toward Heidi.

Heidi looked to her fellow Council members, a devious smile lighting upon her face. She leapt down from the stage, landing nimbly before Jerusa. She took Jerusa's outstretched hand and a deep gasp of shock escaped her.

The crowd of vampire ghosts thronged the room, taking up every available spot. They jostled with one another for position in the room. Jerusa figured many of them had died at the command of Heidi and the other Council members and each wanted a chance for her to see their stricken face again. Heidi scanned the room, her eyes burning with a greedy awe that left Jerusa feeling uncomfortable and dirty. But when her sight fell upon Alicia, glowing with an unearthly light, a shadow of fear passed over her face and she snatched her hand away from Jerusa.

"She speaks the truth." Heidi gave a dreamy glance at the room about her, then looked up at the Council. "She is a blood witch."

Othella, Cot and Mathias were overtaken with delight. After all of their long years, they had finally found something new to entertain them. Marjek, however, just scowled. "Impossible," he said under his breath.

"These spirits are the ones that told you of Suhail?" Heidi asked.

"Yes," Jerusa lied.

"And they can lead you to him?"

"That is how we were able to find Kole after he had gone savage."

"Was it your ghosts that turned Kole savage?" Marjek asked. "He was no young vampire. It must have taken great strength to rupture his heart. Do your ghosts possess such strength? And how did you kill him once he had become savage?"

"I killed Kole," Taos said. "I burned him with my own fire. If you allow me to join the Hunters, then I will burn Suhail as well."

Jerusa turned to ask Taos what he was thinking, but she recognized the stubborn look in his eyes.

"Fools," Shufah said under her breath.

Chapter Twenty-Six

A rumble of laughter rolled through the room like the distant thunder before a treacherous storm. Jerusa watched Taos, expecting any moment for the rage he had been storing up to finally come to a head. But Taos stood with his head held high, enduring their mockery with silent stone-faced strength.

Jerusa hated them. Taos deserved better than this. She didn't understand his desire to join the Hunters, but she did understand wanting to belong, only to be cast aside for superficial reasons. It had been happening to her, her whole life.

"Do you really think you have what it takes to burn a savage like Suhail?" Ralgar asked. A derisive smile spanned his face, but the fury in his eyes sent chills washing down Jerusa's back. "Yes, you are big and handsome, but you are soft. I doubt you've ever been in true battle."

Taos spun to face Ralgar, his pale blue eyes wide, his jaw fixed tight. "Do you wish to test my battle skills right now?"

"I'd love to."

Jerusa could feel the kindling heat of aggression between them. They looked like a pair of bulls preparing to charge. Jerusa wasn't sure if she should cast herself between them or flee the hell-storm they were about to unleash.

"Shut your mouth," Heidi said to Ralgar. His face blushed a bit and his eyes narrowed into slits, but he didn't argue. Heidi turned to Taos. "You say that it was you that killed Kole?"

"Yes."

"That couldn't have been an easy feat."

"No, it wasn't."

Heidi touched his shoulder and Jerusa wanted to slap her

hand away. "Perhaps you would be an asset to us. Both of you." She glanced at Jerusa like a serpent eyeing its next meal.

"Please tell me you aren't serious," Marjek said.

"I am. Our attempts to find Suhail have all failed. We need to try something different. Wouldn't the Council agree?"

Cot, Othella and Mathias didn't speak up, but passed unsure looks to one another.

"The decision has been made," Marjek said. "The fledgling will die and the Crimson Storm will hunt down Suhail."

Heidi circled around Taos, tracing his chest with her fingertips. He flashed an uncomfortable look towards Jerusa. She pretended not to see, but in truth she wanted to rip Heidi's arm off and beat her with it. She wasn't sure why she felt this way. Maybe it was a side effect of not feeding.

"We have already lost five teams," Heidi said. "Are you really going to send in another team, blind and unprepared?"

Ming hopped forward. "The Crimson Storm is not afraid. And we will not fail."

Heidi gave Ming a patronizing look, then turned back to the stage. "Hear me out. If we send the giant and the blood witch with the Crimson Storm one of two things will happen. Either they will help to track him down and snuff him out or they will perish like all the rest. Both sides of the coin are beneficial to us."

Marjek stood in quiet consideration. Jerusa wondered if he was thinking of the third option, the one that Sebastian had warned her of, the one that would clear up all loose ends.

"Very well," he said. "But first, they must prove their worth."

"No," Shufah said. "If you must send someone after Suhail, send me. No matter what he has become, he is still my twin brother. We have always been drawn to each other. If he lives, we will come together again."

"I would never describe a savage as *living*," Marjek said. "And your part in turning Suhail savage is the very reason why you must stay here."

"What do you mean?"

"We believe that Suhail has regained consciousness," Marjek said. "He somehow managed to make it to the nearest quarantine community before the savage blood overtook him."

"How is that possible?" Jerusa asked. She thought of the bite Kole had given her and how fast the venom had flooded her system. Had Silvanus been a few moments later she would have been one of the mindless flesh eaters. "When Kole died, he changed right away."

"I only severed his hand," Shufah said. Her eyes were distant, haunted, as if she were reliving the moment and reconsidering her choice. "Very little of Kole's blood would have entered the wound. Suhail is thousands of years old. The strength of his blood bought him the time he needed."

"The time he needed to do what?"

It was Heidi that answered. "To get somewhere safe. Somewhere that he could change and feed without fear of human intervention. A place he knew we would not expect an attack."

Jerusa's knees trembled and she hoped the others didn't notice. A slithery knot formed in her stomach. She knew the town they were speaking of. The workers that had installed the security system in their house were from that town.

"Did he kill everyone in town?" she asked. She felt weak and distant. A pang of thirst echoed through her bones and she became all too aware of the sound of Thad's heart.

"No, we don't believe he killed everyone," Heidi said. "From what we can tell, he fed on enough to regain his consciousness."

"What happened to the others?" Jerusa allowed half a hope to bloom that the workers she had met were still alive, perhaps relocated to another community or even hiding somewhere in this house.

"After Suhail had what he needed, we believe he proceeded to turn a select group, which in turn fed on the other humans."

"Suhail's army," Jerusa said, fighting the urge to vomit.

"Yes," Marjek said. "That's what the Hunters have

nicknamed this group of savages." He turned an angry eye toward Ming and her group. They shied from the silent rebuff, but made no attempt to deny his accusation. He turned that same blistering stare on Jerusa, but she refused to cower. "Did your spirits tell you this, blood witch?"

"Yes," she said without hesitation. She was getting good at lying.

"Suhail is out there and we can't find him," Heidi said. "He's no longer a mindless wraith, hunting and eating whatever stumbles across his path. The savage in him is aware. It's hiding, planning, waiting for a moment to strike."

Marjek looked with unrequited longing at Shufah. The moment passed quickly, but was no less painful to behold. Jerusa didn't know which was worse, hating Marjek because of the demented tyrant he was or pitying him for the endless misery he had endured.

Jerusa once again felt the true weight of eternity pressing down on her, like the creeping force of a glacier. Was immortality really a treasure to be sought if it was to be spent alone, cut off from those you love, hiding in the shadows, death your only sustenance? Perhaps the High Council would be doing her a favor removing her from this burden. Had she been alone in this, she might go willingly into the fire, but if she could negotiate for the lives of Shufah, Taos and Thad, it would be worth the price.

"If you say my brother still lives, I will accept that," Shufah said. "But if he is to die, it should be at my hands."

Marjek shook his head. "I cannot allow that. Something strange is happening. You remember the last war with the savages. Always before, the savages spread like a foul virus. But in the six months since you infected your brother the only savage attacks have been on the quarantine community towns. These are calculated attacks."

"What does that have to do with me?" Shufah asked.

Heidi sighed, bored with this exchange. "He thinks your

brother will hunt you down, as if a savage has the capacity for revenge. I say we put you on a hook and dangle you where he can find you, but poor lovesick Marjek won't hear of it."

Anger surged into Shufah's face. "So you mean to confine me, so that you can *protect* me?"

"Yes," Marjek said.

"I am neither your prisoner nor your ward. If my brother still exists somewhere within the savage and he has mind enough to seek me out, then you have no authority to keep that from happening. It was you that created us, Marjek. So, ultimately you are the genesis of this disaster. I am going to walk out of this house, with my coven and we will hunt my brother down, and his army."

Marjek's pale cheeks blushed hot. "I forbid it. You will stay within these walls until your brother has been disposed of and if you attempt to cross the threshold I will not only kill your coven, I will take them to the dungeons and cast them into the catacombs."

"Don't be so hasty," Heidi said to Marjek. "I think it should fall to Shufah and her coven to clean up this mess."

The Crimson Storm (except for Celeste) wore masks of bitterness over Heidi's suggestion. They were hungry to succeed where five other teams of Hunters had failed. To place this task in the hands of common vampires was more than a slap to the face, it was a disgrace.

"I forbid it," Marjek said.

"Are you higher than the Council?" Heidi asked. "Does your vote weigh more than ours? I think not. You have been given your way for far too long and look what it has brought us. This whole tragedy has spawned from your obsession with Shufah. We will put it to a vote and if you try to circumvent the laws we established centuries ago, we will take the matter to the host of Stewards and see what they make of your abuse of power."

Heidi's words lingered in the air like the ozone after a lightning strike. The shocked silence was as loud as thunder.

Just as the tension in the room seemed on the verge of

combustion Marjek said, "Very well. Let us vote."

Marjek and Heidi had already claimed polar ends of the debate. They turned now to the other three on the Council, who up until now had been content with silent and safe observation. The trio stood now with sour expressions, eyes darting between the more aggressive members of their arcane order.

Mathias stepped forward.

"I stand with Marjek." He spoke with confidence, but refused to meet Heidi's eyes. "Shufah must stay. Send her coven with the Crimson Storm. Let fate choose their execution."

Jerusa's temples throbbed and her eyes itched. Were her irises encircled with blood, were her lips growing red? If the High Council discovered that she wasn't feeding, then all bets were off. She closed her eyes, slowed her breathing and tried to think of any other place than where she was.

Cot spoke next.

"I stand with Heidi. Send Shufah and her coven to search for Suhail. If they succeed, then they shall win their freedom. If they fail, they will die."

Every eye in the room turned to Othella.

Othella stood, relishing the attention. A devious smile parked itself on her face and Jerusa felt the floor open up beneath her. She closed her eyes waiting to hear Othella's vote. Nothing felt real anymore. It all had taken on the fuzzy, surreal chaos of a nightmare. She would have given anything to sit up in bed, in her mother's house and have all of this dissolve with the sunrise.

Jerusa opened her eyes. The nightmare still played out before her. She pricked her tongue with her fang, drawing a droplet of blood and immediately regretted it. She had meant it as a way of confirming the reality of her situation, like pinching herself, but the taste of blood in her mouth ignited the thirst that had been dozing just beneath the surface of her mind. Her predator's senses snapped into place and had Alicia not placed a warning hand on her should she might have lunged for poor Thad.

Jerusa was now thankful that Shufah had demanded that she and Thad not see each other anymore. She had spent all summer dreaming of the romance that might have blossomed forth had they had a chance to be alone, but Shufah had been right all along. No matter what Jerusa felt for Thad (which was confusing at best), it would not have been strong enough to overcome her thirst.

"Spare us the theatrics," Shufah said to Othella. "Give us your vote and be done with it."

"I stand with Heidi," Othella said, after a moment's pause.

Jerusa glanced about, searching for the verification that her ears hadn't betrayed her. Taos smiled. Though she didn't dare show relief, Celeste's eyes held a glow of happiness that she couldn't contain. In the opposite regard, the rest of the Crimson Storm stood with morose glowers plastered to their faces. Only Shufah's face remained unreadable.

Jerusa couldn't contain her own smile. Sure they were far from safe, but they had won their lives for a bit longer. The rush of exhilaration flooding through her swallowed even the burning thirst gnawing at her bones. She might have broken into a dance had Othella not spoken up.

"I stand with Heidi," she repeated herself, "but first I think they should prove their worth."

It was worse than a punch to the gut. Jerusa might have even taken a few steps backward, but she couldn't feel her legs enough to know. Strange as it seemed, the only thing that felt real to her was Alicia's hand upon her shoulder.

"What do you have in mind?" Marjek asked. Hesitation rested beneath the surface of his voice. The situation was quickly slipping from his grasp. He had built the Stewards, ordained the High Council and now the power of his creation was turning against him.

Jerusa almost felt sorry for him. Almost.

Othella stepped to the edge of the stage and looked down upon Jerusa. "If Heidi says this fledgling is a blood witch, then I believe her. But to send her and her coven out to hunt down Suhail without any proof of their skills seems a bit foolish to me. If they wish to be Hunters then let them face the same tests as any other vampire. Place them in the labyrinth."

A cheer of agreement rose up from the Crimson Storm (though Celeste seemed obligated on her part). Heidi, Cot and Mathias gave their consent. Shufah, as always, refused to react, but Taos stood tall as though this pleased him. Jerusa didn't know what the labyrinth was. She wasn't sure she wanted to know.

Marjek called for silence and the room obeyed. "If that is the wish of the Council, so be it. However, only the fledgling and the giant asked to join the Hunters and only they will face the labyrinth."

"I will not allow that," Shufah said.

Marjek turned on her. The bewilderment in his eyes chilled Jerusa's blood. "You have no authority here. You offered your life for the fledgling and she will live. There will be no more negotiations. The fledgling and the giant have made their choices. If they wish to be Hunters, they must face the labyrinth. You have nothing to offer the Hunters, I'm afraid. Unless you too are a blood witch and have been lying to me all these years."

Shufah's stoic face broke in a moment of resentment for Marjek's words, but she offered no argument.

"I'm sorry," he said. "They must face this task without you. And if they survive, they will go with the Crimson Storm to hunt down your brother."

A shiver of hatred washed over Shufah. Jerusa was thankful the look was not directed at her. She looked on the verge of screaming, but Shufah held her peace.

Marjek turned to Ming. "Confine them to their rooms. Just before sunrise escort them to the labyrinth."

"Yes, my lord."

Ming motioned to her team, then started for the door. Ralgar and Quinn prodded Jerusa and Taos out of the room while Mikael and Celeste closed in behind them. Jerusa glanced back and held on to the sight of Shufah and Thad as long as she could.

Chapter Twenty-Seven

Jerusa sat alone in her room. Well, not exactly alone. The crowd of ghosts filtered in and out in a constant shuffle, but it did little to ease her solitude.

The spirit with the piebald eyes tried several time to get her attention. She looked up thinking he might have some important information to pass on to her, but it soon became clear that all he wanted was to be noticed. She could relate, but she wasn't in the mood. He knelt down waving his hands before her face until, out of frustration, she asked Alicia to shoo him away. Alicia did as she was asked, not only chasing away the piebald-eyed ghost, but all the others as well.

The ghosts skulked away in sullen, slump-shoulder gates, pouting like chastised children being sent off to bed without dinner. Jerusa felt bad for them. Most had been wrongly condemned, murdered by the Stewards and left to linger, invisible in this corporeal world. She wanted to apologize to them, but she didn't have the mental strength just now. If she survived the Council's test, she would try to make it up to them.

Jerusa pierced her thumb with her fang and placed a few drops of blood in each eye. She smeared the remainder on her lips before the wound closed. Dawn would be here soon and they would be coming for her any time now. She didn't want to be caught unaware. This would all be easier if Alicia would just let her feed.

"I'm worried. I feel so weak. So drowsy. What if I can't do what they want me to do?"

Alicia gave her a reassuring hug and Jerusa found that the thirst within her didn't seem to notice that she wasn't touching a living, breathing person. She pushed Alicia back out of reflex. She posed no danger to Alicia, yet the urge to protect others from her predatory nature had become a second nature to her.

Foster appeared in the room close to where Alicia stood. Jerusa smiled at him, but it quickly withered when she saw the bewildered look upon his face. He must have thought she was in danger. He seemed relieved to see her, but something troubling stirred behind his eyes.

"What is it?" Jerusa asked standing to her feet. "Where have you been?"

A knock came to the door and Ming stepped inside without being invited. Foster watched her with cold eyes.

"The sun is not far off. Time to see if you have what it takes to be a Hunter."

Jerusa followed Ming. She looked for Shufah, Taos or Thad as she exited her room, but the hall was empty. Ming led her through the house and down the main staircase. The house was strangely active this close to sunrise, with the gawking faces of other vampires and even the human servants peering at her around every corner. The news of her test had made quick rounds through the gossiping chains.

Taos stood with Ralgar at the large front doors. He smiled at her as she came down the stairs. A quiet paranoia had risen in her that the Stewards would make her face their test alone. She was so happy to see him that she almost skipped the bottom ten steps to run and embrace him. The only thing that kept her in place was the fear that Ming would mistake her excited rush toward Taos for an attempted escape. The Hunters would love to have any reason, even a flimsy one, to kill her and at the moment, Jerusa didn't feel in a rush to die.

Taos brushed a few loose strands of hair from her face. The tenderness of his touch prickled her skin with goose bumps. She gazed into his pale blue eyes. Her stomach felt hollow, her face flushed. Why did she suddenly feel so awkward around him? It still seemed strange to her that they had become such good friends, seeing as how only six months ago they almost tore each other to shreds.

"Are you ready for this?" he asked her.

Jerusa's heart skipped a beat. She couldn't answer him. Ming opened the front door and a blast of artic air rushed in, zapping her energy and plunging her back into the icy waters of reality. One of the black SUVs waited for them under the stone canopy, idling in a plume of its own exhaust.

Ming motioned for them to go. Taos opened the door and allowed Jerusa inside first. The warmth in the cab restored a bit of her strength, but it could not dispel the claustrophobic trepidation gnawing at her. Taos slid in beside her and Ming and Ralgar sandwiched them in close together. Taos reached for her hand. She allowed him to take it, but it felt awkward. Confusing feelings bubbled up and she forced them back down. She didn't have time to think about this right now and she was a bit irritated that Taos chose this moment to be tender to her. Maybe he figured this would be his last chance, which disturbed Jerusa more than his uncharacteristic show of kindness.

Ming told the driver to go and he pushed the SUV into the blowing snow without question. They drove in silence for twenty minutes through the white-cloaked trees before turning up a thin trail that seemed no more than a footpath. The branches of the close trees clanged and screeched along the side of the SUV. The driver pushed on, never slowing until they broke into a tiny opening.

Ming and Ralgar opened their doors allowing the harsh, biting wind to envelope them. They stepped out into the blowing snow and motioned for Taos and Jerusa to follow. They trudged through knee-deep drifts and though Jerusa was well-dressed for the cold it somehow still found its way in through the layers and down into her bones.

The predawn sky was the color of a deep bruise. The sun would be up soon. Jerusa wondered just how close to the light they could come before it started breaking down their cells. A terrible thought caught her and she stopped mid-step. What if there was no test? What if Ming and Ralgar had brought them out here to kill them, maybe bind them in some way and leave them for the sun?

Sebastian had warned her to escape from the Hunters the first chance she got. Should she run now?

That wouldn't work. There was no guarantee that she could find shelter from the sun. And even if she did, she didn't know the terrain—didn't even know what country they were in. The Hunters would have her before the next sunrise.

They marched on, Ming in the lead, Ralgar bringing up the rear. In the middle of the opening Ming halted them.

"Here we are." She bent down, digging in the snow until she uncovered a square metal hatch, buried a foot down. She placed her hands upon two large turning locks set into the hatch door, but she didn't release them. "Beneath the ground is a series of tunnels. There are several other doors like this one, scattered throughout the forest. Do not be tempted to open them unless you want a face full of sunlight."

"What are we supposed to do down there?" Jerusa asked.

"You asked to be Hunters," Ming said with a smug look. "So, hunt."

"There are savages down there?"

Ming didn't answer, but it was clear from the sadist glint in her eyes that the answer was yes. Jerusa wanted to ask how many savages were down there, but she knew Ming wouldn't answer.

"If you survive until nightfall," Ming said, "we will fish you out and see how well you have done." Her eyes hardened. "If you try to escape at any time, we will take your mother and the boy and pitch them down into this pit. Do you understand?"

Jerusa's throat was too dry to speak, so she just nodded.

"Good. Now, blood witch, let's see what your spirits can do for you." Ming started to open the hatch door, but Taos stopped her.

"Hold on. Are we to go in unarmed? Even great, skilled Hunters such as the Crimson Storm don't go into battle without weapons in hand."

Ming eyed him with a crocodile's stare. "My mind is the only weapon I need, but if you must have something."

She nodded to Ralgar. He removed his sheathed skewer from beneath his coat and tossed his skewer to Jerusa. She caught it, amazed at the weightlessness of the weapon.

"I only have one," Ralgar said to Taos. "You will have to rely on those tiny flames you can conjure and your mindless, brute strength. I doubt either will save you. My advice is to kill the girl and take the skewer from her. Or wait until she dies, then try and retrieve it. With it you may stand a chance, but whichever path you choose, I don't suspect we will see each other again."

Taos stood tall. The rest of them seemed diminished in his presence. That haughty, machismo grin spread across his face and this time Jerusa didn't mind it so much. "Oh, we'll see each other again. My face will be the last thing you see before I drive my fist into your chest and crush your wretched little heart with my bare hand."

"Enough," Ming said before Ralgar could answer. "Approach the door."

Jerusa and Taos stepped down into the hole in the snow just on the outside of the hatch door. Ming turned the locks—one clockwise, the other counter—and the sound of heavy pistons, sliding free, groaned up through the ground. Ming wrenched the door up and immediately Jerusa was hit with the stench of rot. Not the normal scent of decay, but of dead flesh too long in the cold. And wafting behind that was the subtle scent of savages.

Jerusa had just enough time to glance down into the darkened pit, feel the fear well up into her throat, before Ralgar kicked her hard in the back and sent her tumbling over the edge.

It was too dark to judge the distance from the hatch door to the ground below. The fall seemed to take forever, long enough for Jerusa to gain her bearings and land cat-like on her feet, yet as she was in the midst of her decent she heard Taos curse Ralgar and jump in after her. He landed awkwardly beside her, a half a moment later. The hatchway door slammed shut above them, the clang echoing off of the tunnel walls in all directions like metallic thunder.

Jerusa was disoriented by the noise and darkness. The silence that followed seemed even more heavy and intense than the closing door, as if she had suddenly gone deaf. She turned side to side unable to get a feel for where she was at. She clutched the closed skewer in her hand while pressing her back hard into Taos. The irrational fear of letting go of him drowned her senses. He was her tether to this world and if she lost her grip on him she would tumble down into this bottomless pit forever.

Jerusa searched the skewer's handle, feeling out every detail, searching for a way to extend the points. It crossed her mind that Ralgar had given her an empty handle to use, but she soon found what she was looking for. She twisted the handle and the two spear points shot out with a quick metallic hiss.

She turned the skewer over and over like some large, dangerous baton. It felt awkward in her hands. She had the speed and strength to use it, but that wasn't the real issue. It was a killing tool and she wasn't a killer, even if she sometimes wished she was.

Light flooded around her and, for a moment, Jerusa thought that Ming and Ralgar had rigged the hatchway door to open on the sunrise. But this light didn't come from the sun. It came from the mob of vampire ghosts crowding the underground corridors.

Though their auras burned bright, the darkness quickly gobbled up the light, leaving Jerusa with not much of an advantage over the savages lurking in the corridors. But she would take what she could get.

Alicia and Foster appeared next to Jerusa. Neither one looked at her, but instead, shuffled off through the crowd of ghosts. They moved in and out, pointing this way and that, speaking in that silent way they had. Before long they had the crowd of ghosts scattering off through the tunnels in a systematic search pattern.

"Come on," Taos said. "We need to move. I don't think it's a good idea to stay here much longer."

"Hold on. Something is happening." Jerusa reached out and took Taos by the hand. A small gasp escaped him as his eyes were opened to the army of ghosts surrounding them.

He looked about in awe. "What are they doing?"

She watched as several of the first ghosts to leave returned, spoke a quick word to Alicia then left again, passing through the stone walls. "I think Alicia has them doing a little recon for us. They're mapping out the area for us."

"I didn't know ghosts did that sort of thing."

"Neither did I."

Alicia and Foster conferred for a moment, then the ghost girl, so out of place in her glowing prom dress in this labyrinth of old stone tunnels, held up four fingers.

"Four," Jerusa repeated. "There are four savages in here?"

Alicia nodded.

"Where are they?" Taos asked.

Alicia motioned for them to follow her, but stopped when the ghost with the piebald eyes whispered something in her ear. Maybe it was a trick of the light—so many different auras playing off of each other—or maybe it was just Jerusa's imagination, but she could have sworn that Alicia's face drained of all color. The ghost girl looked back at them and Jerusa's heart missed a beat. She knew that look well. Nothing good ever came when Alicia had that look.

Alicia motioned for the other ghosts to continue on their mission. She approached Jerusa and took her hand. Taos still held her other hand and he clenched it tight, as though he felt Alicia's energy flowing through Jerusa and into him.

"What is it?"

Alicia held her free hand high over her head, squared her shoulders and puffed out her chest. Over the years, dealing with spirits unable to speak, Jerusa had developed a certain understanding for their wordless gestures. No ghost had ever been closer to her than Alicia, so when she made this little act, Jerusa knew right away who she was describing.

"Thad." The name escaped Jerusa's mouth in a saddened groan. "Thad is down here with us?"

Alicia nodded.

"Is he dead?"

She shook her head.

Jerusa didn't want to ask the next question, but she needed to know. "Is he one of the savages?"

Time crawled to a stop as she awaited Alicia's answer. Centuries unwound between each beat of her raging heart. Galaxies burst into life only to burn out like the coals of a dowsed fire.

Alicia shook her head, but trepidation swam in her eyes. Thad was alive, unharmed for now, but there were four savages loose in these tunnels and unless they found him first . . . well, she didn't want to think about that outcome.

"You know what to do," Jerusa said to Alicia.

Jerusa pulled her hand out of Taos's. He gripped her fingers tight, unwilling to release her, but he allowed her hand to slip from his and offered only a small groan of disapproval.

She grabbed the skewer in both hands and held it out before her. It felt too light, too flimsy to be a weapon, but she supposed it would get the job done. All she needed to do was pin the savages down and let Taos burn them. How hard could that be? She twisted the handle the way she had witnessed Ralgar doing it and four prongs snapped open on each of the long, slender points.

"Let's go get Thad." She glanced back at Taos. "Follow me."

Alicia and Foster started down the tunnel, occasionally sweeping to the side to converse with the other spirits. Jerusa could sense that the sun was up over the horizon, but down here light was a distant dream. Her vampiric eyes were able to glean a little bit of her surroundings and the light from the ghosts helped as well. Still, there were too many corners, too many crevices, too many places for a savage to lie in wait.

The ghosts scoured the labyrinth like an industrious swarm of ants. A calm assurance washed over her. They would not let her walk into an ambush. She tightened her grip on the skewer and a surge of power rushed up her arms, filling her with a warm intoxicating excitement. She had never felt more right, more in her element.

Alicia and Foster took off running. Jerusa darted after them.

They passed through the black tunnels, turning this way and that. Jerusa didn't bother marking where she was at or where she was going. The darkness seemed to gobble up the sounds of her footsteps. The air was cold enough to turn her breath into white plumes. Though she couldn't hear Taos behind her, she assumed he was close on her heels. She was tempted to check over her shoulder, but the predator's instinct within said to keep her eyes forward.

It was a good thing that she listened, because just as she turned the next corner a flood of ghosts pressed through the walls, waving their hands and pointing ahead in warning. Alicia and Foster parted, their backs vanishing through the solid stone walls, giving Jerusa a clear view of what was rushing to meet her.

The savage came at her faster than a striking serpent. As quick as her reflexes had become, Jerusa barely had time to register the beast's blood-filled eyes and snarling teeth as he lunged at her.

Jerusa cried out in shock, thrust the skewer forward and caught the savage in the shoulder. His momentum drove her back, the rear point of the skewer gouged into the stone floor and caught in a mortar joint. She fell on her back and the savage flew over her head like a pole-vaulter. The savage came off of the skewer and flew like a missile right into Taos.

The savage let out a garbled snarl, its powerful jaws snapping like a bear-trap. Taos caught the beast by the throat with one hand while hammering at its face with the other. The savage swiped at Taos with its long, broken fingernails, drawing blood.

Taos clenched his teeth, bent his knees and with one powerful thrust, drove the savage's head upward into the ceiling. A terrible crunching noise echoed through the tunnels and dark trails of blood splattered down onto Taos. The savage continued to claw at Taos in blind swipes that made their mark just as often as not. With a growl of anger, Taos smashed the savage, first into the wall on his left and then again on the wall to his right. He spun in a tight circle, tossing the broken body of the savage down the black tunnel.

Jerusa leapt to her feet. She rushed to Taos's side. The scratches on his face and neck were already healed. The only evidence of his wounds was a few drops of blood on his collar. Jerusa checked him over anyway.

"Were you bitten?"

"No. I'm fine."

"Can a savage infect you by scratching you?"

"I don't think so. Maybe if their fingers are bleeding. I guess we'll just have to wait and see." He winked at her. When she shoved him backward, he said, "I told you that I'm fine. If it infected me, we'd know by now."

He was right. The night Kole had bitten Jerusa she felt the venom start to work immediately. Even if Taos was strong enough to delay the change, he'd still feel it burrowing down into his cells.

The spirits moved about her in an agitated swarm. Alicia motioned for Jerusa, pointing down the hall. Jerusa didn't need to ask what had stirred up the ghosts. She could hear it. The sound of its tattered breathing echoed from wall to wall. The scrape of its body dragging across the stone floor sent the hairs on the back of her neck standing on end.

Taos turned at the same time she did. He reached out to try and force her behind him, but she would have none of that. Her days of playing damsel in distress were over. She forced his arm away, using the skewer to make her point and stepped up beside him.

"It isn't dead."

A small orb of fire burst to life between Taos's palms, its tiny light almost blinding after being in the darkness of the tunnels. "Then let's change that," he said with a smile so pure Jerusa couldn't help but join in.

It felt strange to smile in such a situation, but she couldn't help it. Was she frightened? Yes. Was she concerned for Thad? Absolutely. Yet, all the same, she was excited in a way she had never been before. Even when she had helped hunt Kole she hadn't felt this degree of contentment.

They moved toward the ghastly sounds. She held her breath. They inched forward, yet the noise seemed to ever evade them. Jerusa began to doubt her senses. She turned, walking backward for fear the noise was actually coming from behind. Occasionally a spirit would dart through the walls, on its way to search out other parts of the labyrinth and it was all Jerusa could do to keep from screaming at them to stop startling her.

"There it is," Taos said.

Jerusa turned to look. They hadn't moved fifteen feet from where they had battled the savage, yet it seemed to her as though they had covered a mile in search for it. The creature remained just beyond the circle of light, a deep black shadow swimming in a slightly less black lake. When it finally entered the light a gasp of horror escaped Jerusa.

Chapter Twenty-Eight

The savage groped the stones of the floor, using the mortar joints to pull itself along. Its legs, twisted and lifeless, trailed behind its torso leaving twin smears of dark, polluted blood. It wore no shoes and one foot was turned around backward. Its left arm looked to have a few too many elbows, and a bone protruded through the skin near the wrist, but the creature continued to flip the useless appendage up in an attempt to pull itself along.

Worst of all, however, was the savage's head.

Its skull looked like a pumpkin that had been dropped from a high ledge. Its scalp was peeled away and was lying in tatters around its ears. The beast's mouth continued to snap, even though its jaw was broken. The misaligned teeth ground together and the noise made Jerusa feel as though her soul was trapped in that busted maw.

Still the savaged inched forward with mindless determination, unaware of—or perhaps unconcerned with—its devastating injuries. Jerusa's skin crawled as though she was looking down on a very large insect. It was all she could do not to turn and run down the dark tunnel screaming. She wondered if she would ever get used to seeing savages. Would the squeamish nausea they induced in her ever subside or would she just have to learn to live with it? It wasn't the macabre, sometimes gory, form they took. She had been looking at ghosts and the ghastly way they had died, all her life. No, it was something subliminal. Even the tiniest molecules within her could sense the unnaturalness of the savages.

Taos seemed to share her thoughts because he shuddered in disgust. "That was a little too close. I hope your aim is a bit better next time."

Jerusa's legs went weak at the thought that not only did there have to be a next time, but two more times after that. Maybe more depending . . .

No. She would not allow herself to even consider that ending.

"He caught me off guard," she said. Her voice trembled and sounded strange in the close, echoing tunnels. "It won't happen again." She pointed to the savage. "You're one to talk, though. You almost bashed his brains out. We really don't want these things exploding down here."

"Won't happen again."

Taos juggled the orb of fire back and forth, increasing its size with each pass. The savage looked up at the fire and one of its eyes drooped out of the socket, down onto its cheek. It hissed at the growing flames, but continued toward them. Taos caught the fire in one hand and with a thrust of his arm sent it hurtling toward the savage.

The creature ignited like a piece of dry kindling. It let out an ear-splitting howl, yet continued to claw its way toward them. Taos increased the fire. Jerusa hadn't realized just how cold she was until she felt the heat baking her face. The savage turned over onto his back. His twisted, blackening form swiped at the flames with its good arm. It snapped its jaw one last time before falling still. Soon the savage disintegrated into a pile of ash, bones and all.

Taos reined back his fire, keeping a small orb bouncing between his hands for light. Deep shadows crept back into the tunnels, casting themselves about in impassioned dances.

"Alicia," Jerusa called out. The ghost appeared before her. "Take us to Thad." Alicia nodded and motioned for her to follow.

They passed through the tunnels at a slower pace this time. The other ghosts, led by Foster, continued to pass through the walls before and behind them as they searched for and kept track of the other three savages. Jerusa watched the shadows, clutching the skewer so tight that her knuckles bleached white and the intricate metal handle groaned in objection.

The tunnels all looked the same. There was no way to

distinguish where they were or how far they had traveled from the drop off point. Had it not been for Alicia and the other ghosts Jerusa was sure they would have just walked around in circles, until the savages hunted them down.

A loud click erupted from somewhere inside the walls. Jerusa jumped back just in time to keep from being smashed by a heavy, iron portcullis dropping from the ceiling. It crashed into the floor with a bone-jarring crash, its teeth slipping into sheaths formed into the stone floor.

Alicia stood on the other side of the portcullis. She crossed her arms and shook her head, upset that she hadn't noticed the trap before it had been sprung. She pointed to Jerusa and Taos, asking without words if the pair of vampires could lift the portcullis.

Jerusa grabbed the latticed iron and pushed up as hard as she could. The portcullis didn't even wiggle. Taos extinguished the flame in his hands, casting them back into blinding darkness. He stepped up beside her and took hold of the portcullis. They pushed together, but this was a trap built by vampires, not humans and they knew just what to do to keep the portcullis in place.

"I could try and melt it," Taos said.

"No," Jerusa said. "It will take too long. We need to keep moving." She turned to Alicia. "Can you find another way to Thad?"

Alicia nodded yes, but Jerusa could tell from the look on the ghost's face that the situation had grown worse. There were three savages remaining. It was feasible that with the ghosts' help she and Taos could evade them until sundown. But not with Thad thrown into the mix. Though Alicia couldn't express her plan to them, Jerusa believed that she had been leading them to Thad in a way that would minimize their contact with the savages. That way was blocked to them now.

Taos started to ignite another fire, but Jerusa stopped him. "No. It'll just draw attention to us. The ghosts will tell us if we're near any savages."

Taos didn't seem too convinced, but he agreed.

Alicia led them down too many similar corridors to keep track of. Silence surrounded them, seeping into their bones like the wretched cold. They moved at a crawling pace that grated on Jerusa's nerves. She wanted to scream and go running at top speed. At this rate, Thad would be an old man when they found him.

They came to a long, narrow passage with a low ceiling. Jerusa stood with her hands on the walls, peering into the void with uncertainty. The area was so strait that not only would they have to go in single file, but they would have to slide in sideways and make the whole journey that way. It was a tight fit for Jerusa, but Taos stood a good chance of getting stuck.

"Are you sure about this?" Jerusa asked Alicia. The ghost shrugged her shoulders. "Isn't there another way?"

Alicia pointed down an adjacent tunnel then tapped her wrist as though she was wearing a watch. There was another way, probably several, but this was the fastest.

Jerusa sighed. She checked the tunnel again. "Are you all right with this?" she asked Taos.

"Not really," he said. "If it was up to me, I'd let the mortal fend for himself." Even in the darkness she could see a flicker of the old Taos burning in his icy blue eyes. "But it's not up to me and I go where you go."

It wasn't the best answer, but it was good enough for now.

"All right, let's get this over with." To Alicia she said, "Keep the others on guard. I don't want anything sneaking up on us." Alicia nodded and Foster darted off to conduct the other ghosts.

Jerusa slid into the narrow opening and instantly regretted it. There was no room to turn her body, except for her head. Though she wasn't sure how it was possible, it seemed even darker in here than it did in the other tunnels. She reached out with her hand expecting any moment to find a wall blocking their path. She tested each step, sure the floor would drop off.

Alicia appeared before Jerusa, her aura giving a tiny bit of light. The other ghosts moved in and out of the walls ahead of them searching for any trouble. Despite this small comfort, Jerusa still felt as though the walls were drawing in on her. Shufah had told her stories of the Stewards' cruel lust for torture, of burying vampires alive or sealing them up in pits, to sit in darkness for centuries, until the Stone Cloak overtook them.

She forced these thoughts from her mind before they struck a chord of madness in her.

Jerusa glanced back on Taos and discovered she didn't have it so bad after all. For poor Taos the walls really were closing in. He was pinched in between the walls so that if he wanted to move he had to suck in his chest and stomach just to get enough space to make it another step. Jerusa was short so the ceiling didn't pose a problem for her, but Taos had to crane his neck sideways with his ear pressed against the stone.

Would there ever be a time that Jerusa wasn't causing her friends some kind of discomfort?

One of the ghosts came rushing by, headed in the opposite direction. Jerusa couldn't tell which one it was because it was half in and half out of the wall. Before she could turn her head to question Alicia two more ghosts ran by.

Alicia stood still, her shoulders squared so that they disappeared into the stone walls. She held one hand back motioning for Jerusa to wait. Moments later a large group of ghosts came barreling towards them, flying in and out of the walls like a flock of frightened birds.

"What's wrong?" Taos asked. "Why are we stopped?"

"I don't know. Something ahead of us has the ghosts scared."

"What do ghosts have to be afraid of?"

Jerusa had an idea, but it was too complicated to explain to Taos just now. Her suspicions were confirmed when another group of ghosts passed through the wall behind her and into the other before her, and following them was a pack of dark, not fully formed, shadows.

Alicia turned just in time to see the last of the savage spirits pass between her and Jerusa. She crossed her arms and shook her head. She apparently found the vampire ghosts' fear of the savage spirits just as absurd as Taos did.

"Can you and Foster chase them off," Jerusa asked. "We need the others to keep watch for us."

Alicia nodded, then went off in pursuit of the savage spirits.

Taos squeezed in closer to her without her noticing and when he tapped her on the shoulder she nearly jumped out of her skin.

"I don't know what you are seeing," he said in a whisper. "But we need to keep moving. If I have to stay in this coffin much longer, I'm going to freak out."

She resumed scooting down the narrow tunnel. Without the ghosts' auras the darkness was even more oppressive. Its suffocating weight pressed down upon her like the crushing pressures of the ocean bottom.

A growl cracked the silence, freezing Jerusa and Taos in place.

It had been so sharp and quick that at first she couldn't tell if it had been real or in her head. The growl came again, longer, more menacing this time and there was no denying that it was real.

"Oh, this is just wonderful," Taos said and the fear in his voice was more unsettling than the growls. "Move! Move now!"

Another growl echoed down the tunnel, but Jerusa couldn't tell where it was coming from. One time it sounded like it was coming from behind them, the next from in front. They continued to inch forward, but they hadn't made it very far before a pair of growls sounded at the same time, one from before and one from behind. There was a rolling pitch that came through the growl and Jerusa had the strangest feeling that the savages knew they were there and were talking to each other about their trapped prey.

The savages grunted as they pressed their bodies into the narrow tunnel. She couldn't bring the skewer up, couldn't even square her shoulders. Taos couldn't conjure a fire in these close quarters without the danger of the flames turning against their master. They were done for. No room to fight, no place to flee.

Jerusa pressed back against Taos. Her hand found his and he gently squeezed it. She wished that she hadn't sent Alicia off to chase away those demonic savage spirits. There was nothing Alicia could do to save them, but Jerusa wanted her to be here when she died. Though she knew it was irrational, she feared that her soul would be lost without Alicia to guide her across the void.

The savages were almost upon them. Their bodies scraped against the stone walls. They grunted and panted as they forced their way in further, they screeched when they became lodged. The echoes crashed in upon them making it impossible to tell just how far away they were.

Jerusa wanted to apologize to Taos for bringing him into this. It felt as though she always needed to apologize for something. She knew it was stupid. Her friends didn't blame her for anything. Yet, the guilt was there all the same.

She held tight to Taos's hand, wanted to bring it up to her face, but there was no room. She wished she had just a bit more space. Just enough to reach up and kiss Taos once before they died. She had spent the last six months trapped in a triangle of confusion, her emotions switching rapidly between Taos, Thad and Silvanus.

"I don't want to die like this," she said. "Not like this. I don't want the Stewards to win. I don't want to leave my mom alone with them."

Taos jerked his hand away from hers and brought both hands up as close to his chest as he could. He pushed against the wall with all his strength. His grunts became growls, his growls became screams. The savages called out, excited by the noise and the sound of their approach quickened.

Taos continued his assault on the wall, undaunted by the savages. He thrashed side to side, as much as he could, but nothing happened. Jerusa peered down her side of the tunnel and nearly cried out with shock. A savage crept out of the inky blackness.

The savage's withered lips pulled back in an excited grin. He snapped at her as though he was close enough to sink his venomous teeth into her flesh. He pushed hard, scraping his skin away on the stone and leaving smears of dark blood.

A scream of terror rose into Jerusa's throat, but died when she felt the stone wall give way.

The wall only moved a half an inch, but the fact that it moved at all left her thunderstruck. Taos released some pressure and the blocks in the wall fell back into place. He pushed again and this time the wall moved an inch.

Jerusa dropped the skewer and pressed her hands to the wall. The weapon fell to the floor with a loud clank, the sharp ends retracted and it vanished in the murk at her feet. This brought an almost debilitating sense of vulnerability and she had to remind herself that the skewer was useless to her in this confined space.

Jerusa waited, timing her movements with Taos. When he pushed again, she threw all her strength in with him. The wall moved a few inches this time, concaving and raining broken mortar down upon them. A sense of hope rushed through her, leaving her jittery and dizzy. It was all she could do to not shove again right away. If they were going to do this, they would have to do it together.

She didn't know if the savages on either side of them understood just what was happening, whether they realized their prey was unarmed and making a valiant effort to escape or if they smelled their fear as she sometimes did with mortals. Either way, they called to each other, as if goading the other to hurry. The one closest to Jerusa shoved forward with a hard lurch and came within grasping reach of her.

The savage's vile, festering fingers clawed at her shoulder, but it could come no further. In its lust for her flesh, it had wedged its shoulders against the narrow walls. It screamed with unholy anger and began thrashing so hard that its raggedy shirt tore away and the skin on its shoulders soon followed. Like a trapped beast gnawing at its own leg, it was only a matter of time before it freed itself.

Taos and Jerusa continued pushing the wall. A section of

blocks had slid back, yet the wall didn't seem ready to collapse for them. Taos let out an angry growl and kicked at something. Jerusa couldn't see past him, but she suspected that the other savage had come a little too close for comfort. He never ceased his assault on the wall, however and soon they had gained about six inches of room.

Jerusa's savage lurched forward, his bloody shoulders sliding along the stone and made it close enough to grasp her throat. She tried to kick at him, like Taos had, but she couldn't plant a solid hit. The savage pressed closer and she had to throw up her hand to keep him from getting to her. They had each other by the throat, each trying to tear out the other's trachea.

The savage moved into the wider space she and Taos had made. He squared his shoulders and reached around with his other hand. He hooked a claw-like hand around the back of her neck and tried his best to draw her into his open mouth. Jerusa kept her other hand on the wall, pushing against the blocks. Taos was having trouble staving off his own attacker, causing him and Jerusa to fall out of synch.

Jerusa's strength outmatched the savage's, but her one arm couldn't fend off his two, for very much longer. She tried to keep her arm straight, but the savage's fierce thrashing jarred her hard enough to clank her teeth together. Jerusa couldn't take this much longer. The wall gave more with every push. If only she could get all of her strength into one good shove.

The savage pulled on her and this time she allowed her arm to go limp. The savage fell forward and just as he lunged for her throat, she lurched forward and smashed his face with her forehead. The darkness exploded with white-hot bursts of light and the ground beneath her rippled like a storm-tossed sea, but the savage's hands left her and he stumbled backward.

Jerusa turned, though she was no longer sure she was facing the right direction, pressed both hands against the wall and pushed with everything that she had.

Everything seemed to be in flux. The sound of stone scraping against stone rang out, followed by the sensation of falling. A blast of pain filled her lower half. Instinctively she tried to climb to her feet, but found that her legs were pinned beneath a pile of large stones. Taos was next to her, face down and still.

The pair of savages looked down on them from the hole in the wall.

Chapter Twenty-Nine

The savages spilled from the hole in the wall, croaking in what sounded like horrific elation. They came at Jerusa with deadly speed. Though the darkness was near perfect, she could still see their froth-covered teeth glistening as if filled with unholy light.

Jerusa snatched the first of the savages by the throat and using his own momentum, tossed him over her head and into the black emptiness. She tried to bring her hands down to fend off the second savage, but he was too fast. He grasped her wrists and lunged, biting at her throat.

His fetid teeth came within a fraction of an inch from her before Taos caught him in the side of the head with a thundering blow. The savage rolled several times, regained his balance and scuttled off into the darkness like a spider. Jerusa couldn't see either savage but she knew they hadn't gone far.

Taos kindled a small orb of fire. The heat washed over Jerusa, but when the light hit the ceiling her blood turned to ice. The pair of savages crept along the ceiling and was almost directly above them.

"Taos," Jerusa screamed, pointing at the ceiling. A heavy terror filled her at the sight of the savages crawling along the ceiling, using a series of metal brackets that at one time had held some piece of machinery above the floor.

Taos tossed the orb of fire at the pair of savages but missed. The savages leapt to either side and the fire exploded against the stone. Sparks rained down upon Jerusa.

The savages came rushing in again. Taos jumped to his feet, another orb of fire hovering over his left hand. He thrust it before him in an attempt to drive the savages back, but their hunger outweighed their fear of the flames. They parted, circled around him, then as if on some cue that only they could hear, the two savages came at him. Taos's fire extinguished and the sound of the struggle drifted off down one of the adjacent tunnels.

Jerusa tried to get up, but her legs were still pinned beneath a pile of large stones. She sat up and began to dig herself out, spurred on by the dwindling echoes of Taos's voice. She grabbed the large stones, several weighing more than a hundred pounds and threw them across the room as though they were made of Styrofoam. After what seemed an eternity she had removed enough debris that she could wrench her legs from beneath the rubble. She rolled over and her hand brushed the handle of Ralgar's skewer.

A surge of power rushed from her hand up into her body. Jerusa brought the skewer up to her chest then rushed with all her speed into the darkness.

There was not even the slightest bit of light for her vampiric eyes to absorb and the echoes of the battle were unreliable, so Jerusa focused her attention on tracking Taos by his scent. The smell of his clothing, of his hair, of his blood, called out to her, leading her through the darkness like a tow rope.

Jerusa turned a corner and had to drop to the floor to keep from being hit in the face by a flying ball of fire. The flames exploded against the wall and blinked out of existence.

Taos stood with his back in a corner, tossing fire at the savages, but was unable to hit his mark. His clothes were shredded and a trail of blood ran down his forehead and dripped from his nose. He was spent, his strength waning. He fell to one knee as the savages sprang from floor to wall, back and forth, rushing in alternating attacks that grew more and more difficult for Taos to fend off.

Jerusa's face blushed fiery hot. She ran, but didn't realize it. She screamed, but didn't hear herself. Bursts of light exploded around her as clusters of ghosts followed beside her. They charged like a silent battalion, but they didn't have the weapons to wage war. Only Alicia could help her.

The savages turned, startled by her war-cry. Jerusa was on them before they could charge her. She thrust the skewer forward, catching one savage in the throat. With all her strength she brought the weapon up hoping that the beast's head would tear away, but instead his body followed along. Jerusa had no experience in combat. All she knew were the few moments when she had been lost in blind rage. She misjudged her own strength and drove the skewer up, lodging its sharp point into the stone ceiling. The savage slid down the skewer, its throat catching on the claw-like prongs. It shrieked with rage, lashing out at her, but couldn't pull itself free.

Jerusa wasted no time on the trapped savage, but instead turned her fury on the other one. They clashed together like a pair of tidal waves. The beast was fast, reaching up to snag her arms while lunging for her throat. But Jerusa was faster.

She smashed the savage's arms to the side, snapping the bones like dry twigs and spinning him off balance. She stepped to the side, allowing the fiend to stumble by and caught him by the back of the neck.

The flood of hate coursing through her blood burned white-hot when her hands touched the sticky, rotting flesh of the savage. All thought vanished and for time unknown Jerusa was only aware of the spirits surrounding her.

The ghosts encompassed her, watching with silent rapture and bloodlust. Jerusa took in their faces, the looks of satisfied vengeance burning in their eyes and couldn't understand why this should be so. What were they seeing? Why did they cheer so?

It wasn't until Alicia appeared beside her, placing her hand on Jerusa's shoulder, that the fog of fury burned away. Jerusa looked down on what lay at her feet and had to fight the urge to retch.

Jerusa's hands were slick and shiny with thick, black blood. The gore dripped from her cheeks, painted the front of her clothes. The savage laid at her feet, a smashed, ruined pile of pulp where his skull should have been. The beast's obliterated brains squished beneath her feet and it felt like mud at the bottom of a shallow stream.

The world seemed to fall off its axis and all Jerusa could think was how embarrassing it would be for Taos to see her faint. Embarrassment aside, she might have dropped to the ground regardless had she not noticed the savage's body begin to swell.

Jerusa looked down in horror as the savage's flesh turned the marbled black of an impending thunderstorm. Its body continued to bloat, bursting through the tattered remains of its clothing. Any moment the savage's body would explode, releasing a cloud of deadly vapor that would be impossible for them to escape.

"Taos," Jerusa screamed. She scanned the darkness and found him lying face down beneath the feet of the savage pinned to the ceiling. She ran to him, dodging the grasping hands of the savage and lifted him to his knees. His head bobbed listlessly from side to side and she was disturbed to see the wound in his scalp had not yet healed.

Jerusa shook him, but she couldn't rouse him. She slapped him hard across the face, but he only glared at her with distant, unfocussed eyes. She glanced back at the savage whose skin was now beginning to split from the pressure.

It was over. She had failed the Stewards' test. The truth of it rose up within her like bitter bile. She didn't fear death. It was an old friend to her. But this would not be death. She didn't want to be a savage. She didn't want to scurry around these darkened tunnels feasting on whatever poor souls the Stewards cast down here. Most of all she hated that Taos would suffer with her.

She pulled him in close. Buried her face in his neck. His hot breath caressed her ear, sent chills down her back. Though it added to her list of things to feel guilty about, she was glad that she wasn't alone. Against all odds, Taos had become a good friend. She knew that he had hoped for more. That was why he was down here, wasn't it?

She thought of Thad, lost somewhere in these wretched tunnels. He was either dead or a savage. They never did get the chance to finish their first date. There had been that brief, blissful moment at the prom six months ago, before her thirst had taken hold. Sometimes she dreamt that she had never become a vampire and that he had kissed her on the dance floor.

And what of Silvanus? She whispered his name, but the hope of his appearing died on her lips. Why had he not returned for her? Why did her heart ache so much at the thought of him forgetting her?

She had never felt so sad, so alone. It was a pain far too intense to bear. She just wanted it to be over and done with.

Jerusa took Taos's face in both hands. His pale blue eyes rolled from side to side as though he tracked the movement of something unseen to her. She brushed the loose strands of blond hair away from his face, then leaned in and pressed her lips to his.

Taos's lips were warm, soft. She closed her eyes, held her breath, waiting for the moment when the savage would pop like an overfed tick and all that she knew and loved would be washed away.

Taos flinched in her embrace, startling her, but not enough for her to release him. She pressed further into the kiss. Taos thrashed in her arms, grabbing her by the shoulders and casting her aside. She hit the wall just as the room exploded with light.

Taos was up on his knees, a massive ball of fire churning between his hands. He thrust his arms forward and a spinning torrent of flame washed over the headless savage. Its swollen body burst just as the fire covered it, but the black miasma of venomous blood could not escape. Within seconds, all that remained of the savage was a cloud of glowing embers.

The fire continued to pour from Taos's hands. Jerusa had never seen him produce such an intense conflagration. The heat cooked her face, dried her eyes, made her feel as though her hair would ignite at any moment.

The savage pinned to the ceiling screeched at the fire. Taos flipped over onto his back, slinging the fire around like a whip. Jerusa leapt out of the way just in time to avoid being incinerated.

Taos struggled to direct the fire. His eyes were dull and glassy as he searched for the other savage.

The savage tried to scurry up the wall away from the flames. He pulled hard against the prongs of the skewer and finally managed to pry it from the mortar joint. He turned to flee, but Taos brought the fire down on him before he could get too far. The savage turned to cinders, leaving only the skewer glowing red-hot on the stone floor.

Taos collapsed. Jerusa started for him, but stopped when a noise caught her attention. She stood in heavy silence, listening, hoping she had been mistaken with what she had heard. It came again and this time there was no doubt.

Thad's voice echoed from some distant point. Though she couldn't make out his words, she could feel the terror in his voice. Alicia appeared before her and from the look on her face, the news was grim.

Chapter Thirty

Alicia shot down a side tunnel faster than Jerusa had ever seen the ghost move. She chased after Alicia, leaving Taos face down to fend for himself.

Jerusa pushed her speed to the limit. When she caught up with Alicia the ghost began a rapid cycle of vanishing and reappearing just at the edge of Jerusa's vision. Even though they were traveling at a tremendous speed, it still seemed as though hours were passing, instead of seconds.

She moved through the darkness with the stealth and agility of a bat, leaping over pitfalls or ducking beneath pipework just moments before colliding with them. She had no idea where she was. She didn't care. Alicia wouldn't lead her astray.

Thad's voice grew louder with every step and with it came the unmistakable growl of a savage.

Jerusa rounded a corner and as she did, Alicia vanished, reappearing at the end of a corridor the length of a football field. Jerusa detected movement near where Alicia stood. She rushed forward. Light filled the tunnel around her as the army of ghosts materialized behind her.

Her vampire senses became supercharged, fusing together to show her what the darkness sought to hide from her eyes. Thad was injured. The scent of his blood permeated everything. The injury was not life threatening, however, for his heart beat fast and strong. He had somehow managed to barricade himself behind a door of heavy steel bars, but the savage on the other side crashed vehemently against it, loosening the hinges with every blow.

As she was little more than halfway down the corridor the door exploded inward, missing Thad by inches. The savage—Jerusa could now see it was a woman—barreled in like a spider. Thad stumbled backward and only had enough time to throw up his hands before the savage was on him.

Jerusa caught the savage in the back with all her force, lifting her up off of Thad and forcing her through another steel-bar door, at the other end of the room.

She drove the savage as far forward as she could, but soon their feet tangled and the pair crashed hard to the ground. Jerusa's arms were wrapped around the savage's chest and the rough stone floor tried its best to flay the flesh from her forearms. The savage managed to get her hands up and with a solid shove sent the both of them hurtling into a wall.

It was like trying to wrestle a tornado. The beast thrashed from side to side, smashing Jerusa in the face with her elbows. She snagged Jerusa's hair, tearing out great matted chunks, as she attempted to pull Jerusa's face into her snapping jaws. Her legs worked like pistons crushing Jerusa against one wall, then another.

Jerusa squeezed harder. Tightened her grip. The savage's ribs snapped beneath her thin, leathery skin, yet the pain didn't quench her ferocity.

Jerusa's knees buckled, her grip slipped and the next thing she knew, she was on her back with the savage on top of her. She had just enough presence of mind to bring her hands up. She caught the savage by the throat just in time to evade having her nose bitten off.

The savage tore at Jerusa's face with twisted, broken fingers. Her venomous teeth continued to crack together reminding Jerusa of a distant memory of hearing trees snapping under the weight of heavy ice. She tilted her head up and away to protect her eyes from those wretched claws.

That's when she caught sight of the hatchway set in the ceiling above them.

Jerusa's strength spilled from her in great gushes. She couldn't outlast the savage. She knew what she had to do.

"Thad," she called, though it took her three times before she could draw in enough breath. "In the ceiling! Open that hatch!"

Thad ran to the wall, found a ladder made of steel rungs set in the stone and began to climb. About half way up, he realized what it was she was asking him to do.

"No," he yelled back to her. "The sun is still up. I can't open it. You'll die."

"I'm dead already." Each word felt like a porcupine passing through her windpipe. "Open it. Do it now. I'll hold her."

Thad stood frozen on the ladder, looking down in horror. He couldn't do it. She could see by the look in his eyes that he would rather die than be responsible for her death.

He's so stupid, Jerusa thought. *Why won't he just save himself?*

The strength in her arms was spent. Jerusa was now nose to nose with the savage. It occurred to her that is was how she had ended up with Kole. Except this time Silvanus wasn't going to appear and save her. She closed her eyes, hoping the beast finished the job. She'd rather be dead than become one of them.

Jerusa felt Alicia's hands slide over her shoulders. A thought, floating like a reflection on a murky lake, told her that she had already died. It was over and Alicia had come to guide her to the other side. But then that familiar molten fire filled her bones, rushed outward into every nerve-ending, out through her fingertips and into the savage.

Jerusa screamed, the savage shrieked and for just a moment it seemed that even Alicia cried out in pain. The three women, all undead in one way or another, writhed upon the ground, bound in spectral chains of agony. Alicia's electric assault had never been so intense before. Her eyeballs were melting. Her teeth exploding like kernels of popcorn. She would have begged for death had she been able to form words.

The savage tried to escape from this hellish torment, but Jerusa's hands were clamped down and she couldn't let go. Jerusa climbed to her feet, or maybe Alicia had lifted her up. She couldn't say.

The ghost's hands remained on Jerusa's left shoulder, but she had moved around beside her. All around them the other ghosts swirled in a maelstrom of phantom lights, flashing in and out in a nauseating strobe effect. Jerusa's head swam and her legs trembled as though she bore some vast weight. The pain had gone on too long. She could bear no more.

Alicia pushed her forehead against Jerusa's and the electricity jolted her so hard her heart stopped. The savage lurched from side to side, nearly dragging Jerusa off her feet. Jerusa tried to pull away from Alicia, but couldn't break free.

Alicia grabbed Jerusa under the chin, forcing her to look at her. There was something in her eyes, something hidden behind her own silent agony. Alicia glanced to the left then up to the hatch in the ceiling.

Jerusa thought she understood.

Alicia mouthed the word "now" then pushed away from Jerusa. At the same moment Jerusa shoved the savage with what little strength she had left. Though the laws of nature would have had them simply fall away from each other, they were not natural beings and instead flew apart as though a great concussive blast erupted between them.

Jerusa landed on her back, once again incased in the miry blackness of the pit. She managed to scream out two words before the power of speech left her: "Thad! Open!"

A square opened in the ceiling, giving Jerusa her first glimpse of sunlight since becoming a perpetual creature. Its beauty was matched only by the ferocious wave of heat that rushed over her. It was a thousand times worse than when Thad had blasted her with the UV lamp. Bathing in sulfuric acid would be a spa treatment in comparison.

Jerusa scuttled backward faster than she thought possible and kept moving until she was buried in the inky darkness. The pain eased, but didn't go away. When the hatch had opened, she had been off to the side, out of direct sunlight. The savage, however, had fallen right into the intense golden beam.

Jerusa chanced a look around the corner. The bright light seared her brain, but she had to see.

The sun cast a perfect square column of light upon the floor. The savage lay upon her back inside the square, her arms and legs flailing as though she might swim through the golden light to safety. But there was no escape.

The savage's skin liquefied and pooled beneath her, exposing the muscles and sinew beneath. Her eyes ruptured. Her tongue slithered out of her mouth like a listless snake. Shufah had once described the sun's effects on a vampire as cellular deconstruction. Decomposing while still alive would have been a better description.

That was all of it Jerusa could stand to watch. She pulled back into the darkest corner she could find and waited for the pitiful creature's wails to cease.

It took a long time.

Sometime before the savage completed her journey back to dust Jerusa blacked out. A heavy blanket of darkness, deeper than even the murk of the tunnels, fell over her. Shreds of dreams fluttered in her mind. One moment she was confined inside a rock. The next, all her friends were scattered by the Stewards. Even Alicia had somehow been taken from her. But through all of the visions she heard Silvanus whispering her name.

Chapter Thirty-One

Jerusa awoke, startled. The sun was still out, but the hatch in the ceiling was closed tight and the tunnels had returned to full darkness. Though she could not see, her other senses told her that she was not alone.

Jerusa sprang from the ground in a moment of predatory instinct and caught the intruder square in the chest. He fell backward with a grunt and she followed him to the ground. The thirst raged inside her, pressed further by the scent of his mortal blood.

"Jerusa, it's me," he said in a panicked voice. "It's Thad. Don't you recognize me?"

She did recognize him. She just didn't care. She needed to feed. Nothing else mattered. Not her feelings for him. Not the pain and anguish she would experience after killing him. There was no other choice.

Jerusa thrust her fangs at Thad's throat.

The room filled with light. Alicia clapped her hands on Jerusa's head and another jolt of lightning coursed through her. It was enough to rock Jerusa back, but the pain had lost much of its potency. Thad scurried backward. Jerusa rushed for him, but Alicia cast herself between them, wrapping Jerusa up in a tight embrace.

The spectral electricity came again, but this time there was hardly enough to tingle Jerusa's skin. Was it possible that Alicia had exhausted her power on the savage? Jerusa pressed forward and though Alicia slowed her down, she couldn't stop her from getting to Thad.

Thad sat with his back against the wall, watching this all play out with a look of detached disbelief etched on his face.

Taos's voice echoed through the tunnels. He called out

Jerusa's name. He was drawing closer, probably following her scent, or maybe Thad's, but he wouldn't get here in time to stop her.

Hot tears streaked her cheeks and for once she was thankful for the darkness. That way Thad couldn't see the blood leaking from her eyes only to reabsorb into her face. That way his last few moments of life might not be filled with absolute dread.

She was going to kill him. There was no stopping it now. The thirst had grown too strong. She could think of nothing else but quenching the fiery nest of serpents slithering within her bones. Alicia stayed between Jerusa and Thad, but with every step the ghost lost ground to the vampire.

"I'm sorry," Jerusa said to Thad. "I'm so sorry."

Maybe he thought she was apologizing for involving him in this undead world, or for almost getting him eaten by a savage. Or maybe he understood just what she was saying. Whatever the case, he didn't attempt to escape. He just sat there, staring up at her with his deep, soulful eyes.

Alicia wrapped her arm around the back of Jerusa's head and pulled her face down. Jerusa allowed her cheek to rest on the ghost's clavicle, but continued to drive toward Thad. Alicia had no corporeal body, no flesh or bone or blood, yet she felt wholly there nonetheless. Her skin was hot to the touch. Her bones sat sturdy beneath her soft flesh. Strands of her hair even tickled Jerusa's nose. Why could she feel Alicia and not any of the other countless ghosts she had encountered?

A strong pang of blood-thirst rippled through Jerusa and she would have doubled over had she not been leaning on Alicia. Her borrowed heart raged within her chest and that's when something rather odd happened.

Alicia's aura began to flicker in time with Jerusa's heartbeat. She turned her head, further exposing her neck and Jerusa brought her mouth up without thought. A pulse thrummed within Alicia's neck, as though she had blood and a heart to pump it with.

But that was foolishness. Alicia's body had been placed

below ground almost three years ago. The only part of her still alive was beating within Jerusa's own chest. Yet still, Jerusa's vampiric instincts couldn't seem to discern the truth. She closed her eyes and gave into the predatory nature that now defined her.

Jerusa clutched Alicia tight, so tight that had she been a living person she might have broken her in half. She clamped her mouth onto the ghost's neck and forced her fangs through the skin that wasn't really there.

Jerusa gasped with ecstasy. It was as though someone had filled her with liquid light. The world spun out of existence, leaving her drifting on the ether. The thundering pulse of her heart echoed all around her and her mind filled with images, memories of Alicia's life. Alicia's mother and father tucking her in as a child. Learning to ride a bike. Even the night of her prom . . . the night she never came home.

Jerusa wasn't sure how long this went on. It felt as though she had outraced the earth to the end of time. When she came to, she found herself still clutching Alicia. Her arms fell away, heavy as lead. Alicia stumbled backwards and fell to the floor, her aura now just a thin dwindling light. Jerusa swooned, almost joining Alicia on the floor, but a pair of powerful hands caught her.

"Are you all right?" Taos asked.

She stepped back out of his grasp and nodded. And the truth was she did feel all right. Not just all right, but invigorated in a way she hadn't been since first becoming a vampire. Her thirst was gone. She went to Thad and offered him a hand up, without even the slightest fear that she might attack him.

He took her hand without question and rose to his feet. "What was that? What happened to you?"

"I'm not exactly sure, but I think I just fed from Alicia." She turned to the ghost who looked up at her with a thin smile. "Are you okay?" Alicia nodded, but quickly vanished. The other ghosts stood motionless, watching her with great glassy eyes. Foster stood between the vampire ghost with the piebald eyes and the Monster's fledgling. "Did I hurt her?" she asked Foster.

He looked as confused as the rest of them.

"How can you feed from a ghost?" Thad asked. "Ghosts don't have blood."

"You're right, they don't," Jerusa said. "But she gave me something. I'm not sure what exactly, but I'll take it."

Taos sparked a small fire in the palm of his hand and drew near to her. He took her face in his other hand and turned her head side to side. He stopped and stared into her eyes for a long moment and she couldn't help but wonder if he had any recollection of their kiss. If he did, she hoped he wouldn't bring it up in front of Thad. She felt too good to think about dealing with that drama right now.

"Whatever Alicia did to you," Taos said, "I don't think it's going to do you much good."

"What do you mean?" she asked.

Thad came closer and looked intently at her. His brow furrowed and the corners of his mouth turned down.

"What is it?"

"Your eyes are filled with blood," Taos said. "And so are your lips. Alicia may have quenched your thirst, but you are still starving."

"I'll be fine," Jerusa said. "I'll just drip a little blood in my eyes and on my lips. The Stewards won't suspect a thing."

"No," Taos said in a voice stern as a thunderclap. "You don't understand. The thirst is the least of your problems. Without fresh blood you will cease to heal properly. Your strength and speed will wane. And given enough time—"

"I know. I know," Jerusa cut him off. "If I don't start drinking blood then the *Stone Cloak* will come upon me. You don't have to worry about me. I'll be fine."

"You tried to feed on Thad, didn't you?" Taos asked. His pale eyes glimmered in the flickering light of the tiny flame, making it look as though a turbulent sea rested within each orb.

"Yes, but Alicia stopped me."

"But you almost overpowered her? You were able to fight through the pain?"

"Yes." She didn't like the way his eyes darted between her and Thad. "I think she wore herself out with the savage."

"Is she still weak? Do you think you could fight her off again?"

"I don't know. Why?"

Taos quenched the fire in his palm and snatched Thad by the back of his neck with blinding speed. Thad barely had a moment to shout out in alarm before he was hoisted from the ground and flipped up on his back.

Taos held Thad out to her, forcing his neck towards her face. "Take him. You have to."

"No," Jerusa shouted. "Put him down!"

"You need blood." Taos took a step towards her just as she took a step back. Thad fought all the harder, lashing out at Taos's face with his fists, kicking at his chest, all without effect. "The sunlight burned you. Not bad, but you won't heal fast enough. The Stewards might not notice your eyes or lips, but the Hunters are going to be watching you. They will notice when the burns don't vanish fast enough."

"I'll be fine. Now put him down. Right now! I mean it!"

Her words slid right off of him. "He's dead already. You have to know that. The Stewards have passed their judgment. He won't be turned. Why else did they put him down here if not to die?" A desperate madness rose within him.

"It was a test. Just a test. To see if I could really talk to the spirits. But I won. I beat them. We saved Thad. He's not going to die."

Taos wrenched Thad's head back and the boy uttered a groan of pain. "If you won't feed from him then I will. I will finish what I started. But it should be you. You should feed while Alicia is too weak to stop you."

A long moment passed where Jerusa and Taos stood stark

still, eyes locked, each awaiting the other to make the first move. Even Thad ceased his struggling, either accepting his fate or wrung out from too much adrenaline.

"I won't," Jerusa said finally. "And neither will you."

That was the wrong thing to say to Taos. He bore his fangs with a defiant sneer, then bit into Thad's neck.

Chapter Thirty-Two

Jerusa screamed, though whether from fear or fury even she couldn't say. The army of spirits surrounding her lit up like a flash of lightning, resplendent and dazzling for one brief moment, blinding her to all else.

She was on Taos before she even realized that she meant to attack him. Jerusa punched him in the face, driving his head back and away from Thad's neck. The scent of his blood washed over her, but instead of invoking her thirst, it only fueled her rage.

She sent punch after punch rocketing into Taos's face. He dropped Thad to the ground, tripped on his own feet and tumbled backward. Jerusa was on top of him in an instant, hammering at his chest and face. His nose gave a terrible crunching noise and blood spilled from his mouth. He threw up his hands, but made no attempt to fight back, or to even stop her.

Jerusa's hands became as heavy as a pair of anvils, but she swung them again and again, until her muscles cramped and burned and there was nothing else she could give. She dropped her arms to her sides. She sat astride Taos, heaving and gasping, sure at any moment her lungs would try to escape out of her mouth. Taos's face was bruised and mashed, with one eye swollen up like a tomato. He regarded her from his good eye and a steady stream of tears dripped from the bloody corner. She had never seen Taos cry, hadn't ever thought he was capable of it and it sucked all of the rage out of her.

Jerusa stood up slowly, motioning for Taos to stay where he was. She turned toward Thad, but she didn't dare tempt her thirst by going near to him.

"Are you all right," she called to him.

Thad sat with his back against the wall, holding his neck.

"Yeah, I think so." He turned a set of hate-filled eyes on Taos. "You bit me . . . again."

Taos stood to his feet. All emotion, good or bad, was gone from his face. The tears had vanished leaving Jerusa to wonder if they had actually been there at all. His wounds were already healing and soon would be gone. It made her keenly aware of the stinging sunburn covering her face and hands.

"It won't happen again," Taos said. With that he turned and shambled off to the far corner of the room.

They sat in silence the rest of the day. Jerusa laid on her back in the filth and grime, thinking that she would trade all her vampiric powers and immortality for a hot shower and a full day's treatment at a spa. It was a strange sensation and hard to articulate, but a colossal sense of pride swelled within her. She had been through hell. She had faced the Stewards' test and won.

A bit of her old self rose up like a chilly wind, telling her she had no right to feel this way when her mother lay dying somewhere within the great house. It was her mother's voice telling her this. The voice of guilt was always her mother's. It just didn't sound as loud now.

Jerusa drifted in and out of sleep, sometimes awakened by one of her ghostly entourage hoping to get her attention. After a while, they let her sleep, though that may have been Foster's doing. Alicia didn't appear all the rest of the day, but Jerusa knew she hadn't gone far.

The sun settled beneath the horizon. Jerusa felt its decent and sat up. She opened her thumb with her fang and dripped a few drops of blood in each eye, started to smear it on her lips, but decided to coat her face and arms with it. Despite Taos's prediction, the burns had mostly healed and the ones that hadn't, vanished as her skin reabsorbed the blood.

Another hour passed in silence. The ghosts shuffled around her in agitation and Alicia appeared in front of her, looking young and beautiful as always, save for a weariness in her eyes. Jerusa didn't have to ask. She knew what had stirred the ghosts.

"They're coming for us."

Thad was dozing near the ladder and jumped with a start at Jerusa's voice. He stood up and backed towards her. Taos joined them, standing on her other side. She could feel the competitive heat passing between the two men. She could only imagine the intensity if Silvanus had been there with them.

A wave of sadness passed over her, but she didn't have time to think about him right now.

The hatch door flung open with a loud bang. Icy wind and snow rushed in. Moonlight puddled on the floor, giving the room a dreamlike luminescence. Without noise, five beings dropped into the tunnel below.

"All alive I see," Ming said, with an air of disgust.

"I would have thought at least one of you would have died," Ralgar added. "Even the human survived. How disappointing."

"You did well, blood-witch," Ming said, though the words must have tasted terrible to her. "Four is no easy number, though the savages were still mindless. Tell me, how long ago did you dispatch the last savage?"

"Several hours ago. It was still full daylight."

Celeste couldn't contain her smile, but the other four Hunters shot nervous glances at one another.

"You don't believe me?" Jerusa asked.

"It doesn't matter what we believe," Ming said. "Come with us. The Stewards are waiting."

They climbed up the ladder and out the hatch. The wind whipped at them so hard that a few times Jerusa thought her bare skin might split open. No matter the cold, she would still survive. It was Thad that she worried about. Thankfully, they didn't have far to go. The pair of SUVs was waiting on a thin road, distinguishable only by the break in the trees and a pair of tire tracks. The heat inside the cab was such a wonderful relief that Jerusa almost cried out for joy.

They drove back to the great house in silence. Jerusa had hoped to grab a hot shower and a change of clothes when they got back to the Ice Sanctuary, but as soon as they parked beneath the stone archway, Ming and the Crimson Storm led them to a large room off of the great hall.

Marjek and the other High Council sat on cushioned thrones positioned atop another raised platform. They seemed to like looking down on everyone else.

Shufah sat in her own meek wooden chair at the bottom of the stage. Her tiny amused smile exploded when they entered the room. "You see, Marjek. I told you not to underestimate my coven." She greeted each of them with a hug. She lingered a bit longer with Jerusa, her dark eyes searching for some subtle secret buried within.

Marjek rose from his seat and the other members of the High Council followed his lead. He glared at Jerusa for a long moment before turning his eyes towards the Crimson Storm. "It's obvious that they all made it out alive, but were they successful in dispatching all of the savages?" His handsome features were pulled tight. It agitated him to have to ask about the savages.

Ming stepped forward, head bowed, eyes averted like a chastised child. "Yes, my lord."

"How many savages roamed the tunnels?" Heidi asked.

"Four."

The other four members of the Council seemed impressed by this, but Marjek continued to scowl. Ming glanced upward as though she wanted to say more, thought better of it and returned her eyes to the floor. Heidi told her to speak freely.

"They also managed to kill the four savages within only a few hours of entering the tunnels."

"Well done." There was no cheer in his voice. "It is the decision of the council that Jerusa Phoenix be granted the right to immortality by virtue of her *unique* talent." The word couldn't have been any more painful to him had they been made of broken glass.

To Jerusa it was the most wonderful thing she had ever

heard. A mountain of stress lifted from her and she looked at her feet to make sure they were still touching the floor.

Marjek continued. "The vampire Jerusa and the vampire Taos have earned their places among the clan of Hunters."

Jerusa came crashing back down to earth. She had been so happy to know that she was going to live that she had forgotten what type of life she would have to endure. *Join them if you wish to live,* Sebastian's voice called out in her mind. *But you must escape at the first opportunity, before they get the chance to destroy you.*

"There is no higher calling," Marjek said. "You are now soldiers of blood. Protectors, not only of the vampire realm, but of all that breathes upon the earth."

Jerusa had a feeling they were getting the condensed speech, the one without pomp or fanfare. Celeste stepped before them, holding a ring in each hand. To Taos, she offered a large ring with a broad silver band and a flat face with the Hunters' insignia embossed in bright rubies.

He took the ring, a tight smile upon his face and placed it upon the index finger of his right hand. He looked at it with satisfaction. At one time, it had been his dream to join the Hunters, even though his rugged beauty had purchased his immortality long ago. He had renounced that dream after joining their coven, but did he still feel the same way? That smile left a hollow space in Jerusa's stomach.

Celeste stepped before Jerusa. She held out a ring similar to Taos's, though smaller and designed for a woman's hand. Celeste's hand trembled a bit. She was nervous, but why?

Jerusa glanced up at the High Council. They stared down on her in contempt, except for Heidi who had a morbid look of fascination etched into her eyes. It was a look that left Jerusa feeling like an ameba wriggling beneath the eye of a microscope.

Shufah watched her with a mixture of pride and sadness. She nodded for Jerusa to take the ring, so she did. She followed Taos's lead and placed the ring upon her right index finger. She expected there to be some sort of oath they would have to recite (perhaps for more worthy vampires, there was), but instead, the High Council merely turned without word and started to leave.

"Wait," Jerusa said. "What happens now?"

Heidi was the only member of the High Council to stop and turn. "Tomorrow evening, you will go with the Crimson Storm back to the United States. You will penetrate the quarantine communities and search for the savage, Suhail. I trust you are smart enough to discern the rest for yourself."

"What about Shufah and Thad?" Jerusa sensed that she should be quiet, but after what she had just endured she didn't much feel up to being obedient. "What about my mother?"

"Your mother must stay here," Heidi said. "We still don't know what affects this new blood will have on her. The human must also stay." Though Thad remained standing, Jerusa could see crippling pain in his eyes. "He will serve with the other human staff. When this ordeal is over, then perhaps he can be moved to one of the other communities. He may even earn his right to the blood. We shall see."

"And Shufah?"

"I'm coming with you," Shufah answered. Marjek shot a sullen glance over his shoulder, but said nothing. "At least for a while. I have promised to return once we have made contact with my brother. If he is killed or it's determined that our sibling bond no longer holds any sway with him, I am to report back here."

We're going home, Jerusa thought. She wanted to cheer out loud, but held her joy behind a solemn mask. Not everyone had cause to celebrate. Her biggest fear was over. Thad's had just begun.

Heidi turned and joined the High Council and they exited the room through a door at the back of the stage. The Crimson Storm left through the door they had entered through.

"So, how did you convince them to let you come with us?" Jerusa asked Shufah.

"I just reminded them that Suhail is my twin and my

responsibility. If anyone is going to destroy him, it should be me."

"Is that really what you told them?"

A coy little smile brushed across Shufah's face. "Well, that and I reminded them of how bad I can be for the morale of the house and the living hell I would almost assuredly put them through."

Even Thad managed to laugh at that.

"So, what's our plan?" Jerusa asked.

"We'll do just as the dwarf instructed," she whispered. The shock on Jerusa's face brought another smile to Shufah. "Don't seem so surprised. The dwarf and I have a long and interesting relationship. Not quite a friendship, mind you. More like a mutual respect."

"Who is this *dwarf* and what does he have to do with us?" Taos asked.

Shufah motioned for Jerusa to explain.

"His name is Sebastian. He is an augur with the Watchtower. He said that we should escape the Hunters the first chance we get and go into hiding." She used the word *we* when in fact the dwarf had suggested this plan to her alone.

"I don't think that's a good idea," Taos said. "We'll be outcasts. They will hunt us for sure. We should just go with them, find Suhail and kill him."

"The Crimson Storm will never let it get that far," Shufah said.

"Why not?"

"Because," Jerusa said. "Marjek has given them special instructions. Make sure we die and bring Shufah back here."

Taos looked as though he might argue, but he held his tongue. After a moment of silence he asked, "So what do we do?"

"First we lure them back to our house," Shufah said, a feverish twinkle blazing in her eyes. "I had the security team install a special little feature. Once the Hunters are in the basement I will activate the UV Shield. If they try to approach the exit, the motion sensors will bring a set of UV lamps online until they retreat out of the blast zone. It won't keep them locked up forever, but it should give us a good head start."

Thad shook his head like he had a thought trapped in his ear. "Why would you have something like that installed in your own home?"

"It was for me, wasn't it?" Jerusa asked.

"Yes. The longer your condition continues, the more dangerous you become, not only to yourself, but to us as well."

Jerusa wanted to tell her about feeding from Alicia, how that had taken away the thirst, but the words were like a bad taste in her mouth now and she no longer wanted to talk. Shufah didn't push the conversation, but she didn't apologize for building a secret prison cell in their home, either. Instead she turned to Taos and Thad.

"Once we are away from the Hunters, we will make our way back here."

"Here?" Thad asked. "They'll be after you. Why come back here?"

"To get you, silly," she said with a smile. "And Jerusa's mother, too. I'll not leave you two here one day longer than necessary."

Chapter Thirty-Three

Back in her room, Jerusa ripped off the tattered remains of her clothes and spent the next several hours in the shower. Thank goodness the house had unlimited hot water, because she needed every drop to thaw the ice crystals out of her blood.

Afterward, she sat on the edge of her bed until dawn broke over the eastern horizon. She stared at the heavy steel shutters that protected her from the sunlight. If the Stewards wanted her dead so badly, why didn't they just hit a button and let the light spill in on her?

Her skin crawled at the thought, but she refused to cower in the closet. She was done cowering.

When night began to close in, there came a knock to her door. Her heightened senses told her that Thad was out there. She opened the door and he stepped inside uninvited.

"You shouldn't be here," Jerusa said. "Shufah will be angry if she finds out we're alone together."

"I don't care," he said. "I'm not afraid of you."

"You should be." He still didn't understand just how close she had corne to killing him in the tunnels. "It's not safe for—"

He cut her words off with a kiss.

Jerusa's reflexes were quick enough that she could have easily evaded Thad, but the truth was, she wanted to kiss him, had ever since she had first met him. The heat of his body flowed through her. Her heart matched his. A tickle of the thirst rose within her and her fangs yearned to pierce his tongue, but she willed that side of her away, burying it beneath the last remnant of her mortal self.

A set of hands touched her shoulders and she knew, without

looking, that Alicia stood behind her. Jerusa obeyed the ghost's warning and broke away from Thad before the predator side of her nature could sneak up on her.

Thad didn't seek another kiss, nor did he seem upset that she had broken contact. He merely rubbed her cheek with the tips of his fingers. "Don't be gone too long," he said, then turned and vanished into his own room.

Not long after that, Celeste came to the door.

"It's time to go."

Jerusa had no belongings, nothing to take with her except the clothes on her back, so she followed the augur out, without even a glance back. She climbed into the back seat of the SUV with Taos and Shufah. She didn't notice the cold. She didn't watch as the great house dwindled into the blowing snow. They boarded the jet and took to the air without incident.

Jerusa sat alone. She didn't want any company. She missed her mother. The Stewards wouldn't even allow her to say goodbye.

Taos approached but turned away, possibly sensing her mood. Jerusa was still mad at him for tempting her to kill Thad. That had upset her more than she could say, but that wasn't what was bothering her. She was weary. Not just from the trial in the tunnel or the lack of feeding, but in a way only a person with a divided heart can be.

She had kissed Taos in the tunnel and Thad just before leaving, and though different parts of her leaned toward each man, right now all she could think about was Silvanus. She couldn't shake the feeling that something bad had happened to him.

The jet landed at the same air strip, outside of town, that they had left from. They had only been gone a few days, but it seemed as though a whole life time had unraveled since she had last been home.

The air here was cool, but not frigid. The bare trees danced in the breeze, but at least the fallen foliage wasn't hidden beneath two feet of snow. She had forgotten that it was still autumn here, not yet

Halloween.

From the tiny airport they moved on foot through the forest back toward the house that Jerusa, Taos and Shufah shared. She still wasn't sure how Shufah had managed to convince the Hunters to come back here. Maybe it was because sunrise was only a half hour away. There was no time to find another shelter, let alone make an assault on the nearest quarantine community.

Jerusa felt heartsick as she stepped through the front door. Not far from here, her mother's house sat empty. Debra Phoenix wasn't coming home. Did anyone even notice that she was missing?

Shufah stood talking with Ming, Ralgar and Celeste, discussing the multiple safety features of their basement sanctuary. She did, however, leave out the part about the UV trap she intended to lock them in just as soon as the other two Hunters finished their reconnaissance of the property.

The sky was quickly turning from violet to the soft pink of dawn. Though Shufah's face remained calm and placid, Jerusa knew her well enough to see the signs of stress eating at her. If they didn't get all of the Hunters down into the basement at the same time— somehow without going in themselves—the plan wouldn't work. And if it didn't work, there might not be another chance to escape.

Shufah subtly glanced out the open door. "Dawn is coming. Should we expect your comrades or will they be lodging somewhere else?"

A sullen look of annoyance passed over Ming's face. She looked toward Celeste. "Go find Quinn and Mikael."

Celeste started for the door without question, but Shufah stopped her.

"It's all right. I'll get them. You three go on down and get comfortable."

Ralgar and Celeste started down the stairs, but Ming held back. "What of the giant and the fledgling? Are they not joining us?"

Ming had been a Hunter for a long time. It was in her training to sense impending traps.

"They will be right down," Shufah answered without missing a beat. "Just as soon as they finish securing the shutters and door reinforcements." She didn't wait to see if Ming would go down the stairs, but instead turned to go find the missing Hunters.

Just as she crossed the threshold, Shufah made a quick snap as if something had startled her. "Oh my," she said in a calm, hushed voice as she turned on her heels.

Taos jumped to his feet and Ming emerged from the basement door like a feral beast, but it took Jerusa's weary mind a moment longer to understand what she was seeing.

Two holes, rimmed in blood, had appeared in Shufah's shirt. She dabbed at them with her fingertips, staggered forward, then fell to her knees. That's when Jerusa saw them standing silhouetted in the doorway.

The pair of umbilicus creatures stood smiling—a ring of still-wet blood coating their lips—at the dumbstruck vampires. They were dressed in a mix-matched ensemble of clothing that looked like it had come straight out of the lost-and-found somewhere, but in truth probably came from whatever victims they had come across in town. Their skin was no longer burnt, nor was it the malformed lump of clay that she remembered. They emanated a power that hadn't been there before. Their black eyes drank the light of the rising sun.

Jerusa and Taos rushed the beasts at the same time, but the umbilicus were too fast. In one smooth motion they slipped a heavy black bag over Shufah and pulled her through the door.

Jerusa tried to follow them, but Taos snatched her around the waist. "No," he said. "The sun is up. We can't go after her. She's gone."

Jerusa continued to fight him, to the point that she ripped the door from the hinges and left the jamb in splintered ruin, but he was right. The sun was upon them. She allowed herself to go limp and as Taos pulled her inside, Jerusa caught sight of Quinn and Mikael's bodies on the ground, already beginning to break down in the daylight.

They made it into the basement sanctuary just as the sunlight blasted through the front door. Taos pushed the others down the stairs and Jerusa jerked the steel gate down.

"What are we going to do?" Celeste asked.

"We are going to go after them," Jerusa said, her voice incredulous, yet flat. "We are going to get her back."

"We have orders," Ming said. "You are a Hunter now. We must make our move on Suhail."

"And how long do you think Marjek will allow you to live after he discovers that Shufah is gone?" Jerusa held Ming's fierce gaze. "It won't matter if you wipe out Suhail and his vast savage army. If Shufah dies, so do you."

Ming turned in a fit of rage and the entire house quaked.

"How are we supposed to find them?" Taos asked. "They can move day and night and we have no idea where they are going."

"You said you thought they were Light Bearers, right?"

Taos nodded yes.

"First we find the Light Bearers, then we hurt them until they take us to Shufah." The calm malevolence in her own voice shocked her.

"The Light Bearers operate in splinter cells," Ralgar said. "Even we don't know where they operate from."

"I know someone that can take us to them."

"Who?" Ming asked.

"Silvanus." Saying his name brought a cold chill to Jerusa's flesh. "He knows where the Light Bearers are hiding." She didn't have the heart to tell them that she didn't know where Silvanus was, either. She glanced over at Alicia who stood in the center of the room. Foster stood beside her and behind them was the legion of vampire ghosts. "We'll find them," Jerusa repeated. "And if they've hurt Shufah, I'll make them pay."

The End.

~ 313 ~

About the Author

Gabriel Beyers lives in Bloomington, Indiana with his wife, two children, and two lovable yet destructive dogs. He is also the author of:

Guarding the Healer
Contemplations of Dinner
Predatory Animals
Heart of the Dead: Perpetual Creatures 1

For more information go to www.gabrielbeyers.com.

Correspondence can be made at gabrielbeyers@gmail.com or PO Box 222 Clear Creek, IN 47426.

Printed in Great Britain
by Amazon.co.uk, Ltd.,
Marston Gate.